Bratva Sweetheart

The Ivankov Brotherhood

Sabine Barclay

OLIVERHEBERBOOKS

Published by Oliver Heber Books

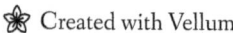 Created with Vellum

There are very things in life that are absolute, but the love between soulmates. May we each find ours.

Subscribe to Sabine's Newsletter

Subscribe to Sabine's bimonthly newsletter to receive exclusive insider perks.

Have you read *The Syndicate Wars*? This FREE origin story novella is available to all new subscribers to Sabine's monthly newsletter. Subscribe on her website.

The Ivankov Brotherhood

Bratva Darling

Bratva Sweetheat (Coming 8.9.22)

Bratva Treasure (Coming 9.20.22)

Bratva Beauty (Coming 11.1.22)

Bratva Angel (Coming 12.13.22)

Bratva Jewel (Coming 1.24.23)

Do you also enjoy steamy Historical Romance? Discover Sabine's books written as Celeste Barclay.

CONTENT WARNING

This book contains one consensual non-consent roleplaying scene.

Chapter One

Tina

Huuhh. Sigh. I thought tonight would be more fun. It usually is when Todd and I go out, but tonight is dragging with no end in sight. We've already been to a bar and a club, and now I'm watching him enjoy a lap dance. We came here for some fun, but they definitely have their second string working tonight. This chick's been grinding on him for like five minutes. I can see he's hard, which is the whole point of why we came. We enjoy a little show, then we go to his place and fuck. But this woman won't leave. Sure, Todd's having a great time, but I'm bored AF.

"I'm getting a drink." I doubt Todd hears me. His hands are dangling at his sides, just like his tongue is dangling from his mouth. He and I have an arrangement that's worked for years, and I'm good with it. But usually, he gets the lap dance, and I get felt up during it. We're both satisfied. Then it leads to awesome sex when we get to his place. He seems to have

1

forgotten me, and to be honest, I don't think I really care enough to make more effort to remind him I'm here.

I know I could signal someone to bring me a drink, but I'd rather look around. I can't help but love people watching in a strip club. It's New York City, so there's usually something shady going on somewhere. Sometimes it's more than just a lap dance. Sometimes it's a guy getting thrown out for trying to make it more than just a lap dance. And sometimes you see the most unlikely people conducting business. I'm certain that's one of the club owners. *Pussycats*. How utterly unoriginal. But damn, he can call this place whatever he wants. He's hot.

"Bourbon on the rocks with a splash of water."

"If you drank vodka, you wouldn't need to dilute the taste."

That voice. It's sin waiting to happen. I look to my left, and the man who'd been in the corner talking to a rather large Italian-looking guy is now beside me. He was hot from a distance. He's Lucifer in a suit up close. Are my panties on the floor? Those blue eyes might have just made them drop. They're certainly wetter than they were a few minutes ago, watching Todd and the understudy stripper. God, I can be a bitch. The girl is just doing her job.

"I had a bad experience with vodka in college. I steer clear."

"Made yourself sick?"

"And if I'd like to continue to enjoy orange juice without being certain I taste vodka, I stay away."

I offer him what I hope is a slightly sarcastic yet sexy smiley kind of smirk. From the way he's grinning, it either worked, or he thinks I'm batshit. Oh! Maybe he did like it. He smells amazing, and now his chest is practically against the side of my shoulder. I can smell the hint of vodka on his breath, and for once, it doesn't make me want to shiver and turn away.

"You didn't look like you were having a good time earlier.

Boyfriend not paying enough attention? Or perhaps too much attention?"

"He's not my boyfriend."

"Your date then."

"Not a date. Those both imply romance. That's not our arrangement. Partners in crime. Partners in fun. Definitely not partners in life." I cock an eyebrow, waiting to see how he responds to me basically admitting that Todd is a fuck buddy. We tried going on a couple dates. We enjoyed each other's company, and we really enjoy having sex together, but no sparks ever flew for either of us.

"So you came for an appetizer, and I suppose you're supposed to be the main course later."

I look back over my shoulder and can't find Todd. He's not at the table I just left. I wonder if he went to the bathroom. He better not be taking care of anything, otherwise, I'll have to do all the work to get him revved up again. Sometimes we enjoy the foreplay, but that wasn't the deal tonight.

"Something like that."

"But only one of you gets to sample. That hardly seems fair."

"It's fine for tonight." Todd and I have been to clubs that allow us to do more than just watch. He might get a lap dance, and I might get his fingers. I might sit on his lap while he fucks me, and I get a lap dance. We're kinky like that, but we've never had a full-on threesome. Women just don't interest me enough for that. Now two guys? One can only wish.

Mr. No Name shakes his head when the bartender approaches, and I reach for my purse. Before I can insist that I pay, he's picking up both of our drinks and turning away from the guy. I don't know what to say beyond a mumbled thanks. I follow this guy, which I know is ridiculous, but I'm too damn curious for my own good. He steers us away from the men in the corner where I first spotted him. There's another man who looks so much like him they could be twins. My mystery man nods to his lookalike before taking us to a corner table on the opposite side of the stage.

"You can see if your friend returns. That way you won't miss him."

There's something about his tone. Those two sentences have more than one meaning. As I meet his gaze, I can see it just as much as I heard it.

"Thank you for my drink. But I usually don't accept drinks from strangers."

"Good thing you watched it being poured. I'm Bogdan Kutsenko."

Oh, holy fucking shit. I thought he might be, but now I know. He's a fucking billionaire. He and his brothers own a slew of strip clubs, casinos, commercial developments, and Lord only knows what else. And I'm fairly certain that whatever else is not even close to legal. I've heard the rumors. Russian mafia.

"You recognize my name. Should I let you go back to your friend?"

"I recognize it. But did I speak, and I didn't hear myself?" I hope my smile is coy since my words sound more sarcastic than I meant. "I never said I wanted to leave. I'm Christina." I never give my last name to strange men. Ever. When his brow furrows for a moment, I know he noticed, but he doesn't push the issue.

The way we're seated in the booth—it's not exactly a booth since there isn't another bench across the table—our shoulders are touching. And now so are our thighs. It's no coincidence. At least not the leg part. His shoulders are so broad that I could almost say it isn't intentional, at least not on his part.

"I almost didn't come in tonight. I'm glad I did," he said.

He's watching me. I can feel it even though I'm looking at the stage. Every time I look into those icy-blue eyes, my pussy tightens. Maybe the club's name isn't so stupid after all. But I can't help myself. There's six and a half feet of gorgeousness sitting beside me, and for some reason, I feel more at ease than I expected. I'm trying not to make an ass of myself, but I'm not nervous or even hesitant. I'm never like this when I meet a man. I'm always cautious. I'm always hyperaware. I'm a single woman living in New York City. I have to be. But I have this uncanny sense that I can lower my guard with him.

"Why did you?"

"My oldest brother, Maksim, asked me to. We had an incident a few weeks ago at one of our regular clubs. He had a feeling something might be up tonight."

That's not what I wanted to hear. I look around, searching for an exit other than the main doors. I'm looking at how many people are between me and my escape paths. I'm looking for anyone who appears least likely to be a threat, assuming they're the most dangerous.

"I didn't say that to make you uneasy. You're not obvious, but I know you've just figured out at least three ways to get out of here."

"Why do you think that?" It rattles me that he knows that's what I did. My dad was in the military before I was born. He's hardly a conspiracy theorist or paranoid, but he taught me a few things before I left home. I rarely sit with my back to the door in a bar. I always know how to get out or where to hide. And I can throw a punch hard enough to get away.

"Because you have the same supposedly neutral expression my brothers, and I suppose I, wear when we're making the same plan."

"And why would you need to do that? You hardly strike me as the type to flee."

He chuckles, and it's smoother than the bourbon I'm sipping.

"Flee? No. But we aren't always welcome places, or sometimes we draw too much attention. We like to know how to leave without a fuss."

"Why wouldn't you be welcome? I would think most establishments would be excited to have such a customer."

"Because I'm wealthy? Yes. Many see dollar signs when my brothers and I arrive. But some places aren't so fond of Russians who clearly sound Russian."

He has an accent, so I'm certain he was born there. But it's not that strong, and his English is excellent. None of that stereotypical "strong like bull" speech. It's New York. I can guess what he means.

"I guess you don't eat at Italian restaurants that often. And you probably aren't shutting down any Irish bars."

"You could say that."

I look down at my now empty glass. I see Todd back at our table, but he doesn't seem to notice I'm still gone. A much more attractive woman is now doing dangerously more than just a legal lap dance. When he reaches for her, I see a bouncer move toward the table. Todd must have seen him too because his hands drop back to his sides.

"Thank you for the drink, Bogdan."

I stand, and he rises immediately. I think someone must have raised him to do that. Stand when a woman does. It doesn't feel like he did it to stop me or to walk me back to my table. If I leaned forward, my nose would come to the center of his chest. He's got to be close to a foot taller than me, so I'm tilting my head back to look at him.

"If he's not your boyfriend, or even your date, would he care if I kissed you?"

The corners of his eyes crinkle as he grins again. His smile is so relaxed and natural, yet now that he's standing with his back to most of the crowd and the door, I can sense he's tense. I shift so I'm standing to his side. He turns, now putting the door to his left and fewer people behind him. His shoulders are no longer stiff.

"Perhaps you should care if I want you to kiss me."

"I definitely do. But I don't need to knock your—friend— out if he gets pissed. That would cause a scene."

Why am I so fucking tempted? When I'm not mesmerized by his eyes, I keep looking at his lips. I'm certain he's noticed. That's why he knows I won't say no.

"I don't want a scene either." I look around, then over my shoulder. I'm looking away when he takes my hand. His is warm without being clammy. I can feel callouses, but his grip is gentle. I could pull away if I wanted, but I don't. I stop when we get to a storeroom door, and he opens it. Now I'm having doubts.

"I'll leave the door open if you want. Or we can go farther down the hall, but someone will see us if we do that."

"Do most women agree to go into dark rooms with you?" My tone has changed. It's challenging.

"No, because I don't invite women into them. I don't make a habit of kissing women where I work. And I know it makes me an ass, but I rarely care that much about shielding a woman from prying eyes."

He reaches in and flicks on a light. I can see there's a fire exit across the room, which will be unlocked and sound an alarm if I push on the door. When I look back at him, I know that's why he picked this room. He wants me to know I have a way out that he can't lock. God. If I saw this in a movie, it would be a slasher film, and I'd be thinking the woman is stupid, that she'll get what she deserves. Yet now I'm walking in.

I glance over Bogdan's shoulder to the door we just passed through. He has his back to it, and I realize that as much as he doesn't enjoy feeling that unguarded, he's doing it for me. If anyone walks in, he's so much bigger than me, they won't see me. That could feel threatening, but for reasons that surely are insane, it's reassuring.

"If you don't like anything, stop me. I'll step away and won't try to stop you from leaving."

I nod as he places his hand on my waist. His other one cups my jaw, his fingers in my hair. For such a large man, he's so gentle. It seems completely at odds with his appearance and knowing he owns a strip club. He's not skeezy. Suave is more like it. I tilt my head back, and the feel of his lips against mine is like an electric current surging through me. I'm opening my mouth to him, wanting more without even thinking about it. He's not rushing anything, but at the same time, I feel like he's ready to devour me. I want the same as my hands slide up his arms and around his neck. He pulls me against him, and I can feel how hard he is already.

Endowed. Very, very endowed. That's all I can think as I press myself against him. The moment our bodies fully align, the kiss explodes. I can't get enough, and it's like an out-of-body experience. I'm floating above myself as though there is a world around us, but we're detached from it. It's just us. It's heady and arousing.

Yes! His hand is on my ass now, and I can't help but moan. He's squeezing, and it's only making me want to rub myself against him. Each moan is making him increase his hold, and it's almost painful, but damn, it feels good.

"What do you want, Tina?"

Tina? No one calls me that. At least not since I was in kindergarten. By then, I was certain I was too old for nicknames and refused to be called anything but my full name. But coming from him? He can call me whatever the fuck he wants, as long as he keeps kissing me.

"You."

Well, I didn't mean to say that out loud.

"Do you? Because I'm not fucking you in some storeroom."

"Your office?" I'm only half joking.

"No. I do not need one of my brothers or cousins walking in on us. I want you naked and in my bed. I don't want anyone else seeing you."

It's possessive and way too forward. And it sounds perfect. I know it's not the soundest judgment, but I've gone home with a guy before when I haven't known him nearly long enough. When I was younger, it was straight foolishness and a ridiculous sense of being untouchable. I haven't done it in years. But everything about Bogdan makes me feel like I'm safer with him than without. Which is utterly absurd if he is Russian mafia.

"I came with someone."

I have to remind myself of that. I don't want to. But I should get back to Todd. He has to be wondering where the hell I went. He probably thinks I already ditched him. One more kiss first.

"What do you want, Tina? I know I want to be inside you right now. But I won't fuck you against a wall in a strip club. That feels wrong."

"Why?" I'm trying to think straight.

"Because you deserve better."

I didn't expect that answer. Not the words or his tone. It's soft. He's kissing my cheek and jaw as he tucks hair behind my ears. When he kisses my neck, I'm ready to give in.

"I have to tell Todd our plans have changed. I can't just leave."

"Fine."

Bogdan takes my hand once more with a gentle grip, which

doesn't match how he was holding my ass a moment ago. He looks both ways before we step out of the storeroom. He turns off the lights and pulls the door closed. I can't see Todd, but Bogdan points to the mezzanine. This is where the high rollers go with the best dancers. They give fully nude lap dances up here, but it costs. It's not the sort of thing Todd is usually willing to spend on. But the moment I get up to the second floor, it's obvious he's in the middle of more than just a lap dance. He's fucking the first dancer we saw. Like full on. I can see his pants are unzipped and his fingers are digging into her hips.

"What the fuck, Todd?" I'm pissed. I shouldn't be since I'm about to leave with another guy. But at least I came and found him to tell him I'm not going home with him. He looks at me and laughs.

"I figured you were slutting it up with that Russki I saw you talking to. You can get wet where you want, and I'll get hard."

"So fucking her is going to keep you hard? That's not been my experience. I'd be waiting a good hour and a half for you to be ready again."

"You know how much I love you sucking my dick. That should do the trick. It's a better use of your mouth than listening to you bitch at me."

Before I know what's happening, the woman is plucked off Todd's cock, and he's being pulled out of his seat. Bogdan's fisting his shirt and shaking him.

"Don't ever speak to her that way again. And I'm banning you from all clubs my family owns. You are not allowed to fuck the dancers, and you know that just like any other guy who comes in here. You want to do that, you do it away from here." Bogdan lets go and spins around to the woman. "Zora, get your shit and go. You're fired. You know the rules. We aren't running a fucking whorehouse."

Bogdan signals to someone on the floor below us, and two men who look remarkably like Bogdan but nothing like each other come upstairs. With his voice low and in Russian, Bogdan speaks to the men. I don't know what he says, but one takes off his suit coat and puts it around the woman's shoulders. The other grabs Todd's arm while my former fuck buddy tries to fix his pants. He turns back to me as the guy starts to drag him away. He should have listened to Bogdan.

"Did you fuck him already, Christina? Is that why he's trying to measure dicks?"

I laugh. "There's no comparison. There's a reason I'm going home with him and not you. Don't call or text. I'll block you."

"Don't be a bitch about this. It's not like either of us is cheating. We can hook up tomorrow. Just come over."

"I told you not to speak to her like that." Bogdan has clearly heard all he's willing to. His bouncer is still holding onto Todd's arm, but Bogdan steps in front of him. "Run your mouth again, and I will make sure no bar, no club, and no strip joint ever lets you in the door. Don't underestimate me or my reach."

"Christina, come on. Call your dogs off. You have a nice cunt, but it isn't worth all this."

I step between Bogdan and Todd before Bogdan can kill him. There's simmering rage there.

"You don't get it. Fuck whoever you want. I don't care. But you're a fucking idiot to do it in a strip club. And I might not mind dirty talk when we're alone, but what you've said, and other people have heard, is a no-go for me. You don't get to insult me because you aren't getting your way. Do not call or text. I'm serious."

"Or what? You're going to get your mafia boyfriend to whack me?"

"Who even talks like that? Go away." I turn to Bogdan and slide my hand into his. I tug him toward the stairs, not interested in what happens to Todd. I just want to leave. Bogdan hesitates, but then he follows me. When we get to the first floor, he leads me to the main door and points to a chauffeured sedan. I climb in and sit back, closing my eyes for a moment. When I hear the door close, I wonder what I've gotten myself into.

Chapter Two

Bogdan

What the hell am I doing? I never take women home with me. I don't hook up with random women either. I was ready to bust that guy's face over what he said. She's hot and sexy, but I have never gotten in a fight over a woman. She's not looking at me since she has her eyes closed, which is good. I need a moment to slow my heart down. I have three older brothers, and we immigrated to America with next to nothing. I have never been possessive or protective of anything. Not true. I'm protective of my family, but that's different. I would have totally overreacted if she hadn't pulled me away. Why am I being like this?

"Tina?" I need to know how upset she is. When she opens her eyes, she smiles, and I seriously think I might come just looking at her. She looks at the partition glass, then back to me. It's early fall, but it's still warm. She's wearing a miniskirt that is practically around her waist as she straddles my lap.

"Thank you for defending me."

She's kissing my neck and up to my ear. My dick twitches as her breath hits my ear and her teeth tug at my earlobe. Oh fuck. Now she's flicking it and sucking. I know what she's hinting at, and if this is even a fraction of what her mouth can do, I might propose tonight.

"Anytime, *malyshka*." As my hands glide up her thighs and under her skirt, the endearment feels natural. I've never said it before, but somehow it fits.

"What does that mean?"

"Baby girl." I watch her reaction. Heat flares in her eyes before she leans in for a kiss. She tries to grind on me, but my hands hold her hips in place. I feel her hesitation, then she stops. That's when I make her move. I control the speed and motion, and I feel her melt against me. She's letting me, and I'm pretty damn sure she likes that I'm taking the lead.

My fingers slide beneath her thong and along the divide between her ass cheeks until my fingers find her pussy. She's soaking wet. It's a good thing we're going to my place, because I suspect I'm going to have a wet patch on my pants when she gets off.

Gets off. That's exactly what I'm going to make her do before we even get to my door. Fuck, she's tight with only two fingers. She's going to squeeze the cum out of me once we're fucking.

"Kegels."

"What?" I don't know what she's talking about.

"Kegels. They're an exercise to strengthen a woman's vag. Don't worry. You'll fit."

She winks at me. That's it. I flip her around, so she's lying on the seat, and I'm kneeling on the floor. I pull her panties down, and she reaches for them. I look at her as if I'll hand them over. Then I stuff them in my pants pocket.

"Mine now."

The way her eyes widen tells me she understands I mean more than the obvious, just like earlier. Before she can disagree, I'm licking and kissing the inside of her thigh, nipping along the way as I make it to the promised land. The first sip is like the nectar of the gods, and her moan spurs me on. I know I have a five o'clock shadow that's rubbing against her pussy lips, and from the way she's trying to get closer, she likes it. Her hand is in my hair, and now she's trying to press me closer. I snag both her hands and flip her over.

The smack I lay on her ass is loud, but not hard. I'm ready to roll her back over when she pushes her hips up. It's an invitation, and I accept. I spank her again, a little harder. She shudders but pushes her ass toward my hand again. I rain down three more hard slaps while I have her hands pressed against the small of her back. She's already crossed her wrists, and I know she's done this before.

I release her wrists after one more spank. I spread her ass cheeks, and I lick her from top to bottom. I have no mercy now that I know she likes it rough. I suck her clit until she's shaking. She's not ready when I thrust three fingers into her. I'm careful. I don't want to hurt her. But I do want to dominate her. I know when she's getting close. I can feel her tightening around my fingers again, and she's dripping into my mouth.

"Can I—can I see you when I come?"

Her question is whispered, but the need is loud enough. I want to watch her face as I give her, her first orgasm of the night. I'm going to keep her coming over and over, and a couple might be while I'm riding her doggy style. But this first one feels significant. I turn her over, but she keeps her hands beneath her back. I look at her and raise an eyebrow. Let's see what she does now.

"Please, sir."

And there it is.

I press my mouth back to her pussy and work her clit until she can't help herself. She's raising her hips off the seat, and her hands are now in my hair and pushing my head to her cunt. I let her. She'll make up for it later now that I know at least part of what she likes. I work her until she's spent and panting. I scoop her into my arms and settle her on my lap. She burrows her face against my chest as she tries to catch her breath.

"Thank you." It comes out as a hoarse whisper, but the sincerity is clear. She inhales deeply before pushing away. She tries to get off my lap, but the car stops abruptly. I pull her tight against me to keep her from falling. There's something in her eyes as she looks up at me. I think she sees it in mine. I don't know what it is, but she's different. The moment ends as the car continues to approach my penthouse. She eases off my lap and kneels before me. Her hands are behind her back, and her eyes are lowered, but I see the smile. It's the same sexy smirk she gave me when we met.

Fuck me. This time, when the car stops, I look out the window. We're at my place. I sigh. Hopefully, she's in the mood to oblige once we're upstairs. I help her onto the seat and knock on the window. The door opens, and I slide out before reaching in to give her a hand. I nod to Stefan, my driver, before I lead her to the door. A sedan pulls up behind mine, and my cousin Anton gets out. I see Tina's confusion as she recognizes him. He has an apartment in my building, but I doubt he's going to spend the night at his place. He doesn't often and never alone. But he keeps his relationship discreet. It's safer that way for both of them.

"Tina, this is Anton, my cousin."

"Nice to meet you." She smiles at Anton as we get in the elevator. "I thought you look a lot alike. But what about the other man? He looked like you too, Bogdan."

"That's my other cousin. Sergei. Anton is from my father's

side, and Sergei is from my mother's." Anton looks ready to murder me. Why the hell am I telling her this? I shouldn't have even used his name, let alone told her half my family tree. Now she's looking at me, wondering why Anton is glaring at me. I wrap my arm around her and pull her against me. I drop a kiss on her head, and it surprises me. It's affectionate when I meant only to distract her. I catch Anton rolling his eyes as the elevator pings. We're at his floor.

"Have a good night." Tina offers my cousin a smile. Anton is a good-looking guy, especially when he smiles. He can charm just about anyone. If I didn't know him better, I might be jealous. But I know neither he nor Sergei are competition. When we're alone again, I tilt her chin and swoop in for a kiss. I know she can taste herself, and I smile when she grimaces. Apparently, she doesn't think she tastes as good as I think she does. We're forced apart when we reach my floor. Unlike two of my brothers' places, the elevator opens into my apartment. Aleksei and I prefer it, since no one can burst in without us knowing they arrived on our floor. Maksim and Nikolai prefer having a door between them and anyone who arrives on their floor. All of us have security cameras and bodyguards, so no one is coming near us regardless of our floor plans.

"Who's this?" Tina looks down as a silver cat brushes against her ankles. She squats and pets the cat's side before scratching between its ears.

"This is Cleo."

"Cleo?" I can hear she's trying not to laugh. Then her smile falls, and her eyes sweep my apartment.

"Ex-girlfriend, Tina. When we broke up, I got the cat." I knew what she was thinking. She nods, but I can tell she's less certain than she was a moment ago. "That was three years ago. I haven't seen her in ages. No one's going to barge in, and there's no one I'm missing."

"I didn't say anything."

"You didn't have to."

I stroke the back of my fingers along her jaw. It's a soft touch, so she's unprepared when I pull her against me and wrap my hand in her fiery hair. I would never call it carrot out loud, but it's a rich red and orange that I already know is natural. Her pussy is bare, but I could see a hint. Her eyes are a deeper tone than the bourbon she drank earlier, more like a whiskey.

"Are you always good at reading people who don't want to be read?"

"Yes. It's an important skill for business." I can guess what type of business she's assuming, and she wouldn't be far off. Though I'm fairly certain whatever she's thinking pales compared to what I've done over the years. "That's not the only place where it's important."

She bites her lip, and I can tell she's hoping I don't make her say it out loud.

"Do you want vanilla tonight or not?" She shakes her head. "Do you trust me to read you well enough to give you pain and pleasure?" She nods. My expression darkens.

"Yes, sir." She looks toward a closed door. "How'd you guess? I mean, I know you were testing me by how hard you could squeeze, but how did you know in the car that I would call you sir?"

"I wasn't sure, but I'd hoped you like what I do."

She nods before looking at a second door. This one leads to my room. The other was to my office. She inhales deeply, and her breasts press against my chest. I sweep her into my arms, and she squeals before giggling. She tucks her face against my chest again, but I can feel her laughing. The sound goes straight to my dick. She looks back when Cleo meows, and I know the little beast is pissed at being left alone again. But there is only one pussy I'm interested in tonight.

As I put her back on her feet beside my bed, I'm trying to decide what I want to do. She steps back from me and kicks off her heels. She unties the halter top from around her neck and pulls the shirt over her head. I knew she wasn't wearing a bra, but I didn't expect the pasties. She's quick to turn around and take a step back to me. I gladly unzip her skirt and push it down to the floor. I still have her thong in my pocket. I am not giving it back. I suspect I'll be jerking off to it a lot until the next time I see her.

When I step close to her and slide my hands over her taut belly and up to her breasts, she reaches behind her and unfastens my belt, then my pants. I'm massaging her tits, and glorious ones they are. They fit in my hands, firm and full. I don't need to look to know they're real. She rests her head against my chest, and it's the third time she's done that on her own. It feels like it belongs there, and she didn't fight me in the elevator when I pressed it to me. I peel off the pasties as I kick off my pants and shoes. Regrettably, I have to let go to pull off my socks and boxer briefs. I hurry to shed my suit coat and unbutton my shirt. I'm naked and harder than I can ever remember.

One hand goes back to working her tits while the other squeezes her ass. I'm no longer gentle. I graze my teeth along her neck until I reach the crook and press my teeth into her flesh. Not deep enough to leave a lasting mark, but enough to remind her I'm in control. But I need to be sure one last time. I turn her to face me.

"Tina, you said you don't want vanilla. What're your limits?"

"Short of any R. Kelly kind of kink, I don't really have any."

Everyone has limits. We might not get to hers tonight, but I plan to discover them, eventually.

"Do you have a safe word?"

"Yes." She pauses when I expect her to tell me.

"What is it?"

"I don't want to use that one with you." It's more like she's talking to herself than me. "Olives."

"That's your safe word?"

"Yes. I don't like them, so I would never ask for them. And I've never used it before."

As I gaze into her eyes, I see that's important to her, and I realize it's important to me, too. I don't want to share that with someone else. It's obvious neither of us is a virgin, especially not after what I know were her original plans for the night. I can't change that we've both been with other people, and I don't even care. But having a word that is just ours seems special. I didn't even think that much about it when I started dating my ex-girlfriend.

"Sir, may I?"

Tina's looking down between our feet, and her hands are behind her back once again. I nod, and she sinks to her knees. I palm my cock and stroke it twice, a drop of precum leaking from the tip. She opens her mouth but waits. I guide my cock to her, and her tongue licks me.

"Snap if it's too much."

She barely nods before my hand cups her jaw, my thumb on one side and my fingers on the other. My free hand fists her hair as I drive my dick into her mouth. Her lips wrap around me, and she sucks. Holy fuck. I watch her eyes close as she works me, her head bobbing. This is going to be over way too soon. And I want to get off from pleasuring her, not the other way around. I tug her head back, but she refuses to let go.

Instead, she works me harder, sucking me practically down her throat.

"Enough, Tina." It's a command. One she purposefully ignores. "*Malyshka.*"

Her eyes pop open, and she sits back on her heels as she releases me. I reach over to the bedside table and pull the drawer open. I hand her a condom and wait for her to put it on me. She's a tease even doing that. She eases it down my shaft, and I'm ready to go insane. I lift her off the floor and into my arms, guiding her legs around my waist. The tip of my cock is ready to slide into her pussy. I spank her, making her jolt up, then slide down my cock.

"Oh, God."

She's clinging to me as she moans. I spank her again and again, each one a little harder than the last. I can feel her wanting to move, but my arm around her waist holds her in place. I'm rocking my hips, but I'm not thrusting the way either of us wants.

"Who is in control tonight, *malyshka?*" I give her a particularly hard slap that makes her whimper. I kiss her, and she melts around me. Her arms and legs tighten. "Who's in control, baby girl?"

"You, Daddy."

I nearly drop her as we climb on the bed. Her shock matches mine. Clearly, she hadn't planned to say that.

"That's right, *malyshka*. Daddy decides what his baby girl gets. Right now, I think you need a rough fuck."

She nods as I plow into her. I might lead, but she definitely follows. She's taking each thrust, raising, and rolling her hips to take me deeper. I've had enough sex to know good from bad, but this might be the best I've ever had. No woman has called me Daddy before, either. I didn't know it was my thing until Tina said it.

"More." She's looking up at me as her nails dig into my shoulders. I think about pinning them above her head. Next time. Right now, I'm enjoying how it feels to have her cling to me. I thrust harder and faster, and she practically comes off the bed as her back arches. Her mouth opens in a silent scream.

"Let me hear you. I want to know I made you come."

"Yes, Daddy!"

That's all it takes for me to explode.

My arms are shaking as I roll over and pull the condom off. I toss it into the trash beside my bed before looking back at the glorious redhead lying next to me. I lift her to straddle my waist before I sit up. It's an intimate position I haven't been in for years. My cock is already thinking about coming back to life, but for right now, I just want to kiss and be close to her. That's not me. I don't cuddle. I don't need post-coital affection. At least not before tonight. My lack of interest in it was a huge sore spot with my ex. With Tina, I can't seem to let go.

"Bogdan?"

"Mmm." I kiss behind her ear as I stroke her hair. She rests her cheek on my shoulder and sighs.

"I've never called a guy that before."

"I thought it surprised you."

"It did. Is that what you like to be called?"

I lean back. Her voice sounds unsure, and I don't like that she feels uneasy with me. That's the last thing I want.

"No one has ever called me that, and I've never called a woman *malyshka* before."

"Are you a Dom?"

The word makes me hard. Or rather, it's Tina saying it that makes me hard. Before I answer, I grab another condom. I hold it up and wait for her to decide. She nods and takes it from me. She rolls it down me before rising on her knees. She slides down my dick, and I can't help but groan. She feels better than anything I ever imagined. But I'm content to just hold her for a moment.

"No. I like to be in control, and I like kink. But I'm not a Dom. The few relationships I've had in the past have been traditional."

"You asked what my limits are. What do you like?"

"I like to use restraints. Handcuffs, spreaders. I enjoy spanking, as I'm sure you've figured out. What about you? Are you a sub?"

"No. And I'm not a little. I'm not submissive at all during sex. I don't always take charge or anything. But tonight... I enjoy spanking, especially with a paddle, flogger, or riding crop. I suppose my limit is birching."

My hands cover her smooth ass, unable—or rather unwilling—to imagine the welts that would come from a caning. I might want to see her ass fire-engine red, even with some mild welts, but not what comes from that kind of spanking.

"I like restraints, too."

I sense there is something else she wants to say, but she keeps it to herself. I suppose we don't have to share all our fantasies at once.

"I never considered you as a little. But neither have I ever considered myself a Daddy dom. I enjoy hearing you call me that, though."

I kiss her and move her on my cock. She's riding me on her knees, but she soon shifts to straighten her legs. It brings our bodies closer together, even more intimate than a moment ago. She shivers as my fingers play along her spine.

"I like that, Daddy."

"Whatever you want, *malyshka*."

This time is vanilla. It's slow, and we watch each other. Our touches are almost tender. We rock together, and I guide her again. She's content with my rhythm, but it's not long before I can feel her eagerness build.

"Bogdan, please. I need to come."

I suppose if she were my sub, I would punish her for saying my name. But I love the sound of it as she whispers beside my ear. I lean back, and she once more shifts to kneel again. I lace my fingers with hers, but I no longer set the pace.

"Take what you need, *malyshka*. Ride me how you want."

She doesn't waste a breath as she moves how she needs, and I feel her muscles clench around me as she comes. We're there at the same time. I hadn't expected that, not coming at the same time, or something that was actually tender.

We're breathless as she rolls to lie on her side. We share brief kisses until we stop panting. My hand rests across her ass just before her hand explores my chest and back, finally stopping as she comes to my ass.

"You said you like restraints." She glances at the headboard and sees where some of the wood is chipped. "Would you cuff me to your bed and have your way with me, sir?"

"Back to sir?" I tsk at her before rising and rolling her onto her belly. "Don't move, baby girl."

I open the bedside table drawer again and pull out a pair of handcuffs. I have a moment of hesitation when I think about the other women who have worn these. Somehow, I don't like the idea of reusing them with Tina, but she asked, and they're what I have. I snap them around one wrist before looping them over the crossbeam, then closing it around the other wrist. I grab a paddle and stand beside the bed.

"What do you call me, *malyshka*?"

"Daddy."

"What did you call me instead?

"Sir."

"Am I your Dom?"

"No, Daddy."

"How many paddles do you think you deserve?" I want to gauge what she can take.

"Ten, Daddy."

That's more than I expected. I start with two fairly light ones, one on each cheek. Her expression tells me she thinks they're lame. I grab her hair and tug back.

"That is not a very polite expression, baby girl."

"Does that mean more spankings?"

"Cheeky."

I land five to each cheek, leaving her ass a bright red. I'm not so light-handed with those. She kicks her feet several times, but she never tells me to stop or uses her safe word. I look toward the drawer and notice the massage vibrator I have. I can't bring myself to use that when I know I used it with my ex. It's clean, of course, but I draw the limit with that. Instead, I grab an extendable spreader. I flip her so she's on her back again, her wrists crossed and still fastened to the headboard. I attach the bar to each ankle and climb onto the bed between her thighs. I give no explanation or warning before each thing I do. I latch onto her clit and suck. She squeals and writhes, unprepared for the sensation when I know her clit must be sensitive from already coming three times. I'm relentless. I drive her to the edge and pull back. I do it over and over as sweat beads along her hairline and her cheeks grow flushed.

"Daddy, please. I can't take any more. I need to come."

"If it's too much, use your safe word."

I know she won't, and she doesn't. When I know she truly has come close to her limits, I slide a condom on, and drive into her. She can't move beneath me. Between the restraints and my weight, she's pinned. And she's begging again. She tugs against the handcuffs, but she keeps chanting "yes."

She has no control, and we both love it. Our gazes are fixed to one another, and nothing else exists. If I could keep her chained in my bed forever, I would. That would satisfy all kinds of fantasies.

"Daddy, I'm coming."

"Me too, *malyshka*."

We say the same thing to each other over and over until it's four o'clock in the morning. Thank God it's now Saturday. I don't have to go back to the club until nearly eleven tonight, and I know Tina doesn't have to work. Or at least I assume she doesn't. I realize I don't even know her last name as I drift off.

Chapter Three

Tina

"Good morning."

"Mmm." I feel Bogdan's lips on my shoulder, and I sigh. I'm comfy and completely content.

"I'm going to take a shower."

He swats my backside, and I roll over as he gets out of bed. He has the most magnificent body I've ever seen. And I've seen quite a few. I was a swimmer in high school and college, so I spent a good chunk of my life around half-naked athletic men. None hold a candle to Bogdan. I watch him close the bathroom door, then the shower turns on.

Fuck! Shower? I stayed the whole night. I fling back the covers and glance at the clock. It's eight o'clock. I never linger this long after the sex is done. Granted, that was only four hours ago, and I passed out hard. But still. I scramble to find all my clothes. I'll be doing the walk of shame in the daylight. I prefer to slide into a cab or Uber in the dark. Slide. Humph. Slip away in the dead of the night is more like it. I'm looking for my thong when I remember Bogdan has it. I glance at his pants and grin. He can keep it.

I can guess that he expects me to join him, and it's *so* tempting. Morning sex and shower sex combined and with Bogdan sounds like a special slice of heaven. But I can't stick around. It'll just be uncomfortable once it is time for me to go. We'll just be looking at each other, and there'll be fake promises to get together, or the awkward goodbye when neither of us wants to do this again. Well, I would do it again if it wasn't always meant to be just a one-night stand.

Cleo is staring at me, and I wonder how many other women she's watched do the same thing. Somehow, I bet Bogdan has to chase most women out of his place. I don't know another single man who has a cat. Not what I expected last night, and it still surprises me this morning. I can't help but giggle as the elevator arrives. As I step in, I can only imagine what he's going to think when he comes out of the bathroom, and I'm gone. That just makes me pray the elevator would move faster.

I don't look at the man at the concierge desk, but I nod. But I'm forced to stop when I pass Anton at the door. He looks like he just came from a run, and I see the other guy from last night jogging away. Bogdan said they were his cousins. I smile at Anton and murmur "good morning" before hurrying outside. I was so impatient for the elevator to move that I didn't think about ordering an Uber or Lyft. Thank goodness Bogdan lives in an urban enough area for me to hail a cab. He actually lives in one of the most expensive high rises in Manhattan. Strip clubs apparently earn well.

I hear his voice as I open the cab door. I tell myself to pretend I don't hear him, but I can't help it. I look back and wave, but I nearly fall into the car when I take in how fine he looks in a tight t-shirt and jogging pants. But it's his face. He looks like an avenging angel. Far too perfect looking, but furious. I slam the car door closed as I give the cabbie my address. I'm leaving with fond memories. But he's left pissed.

"What do you mean, I have to go to this site?" Fuck me.

"Jeremy is out sick, and the site is due for inspection. They won't get the next set of permits on time if someone--and by that, I mean you— doesn't go out there."

My boss, Tom, looks about as excited as I do. It's the last place I want to go today, but I don't have much of a choice. There is no one else available. The only reason I can inspect the construction site is because the two builds I was supposed to visit are delayed from material backorders.

"Fine."

Fuck me. Fuck me. Fuck my fucking life. I'm thinking this the entire way from my office in the Bronx to the job site. I love my job, but I hate my office. I live in Queens, but I commute every day. I would rather take public transportation, but considering the amount of crap I have to haul around with me and some of the tools I carry, it isn't practical or safe. I am one more promotion away from moving to the City Planning Commission's Central Office in Manhattan. It'll still be a commute, but I won't have to drive as much. I'll miss going to job sites, but I sure as hell won't miss my boss. And I would love the raise. Fucking student loans. Loans and this inspection. Fuck me.

I pull up alongside the portable trailer that houses the site office. I look around and breathe a little easier thinking I might get away with a conflict-free morning. I grab my hard hat and clipboard. As I step around my truck, it starts. I see the men staring and talking about me. A few even point. I'm already one of a few women on a construction site. Having red hair doesn't help me blend in. Whatever.

I knock before opening the office door. I'm greeted by two men who have familiar dark hair and ice-blue eyes. My stomach knots. They don't know who I am, but I know who they are. And it's not just because of the rumors about them being mafia. Oh, no. That doesn't matter at all. But as I look around, I realize *he* isn't here. I swallow my sigh of relief.

"Mr. Kutsenko, I'm—"

I don't get to introduce myself as I hear two men's voices approaching outside, and I know one of them without a doubt. I steel myself for the inevitable as the door opens.

"Where the fuck is Jeremy? I don't have all day."

And there he is. His hair is windblown, and he's clearly already annoyed. But he's even better looking than I remembered, and I've been remembering a lot over the past two days.

"Tina?"

I watch him look me up and down, taking in the hard hat under my arm and my steel-toed boots. He looks baffled before our gazes meet. Then there's pure blue-hot flames blazing at me.

"Mr. Kutsenko—"

He marches to me before I can get any further into my introductions than the first time I opened my mouth.

"No."

It's a single word, but it feels like it carries the weight of the world. He puts his hand on the small of my back and gives me a little push toward the door. I consider digging my heels in, but this is a scene I'd rather not act out in front of all three of his brothers. He opens the door and keeps his arm outstretched until I step onto the metal stoop. His hand stays on my back as he hurries me down the stairs and around the side of the trailer. No one from the site can see us, and I glance up to be sure there are no trailer windows facing us. We're as alone as we can be with a hundred crewmen and three Kutsenkos around.

"What are you doing here?"

"Jeremy is sick. I'm inspecting today. I apologize for being late, but I didn't know I was coming here until I got into the office this morning."

"You just happen to wind up here."

"Yes, Bogdan." I can't help but snap at him. "Do you think I went to my boss and said, 'Pretty please. Let me go to the job site where the guy I fucked a couple nights ago might be'?"

"Fucked and ditched. You assumed you'd never see me again." I shrug, and his eyes narrow. "*Malyshka*, I didn't take you for a coward."

"I'm not. I don't owe you any explanations for why I left. I wanted to, so I did."

"No. You ran away. You thought it would be too hard or too awkward, so you ran. You saw me, and you heard me. You fucking waved."

"What was the point of going back? Were we going to have breakfast? You'd already showered, and I was already dressed. Morning sex didn't seem likely."

"Tina—"

"Bogdan!"

I look past his shoulder and lean around the corner to see a man on the stoop. It's the brother he arrived with. Bogdan shakes his head and holds up his hand.

"We'll be there in a minute."

"Bogdan, we nee—"

"Tina." He crowds me, but I don't want to move when he steps so close our shoes touch. "If I put my hand between your thighs, you'd be wet for me."

"Just like you're hard for me?" I try to sound snide.

"Yes. Like a fucking pole. Tell me you didn't think about me once this weekend. Tell me you didn't remember what it

31

felt like with me inside you. Tell me you don't wish to feel that again. Tell me the fucking truth."

I close my eyes and tilt my head back before I exhale.

"Of course I thought about you. But it was a one-night thing."

"Why?"

"Because I usually don't sleep with guys on the first date, so it wasn't a date."

"Then let me take you on one, and we won't have sex that night."

"What?"

"Why did it have to be only one night?"

"We met at a strip club. Is that where you met your last girlfriend? It's not exactly where solid relationships usually start."

Something flickers in his gaze before he shakes his head.

"No, I didn't meet her there. I'm not your employer, and you're not my employee. We both happened to be there. Isn't that how most couples meet? They happen to be at the same place. Does it really matter where that place was?"

"I arrived with a guy. You know what my plans were."

"So you came home with me just to get laid? I don't think so. If that were the case, you would have given Todd a pass and fucked him instead of me. If that were the case, you would have told me to fuck you in that storeroom. You came home with me because you knew it was something else."

"What something else, Bogdan? You're reading too much into this."

It's his turn to sound snide.

"If it was nothing, then why'd you call me Daddy?"

I jerk backwards and hit the chain fence behind me. I glower at him, but I don't push him away when he rests his hands on my waist or when he kisses me behind the ear. I close my eyes and try not to melt. I've thought about him nonstop since I left his place. I regretted running away as soon as the cab pulled away from the curb. But I couldn't go back. I refused to be desperate and go to Pussycats the next night, hoping to find him.

"Why?"

"You ask that a lot."

"Then give me a proper answer, Tina. Why?"

"Because it felt right."

"Exactly. And that's why I called you baby girl."

"What do you want from me, Bogdan?"

"A date. Let me take you out, and if you don't enjoy it, then I'll leave you alone."

My phone rings in my back pocket. It's my office ring tone.

"It's work. I have to answer." I pull it out and slide my finger. "Hello."

No... Fuck...Wonder-fucking-ful.

"Yes, Tom. I'll let them know. I'm here now and keeping them waiting. I need to go."

"What's wrong, Tina?"

Bogdan's voice is velvet, like it was several times that night. His arm is around my waist now, and I love it. But I force myself away and shake my head.

"Jeremy has meningitis. He's going to be out of work for weeks, most likely. My boss permanently reassigned me. Bogdan, I can't go out with you. It's a complete conflict of interest. I could get fired."

"I know, *malyshka*."

He kisses my forehead and then kisses my lips. I open to him, regret and frustration multiplying. I finally admitted that I want him, and I was even about to agree to a date. Now it's either nothing or it'll have to wait for who knows how long. I drink in his kiss, savoring every moment, until a throat being cleared interrupts.

"Niko, I swear."

"Bogdan."

"Maks, I swear. Give me two more minutes."

"Bogd—"

"I said two minutes."

I see the man's surprise, and I'm shocked at Bogdan's tone. He shakes his head and sighs.

"I'm sorry, Maks. Just give me two more minutes, please. We're almost done talking. I'll explain later. Please."

"Fine."

Bogdan looks back and watches his brother walk away.

"Tina, I know we have to go. But I'm not taking back my invitation. If you're still interested in me when you're through, then it'll stand."

"And if you're the one who doesn't want to go on the date?"

He looks at me as if I've lost my mind. Maybe I have. He walks beside me as we head back to the trailer. Once again, he opens the door for me. This time, I see not only three men who are clearly his brothers, but I recognize his cousins. As if one of them isn't intimidating on sight, but six of them? It's almost too much. There's not a bad looking one in the bunch, but I'm acutely aware of Bogdan standing next to me. And it's not just because we've already slept together. There is something in him that's like a magnet to me. None of the others tempt me, despite all of them being gorgeous.

"Mr. Kutsenko, I'm Christina MacNally. I'm here in place of Jeremy Hanson."

"Irish?"

I'm not sure who mutters that, but I lift my chin and glare.

"No. It's *Mac*Nally not *Mc*Nally. I'm Scottish, not Irish."

"You don't sound Scottish. And the red hair." I realize it's the brother who didn't come in with Bogdan or come outside looking for us.

"I dinna ken who's who amongst ye lot, but I ken ma ma and ma da are Scottish."

I can sound just like my parents and our family, even if I was born and raised in America. And why do people assume only the Irish have red hair? I watch the surprise on all their faces since I know I sound like I'm newly arrived from Edinburgh.

"I will be taking Mr. Hanson's place while he is out of the office. I won't delay you any further. If you could point me in the right direction, I'll start my inspection and get out of your way."

"Ms. MacNally, we've never seen you at a build site before."

It's the guy Bogdan called Maksim. I notice he has a wedding ring on, and he appears to be the oldest. I glance at Bogdan before focusing on his brother.

"I didn't know you've been to all the build sites in New York."

"She reminds me of Laura." That comes from Sergei.

I don't understand why a few of them are laughing, but I assume Laura is Maksim's wife from the way he tries to glower, but his lips twitch.

"Ms. MacNally, this is my oldest brother, Maksim." Bogdan points to each man as he introduces them. "These are my other brothers Aleksei and Nikolai, and these are our cousins Anton and Sergei. You saw them the other night."

I shoot Anton a look when I see him open his mouth. I'm certain every man in that trailer will know I slept with Bogdan within two minutes of me walking out. I don't need it pointed out while I'm there. He merely grins at me. I'm about to turn toward the door when I catch Anton looking at Sergei. I don't know what to make of the silent exchange, but something is off. I look up at Bogdan, but he's watching me.

"I'll take you around."

It's not an offer. I'm not in the mood to argue, so I nod and follow Bogdan from the trailer. It's not long before the other Kutsenkos follow us. It's like walking amongst a hoard of dark-haired Vikings. I have never felt so short as I do, standing among these men who are all close to a foot taller than me. The workers are watching me, and I see them laughing. I don't need them to like or respect me. I only need the Kutsenkos to respect me. But it's annoying.

"Bogdan, do all of you usually follow Hanson?"

"No." He looks at his brothers and cousins, then shakes his head. They fall back, giving me space to meet the foreman, Jim. He shows me the designs and starts pointing things out to me as though I'm new.

"These girders support the cross section that'll go up as soon as you sign off." He points to a pile of massive metal beams. "We'll use the crane to get them up and lay them horizontally."

"Really? And I assumed your men still carried them up wood ladders." I look down at the designs, then up at the roofing that's going in. "Why aren't you using cleat holes on the rafters to tie the wires? Why are you boring holes you don't need? Seems like a waste of time."

"We need holes to pass the wires through."

Patronizing turd. Please, mansplain some more.

"No, you don't. You can fit diagonal tie wires directly to the rafters by using the cleat holes on the underside of the top flange. That's what they're designed for. It's faster, so fewer days on the site." I look at Bogdan when I mention that, since it'll save his company money. "And it's more structurally sound."

"But it doesn't have to be done that way."

Jim isn't pleased. But then, neither am I.

"It doesn't. But it's the right way." I make a note on my clipboard. It's not something that will cause them to fail the inspection, but I want to remember it later. I know Bogdan is trying to read what I wrote, but he won't understand my shorthand.

I step away from the table where the plans are spread and move toward the actual construction. I have a list of corrective actions they were to take after my predecessor's last visit. I'm also here to look at the second story and above flooring and sheathing. I'm agile and coordinated, moving from one portion of the growing building to another. I ask questions when I need to, but mostly I'm silent. It unnerves both guys. By the time I've seen everything, I'm dreading talking to Bogdan. We head toward the trailer, and I take off my hard hat.

"Who spends the most time at the sites or usually deals with the inspectors?"

"Niko? Why?"

I stop and turn toward him. I look around and keep my voice low.

"Before I make any assumptions and make an ass of myself, I need you to tell me the truth, Bogdan. It's my job we're talking about."

"What is it?"

I think about how I want to phrase this. "Do Niko and Jeremy have any agreements?"

"Agreements? What the hell, Tina? Do you think we're bribing city officials?"

Now it's my turn to give him a look like he's simple.

"Not when it comes to the building's quality."

"Bogdan, there are several issues that I spotted that could shut you down. Worse, they could force you to tear down some sections and start over. They never should have gotten to this point. Previous inspections shouldn't have passed, and several of the corrections from the last inspection haven't been made properly." I run my hand over my hair, that's pulled back into a ponytail. "Do any of you have formal training with architecture and construction?"

"No. We all worked construction when we were teens, but none of us specialize in it. That's why we have a foreman."

I cringe. I turn back to the trailer and sigh as he opens the door for me. If nothing else, his etiquette is impeccable. I look around and try to remember which brother is Aleksei and which one is Nikolai. I think I know.

"Mr. Kutsenko, your brother said you handle most of your company's build sites. I have some concerns. There are several things that need fixing immediately. If they aren't, you fail the inspection, and I have to shut down the build."

"What problems? There weren't any issues when the last inspector was here."

"Yes, there were. But for whatever reason, he said nothing. Or nothing was done about them." I lock eyes with Bogdan's brother, and I can see he's furious.

"Niko," Bogdan warns.

"Mr. Kutsenko—"

"It's Niko, or else you'll get all of us answering at once."

"Thank you. How long has your foreman been with your company?"

"He started just before we broke ground."

"He looks and sounds like he's experienced, so there can only be a few reasons there are so many problems. Either he's incompetent or lazy, or he doesn't care, or he's getting something out of doing a poor job. Whatever his problem is, he's already costing you money. Now he's going to cost you even more."

"What do you mean?"

I set the clipboard down on a desk and place my hard hat on top.

"I noticed right away that the girders have cleats for cross tie wires. He's having your men drill holes to pass the wires through. There's no need for that. It's slowing the job, which means you're paying for more days of work and machines than you need. Now, I've found things threatening the structural integrity of the entire building. He's ignoring them and cutting corners. I can give you a list of seven things that you can fix by the end of the day. I'll come back at four-thirty and do another sweep. If they're fixed and up to code, I'll sign off on the inspection. If they aren't, I can't. I'll lose my job if someone comes after me and knows I said nothing. And I'll definitely lose my job if there's an accident, and I said everything was up to code."

The men are silent, but I can tell they all have plenty to say. They just won't until I leave. But I can't go until I know what they intend to do.

"I'll step outside, or you can speak in Russian, but I have to know which way this is going before I can leave."

The floodgates open. I don't understand a word of what they're saying, but no one sounds pleased as they go back and forth in Russian. I hear the foreman's and my colleague's name several times before they finally all look at me. Only Sergei has blond hair, and only Anton has brown eyes. Otherwise, it's six versions of the same face looking at me. It's uncanny, and right now it's seriously unnerving.

"Tell us what we can do today to pass. Then we'll sort out everything else." Bogdan's face is drawn, but his tone is encouraging.

"The first thing I would do is get a new foreman. But here's my list." I hand over the form that was on my clipboard. I give Niko my business card. "Call or text when you're ready for me to come back, otherwise, I'll be here at four-thirty."

I gather my things and offer a grim nod. No one's in a good mood. I'm not thrilled that I need to come back. I don't want another run in with Bogdan, and I don't want to make a second trip out here. I can't go back to my office either, or my boss will want my report.

"Ms. MacNally?"

I look over at an older man approaching me as I walk to my truck. Bogdan stepped onto the trailer stoop. But someone is still talking to him inside.

"Mr. Litov, hello. I didn't realize you worked for the Kutsenkos."

"Sometimes, yes. Sometimes, no."

"But you're not the foreman. You were at the last site I saw you."

"I was there, but that was houses. This is office building. Not same thing."

"It's not, but I know your work and how you run a project." I walk toward the man who's got to be in his late fifties, if not early sixties. He's a little hunched over, and his face is leathery from too many days in the sun. But he's clearly still strong, and he's intelligent. He shouldn't be a regular day laborer.

"Not my project to decide. Have good day, Ms. MacNally."

I dart back up the stairs and brush past Bogdan as I return to the office.

"You have Anatolii Litov here. He should be your foreman."

"He's never done an industrial or commercial job before, only residential," Niko points out.

"I know, but he's good. He's honest, and he knows what to do. You have my list. Take him around and let him look for himself. If he spots even half of what I did, sack Jim and make Anatolii your foreman." I shrug and turn back to the door. This time, Bogdan follows me to my truck.

"The city has certainly upgraded."

"Check the plates. This isn't the city's. It's mine."

"Really?" Bogdan looks along the side of my quad cab truck, noticing the hydraulic step that I just activated. He notes the bed liner and the rolled back cover. I know he noticed the electric liftgate. When he turns back to me, I have the driver's door open and one foot on the step. I don't love driving a truck, but it goes with the territory of being in mud and rain a lot. I often have to haul things that wouldn't fit in a regular SUV, and no compact car would make it over the uneven ground that I'm constantly on. "It's an awfully big truck for a baby girl."

"I can handle it."

"I know you can, *malyshka*."

I don't think we're talking about my truck anymore. At least, I'm not. But the shitshow I've seen today means I have to tell my boss something to keep Jeremy from returning. That could mean it's even longer before we can see each other again. That or I have to convince Tom to assign someone else.

"I'm sorry I had to be the bearer of bad news today. But I'm not exaggerating about how serious this is."

"I know you're not. It's inconvenient, and it pisses us all off that the work has been shit. But that's not your fault. You're saving us in the long run."

"I hope so." I glance down before I meet his gaze again. "Should I try to get someone else assigned?"

"Do you think I don't want to see you now that you pointed out the problems?"

I shake my head. "We can't go on that date until I'm no longer assigned to this project. I have to tell my boss at least some of the issues, or Jeremy will come back once he's not sick anymore. If I don't get someone else, we might not go out until the entire job is done. That's months."

"I am not waiting months to see you again, Tina. I'll lose my mind. I don't even want to see you drive away today, let alone know I can't see you for at least three more months."

"I don't want that either. I'll talk to my boss and see what I can do."

"*Malyshka*, I'm usually at Envy on Mondays and Tuesdays, or Ivy on Wednesdays and Thursdays. I only check on the strip clubs on the weekends. Maybe we'll run into each other again."

"I'd like that, Daddy."

We both look around, like kids who know they're about to get caught, but plan to be naughty, anyway. Using the car door to shield us, he tugs at my belt and pulls me close. His lips meet mine as his hand cups my pussy. I keep my moan quiet, but I let him know I like the feel of him touching me. I feel the zipper pulled down, and then his fingers are in me.

"Daddy's going to make you come."

I look around, but blessedly, no one is looking in our direction. I'm trying to think of something to say, so we look like we're having a conversation if anyone notices us. But I can't think straight.

"Daddy," I whisper as I feel it. "I'm coming."

Bogdan pulls his hand out of my pants and licks his fingers. "I'm going to be starving by the time I eat your little pussy again."

I sink back into the driver's seat and turn on the truck before I lower the window. He pushes the door closed and leans against the open window. He gives me a quick kiss before I pull out of my spot. It's going to be a long ass day, and I'm still horny as hell.

Chapter Four

Bogdan

That was not how I expected my morning to go. I couldn't have imagined in my wildest dreams that I would open the trailer door and find Tina standing there. I couldn't stop staring. She'd pulled her hair back, unlike the night we met. She wore a button down with a sweater over the top, only her collar and cuffs showing. Her black trousers were professional, but sensible. I noticed the steel-toed boots that were clearly well broken in, and the hard hat. A hard hat is not meant to be sexy, but it sure as hell was when she wore it.

I nearly fell to my death three times because her ass distracted me too much while we walked along the scaffolding and beams. She moved with the ease of someone familiar with the precarious walkways. I'm nowhere near as comfortable as she is. She asked insightful questions that I couldn't answer, and as it turns out, ones Jim barely could. From her notes, it looks like his answers weren't always honest, either. She's observant. I noticed that when we met, but she takes in a lot of details and seems to catalog them, not forgetting a single thing.

She didn't talk a lot, but I'm certain she had plenty to say. Circumspect. I remember learning that word in the eleventh grade. My teacher told me I should be more circumspect when teasing my friend about getting laid after prom. While I couldn't stop staring, it was as though she didn't know I was there. But she did. She was dripping for me by the time I got in her panties again. The way her eyes turn into warm pools of dark chocolate when I make her come. The way her breath hitches, and she holds it as she welcomes the pleasure. I want to see it over and over.

Thank God I'm in my car alone as I head to Envy. The privacy glass is up, and my hand is around my cock. I'd rather be fucking her or enjoying her mouth on me, but my fingers still smell like her. Being inside her was like I'd finally found my dream home. We fit like we were made to match, and nothing has felt better. Her name is on my lips as I squeeze my eyes shut. Damn, that felt good. I'm quick to grab some tissues and clean myself up before the car stops in front of Envy.

I've had a few long-term relationships. I'm the only one of us who's a serial boyfriend. My brothers, at least until Maks met Laura, never settled down. It had been five years since Maks last had a girlfriend, and that was way more business than pleasure. The former members of the Elite Group decided who would make Maks the perfect bratva wife. Unfortunately, she also made the perfect mattress for half the men under Maks's direction. Aleks and Niko refuse to get close to women because our lifestyle isn't conducive to romantic relationships. Every girlfriend I've had has always complained that I'm emotionally closed-off and refuse to share my life with them.

I can't. The rumors are true. We are mafia. We are the Russian bratva in New York City. Our mother and father did what they could to keep us away from the brotherhood, but my father died fighting the Chechens when I was really young. We came to America, and it didn't take long for the Ivankov bratva to hear who we were and about our ties to the Podolskaya bratva back in Moscow.

Vladislav Lushak was *pakhan* back then. The man was a brutal bastard. He'd been former KGB, like my father, but he was the stereotype of a ruthless Russian killer. He loved every time someone took a last breath. He relished training boys to become *boyeviks*, foot soldiers. He made Maks his protégé when Maks beat the shit out of a guy trying to kill me. Maks became a prized bare-knuckle boxer and Vlad's money-maker. We all learned to fight and shoot, but as the oldest, Maks caught Vlad's attention.

Sergei's mother is my mother's sister. They were already here when we arrived. Anton's father was my father's brother. They arrived a few months after us. We've always been a close family, so it was natural that when Maks became *pakhan*, we would all take our places beside him. He didn't inherit the position. He took it. Vlad started paying too much attention to our mom. When he crossed the line, he paid for it. He'd already cost the bratva millions in his bad business ventures, but he made it personal when he even looked in Galina Kutsenko's direction. I believe it's the only time our father would have been proud of our violent ways. Kirill Kutsenko wanted better for his sons, but we are who we are. We are what life made us.

We've all risen through the ranks, but now Aleks, Niko, and I serve beside Maks as members of the Elite Group. Our job is to keep Maks's decision making in check, but more often than not, he asks for our opinions and accepts them, even when he doesn't like them. We are equals in our private business ventures. Anton and Sergei are the two spies, as we call their positions. Sergei is the *sovietnik*, or the one who runs our support team. He's an intelligence gatherer, and there are few people who can hold out when he demands information. Anton is the *obshchak,* or the man who oversees the security group. He's our chief enforcer. He makes sure our less than legal enterprises run smoothly and are virtually invisible. They've always been the perfect pair, always in sync and unstoppable.

I've never told a single woman any of that. I can't. But something about Tina makes me think I could. I'm infatuated. That's what's wrong with me. I know my sister-in-law is aware of almost everything. Maks keeps nothing from Laura unless it's protecting her. She knows who we are and what we do, but none of us tell her the darker details. I can't imagine confessing to Tina what I'm capable of. I might feel like I can trust her to know we're bratva, but I never want her to discover how I can kill with a clear conscience. She'd never think of me as anything but a monster.

As I walk into Envy, I wonder if she'll take my blunt hint. I couldn't stay at the job site since today is payroll. I need to get my work done, so I'm locking myself in my office until the club opens. I also can't be there when she returns because I'm likely to make a fool of myself and beg her to come here tonight. It's not a date if we happen to be in the same place. The rational side of me knows seeing her will end up with us doing more than just talking, which is exactly what could get her in trouble. But the healthy male side of me wants her.

Focus. You need to run payroll and pay the quarterly taxes. You can jerk off again later.

"Who are you looking for? Could it be a fine little redhead?"

Sergei nudges me as I stand in the back corner, surveying the growing crowd. It's only a Monday night, but we run ridiculous happy hour specials that always get people in the door. It gets them drunk fast enough that they don't notice when the prices triple. They're having too much fun with the music and dancing, and they're too inebriated to realize how much more they're spending. There are the regulars who clearly don't care that they overspend. Then there are the ones who are once bitten, twice shy. They won't come back again once they realize their wallets are empty or they maxed out their credit cards. There's enough of both to keep us profitable.

"Isn't that Salvatore's nephew Carmine?"

I follow Sergei's gaze and recognize a guy close to my age. What the hell? It wasn't that long ago that Salvatore's men attacked us here. A group of Italians burst in, busted up some windows and the main bar. Fists were flying, a few knives got pulled. It got nasty fast. But they were fools to try when it's well known that we don't tolerate fights in our establishments. We have more security than most night spots. The fight didn't last long, and none of us got seriously hurt. The Italians couldn't say the same. And thank God Laura was there that night. She's a badass lawyer, and she knew the detective since they'd been neighbors as kids. She kept all of us bratva out of jail that night and sent the detective chasing his tail.

"What's he doing here?"

I watch him walk over to the bar with two women. I don't recognize either of them, which means neither of them is the woman Carmine's supposed to marry. I saw her picture on Insta. We all have ghost accounts to keep track of our competition. I'm certain they do the same for us, but none of my brothers nor my cousins have real social media presences. Laura toned hers down when she started dating Maks. We have just enough not to look suspicious. Mostly, we post the typical guy photos of us at the gym.

He can't be alone. I mean, he has to have bodyguards with

him. I spot the guys easily. There's three of them. Their clothing makes them blend in, but the way they stand, the way they move, the way they keep scanning the crowd makes them stand out to me. They look the same way Sergei and Anton look when they're guarding us. That many bodyguards make me suspicious. Is trouble following Carmine, or do they expect us to make trouble with him?

I look around and easily spot two of my other cousins. Pavel is Anton's little brother. He's two years younger than Anton, which makes Pasha and Niko the same age. On the other side of the dance floor is Sergei's brother, Michail. Misha and I are the same age. Both of them have risen in the ranks alongside me. But our different relations with Maksim put us on different leadership paths within our bratva. Both Misha and Pasha are now *avotoritet*. The English equivalent is a brigadier. They lead their own groups of men when we have jobs that need discretion, and they're in charge of all the bouncers at our clubs and bars.

"Misha's watching him."

Sergei sees the same thing I do. Ever since the attack here a couple months ago, we've doubled our security.

"Kutsenko."

"Mancinelli."

What does he want? Pasha's inching toward us, and I can see Misha crossing the dance floor. Sergei slides his hand into his pants pocket, and I know he's holding his knife. I cross my arms.

"I'm here with friends. I'm not looking for trouble."

My only reaction is to raise my eyebrows. Carmine and trouble have gone together since we were kids. He's like Pig Pen and the cartoon character's cloud of dirt. Trouble follows Carmine exactly the same way. He looks back at the women chatting at the bar before his eyes meet mine.

"My uncle sent me."

"And you just made it a threesome in the meantime."

Carmine shrugs. "Looks less suspicious, and you run a good club. Why not kill two birds with one stone?"

"Your uncle's got balls sending you here after the last time he sent anyone."

"And your brother had balls thinking he could come to one of our restaurants with his little side piece and be welcome."

"Motherfucker. You know that's my sister-in-law you're talking about. You are trying to cause trouble. Tell me what you have to, then leave. Don't waste my time, or I'll throw you out on your ass and fuck both your women."

I'll do the former, but I have no interest in doing the latter. Maybe a week ago I might have considered it, but not now. I'll find another way to fuck with him if I have to.

"No, you won't. I hear there's a new woman you're into. I like redheads as much as you do. Maybe you should introduce us."

How the hell does he know about Tina? I force myself not to react. I act as though I don't know what he's talking about. I can't let him see how much that bothers me. If Tina's on the *Cosa Nostra's* radar, she's already in danger.

"What does Salvatore want his little messenger boy to tell me?"

"Funny. There's some real estate my uncle wants. Sell it, or we'll visit a few more of your fine establishments."

"We closed for half a night. That's all your uncle's little tantrum did. His friends at the city planner's office may have delayed that job, but they haven't delayed all of them. You've already played your hand with the clubs, so we've added extra security."

I nudge my chin toward what's happening behind him. He spins and finds his three bodyguards corralled with seven of my bouncers nearby. Neither side is talking to the other, but neither are the Italians free to move around. The protection Carmine came with is useless, and he knows it. He looks to the women who are watching him now, and it's clear they're getting bored. I nod at Pasha, who approaches the women and soon orders them both a drink. They've probably already forgotten about Carmine. Pasha is the best looking of all of us. The man breathes and women melt.

"Don't come to my business and think you can issue threats, Carmine. Leave. Go run home to Salvatore and let him know that it's going to cost him a shit-ton to derail all our builds. It'll bankrupt him before he makes a single dollar off what he wants to take from us. Sergei, remind Carmine how to find the door."

My cousin chuckles and steps forward. He's at least six inches taller than Carmine and nearly twice as broad across the chest. Sergei's favorite pastime is weightlifting. He might enjoy running with Anton, Misha, and Pasha, but give him a weight room, and he's happy. He steps so close that Carmine's nose is practically in his chest. It forces Carmine to take a step back, then another as Sergei herds him toward the door. Carmine spins around and gestures to the women, but they don't see him. They're already halfway in love with Pasha. It's not until he's outside the club before my men step away from his bodyguards.

The men are barely back in their places before I hear raised voices, then the sound of glass breaking. It's easy to see the three drunk chicks going at each other. I can practically hear all my bouncers groan. No one enjoys breaking up girl fights. Women don't care who's in the way. They will swing and scratch regardless of who tries to intervene. Men might break bones or knock each other out, but women are vicious. I'd rather go ten rounds with Maks in the ring than get in the middle of the shitstorm brewing right now.

Wonderful. One's got a fist full of hair while another has her hand wrapped around the first girl's throat. The third one is screaming her fucking head off at the second chick. Everyone is watching them, and my guys are trying to break it up while touching none of them. None of my bouncers want one or all of them claiming assault when this is done. They'll probably be besties again by morning, and my men will face the cops.

"Ladies."

I step between the third woman and the two ready to duke it out. None of them looks at me. The one screaming leans around me to keep running her mouth. I can't even understand half of what she's saying. I'm pretty sure it's English, but her Brooklyn accent is so heavy, I can't catch everything. And people say I sound like a foreigner.

"Let go before I call the cops. You can let my men escort you to cabs or Ubers."

"Or what?"

Loudmouth looks at me and puts her hands on her hips. The other two notice me and how their—friend?—is mocking me. I'm twice the size of all of them, but chatterbox doesn't seem to notice like the other two do.

"Who the fuck are you? Where's the manager?"

"Let me guess. Your name is Karen."

People around us watching think I'm funny, but the three women don't. Now all three of them are ready to have a go at me, which is fine. Now they aren't fighting each other.

"I want to see the manager, asshole."

"He's not available, but I'm the owner. Do you have a problem?"

I offer her the most artificial smile I've ever worn, and it only pisses her off more. Even better.

"Yeah, I have a problem. I—"

"Then it would be a good idea that you listen to me and leave. If you don't like it here, don't come back. Now, order an Uber or go get in a cab. But if the three of you aren't gone in the next thirty seconds, I'm calling the cops."

"Asshole."

"Doesn't change the fact that I own the place. Out." I turn to the other two women, who are now practically shaking. "I don't give a fuck what's going on between the two of you. Fight on the sidewalk for all I care, but get your friend out of here. She's pissing me off."

"He can't talk that way to us."

I roll my eyes, but then I can't help but laugh when the hair-puller blurts out, "He's a Kutsenko. He can talk however he wants. Better he's talking than drowning us in the Hudson with cement shoes. Come on."

The fight seems to be forgotten as the two combatants drag their friend to the door. I can hear some comments, which takes effort over the music that's still booming, but I don't care. If it's not our bouncers keeping the peace, then it's our reputation that keeps people from causing trouble in our clubs. I make my way to the bar and order a Sprite. I only drink at work for appearance's sake when I'm in the middle of a business deal, and that's usually at the strip clubs. When I'm the manager on duty, I don't touch alcohol.

"That was annoying."

Pasha's standing next to me now. He's shaken off Carmine's dates who'd started hanging on him. He gets a Coke and turns to lean back against the bar. I'm watching the crowd through the mirror behind the bar.

"Which part?"

"All of it. But I learned Carmine's been talking a big game."

"Oh?"

"Mhmm. Seems like he's been spending way more than what's in the allowance Salvatore probably gives him. The dude doesn't work, so his uncle must just give him money. One girl was showing off the bracelet he gave her a few days ago. The other was telling me about the hotel room they're supposed to go to tonight. You and your brothers may be billionaires, and the rest of us are doing more than just fine, but none of us are throwing around money like that."

"That's why we're what we are. All of us have earned the money we have one way or another. Carmine's Salvatore's little bitch. He does whatever his uncle tells him to, which is barely anything because Salvatore knows the guy's worthless. The rest of the time Carmine thinks he's the next John Gotti. He doesn't see how his uncle owns him. None of what he has really belongs to him. He has it because Salvatore lets him. And Salvatore is no fool. He sent Carmine tonight because he doesn't care if his nephew gets the shit beaten out of him. He probably hoped we'd do that. It would give Salvatore an excuse to wage a full-on war and blame us. For a man who likes to look macho, no one plays the victim as well as Salvatore Mancinelli."

"Do you want me to talk to Sergei? He can assign me to watch the shithead."

"Yeah. Let me know if you learn anything, but report straight to Maks."

"Isn't he going on his honeymoon in a few days?"

I look at my watch. Shit. I forgot about that. Their wedding was two weeks ago, but it was basically an elopement. They delayed the honeymoon because they'd just come back from a weekend away in Turks and Caicos.

"Report to Aleks then. But email Maks. He probably won't be checking it often, but at least the info will be there if he does."

"I never imagined he'd get married. I can't believe he did while Misha and I were in Moscow."

"I know. None of us liked that, but it was a blessing in disguise that you were. You dealt with Nadia for us. Meeting her flight and making sure she made it back to her boyfriend was perfect timing."

Pasha snorts. "You make it sound like it was a courtesy. She was pissed when she spotted us. And her boyfriend? Fuck, I almost felt bad for the bitch. But after what I heard she pulled, moving into Laura's building, and showing up at their wedding, she got what she deserved."

"I didn't imagine Maks would get married either, but he and Laura are perfect together. They get each other in a way I've never seen with another couple, not even my parents or yours."

"What about Tina? Anton told me about her. Apparently, she's not easily intimidated. All six of you? Even I know that can be a lot."

"What about her? We met the other night and hooked up. She happened to be the inspector today."

"Bullshit. Anton says he saw her leaving your building the next morning."

"So?"

"He also said you were pissed as shit when you chased after her, and she waved from a cab. Then she shows up at the job today? That had to have shocked the shit out of you."

"You could say that."

"Anton said you followed her around like a little bitch."

"Your brother says a lot. Maybe he should keep some of his stories to himself." I scowl at my cousin, but I know if Anton hadn't told him, then it would have been Sergei or my brothers.

"What're you talking about?"

I look over at Misha, who's already grinning. He knows exactly what we're talking about.

"Nothing."

"Come on, Bogdan. Are you really going to call the woman of your dreams nothing?"

"Shut up, Pasha."

I might want a vodka after all. With Frick and Frack now ready to have a go at me, I'm screwed. My cousins are all so close in age to me and my brothers that it's really like having seven brothers instead of three. I won't hear the end of it until I confess what they both clearly already know.

"Bogdan, just admit you're into her. You haven't had a girlfriend in three years. Before that, you always used to be with someone. By my calendar, you're long overdue."

"Shut up, Misha."

"What?"

"Tina's different. Leave off."

"So not girlfriend material? She must have been a good lay if you're still sniffing around."

I turn toward my cousin, and he takes a step back and puts his hands up.

"Dude, I didn't know. I didn't get what you meant by different. Now I do."

"Don't talk about her like that. She's not just a piece of ass."

"Anton said that's how she treated you, though. He said she didn't even say goodbye that morning."

"What she did or didn't say to me is none of anyone's business. I'm into her." My cousins snort. "Assholes. You know that's not what I meant. There's something about her that's different from my past girlfriends. I can't tell what it is yet, but I'm hoping to get the chance to find out. But as long as she's assigned to our project, I can't. At best, she'd get reprimanded. At worst, they could fire her if we date right now."

"Are you just going to wait it out, then?"

"Yeah. There's not much else I can do right now. But she's already said she wants to go out with me."

But apparently, she doesn't want to see me tonight. That stings. Did she change her mind? Or did she just tell me what I wanted to hear? No. She's not a liar. She could have lied several times since we met, and she hasn't. Evasive, yes. Liar, no. If she changed her mind, then...Part of me wants to force her to change it back in my favor, and part of me thinks I should back off. All of me—or at least, all of my dick—just wants her.

No, it's all of me. The sex was mind-blowing, but that wasn't just because we're physically attracted to each other. It was more than that. And today. It shocked the shit out of me to find her in the trailer. I thought I would be pissed, but all I wanted was to hold her.

"Hello?"

I look at Pasha and realize he's been talking, and I totally tuned out.

"Sorry. My mind wandered."

"Yeah. To that hot little redhead who just walked in."

Chapter Five

Tina

Bogdan spins around from the bar and spots me immediately. I'm with a couple friends, but it only took me a moment to find him.

"I see someone I know. I'll be right back." I head to the bar but stop when I notice the two men with Bogdan. "Your family genetics are incredible."

One looks just like Anton, and the other looks just like Sergei, which means they look like the Kutsenko brothers, except the guy who must be Anton's brother has dark eyes, and the guy who must be Sergei's brother has blond hair.

"Tina, these are two more of my cousins. Pavel and Michail."

"Call me Pasha, and he's Misha."

Bogdan's cousins shake my hand before I step closer to Bogdan. We hesitate, then I'm in his arms where I belong. His cousins disappear as I sense him inhaling my citrus scent. It's grapefruit and oranges. He'd said it was delicious when he kissed every inch of me.

"*Malyshka*, I thought you might not come."

"I doubt that."

"You know what I meant." He can't seem to help but laugh.

"Who's this, Christina?"

My friends are standing behind me now, so I can tell he's being careful not to have his hand too close to my ass. I step back and turn around, but I don't move away from Bogdan. His arm is around my waist.

"Kelsey, Tracy, Sarah, this is Bogdan. Bogdan, these are three of my closest friends."

"Three of? We are your closest friends." Sarah teases me. "It's nice to meet you."

He's forced to let go of me so he can shake hands. He signals the bartender, and we order our drinks. The girls are watching me like a hawk, and I'm certain they're dying to know why I went straight to him and why we were hugging, since I haven't told them anything about him.

"Remember how I told you what a disaster Friday night started out as?" I take a sip from my cider and lager. "I met Bogdan that night, and we hung out."

The girls know exactly what I don't say. They look him up and down, and I can tell Kelsey and Sarah approve, but Tracy doesn't look so convinced. Bogdan must see it too.

"We had a good time, and I recognized him when we walked in."

I can tell he's wondering why I didn't tell them I knew he would be here. He's wondering why I'm making it seem like a coincidence.

"Good thing you told Todd not to come with us."

And there it is.

"You saw Todd tonight?"

"Yeah. He texted Tracy and asked if we were doing anything tonight. She didn't know yet that I told him to leave me alone. She mentioned we were going out to dinner, and he showed up."

"Did he bother you, Tina?"

I turn back toward him and sense he caught himself before he called me *malyshka,* and I think he realizes no one else calls me Tina. I think he's also trying not to get angry, but he knows Todd manipulated my friends and me.

"Not for long. Christina was having none of it."

Kelsey answers for me, and he only nods. My eyes lock with his, and I'm silently begging him to let it go. I think he will because that's what I want, but only this once.

"He thought I might have changed my mind. I made it clear that I hadn't. That ship has sailed and sunk. I'm not interested in that kind of arrangement anymore."

He's wondering what I'm saying. Am I saying I want something else?

"I told you, you could do better." Sarah darts her eyes to Bogdan.

"It was never a question of not being able to do better. It suited me then, and now it doesn't."

"Does Ja—"

Tracy snaps her mouth shut and looks away. I know Bogdan's looking down at me, but I'm shooting daggers at my friend. He keeps his voice low as he leans toward me.

"Does who know that?"

"No one."

I don't look at him. I keep glaring at Tracy, who's now studying the ice in her drink. I finish my drink and put it on the bar before I turn to him.

"I suppose you're working tonight. We're going to go dance, but I'll look for you before we leave."

The music suddenly gets louder during a drum solo. It gives him a reason to whisper in my ear.

"Do you have another fuck buddy, *malyshka*?"

"No. I have an ex-boyfriend named Jared who wanted to get back together but would settle for being that. I'm not interested in either option, so I told him I didn't need a second fuck buddy. He doesn't need to know I ended it with Todd, or he'll think he can slide into his place."

"Or he could know that you're interested in someone else."

"Someone I can't go out with for another two weeks."

"Two?"

"Yeah. I'm going to work on my boss, so he'll assign someone else, but no one can take on the case right now. I told Niko when I went back this afternoon. I'm guessing you haven't talked to him yet."

"No, why?"

"It was kind of ugly."

"What do you mean?" I'm sure I look like I don't want to answer. He makes sure I know he expects an explanation. "*Malyshka*."

"Jim got really pissed when Niko fired him and hired Anatolii instead. I was just pulling up when it happened, and Jim saw me arrive. He lost his shit and said some stuff he shouldn't have. It pissed Niko off, and there was a big scene."

"What did he say?"

"Let Niko tell you. I don't need to be in the middle of that part of your company business."

"This isn't just company business when someone insults you. What did he say?"

"Bogdan, please. I really don't want to talk about it. Niko handled it, and it's over. I had a shit day, and tonight didn't start out much better. The only good part has been seeing you. Can we talk about what happens tomorrow? I have to go back to the site. Will you dance with me?"

My eyes are pleading with him. I know my friends are watching us, trying to figure out what we're talking about. I don't want to argue with him, and dancing with him is probably the only way I'm going to touch him tonight. He nods, so I lead him to the dance floor. It isn't long before the girls are dancing in a group with other guys. He pulls me close and slides his thigh between my legs.

"Fuck, Bogdan. That feels good."

We're leaning close, so we can hear each other. His hand is on my lower back, pressing me against him. I'm grinding on his thigh, reminding both of us of how good it felt to fuck three nights ago. Two weeks might kill me.

"What does my baby girl want?"

"You, Daddy."

Our gazes meet before our lips do. Then it's a wildfire. My hands are sliding up and down his chest while he moves me on his thigh. He's guiding me, controlling how much friction I get. He can tell I'm getting frustrated because he won't let me get all that I want. But we both freeze when my hands slide under his suit coat and over his ribs. I pull back and shake my head. I'm desperately looking for my friends before I look back at him. I didn't feel his gun when I hugged him at the bar. My arms were around his waist and low enough not to feel it in the holster beneath his arm.

"Tina, come to my office, and I'll explain. It's too loud in here to talk."

He's practically screaming now. I look at my friends for so long I'm sure he thinks I'm going to refuse. I won't look at him, but I nod. I let him take my hand and steer me to the back of the club. The door has a code that he punches in and opens for me. I step inside and take in the comfortable couch against the side wall. I bet he's taken a few naps there. I notice the couch that's more like a bench that's pushed against the wall with the door. I bet more than one employee or guest has been ready to shit themselves while sitting on that one. I check out the desk with the two monitors.

"Somehow, I doubt most club owners carry guns."

My arms are crossed, and it's not because I'm pissed. It's like I put up a wall between us, and I'm keeping myself safe from him. He looks like he hates it. I know I do, but this is fucking freaking me out. He points to the comfortable couch, then takes a seat on the plank. He's giving me space, but all I want is for him to pull me onto his lap. I'm surprised, then disappointed, when he doesn't sit next to me. My hands are in my lap, and I'm staring at them.

"Can I sit next to you?"

I think he's trying not to assume anything. I nod, but I'm not looking at him. He moves over and puts his hand on top of mine. When I don't pull away, he lifts me onto his lap. I lean against him, but I shake my head. Mixed messages, but I'm more confused by myself than with him.

"*Malyshka,* I think you know why I have it."

"Are you really Russian mafia?"

"Bratva. Yes."

"What does that mean? I'm guessing it's not exactly like the movies."

"No. Not exactly." He tries to soften what he's going to say with a smile. "We don't sit in back rooms, smoking cigars, and planning the next shoot out."

"I figured. Why do you have a gun, Bogdan?"

"Because they have a way of convincing people not to shoot me first."

"That's not funny, Bogdan. I don't need quips or jokes. I

need to know whether—how much—danger I'm in being with you."

"Truly, hopefully not much. But I can't say I'm not dangerous. I hoped we could go out a few times before I needed to explain all this to you. If you ended up not being that into me, then I wouldn't have to explain anything."

"I think you just wanted more time to figure out what to tell me, how to make it sound like not a big deal."

"It is a big deal, Tina, and I know it. I've never told anyone flat out like I did just now. Knowing that puts you in danger, but it's just as dangerous for me. You could call the police right now or go straight to them. I'm trusting you, Tina."

I inhale so deeply that I can feel his shirt buttons against my chest. I nod but say nothing to contradict what he just admitted.

"Owning night clubs and strip clubs is dangerous enough because of the clientele and the large amounts of money. When you add who we are to it, then you get a situation where carrying a gun is wiser than not."

"You weren't carrying one the other night."

"No. But I was armed, Tina."

"You were?"

"I had a knife in each pants' pocket."

"Are you carrying one tonight?"

"Always, *malyshka*. All of us always carry at least one knife."

"Do you use them often?"

"The gun, no."

"But you use the knife?"

"Sometimes."

"You're being cagey, Bogdan. I don't like it."

"I didn't plan to tell you any of this tonight. I'm trying to figure out as I go along what's safe to tell you."

"Are we only ever going to your place or one of your clubs? Is it safe to go places with you?"

"It is. But being with me means having a bodyguard, Tina."

"What?"

I try to get up, and he doesn't stop me. I rush across the office and lean against the wall, as far away from him as I can get. I watch him as he stands, but he doesn't move closer.

"You've met my cousins. One of them would be your bodyguard. Most likely Pasha or Misha, since Sergei is usually with Maks's wife, Laura. Anton takes turns with my brothers and me."

"What does that mean? Someone follows me everywhere. How do I do my job?"

"Since I'm guessing you won't want a car and driver to take you to and from work, then Misha or Pasha follow you in their cars. They wait outside your office building and go to job sites with you. They stay in the car or just out of sight. They keep watch. They're only visible to anyone else if someone is a threat to you."

"So every day until we break up, I have a shadow."

"Why are you assuming we'd break up?"

"Do you see yourself with a lifelong girlfriend? A wife? Somehow, I don't think too many men in your position marry."

He can't look at me. Is he going to say that eventually almost all of them marry? How else do they get the next generation?

"Tina, I don't know what the future holds for us, but I want to find out if there is a future. That means protection for you."

"Am I going to be a target?"

"It's complicated, Tina. That's the best I can say. I don't want you to be, and I'll always do everything I can to keep you safe."

"How did you explain this to your other girlfriends?"

Now he really can't look at me. He presses his lips together, between his teeth, as he thinks about what to say.

"You didn't tell them, did you?"

"You read me too well, *malyshka*. No, I didn't."

"Even the one who gave you the cat? You must have been pretty serious."

"We were. But I knew I didn't see a permanent future with her."

"Then how can you say you were serious?"

"Because we were together for three years."

"Did she know you weren't planning to make it permanent? Or did she believe you were going to marry her?"

He sighs. "I always changed the subject if she brought up marriage until she stopped. That's part of what broke us up."

"Part? How did she not know who you were for three years?"

"Because I never completely trusted her. That's why I never told her I was bratva. And she said I was too emotionally unavailable. I was."

"Was? Or am?"

"Was, *malyshka*. I'm sharing things with you I never imagined I would with a woman before our first date."

"Well, we did fuck."

"*Malyshka*." He crosses the office and fists my hair. I don't fight him as he holds me in place. I love his dominance too much. "Don't be flippant. If it was just fucking for the sake of getting off, you wouldn't be here right now. We both know this is something else."

"Maybe it is. But what exactly is that?"

"I don't know. What I know is that I will do whatever I have to when it comes to protecting you. I know I want to spend more time with you. I know my intuition has been right my entire life. It's why I'm still alive, and it's telling me I can trust you. That you're special."

"I need to think about all of this. It's a lot, Bogdan."

"What do you need from me, *malyshka*?"

I shake my head, and I think he can feel my uncertainty and sadness as though it's his own.

"Time, Daddy."

When I look up at him, there are tears in my eyes. It feels like the entire world is crashing down around me. He looks just as worried, as though he fears this is over before it ever started, as though I'm going to walk out right now and never come back, never let him come back.

"I'll give you whatever you need, baby girl."

I nod before I fall into his arms. He holds me tightly. I close my eyes as my heart feels like it's shards poking into my lungs and ribs. I wrap my arms around his waist and burrow into his chest. I think he loves how I do that because he always relaxes. It's like I can't get close enough.

"What am I supposed to do when I feel like I need time and I need you? I'm scared."

"Of me?"

"No. Not even a little. I'm scared of what this means to be with you. I'm scared of what might happen to me if something happens to you. I don't know that I can bear that. I'm scared that I'm making a mistake trusting you. But I'm not scared of you."

"Take whatever time you need, *malyshka*. I'll be here if you're ready."

"If? You don't think I will be?"

"I didn't want to pressure you by making you think I assume you'll want us."

"You're not. I just need to think this over."

"Do you want me to keep my distance, Tina? Do you want

me to stay away from the job site when you're going to be there?"

"No." I don't think before I answer. "I want to keep getting to know you, not avoid you. I need time to figure out what I think about all this, and I can't do that if I never see you or talk to you. But I'm not ready to say whether I can date you."

"Fair enough, *malyshka*."

What else is there to say?

Chapter Six

Bogdan

Last night drained me. Between dealing with Carmine and then seeing Tina, I'm wiped. I wish I could stay in bed and pull the covers over my head like when I was four or five. I would pretend I wasn't there, as though my parents couldn't find me if I hid. But they did, and I had to face the day. Except now, at twenty-seven, my mom isn't greeting me with a kiss and breakfast. Instead, I'm at the gym with Maks, Aleks, and Niko. Our cousins will be here soon. I'm on the treadmill next to Maks while the others are already lifting. Maks and I are warming up before we get in the ring.

Vlad trained all of us to fight, but he trained Maks to win big money. I'll never forget the first time I knocked him on his ass. He'd always gone easy on me as his baby brother. It felt like it took forever before I could really hold my own. I was a week past my twentieth birthday, and we were here one morning. They were all giving me a hard time because I still only needed to shave twice a week. I got so pissed that I took it all out on

Maks. It took me three rounds, but I landed a left hook that sent him sailing into the ropes, then laid him out cold. It may be one of the proudest and most terrifying moments of my life. I nearly shit myself when he came around and opened his eyes. I thought he would kill me. He stood up, glared at me, then burst out laughing.

But no one's laughing today. I'm lost in my thoughts, and my brothers are still dealing with the fallout from three dead women being found on one of our construction sites a couple weeks ago. It's the land Carmine was talking about last night. That dumbass detective was sloppy. He might have tried to make it look like it was the Italians, but he didn't examine the bodies he dumped too well. They led back to his family, the Colombian Cartel, instead of *Cosa Nostra*. But it ground the project to a halt, and Salvatore is benefiting from it. We've tried to reassign the men to other sites, but we can't use all of them. Salvatore was banking on that, so now he's poaching them from us. Men with families to feed are only loyal to whoever pays them on time.

"You ready?"

Maks's voice barely registers. I stop the treadmill and hop off. I'm still lost in my own thoughts as Aleks wraps my hands and wrists.

"You better stop daydreaming, or you're going to scare your girlfriend after Maks is done with your face."

"She's not my girlfriend."

Now I really sound like I'm five again. I wish she was, but who knows what's going to happen next? I promised to give her time, but I didn't promise not to have someone guard her. Pasha agreed to start today after we finish working out. It's barely five, so I think we have plenty of time before she gets to work. I don't know where she lives, but I know Sergei could find out in a heartbeat. Pasha will once he follows her home tonight. I have to tell her, or she won't forgive me if she realizes I assigned someone to her and didn't warn her. But Misha noticed a couple more of Salvatore's men who were way less conspicuous than Carmine. I'm certain they saw me with Tina, and it's got me spooked.

"Come on, lover boy."

"Shut up, *starik*." Old man.

I follow Maks into the ring, and we take up our position. He's laughing as I grumble. Of course, he's having fun. He has a beautiful bride waiting for him at home. Laura's probably still asleep and will be until he goes home to get ready for the day. That, or she's already at her gym, swimming laps. Either way, he has someone, and he's baiting me because I don't. And it's fucking working. I can feel my temper rising.

"Don't be pissy at me because you didn't get laid last night."

"I'll remind you of that the next time you fuck up with Laura. It's been, what, five minutes? You're past due."

"Fucker."

Maks's right fist comes way too close to my left temple before I duck. I shouldn't have said that. They love each other, but saying they've had a rough beginning is like saying there's a bit of water in the ocean. I don't envy Maks his position as *pakhan*. I've never wanted it, and I'm not sure Maks ever did either. He rose to the occasion, and he's the best leader we could have. But it's not an easy job when you love your family, especially your wife. He has to juggle what's best for the brotherhood and what's best for Laura. They're not always the same, and he's still learning to be a husband. Apparently, it doesn't come as naturally as my father made it look. Or none of us were old enough to remember what the early years were like for my parents.

"Sorry."

I can admit when I'm wrong. I might mean to bust his balls, but I don't need to take out my bad mood by using Laura.

"What's the deal with her, anyway?"

"I like her."

"I could tell. You practically bit my head off yesterday."

"I didn't expect to see her in the trailer. We had some stuff to resolve."

"Like how she sneaked out of your place while you were in the shower?"

"Something like that."

"What about last night?"

"Holy shit. Which one of them was texting you the play-by-play? How do you even know about that?"

"Sergei. And he wanted to know if I should agree to whatever detail you want assigned to her."

"Could have let me ask first."

"Figured it would save time."

We're dancing around, throwing punches, and we're both breathing heavier.

"So?"

I'm getting impatient.

"So what?"

"Do you agree she can have one?"

"Will she accept one?"

"Don't know. I mentioned it last night but didn't tell her she'd have one for sure."

"It won't freak her out?"

"It might, but she knows I'm already thinking about it."

"What's so different about her? You've had bodyguards for your girlfriends in the past, but you've never asked for one this soon or told them about it before even arranging it."

Maks stops and lowers his hands. I wipe my forearm across my forehead and lean back against the ropes.

"How'd you know Laura was different?"

Maks shrugs. We've all asked him that question before.

"You mean besides standing up to me the day we met and threatening to bury me if we're into sex trafficking? I don't know. Something inside of me just understood that she will always be the only one for me."

"That's how I feel about Tina. With my previous girl-friends, I was always attracted to them, and they were fun and nice. I enjoyed their company in and out of the bedroom. But something always held me back. Something always made me keep them at a distance. I assumed it's because of who we are. And I guess that's part of it. But with Tina, I don't feel that way. None of us trust easily or quickly, but I feel as though I can tell her anything. I feel like she gets me. I know that sounds lame since I barely know her, but—"

"It doesn't sound lame at all. It sounds familiar. We all know my past with Nadia. I didn't trust her, and that's why I knew I would never marry her. She and I got what we needed out of what was an arranged relationship. But there was no way I would have committed the rest of my life to her. I barely dated after Nadia and before Laura. I wasn't interested, and I met no one who made me want to find the interest. Then along came Laura. I knew before that fucking meeting was over that I needed to get to know her. If she hadn't come into Envy that night, I would have searched for her. Then she ordered me to let her out of the office and into an active crime scene. After that, I felt like I couldn't breathe without her."

"You were a mess that week that she wouldn't talk to you. I've never seen you like that."

"I felt like I was ready to crawl out of my skin. The only reason I wasn't camped outside her door was because Mama said it would only make things worse."

"She was right."

"I know. But that was the longest week of my life."

"I have to wait at least two weeks before we can go out. Until her boss assigns someone else to our project, it's a conflict of interest. Neither of us wants to jeopardize her job."

"Are you coming to the site today?"

"Yeah."

I see Maks's surprise.

"I asked if she wants me to stay away, and she said no. She wants time, not distance. Since the site is the only place where we have a legit reason to be around each other, then that's the best we can do. I'm content to just watch her. She fascinates me. I can tell her mind is constantly on the move, even when she's quiet. She's observant. She's confident. She knows enough to run circles around Jim."

That makes me think about what she told me in the office. I look over at Niko, who's walking over to the ring. I haven't talked to him yet, and I don't know who else was around when he fired Jim. I didn't push Tina, but I still want to know what they said.

"Niko, what happened with Jim yesterday?"

My brother freezes. So does everyone else. Our cousins are here now too, and they all know whatever it was. I'm the only one who doesn't.

"He got angry and ran his mouth."

Niko takes a long drink from his water bottle. I just stare at him. He has to come up for air at some point, or he'll run out of water first. I can wait. When he finally lowers the bottle, his expression is grim.

"Tell me, Niko."

"You really don't want to know."

"Don't I? Because now I'm fucking positive that I do."

I pull the Velcro at my wrists free with my teeth and unwrap my left hand, then I do the same for my right. I toss my gear on the floor after stepping out of the ring. I'm practically in Niko's face, and every second he makes me wait, the angrier I'm getting. Whatever Jim said, they all know it's going to infuriate me. But making me wait is only getting me close to exploding before they even deliver the bad news.

"He made some comments about her body, then he asked if she was involved with only you or if she'd been with the rest of us. He mentioned he might want some time with her when she's not with you. He—"

"Fuck this, Niko. Just tell me what he said."

"Bogdan, you're going to lose your shit. I already fired him, and I made sure no one will hire him. I even told Salvatore and Enrique."

"Now you better fucking tell me if you thought what he did was bad enough to tell the *Cosa Nostra* and the Cartel. Did he fucking threaten her?"

"Yes."

I spin toward Aleks, who hands me a bottle of water. I look at it as though I don't know what to do with it. I toss it on my gym bag. I could already feel the plastic crumpling under my grip.

"And no one thought they should tell me last night? Maks, what the hell? She should have a bodyguard with her now. She shouldn't have gone home alone."

"She didn't." Now it's Sergei's turn to tell me what no one else has. "I made sure she got home safely, and I stayed outside her building until ten minutes before I got here."

"And now she's alone again."

"No." Sergei shakes his head. "Stefan is half a block down the street from her house. He has a clear view and will text me when she leaves for work."

The blood is pounding in my temples. I'm so far past pissed, I don't even know what to call how I feel.

"Whatever he said was bad enough for all of you to discuss it behind my back and set a security watch on my woman, but no one thought I should know."

"Your woman?"

"Niko, I swear. If you don't want Mama weeping over your grave tonight, fucking tell me what the fuck happened. Don't fuck with me. I'm not in the mood."

"Fine. He said he wanted to know if she'd only sucked your dick or all of ours. That if you'd been any good at fucking her, she'd know her place, and it isn't on a construction site. He said she'd be the one to bend over and take it in the ass before he ever did. He threatened to tell her boss that you fucked her on the job, and that he walked in on you. He said he'd get her fired because he has friends who would report her for failing to follow inspection protocol on their sites. He told her to show him her tits, and he might forget about her getting him fired. He said he'd even make sure none of his friends heard she was the reason if she sucked him off."

"Who the fuck even talks like that at work?"

My voice is barely more than a whisper. If I didn't know that my family would never lie to me about this, I wouldn't believe a word Niko said. It's too outrageous. It's too unreal.

"Someone who knows a little too much about us, Bogdan."

I look at Aleks in confusion.

"He knows about the laundering. Apparently, his brother-in-law has a big mouth. The guy told Jim about how we use the clubs as a front."

"Who the hell is his brother-in-law?"

"Leo Popov."

"That piece of shit? I thought he went back to Vladivostok when his Green Card expired, and he couldn't get it renewed since no one will hire him."

"He did, but not before he sang like a fucking canary to Jim."

Leo Popov was a low-level petty criminal for years. But he was useless. He spent more time in jail than out. When he started costing us a small fortune in bribes to keep him from getting arrested, it was time to let him go. He wasn't around enough to know real details about our money laundering, but he's not wrong that we do it. And now Jim knows too.

"Fine. Jim knows about the money laundering. I want to know why he let so much shit slide and how he got Jeremy to pass all the inspections."

"So did Ms. MacNally, and that's what set him off. Apparently, Carmine's been paying him and Jeremy. When he wouldn't tell her what other corners he'd cut, she said she'd get his license revoked. He lost his mind and just started yelling at her."

"And you just let him."

"No." Niko looks insulted. So what? "None of us were there when it started. I fired him and watched him walk to his truck. I went to talk to Anatolii and told him he's the new foreman. Jim followed her to her truck and laid into her. I didn't know Anatolii could run that fast. He got to her side before me. He broke Jim's nose."

"Fine. What else happened? You just let him leave, then sent Tina on her merry way."

"Fucking-a, Bogdan. No. Ilya followed Jim, and Stefan followed her. He lost her in traffic after she left her office. But Ilya was outside Jim's place the whole night. The man never left his house. I called Salvatore and Enrique. They're both old school. They like to keep their women out of things, so I knew they'd be pissed to know he spoke that way in public."

"And in the process, they now know about Tina. She's not my wife, Niko. She's not protected. We all know what almost happened to Laura when she was only Maks's girlfriend. Tina's not even my girlfriend."

"I didn't tell him who he said it about."

"You didn't mention it was a female inspector from the city planner's office?"

"No. I said he went off on a woman working at the site. He got pissed because she pointed out safety issues that got him fired."

"Why didn't you tell me this last night?"

"Because she asked me not to."

"She asked you to lie to me, so you did."

"I didn't lie."

"By omission you did."

"Are you as pissed at her as you are at me?"

"No. She doesn't know any better. She doesn't know the danger she could be in. She doesn't know what's at stake if Jim spreads her name around. She's not bratva, but you are. You should have told me." I turn toward Sergei. "Text me her address now. I want someone taking Jim to the warehouse before I'm out of the shower."

I don't wait for anyone to agree or disagree with me. I grab my bag and storm into the locker room. I need to see Tina, then I'm going to where we conduct our most unsavory business. We own a warehouse in Queens near the Flushing River that isn't on any city planner's map or on any of the deeds recorded by the city. It's where we interview and dispose of people who complicate our businesses or who threaten our families. There's more to Jim's story than what I just learned. And even if there isn't, he went too far. Visitors to the warehouse never leave the way they arrived. I don't know yet whether it'll be the vat of acid or the meat grinder, but what little remains of Jim when I'm done with him will be in the Flushing River by tomorrow morning.

I hear my phone buzz as I yank off my clothes. I glance down at the screen and see it's a message from Sergei. I'm in and out of the shower in less than five minutes. I'm buttoning my shirt cuffs as I walk back onto the gym floor.

"I don't know when I'll get there, but I want him waiting for me. Fuck him up a bit, but not so much that he doesn't register every bit of pain I inflict."

"She won't want you to do this, Bogdan."

"She won't know. You don't tell Laura all the grisly details, Maks. Why would I tell Tina?"

"She's not stupid, Bogdan. She's already figured out more than you probably realize. That's why she didn't want Niko to tell you. She might not know the grisly details, but she'll guess what you're going to do if you don't calm down before you see her. If she was freaked out last night by whatever you talked about and wants time to sort things out, this won't make anything better."

"I never thought she was. But this changes things. She doesn't have the luxury of time now. Who knows who Jim talked to last night? Just because he stayed home all night doesn't mean he stayed quiet. I won't tell her what I have in mind for him, but now there's no choice but to have men assigned to her. She has to know, or it'll scare her even more when she notices strange men following her, because she will notice. If she had my number, she'd probably already be calling me about why Sergei parked outside her house all night."

I don't wait for anyone else to talk. I run to the parking lot and toss my bag in the back of my Audi. It's still early, so there's next no traffic as I leave Manhattan and make my way to Tina's place in Queens. It's not too far from where Laura used to live or where my mom still lives. I'm scanning my mirrors constantly, making sure no one is following me. I drive past her house and park around the block. My car has a lot of custom features, including being silent when I lock and unlock it. The headlights don't even flash. The sun is just coming up as I pull my pistol from the holster at my back. I grab my gym bag, hoping it makes me look less suspicious since I'm dressed for the day and out walking without a dog at six o'clock in the morning.

I walk around Tina's house, checking the fencing and gate before I let myself into the backyard. There's a light on upstairs, so she must be awake. If she's going to argue with me about coming in, then I want to do it in private with no one seeing me standing on her front porch. Her neighbor's dog barks, but I ignore it as I jog up the steps to her backdoor and holster my gun. I knock three times and wait. Nothing happens. I knock again, but I take a step away from the door and lean back. Tina's looking at me from her bedroom window.

"Let me in, *malyshka*. We need to talk."

Chapter Seven

Tina

I hear the gate open from my open bedroom window. I just finished brushing my teeth, so I grab the yoga clothes I already have on my bed and throw them on before I creep to the window. I push back the curtain and look down. I should have known.

"Let me in, *malyshka*. We need to talk."

Yes, we do. And there's no point in refusing Bogdan if I don't want the entire neighborhood to hear us. I hurry downstairs and open the door, but only a crack.

"What do you want, Bogdan? I'm on my way to work out."

He doesn't answer me. Instead, he pushes the door open and steps inside. I could stop him, but I don't really want to. I've been thinking about him all night, driving myself crazy. I take a step back, then another and another, until he has me against the kitchen doorframe. My hair's in a ponytail that he wraps around his fist. I think he's going to kiss my lips, but he grazes his teeth along my neck as his fingers dig into my hip. It's not just his hold on my hip and hair that immobilizes me. It's his mere presence. I don't want to get away.

"You should have told me the truth, baby girl. Don't keep secrets from me."

"You mean, don't do what you do."

"You know that's not the same." His hand's down the front of my yoga pants, and his fingers are sliding between my thighs. "You're wet for me, *malyshka*. Have you been thinking about me?"

"You know I have."

When he nibbles my ear, I can't help how my pussy tightens around his fingers. Everything from my belly button down contracts, desperate to hold him there.

"Then why didn't you tell me the truth?"

"Because I was scared of how you would react."

"And don't you think it terrifies me to know someone threatened you?"

"You terrified?" I scoff, but I feel the tension radiating from him. His fingers move harder and faster, punishing me for dismissing his feelings.

"Anything that could hurt you terrifies me, Christina."

He's never called me that before. He leans back, and our eyes meet. They are truly windows to his soul. I can see everything. His fear, his frustration, his need to protect me, his desire.

"I knew it would upset you, and I didn't want that. He was a douche, but it's over. You didn't need to have someone follow me twice."

"I didn't. That was Niko's decision. I only found out about that an hour ago. I was going to assign someone to you anyway, but I wanted to talk to you about it first. I thought I could do that at the job site. Things changed."

He's still working my pussy as he pushes down my tight pants and thong. I kick them free of my legs.

"Take your shirt and sports bra off, *malyshka*. I want to see all of you."

The moment I'm naked, he's sucking my breast. Holy shit, that feels amazing. I'm holding it, offering it to him as my back arches away from the door jamb. My other hand is in his hair, holding him there, but with no pressure. I'm not in control, and we both know it.

"You should have told me last night. You had the chance, and you made it seem like nothing. I know what he said. It wasn't nothing. It was bad enough that Niko made some calls. That asshole won't be allowed on any job site in New York. No one will trust him not to threaten them or the women they employ if he gets pissed."

I moan in protest when he pulls his fingers out, but he spins me toward the wall and spanks me before I know what's happening.

"Open your legs."

It's not a suggestion. He angles himself so he can spank and finger me at the same time. Each slap presses my clit against the wall. He's stroking the spot he found our only night together. And my ass is already on fire, one spanking coming right after another.

"Bogdan, I need to come. Please."

The moment the words are out of my mouth, I regret them. He pulls his hand away and spanks me twice more before squeezing just above my clit. I whimper with need.

"You don't get to decide. You know that about us already, Tina."

And then he's inside me. He's thrusting into and spanking me, but now it's for pleasure, not punishment. He's bare, and that's a first. We talked about it that night. He knows I hadn't been with anyone for three months before that night. That was why I'd decided to see Todd, and that asshole was the last guy I slept with. Even though I've never had sex without a condom, I get tested every so often. I did that two weeks ago, plus I have an IUD. He got tested a couple months ago and hasn't been with anyone since. But we still used condoms that night. This is so much more intimate.

"You can feel the difference, can't you?"

"Yes, Daddy."

"You're going to take my cum, and you're going to feel it drip down your leg when your pussy's too full to hold all of it. Do you know why, *malyshka?*"

I shake my head, and he tugs my hair that he still has wrapped around his fist.

"Because you're mine."

Holy fuck, that's the hottest thing I've ever heard. He says it in that tone he used the first time he talked to me. He's leaning forward, his chest pressing against my back as he talks beside my ear. Right now, I'll be whatever the fuck he wants. He's fucking me hard, and I'm so close again. And then it happens. He comes and stops thrusting. He pulls out, and just like he said it would, his cum coats my thighs as I press them together, trying to ease my throbbing clit. He spins me around and finally kisses my mouth. It's fierce as he pins my hands above my head.

"You need to come so badly it hurts, doesn't it?"

"Yes. Are you always this possessive?"

"Never. Not with anything I've ever owned or any woman I've ever dated, to where they've complained that I don't show I care enough."

"Then why me?"

"I don't know."

He lets go of me and steps back. I can feel the tears welling in my eyes. Part of it is sexual frustration, and part of it is suddenly feeling abandoned after having him touching me so intimately. He pulls me against him and tucks my head against his chest. This is what I want. As much as I enjoy our sex—it's the best I've ever had—I need his comfort, too. He's still hard, so he lifts me, and I wrap my legs around his waist as he thrusts into me. He walks us to a kitchen chair and sits with me on his lap.

"I still need time, Bogdan. Even more so now. This is fucking confusing. I know I want you, but I don't know if I want everything that comes along with it. It scared the shit out of me when I realized I was being followed back to work yesterday. I thought it was Jim at first, but then I noticed it was a black sedan, like the one we took back to your place. I thought you ordered someone to follow me because one of your brothers told you what happened. I thought it was because you were angry with me or something. The guy was there when I came out of work. He nodded to me. That's when I realized he was there to guard me. That freaked me out, too. I made sure he didn't follow me home."

"You still came to Envy last night, and you didn't confront me."

"I thought about it. But it didn't feel like the right place with my friends around. I recognized Sergei when I left Envy. Did he spend the whole night outside?"

"Yes. Tina, I'll give you the time you need, but I still want someone to watch you. Until I'm certain Jim won't cause any trouble for you."

"Did Niko have someone follow him too?"

"Yes. He stayed home all night, but I have no way of knowing who he might have contacted. I want you to call in sick."

"I can't do that."

"Say your truck broke down."

"No, Bogdan. I'm going to work. That's too much."

"And if I want to spend the day watching you come?"

"Then you have to wait until I decide if that's what I want."

"I already know you do. That's not the part you need to think about, is it?"

He has a point. That's the only part that's crystal clear to me. He stands and lays me on the table. He's slow this time, but he thrusts hard enough to make the table shake and creak. He moves us to the floor, and I can't help but think this is crazy, that only people in movies do this. But it's hot, so fucking hot. He pulls my leg over his hip while kissing my neck. He has me pinned beneath him like that second or third time we had sex. He's gentle, but he's in control. It's heady to submit and fuels my pleasure as much as the way he's touching me.

I've had kinky boyfriends before who liked to spank during sex, and I've played along. I've kneeled before them and kept my hands behind my back. I've called them sir. But inside me, part of me has always rebelled, reveling because I'm silently in control when they think I'm not. Bogdan is the first man that I have ever completely surrendered to, and I know he's aware of what that means, that he treats my trust as something precious. This situation outside our little bubble is a mess, but in here, I've never felt safer. The gun didn't make me feel safer last night, but the moment I'd hugged him when I saw him, I'd felt better. After a shitastic day, I only felt relieved when he was holding me.

"Daddy, I need to come."

"I know, baby girl. Let me feel you."

He's balls deep, and now he's rocking into me, not letting up on my clit. My body tries to arch beneath him, but he's still holding me tight, his arm now wrapped around me. My whole body goes stiff, and my toes curl. My pussy is squeezing him so tightly that I feel him coming. I'm moaning, and he's groaning as we orgasm together.

When we're done kissing and stroking each other's back, he stands and takes my hand. He leads me upstairs, and I point to my bedroom. He takes me inside and into the bathroom, where he strips. We don't say a word until the shower is running, and we step inside.

"I know you've already showered, Bogdan."

"But I haven't showered with you."

I know he doesn't mean just today. I know he'd thought I would join him that next morning. I wish I had, especially as he massages my scalp as he washes my hair. He guides me under the showerhead as the suds wash clear. Then he's lathering my body with my bath poof. He's thorough. So thorough that I'm needy again, and he knows it. He goes down on me, and I watch him. His tongue is a national treasure. But for the first time, it really isn't enough.

"I need you inside me, Daddy."

He's happy to oblige as he lifts me again and wraps my legs around him. I lock my ankles and rest my head on his shoulder. He's letting me move with him as I kiss his neck and shoulder. Why is there this affection and tenderness between us already? Why does this feel so natural and soothing? Sex has never, ever been like this time.

"*Malyshka*, I will give you whatever time you need, but we both know we're meant to be together. This feels too right, too natural for our bodies to be one."

He's thinking the same thing I am.

"I know, Daddy. But it doesn't make the rest of the world understand that. I'm going to work today, and it's all going to come crashing back down on us. We can't hide forever, and the rest of the world might not be as convinced as we are."

"Will you accept a safety detail?"

"Yes, Daddy. If that's what you think is best."

I don't know his world yet. If my mafia—man—thinks I need guarding, then I'm a fool to refuse. I want to live long enough to see what's between us. He's probably totally overreacting, but he cares enough to react. None of this feels like he's acting out of duty or guilt.

"Come on me again, *malyshka*. I can feel you're close."

"I want to feel you come inside me again, Daddy. I only want you. No man's ever come inside me without a condom, Bogdan. My pussy really is yours."

And that's all it takes. We're clinging to each other as our bodies shudder. Each time just gets better, and each time, I fall for him a little more.

Despite being an early riser and Bogdan arriving at the ass-crack of dawn, I get to the office with only a couple minutes to spare. I want to be there before my boss arrives, since I need to plan what I'm going to say. He wasn't here when I returned after my second trip to the job site. Niko worked miracles in the few hours I gave him, and he rectified the most immediate concerns I had. It surprised me that he got that much done, but he'd quietly tasked Anatolii with fixing the smaller structural issues while he called Jim in for a planning meeting. I think that's part of what triggered Jim when Niko fired him. He'd just spent three hours going over plans that he now isn't involved in. I'd be pissed too.

I get to my desk and start my computer as I review my handwritten notes. These aren't the ones I'll share with Tom. I entered several things yesterday when I got back to my truck and my laptop. They're the things that will get the Kutsenkos the next level permit. The things that could get them shut down for weeks, if not months, I'm keeping track of and keeping to myself. I need to give myself enough time to shelter the project while they make corrections, but I also need to convince Tom to hand off this assignment to someone other than Jeremy or me.

"Good morning, Christina."

"Morning, Tom."

"How did things go with Kutsenko Partners?"

"It went well, but they need a little more time to finish up a few things with the floor system. I'm going back this afternoon to see what they get done."

"Was there a lot?"

"Not really. Just a few things that I suggested they take care of now to prevent any issues later."

I debate whether to mention that Niko fired Jim. I don't know what Jeremy may or may not have told our boss about this project and the crew. I don't want to give too much away.

"I heard they fired their foreman yesterday and made some day laborer the boss."

How the hell does he know that already?

"News travels fast."

"Yeah. I've known Jim since I was out in the field."

Fuck. Then how much about the site does he really know? Does he know Jim and Jeremy are in cahoots with Mancinelli? Does he think I'm being cagey?

"Yeah. But Anatolii Lotov isn't just some day laborer. He's been a foreman on several residential projects assigned to me. This is just his first time doing an industrial job. He has tons of experience. I don't foresee any issues coming up because of him."

Tom's gaze hardens. He must know some issues. But why? Is he getting paid off too? Why hasn't he stopped Jeremy from issuing the permits?

"I'm sure that'll be a surprise when Jeremy gets back."

"Any idea how long he's going to be out?"

"A few weeks."

"I can keep this on my caseload for now, but when the two community center projects get back on track, I won't be able to keep the Kutsenkos. That will probably be before Jeremy gets back."

"When do you think that'll happen?"

"A week or two at most."

"Who do you suggest?"

"Anthony probably has room to add them."

I trust Anthony. He's not the type to accept a bribe. I know people have approached him in the past, and he's made some enemies because he won't cave. But he's also someone who's totally by the book and will shut down the Kutsenkos' site.

"Fine. I'll talk to him today. When are you heading out?"

"Ten minutes. I have five sites to check today."

I'm going to visit the Kutsenkos in the middle. If Tom checks, it won't look like I'm favoring them. I'm probably worrying about nothing, but I'm feeling anxious about this whole thing. I need to talk to Bogdan, or probably Niko, about how well Jim and Tom know each other. Is Salvatore's reach longer than they realize? Probably.

Tom heads to his office while I gather what I need for the day. I'll wait until I'm in my truck to call the first foreman to let him know I'm on the way. Unless it's strictly a surprise visit, I try to let crews know I'm coming. It puts me in their good graces and makes everyone's life easier. I'm not looking for anyone's attitude this early in the morning. I'm still enjoying a post-coital high, and I'd prefer not to come down from it.

I'm about to walk out of the office when Tom stops me. He has a coffee mug in one hand and the other arm crossed. He looks smug. What now?

"Those issues the Kutsenkos are having must seem like nothing to them compared to the bodies found at their Queens site. I heard it was a hit job. Some hookers got dumped there. I wonder who did that."

"Considering Salvatore Mancinelli's been eyeing that property and filing grievances with the Queens office, I would guess him."

I watch his reaction. Something flickers in his eyes. I keep wondering what he knows and why he knows it.

"Keep your eye out for any arms or legs sticking out of the ground."

"That's morbid."

"You never know with people like them."

"Like them? The Mancinellis?"

"Yeah, and the Kutsenkos. You must know their reputation."

I know it's more than a reputation.

"Yeah. Who hasn't heard of the Mancinellis?"

"Salvatore's not so bad. He treats his men right and pays on time. He keeps a clean site that doesn't get shut down."

"Why would his sites get shut down when he takes care of business on someone else's build?"

Why are we even having this conversation? We both know this isn't idle gossip. He's maneuvering me.

"The Russians are the ones who like their women. I doubt it was the Italians."

I snort. "Italians don't like women? Don't let them know that. I thought that's how they made their reputations. Women and indestructible buildings. Then again, just like not all Italians are the stereotype, neither are the Russians. They're not all into sex trafficking."

"How do you know?"

"Because it's ridiculous to assume they all are. That's like saying all redheads are Irish. I'm Scottish."

"Just be careful."

"Thanks, Tom."

That's the weirdest conversation I've ever had with him. I'm dissecting it throughout the day until I reach the Kutsenkos' project. I head to the trailer and knock. I recognize Niko's voice telling me to enter. Only he and Bogdan are there. They both rise, but Bogdan stays where he is. I appreciate the professionalism, even in front of only his brother, but I hate it too. After what we did a few hours ago, it feels cold. I watch Bogdan look at Niko, who says he's going to check with Anatolii to see what they're working on and what they can show me.

"*Malyshka.*"

That one word. Bogdan's voice fills all my senses. I can see us together in his bed and on my kitchen floor. I can hear his grunts as he thrusts into me. I can feel the way our skin slides against each other. I can smell his expensive cologne, a scent that will always make me think of him. I can taste myself after he goes down on me.

"Daddy."

Somehow, we're together. I don't remember walking closer or him moving around the desk. But we're hugging, and all feels right in the world. I'm aroused the moment I see him, but for once, I don't feel like I need to jump his bones. I can feel his cock is hard, but he's not making this sexual either. It's affection. The kind I haven't felt with a guy I've not even been on a date with. It's the kind that I should have felt with past boyfriends after months of dating, but rarely did. I close my eyes and exhale.

"Can I call you Bogdi when we're alone?"

I'd searched for Russian terms of endearments last night in the Uber on my way to meet my friends. I'd searched his name to see what it meant, and I learned that was a nickname.

"Of course, Tina. I don't call you by your full name. Though I never asked if I could."

"No one else calls me that. I like it when you say it."

"And that's how I feel about Bogdi. I haven't been called that since I was a kid. It's yours alone, *malyshka*."

"I like that." I lean back. "I think we're kidding ourselves if we say we're waiting to date."

"I know. There's too much between us, and we can't stay away."

"I think Anthony Lake is going to take my place in two weeks. My boss is going to hear about us. Maybe I can take some of Anthony's projects sooner, and he can be your inspector by the end of the week."

I feel Bogdan sigh. I won't like what he says.

"Anatolii found more issues this morning. If we get a new inspector now, he'll close the site. Niko thinks we need those two weeks to get everything up to code."

"What's wrong now?"

"Looks like Jim had the guys cut some corners with laying some flooring. Anatolii's already talked to the crew about why no one spoke up. Apparently, Jim used threats. Some of our workers aren't here legally, and Jim found out. Many of them don't speak English well, so they rely on the others to interpret. They're not comfortable pushing back against people in authority. Their past has taught them not to trust that they'll be safe if they speak up."

"They didn't think they could come to you or your brothers?"

"Not with the threats Jim made."

It's my turn to sigh.

"I need to talk to Niko and you. I think your problems are bigger than Jim and Jeremy. I think my boss is involved."

"Shit. Okay."

Chapter Eight

Bogdan

We head outside, and Tina grabs her hard hat and clipboard from her truck. We walk the site with Anatolii, and she takes notes. Niko kept the crew really late and started practically at dawn to have completed what they did. The mood is completely different now that Anatolii is in charge.

"Ms. MacNally, we'll work on stiffness of floors. Plans didn't call for asymmetrical layout of braced frames, but it looks like Jim may have ordered that."

"That would cause twisting. How stiff was the flooring going to be?"

"Too. It would make floors twist much sooner."

"And it would be grounds for a lawsuit." Tina looks at Niko. "Patterson Deliveries could claim construction flaws and take you to court. They would likely win."

A company based in north New Jersey owns the flex building we're constructing. It has a high ceiling on the first floor for a warehouse, but the next two floors are mostly offices and meeting rooms. It would be one thing if we were building this for ourselves, but we're not.

"What needs to be done?"

Niko looks like he's ready to pace.

"Boss, we just follow plans. We caught this in time."

"All right. Then we can keep moving forward."

"Yes. Based on what I've seen today, you shouldn't have any more major problems as long as you follow the architectural plans. It shouldn't take two weeks to get back on schedule."

"Ms. MacNally, how did you get into construction?"

I know Niko's been dying to ask that question since the moment she walked into the trailer the first time.

"I have a Bachelor's in Architecture and planned to become one, but I realized I enjoy being on sites more than I enjoy drawing pictures of them. I have a Master's in Construction Management. I make less in urban planning for the city, but it's stable work. I enjoy knowing when I'm getting paid, and so does my mortgage company."

With a cocked eyebrow, we all know she means more than because of the weather. Being a female foreman isn't as unheard of as it was twenty or thirty years ago, but it's still not the norm. It would be unlikely for her to have steady work, even during good building weather.

"How long have you worked for the city?"

There's still a lot we don't know about each other, and she said she wanted us to get better acquainted. I suppose my first question for her should have been how old is she. I'm guessing late twenties like me.

"I interned for two years in college, and they have employed me for five. I started as a surveyor, then moved into my current department when I finished my Master's."

I realize that's something else she doesn't know about me. She doesn't know I went to college too.

"Ms. MacNally is very smart woman, Mr. Kutsenko. We're lucky she came here."

Anatolii goes back to work, giving instructions to a forklift driver. Niko stays with Tina and me. She blurts out a question.

"How old are you?"

She takes me by surprise, but I smile. I was just thinking about the same thing.

"I'm twenty-seven, Niko's twenty-eight, Aleks's twenty-nine, and Maks's thirty."

"Your poor mother."

She speaks without thinking, but Niko and I laugh and nod.

"Where'd you go to school, Tina?"

If she interned for the city, probably somewhere nearby.

"NYU for architecture and Colombia for construction management."

"And you work for the city?"

I hear Niko's shock. She went to excellent programs.

"I do. I work year-round with no gaps. I know I'm getting paid regularly without delays, and I know how much, with no doubt. I like stability, and so does my retirement fund. I have a mountain of student loan debt. Working for the city and being a civil servant isn't exactly a lucrative job. Yet. My goal is to work in the Department of City Planning's main office for a couple more years before moving over to the Department of Buildings. I wouldn't mind being Commissioner one day.

"Not relying on a measly inspector's pension?" Niko grins.

"Hardly."

She catches Niko and me glancing at each other before I turn to her. She doesn't know what it means. But we're both thinking we should hire her like we hired Laura as our corporate legal counsel.

"You said you needed to talk to Niko, too. What's up?"

"We should go inside."

She follows Niko with me behind her. I know Pasha was at her house by the time we left this morning. He pulled up behind her when she got here. It doesn't surprise me that he's in the trailer when we return.

"My shadow. How'd you get stuck with such a boring job?"

"It's definitely not boring with the way you drive."

She laughs, but I scowl.

"She's freaking Mario Andretti in a three-ton truck."

She shrugs one shoulder.

"I'm sure you heard it speed up, and I know how long it is."

"Everyone within a block hears that beast rev."

"I know. I love it." She grins. "It roars. Petty power trip, I know. But I think it suits me."

"He's not stuck with you, Tina."

I'm standing just behind her, so I whisper. My breath tickles her neck and nearly makes her shiver, but she catches herself. I'm close enough that if she turns around, our lips will meet. Too bad Niko and Pasha are here.

"He's right, Ms. MacNally. I'm not stuck. Bogdan trusts me, and that's important to me."

She looks back over her shoulder, and I brush a quick kiss on her temple.

"There are only seven people I trust with your safety, and they all share my blood, *malyshka*. You can trust Pasha with anything. If you ever need to, he won't disappoint."

"Thank you." She whispers that, but mouths, "Daddy."

She nods, but she can't look away. I place my finger beneath her chin and press a kiss to her cheek. Her lashes flutter against her cheekbones. I drop my hand from her chin but rest it on her waist. She shifts so she can see all three of us but stays within reach before she tells us what she learned at work that morning.

"I think my boss knows what's going on here. He said he's known Salvatore Mancinelli since he was in the field. He didn't argue when I suggested Anthony take this project, but he dropped hints that he knows Jeremy and Salvatore are connected. I think Tom might get paid just like Jeremy and Jim."

"It wouldn't surprise me. Salvatore's paying half the employees in the Queens office. The city planner shut us down a few weeks ago."

"Is that the same site where they found the bodies?"

All three of our faces become inscrutable. None of us shifts our gaze from her. We have our own type of silent communication among us. There's definitely plenty she doesn't understand.

"Yes." It's Niko who answers. "I suppose that sort of news doesn't stay in one borough."

"Tom mentioned it. He implied it was a Russian thing. He said they were hookers, and he implied you're into sex trafficking."

"Do you believe him?"

She spins toward me. She's pissed.

"You may do some questionable things, but do you think I'm so lacking in morals that I'd be doing some guy who sells women for sex?"

"Tina."

"Don't do that. Don't you think that if I believed you were into that, that I would be too scared you'd sell me to go anywhere near you? Or am I not good enough to bring a high price, and that's why you—"

"Finish that, and I will take you over my knee. I don't care who sees."

I hiss in her ear, but I'm certain my brother and cousin hear me. Her glare challenges me.

"Out."

Pasha and Niko don't hesitate. They're out of the trailer as I pull her to a chair and sit. I don't ask before I unfasten her pants, and she doesn't resist. She knows what's coming, and I think she needs it more than just wants it. It's been one confusing encounter after another since she met me. I sense she feels ungrounded and anxious. A spanking puts me in control, and right now I think she's happy to cede that to me.

I draw her over my lap and squeeze her ass before stroking it. I do that three more times before dipping my fingers between her legs.

"You don't get to come, *malyshka*. This is most definitely not about pleasure. Do you know why I'm spanking you?"

"Yes, Daddy."

"Why?"

"I insulted you in front of your family, and I insinuated you sell women."

"You did. And you insulted yourself by suggesting I would ever think so lowly of you. I know you don't believe my family and I are sex traffickers, but it hurts that you would imply that, even in anger."

"I'm sorry, Bogdan."

"I know, but I'm still spanking you, Christina."

She fights against me to sit up, and I let her move.

"Please don't do that. Please don't call me that, even if you're angry with me."

"Why?"

Her voice is soft, and I'm taking her seriously. She's agitated in a way she wasn't before I used her full name.

"It feels so distant and uncaring. No one else calls me Tina, only you. I don't want to be someone you can push away like that."

"I have you over my lap, ready to spank you. I hardly think I'm pushing you away."

"Emotionally. That feels like a worse punishment than a spanking."

"I only wanted you to know I'm serious. I'm not distant or uncaring. Just the opposite. I've never cared this much. There's enough in my life that'll make you think I'm a monster, but I don't harm women."

"Can I ask you one question, then I'll take my spanking without complaint?"

"You can always ask me anything, Tina. I'll do my best to answer. If I don't, it's because I think it's too dangerous, not because I don't want to."

"When you do these things that you say make you a monster, are you doing them because you like the way it makes you feel or because you have to for your family and your people?"

"Always the latter, *malyshka*. I admit sometimes it's satisfying. But I have no compulsion to hurt people. I derive no pleasure from it. It's part of my job, and my job is to support my family and the bratva. I would walk away from these things if I could, but I will never walk away from my family. You know why none of us can leave."

"One more question."

"All right."

"Can I ask you more later?"

"Yes, baby girl. Like I said, I'll do my best to answer. Tina, I've never encouraged another woman to learn about this part of me. I've never openly admitted it, and I've never answered any questions that came from guesses."

"But you do for me."

"Yes. I don't want you to leave me because I'm emotionally closed off to you. I don't want you to leave me because you think I'm deceitful or untrusting. I've been all those things in the past. I have no desire to be that way with you."

"After my spanking, I'd like you to kiss me, please, Daddy."

"I will, *malyshka*."

She repositions herself and waits for the first slap. It must sting because she tenses.

"You are going to get ten on each side, Tina. I consider what you said serious. I'm not angry at you. I will never spank you out of anger. But that wasn't cool. My family and I didn't deserve that, and it didn't make you look good.

"I know, Daddy. I'm sorry."

"I know that too, baby girl."

I'm unrelenting with my strength. I know I would cause her real harm if I wanted, but I'm careful where each blow lands. It's enough to make her think twice before being spiteful without being more than she can bear. After every two on each side, I rub some of the burn away. It gives her a breather, too. But I follow through on what I said. Ten on each side. The trailer fills with the sound of skin hitting skin and her soft whimpers. When I land my hand on her horizontal crack, she can't help but kick her feet, but she never tries to stop me. She keeps her hands wrapped around my ankle. I think she's fighting the need to cry because she probably doesn't want anyone to see her with red and puffy eyes.

"It's done now, *malyshka*. Let Daddy take care of you."

I roll her over and nestle her against me. I widen my legs, so her sore ass doesn't rest against my pants. They probably felt smooth enough against her belly, but they must be like sandpaper on her fiery backside. I stroke her hair and kiss her forehead until she's not panting anymore. She tips her head back, and my kiss is tender. My hand is caressing her ass, and she melts. If her eyes weren't already closed, they would be. She seems exhausted but content.

"I wish I could take a nap with you right now, Daddy."

"Me too, baby girl."

"I want you to come over tonight, Bogdan. But we both know that's a bad idea."

"And it would be worse if you came to my place."

She sits up straighter, so she can see my face.

"I won't run from you again, Bogdan. You don't need to worry about that."

"That's not what I meant at all. I didn't even think of it, though going to your place would mean you can't get away."

I grin and waggle my eyebrows before kissing her neck.

"What did you mean, then?"

"If you come to me, then you've made a willing choice to spend time with me. You made the effort to come to me. If I show up at your place, you could argue I didn't give you a choice."

"Should I be worried about someone seeing me at your place?"

"Right now, maybe. Carmine Mancinelli came to Envy last night. He knew of you. I'm not sure, but I assume Jim's already reported to Salvatore, who told Carmine, so the prick could antagonize me."

"Do you think Jim actually knows about us? Or was it just the same as when he confronted me here?"

"I don't know. But Niko called Salvatore and another syndicate leader to warn them that Jim isn't safe to have around women on their sites. They'll take that seriously. It probably pissed off Salvatore that he got fired. He won't like that he received a call to say Jim's a risk around women. To a certain degree, he's old school Italian. Women are untouchable to him and must be treated with respect. He's said things to Maks before to goad him, but he doesn't know about you specifically. At least, not from Niko. My brother just said a woman on the site. Salvatore won't put up with Jim harassing any of the women who work for him."

"Thank heavens for small mercies."

There's sarcasm dripping from her words. But it reminds us of why we came back to the trailer. We still need to finish talking to Niko. I help her to her feet, then pull her pants up and fasten them while I kiss her forehead. When I'm done, I cup her jaw in both hands.

"Tina, we'll figure this out."

My kiss is soft at first, then we're ready to paw at each other. If we didn't hear stomping coming up the metal steps, we'd probably be fucking on Niko's desk. We pull apart as the door opens. Neither Niko nor Pasha look at Tina, keeping their focus on me. I nod, so they come inside, and Niko updates us.

"I talked to Sergei. He's looking into Tom's connections to Salvatore, Jim, and Jeremy. Ms. MacNally, what else needs to be fixed before another inspector comes out?"

"Please call me Christina. It seems pointless to be so formal. And if Anatolii finishes what he has planned today, you're in good shape. Your crew does good work when they aren't being told not to. I'm surprised but pleased. I thought it would take more time."

"They're working late and coming in early until we're back on track. Only a few aren't interested in overtime pay."

"Just make sure you stay within union hours. You don't need that headache." She adds as an afterthought, "Even if you're not exactly unionized."

Chapter Nine

Tina

I watched Anatolii clap Niko's shoulder and squeeze when we were on the site. It was a paternal gesture, and I wondered how long they've known each other. I know nothing about Bogdan's parents, so I don't know if their father is in the picture. But Anatolii's gesture gave Niko the reassurance he needed while I was there.

When I sat on Bogdan's lap after he spanked me, and I looked into his blue eyes. They were as fathomless as the Atlantic Ocean. I could drown in them, and he'd be my only life preserver. Maybe baby girl is a common endearment in Russia, but I'm not ready for anyone but Bogdan to hear me call him Daddy. I don't think I ever will be. That's too intensely personal for me.

Now I can't get the idea out of my head about him coming to my place. He's right. I couldn't run away, and I have nowhere I'd rather go. I look at the empty spot next to me on my sofa, and I wish Bogdan was filling it. I don't want to think about how empty my bed will feel yet again. I wake up each morning not remembering all the details from my dreams, but I'm aroused. I must have sex fantasies about him.

It's Taco Tuesday, and the girls want me to come out with them. I'm in sweatpants with my hair pulled into a messy bun. I was going to watch some reality TV, but now I want a distraction. I grab my phone and open an ongoing group chat with Tracy, Sarah, and Kelsey.

Me: I hear fish tacos calling my name after all.

Kelsey: Señor Poncho's. Be there in 30 minutes or I'm eating all the chips and guac.

Sarah: You'll do that even if she's early.

Kelsey: I know but at least it's fair warning.

Tracy: If we get there first, do you want us to order you a drink?

Me: Yeah. Skinny margarita.

Tracy: Sugar, no salt. I know.

Me: Thanks. I'm gonna get changed and head out.

I'm in jeans and a sweater top in five minutes. I add a little makeup, but I leave my hair in a messy bun. I'm about to head to the subway when I realize Pasha is waiting somewhere. I step outside and look around. I spot him and hurry to his car.

"What's wrong?"

He's out of the car the moment he sees me facing him. He meets me before I can cross the street.

"Nothing. I've decided to go out with some friends tonight, and I was going to take the subway." From how his expression changes, I know that won't happen. "Bogdan wouldn't approve, I take it."

"Only if you let me stay at your side."

I sigh. That's better than absolute refusal.

"Let me drive you wherever you're going."

"You're not my chauffeur, Pasha."

I feel badly now. As though getting stuck watching my house isn't lowly enough, to be my driver...That seems insulting.

"I don't think that I am. Christina, what I said back at the site is true. I'm glad Bogdan trusts me to protect you. We're as close as brothers, not just cousins. You're important to him, so you're important to me. I'd feel better if you let me drive you. Are you staying in Queens or going somewhere else?"

"Brooklyn."

"Hop in."

I'm not sure if I'm supposed to ride in the back or next to him. He decides for me and opens the back door. The privacy glass is already up. So much for not being my chauffeur. I push the button and lower the divider. I give Pasha the address and sit back. Neither of us raises the glass. There are a ton of questions I could ask him, but I know I should wait to talk to Bogdan. I fear the silence will be awkward, but it's not. It's nice to sit back and just look out the window. Pasha opens the door for me when we arrive at Señor Poncho's. I see the girls immediately, and they see Pasha. Their eyes dart between Pasha and the sedan, and me.

"Who's that?"

Sarah mouths her question as she stares at Pasha. He's looking at Kelsey and smiling. He's almost as hot as Bogdan, and if I didn't know his cousin, Pasha would probably make my panties drop.

"Hey, girls. I don't remember if you saw Pasha at Envy last night. He's Bogdan's cousin."

"Hello."

Did he just make his accent thicker?

"Are you going to join us?"

Sarah's perplexed, and I don't blame her. Last night, I'm hugging Bogdan then dancing with him. They saw me disappear with him and probably assumed we hooked up somewhere. Now I'm with his cousin. Even though I got out of the back of the car, and he opened the door, it looks suspect.

"Afraid not. I was headed in the same direction, so I offered Christina a ride."

"In the back of the car?"

Sarah will not let it go.

"He had a call to make, so I wanted to give him some privacy."

She accepts that. I look back at Pasha, and he slips me a card. It has his number on it. I assume I'm supposed to let him know when I want to go home. I nod before following my friends inside.

"Spill it. Why are you with one guy one night, then his cousin the next?"

"And how are they so fucking hot?

Tracy, then Kelsey, fires off the questions the moment we slip into a booth.

"Like Pasha said, we were going in the same direction, so he offered me a ride. He saw me headed to the subway while he was driving. He stopped to say hi. When I said I was coming to meet friends in Brooklyn, he said he was headed here too. It was a coincidence, but it sure as hell beats the subway."

"And Bogdan won't mind?"

"Kels, I think he would mind more if he found out Pasha left me to take the subway when he could have given me a ride. They're all pretty chivalrous."

"But you barely know Bogdan, and you got in the car with a practical stranger."

"As opposed to an Uber or Lyft, Kels?"

"That's not the same, and you know it. What if he

kidnapped you?"

"Bogdan would be pissed."

"What if he kidnapped you and was taking you to Bogdan to do unspeakable things?"

I blush to my roots. We did some pretty unspeakable things the night we met, and I loved every one of them.

"Holy fucking shit." Sarah slaps the table. "You've already had sex with Bogdan, haven't you?"

I say nothing. They must feel the heat radiating from my cheeks. I'm sure I'm fucking red as a tomato. My fair skin doesn't help.

"When?"

Kelsey just won't give up. I wonder if it's because Pasha was looking at her. Does she want to be sure nothing is going on with him?

"We hooked up the night we met, and we like each other."

"Did you meet him at the club or bar that you went to with Todd?"

"It was a club." I'm just not saying what kind. "I thought it would be a one-night thing. You know I don't do that often. Turns out we get along and enjoy each other's company beyond sex."

"So are you dating?"

"Not exactly, Trace. It's complicated. My work and his work overlap, and it would be a conflict of interest if we started dating right now. When I'm no longer assigned his company's project, then we can try dating."

"In the meantime, you're just banging."

"You're so eloquent, Sarah. And no. We're not just banging."

"Because you're not having sex, or because it's more than just casual?"

I think about the sex we had on my kitchen floor, then in

my shower. I think about the fact that I've known him less than a week, but I feel like it's been a lifetime. When I went home with him on Friday night, I was certain it was lust at first sight. Then I thought it was a sex hangover mistake the next morning. Yesterday, it was like—I don't know. Love at second sight? It's just fundamentally different from how I've ever felt before. Other than saying it's Bogdan, I don't have any reason for it to be the polar opposite. My relationships have usually developed slowly, with a handful of flings or one-night stands in there. Never did the two intersect before.

"Both." We shouldn't have any more sex because that's way worse if it gets out at work. "I hope Bogdan and I last once we get started."

"He's really that special to you?"

"Yeah, Trace. He is."

"He seems kinda dark."

Sarah's hesitant with her comment, and I think about making a quip about his brown hair to lighten the mood. But she isn't wrong. There's a broodiness about all the Kutsenkos, and there's a legit air of danger to them. That's what Sarah's talking about. It radiates from them, and rightfully so.

"He's a businessman. No nonsense. I suppose it can make him seem aloof."

"Or like a mobster."

My stomach knots at Kelsey's flippant comment.

"Like some Wall Street corporate mogul."

I like Tracy's assessment more. I shrug, grateful that our waitress arrives to take our drink order. The conversation blessedly shifts away from Bogdan and me. Sarah's boyfriend is taking her to meet his parents this weekend in Pennsylvania. She's nervous since she's only seen them over video calls. We give her a pep talk over tacos, chips, margaritas, and beers. I'm a little tipsy by the time we settle the check. The bartender was a little heavier handed than I realized. I duck into the restroom and pull out my phone. I punch in Pasha's number.

Me: It's Christina. I'm going to Uber home. No subway. Promise.

There's no immediate response, so I head back to the front of the restaurant. All four of us have our phones out and are ordering cars. We each live in a different borough, but we met in college. We lived on the same floor, and Tracy was my freshman roommate. I'm about to finish the request when a text notification flashes.

Pasha: I'll be there in a minute.

Me: You don't need to. My friends are going to ask too many questions if you come back.

Pasha: I'm still going to be there in a minute. I'll follow the car.

Me: That seems pointless. If you have the night watch, just go to my place.

Pasha: No. I'm half a block away. I can see you in the doorway.

Marvelous. My red hair, I'm sure.

Me: Fine. I'll just say my Uber is a few more minutes away than anyone else's.

"Who're you texting?"

I don't expect Tracy's question, and I nearly jump out of my skin.

"Is it Bogdan?"

Sarah's sing-song voice makes me laugh. If only it was. We wouldn't be arguing about me getting in the back of his car. I just smile and shrug. Let them make of that what they will.

"There's my Lyft."

Sarah's the first to leave, then Tracy.

"I'll make my car wait until yours gets here."

I appreciate Kelsey's offer, and we've all done that for each other before.

"Nah. It's well-lit here. I'm not worried. I'll stay right by the door."

"You sure?"

"Yeah."

"All right."

We exchange a quick hug before she waves to her approaching Uber. Once the car is out of sight, Pasha pulls out and stops in front of the restaurant with the passenger window down.

"Thank you."

I speak before he even gets out of the car. I know he's going to open my door, but I get to it first. I don't enjoy feeling as though he's a servant or something.

"You're welcome. Have a good time?"

"Mhmm. Is Bogdan home?"

Pasha hesitates.

"No."

"Is he at Envy?" Pasha shakes his head. "Ivy" Another shake. My stomach sinks, and I have a spike of jealousy. "Pussycats?"

"No. We had a family issue come up that he's taking care of."

"Is everything all right? Does he need anything? Do you or your family?"

"No. But thanks. He has everything under control."

Of course he does. He programmed his number into my phone this morning while I got ready. I pull him up in my contacts.

Me: I hope everything is okay. Pasha said something came up with your family. Let me know if you need anything.

I wait, but there's no response. There isn't one by the time I say goodnight to Pasha and go in my house. There isn't one before I turn out the light and try to fall asleep. There isn't one in the hour that I lie trying to get my mind to stop. There isn't one when I get up.

I decide to call him when I'm on the way to work, but it goes straight to voicemail.

"Hey, it's Tina. I'm checking to see if everything's okay. I don't know if you got my text, but Pasha said there was a family issue. I know you're busy, but I just wanted to let you know I'm thinking about you."

I hang up and head into work. As the day progresses, and I don't hear from Bogdan, I wonder what's going on. But I'm busier than usual that day since I have a site that doesn't pass inspection, and I have to write up a report. Tom's keeping his distance, which for today is just fine with me.

He's ghosted me. It's been a week and a half, and I haven't heard a peep from Bogdan. It hurts. Like a lot. Like a lot a lot. I've cried a few—several—times. I have no idea what to make of the situation. I've been to the Kutsenkos' job site twice this week. The first time, only Niko was there. He said the same thing Pasha did. Almost word for word. The second time was yesterday, and Aleks was there too. Apparently, Maks just left for his honeymoon. I wonder if Maks being gone is keeping Bogdan busy. But when I ask about him, Aleks and Niko are even more evasive. They just said he's busy, but he'll let me know when he's not.

This sucks. I got Anthony to take over their case today, and it doesn't even matter anymore. I've added to my work just to get rid of one case. I'm going to be driving all over the fucking

Bronx for the next month. Anthony's cases are at the opposite end from where mine are. I'm going to have to drive back and forth. Hopefully, I can schedule them, so I don't spend all day in my truck for the next month.

It's Friday and Lady's Night at The Hangar Club. When isn't it since it's a male strip club? Fuck Bogdan. Obviously, he doesn't care about me. He couldn't even bother to text me and say he isn't interested. He couldn't have one of his brothers or cousins tell me it's over. He blows me off, and I'm just supposed to get the hint. Well, I did.

The girls and I are all done up. I got my eyebrows done during lunch today, and my makeup is perfect. My already straight hair is sleek and straightened, hanging to the bottom of my shoulder blades. I have on four-inch heels and a miniskirt that would make my parents *plotz*. If I weren't twenty-six, they would ground me if they could just for owning the damn thing. My tank top has a deep v down the front that reaches the bottom. The spaghetti straps connect to a thin strip of fabric around my waist, leaving my entire back bare. It's chilly in late September, and there's no way I'm walking along any sidewalk with my tank top showing, so I have a cardigan. The short skirt is bad enough, but I'm not a total idiot.

I haven't been out at night since Taco Tuesday last week. The girls tried to get me to go out over the weekend, but I wasn't interested. I had important plans: moping. But I'm over that now. He might not see me looking this good, but it still feels a little like revenge. It's a boost for my crushed ego. Pasha doesn't look pleased when I come out of the house and immediately get in an Uber. I'm not sure if it's the car service or my clothes. Probably both. I know he's following me into Manhattan, and he can follow me right back to Queens later. Misha's had the day shift ever since Bogdan disappeared. I told Aleks and Niko to call off their guard dogs, to which I got stares that would have burned a lesser woman to ash. I told them the truth. It's ridiculous to have anyone guard me if Bogdan isn't into me anymore. Neither responded, and I still have the cousins in my shadow.

Fine. The only regret I have about not being in the car with Pasha is not seeing and hearing his reaction when he realizes where I'm headed. But his scowl's clear when I spot him leaning against the building corner when I look around. He even shakes his head, but I ignore him. I'm not letting some bad-tempered Russian hottie ruin my night with a bunch of equally hot but in far better moods strippers. A guy in just jeans and cowboy boots shows us to a table near the stage. Sarah hands me a wad of ones.

"It took a whole lot of explaining to get Chris to calm down when he saw all this cash. I had to tell him like five times that I was bringing it for you three."

"I can't believe he's okay with you being here."

"Much to everyone's disappointment but his, male strip clubs aren't fully nude like female ones. I told him it's the same as the beach or a pool. I can't see anything more here than I would either of those places."

"And he bought it?"

I laugh when she rolls her eyes. Clearly, the answer to my question is no.

"I told him about your shitty experience with you-know-who, and he became way more understanding. I should have led with that."

Our first round of drinks arrives at the same time as the first dancer takes the stage. He's my type. They're all ripped, but this guy is broad shouldered with a super tapered waist. He looks like he played soccer or was a swimmer. He also has dark hair. The build and dark hair remind me of someone, which makes me drink way too fast. I slow down when a blond guy comes on stage. He's hot for sure, but I'm not as into him. Doesn't stop me from tucking a couple dollars in his banana hammock when he comes to our table. Four more guys come out and do their thing to various popular songs.

The first guy comes back, and I would gladly save a horse and ride that cowboy. He drops his Stetson on my head before squatting so his dick is right in front of my mouth. Tempting, especially after the six drinks I've had. The fruit punch has already gone to my head. I tuck five bucks into the front of his G-string, so the bills hang over his cock and wave at me every time he moves.

Just before the end of the night, all the guys make their way into the audience, offering lap dances. You-know-who makes a beeline for me, and I don't refuse. I'm enjoying it until he tries to stick his hand up my skirt. I snap my legs shut and shake my head.

"Christina."

Tracy points toward the door. Pasha looks like he's ready to murder the guy, and he's pushing through the crowd. I shake my head at Pasha and push back my chair.

"Dude, no. The dance is great, but I'm not looking to get felt up."

"You sure, mama? I bet you're wet."

That might be true, but that's none of his business. And it's likely as much from thinking about Bogdan all night as it is any of these guys. I keep picturing him while he's fucking me and comparing that to the guys on stage. Between the two, I'm surprised I haven't come just sitting in my chair.

My phone is on the table, and it vibrates. I turn away from the dancer, who gets the hint and moves onto the next table.

Pasha: It's time to go.

Me: Not it's not. I have another 20 minutes until closing. They just said last call.

Pasha: He knows.

My gaze darts to Pasha, who's back by the door now. I look past him, but the tinted glass keeps me from seeing outside. There is only one person he's talking about, and I'm pissed that Pasha called or texted him. He had no right to do that. I get up to tell him as much, but I take a moment to get my legs under me.

"You okay?"

"Yeah, Kels. I'm not all the way drunk, but I'm nowhere near completely sober."

"None of us are. We should call Ubers now."

Sarah is the responsible one tonight, and I know it's because she isn't having as much fun as the rest of us. She laughed and drank along with us, but I could tell none of what she saw impressed her. She has a boyfriend she's probably going to marry waiting for her at home. For us single ladies, well, I enjoyed myself. Thinking about Bogdan is a double-edged sword. Picturing us having sex is fucking hotter than all get out. But thinking about him in general hurts my heart. Every time I got sad, a new dancer distracted me. Then I thought about Bogdan fucking me. Around my mind went all night. I'm fucking horny and a little sad. But I'm glad I came out with the girls, and I'm glad we came here.

"Isn't that Bogdan's cousin at the door? Does he work here?"

Kelsey points, and I cringe. He looks like he could be a bouncer here if he didn't have a shirt on. So much for him staying out of sight.

"No, he doesn't work here."

"Is he following you? What the fuck?"

"Calm down, Tracy. There was an incident at their job site a week ago with a foreman they fired. He said some shit to me. I didn't take it as a serious threat, but Bogdan and his brothers refuse to take any chances. Pasha's around sometimes to keep an eye on me and make sure I get home safely."

"Are you dating him now? Like did he volunteer?"

"No. Bogdan assigned him."

"Why? You never even dated. He ghosted you, but he has someone following you. Don't you think that's effed up? Just how bad was this guy?"

"I don't know. But Pasha keeps his distance, and it makes all of them feel better to know one of their former employees can't do anything to me. It's not just Bogdan."

"How much longer is he going to be around?"

"Kelsey, just ask him out."

The booze is making me short-tempered.

"Do you think he'd say yes? Have you asked him?"

"No. He and I don't chat. He looks at you a lot, so maybe he's interested. I'm not getting in the middle. If you want him, go ask."

"I suppose you won't need an Uber with your bodyguard to take you home." Sarah glances at Pasha as she speaks.

"Probably not."

"Let's go before it gets crowded outside."

We follow Tracy's suggestion and head to the door. I hang back with Pasha after I hug my friends goodnight. When I step outside, there's a black sedan double parked with a backdoor open. There's a guy I don't recognize standing next to it. I look at Pasha, and his expression is the grimmest I've ever seen. I turn back to the car and wonder if I really want to get in. I'm stalling. Then Bogdan's climbing out and standing by the door. He buttons his suit coat and looks at me.

I don't know what propels me forward, but it's as though he's lassoed me with some invisible rope and pulls me to him. I have no way to resist.

"It's time to go home, *malyshka*."

Chapter Ten

Bogdan

One fucked up thing after another has kept me at the warehouse for more than a week. When we're at the warehouse, our cell phones are off. Not just to avoid distraction, but so we can't be tracked. There's one phone always there, but it's rarely used. We keep fresh clothes and stuff for showers. We're all about the same size, so the clothes are pretty interchangeable if need be. I've barely slept in the past nine days since I arrived to see Jim. He squealed like a little bitch within five minutes of me being there. He confirmed Tina's suspicions that Tom is on Salvatore's payroll just like him and Jeremy.

Sergei is an intel wizard. Most people look at him and assume he's just a muscle-bound construction worker. He likes that impression. No one guesses he's a skilled hacker. He's made Jim look like an embezzler who ran off to Mexico with some of our money. No one will look for him since he doesn't have a wife, kids, or much close family. Right now, his dust has already disintegrated in the Flushing River.

I made him suffer for a couple days, but it was over quickly once I was done with him. However, it wasn't over so quickly when dealing with the men Aleks brought in. They were involved with several threats against Laura and Maks. It's taken a while, but we've been inching closer to knowing who hired a ghost hitman. I didn't intend to be away from Tina for so long, but we lose track of time when we're working at the warehouse. And the man I become is the man I warned her is a monster. I don't want her anywhere near me when I'm like that, not even on the phone or through a text. Aleks told me he and Niko assured her it was just some family business and that I would be in touch as soon as possible.

It's Friday, and I'm hoping Tina's at home. I want nothing more than to see her and hold her. I've missed her so much. When I wasn't concentrating on whomever we strung up on a meat hook in front of me, I was thinking about her. I was so tempted to call her, but I couldn't. I've just gotten in the car and turned my phone back on. Stefan's driving, so I open my texts.

There are four from Tina. The first two hope that I'm all right and ask if I need anything. The second two are asking why I'm ignoring her. Then I listen to the voicemails. Fuck me. There are three. The first one is like the first two texts. The third sounds frustrated, and the fourth sounds like she's on the verge of tears. I'm about to tell Stefan to take me to her place when I decide to see if Pasha is there. Maybe she went out with her friends.

What the ever-loving fuck? Why is Pasha's phone outside the fucking Hangar Club in Manhattan? She went to a mother-fucking men's strip club. Considering where we met and where

I sometimes work, it shouldn't shock me. But it does. She didn't wait long to get over me.

She thinks you ghosted her, you asshole.

Me: I'm coming to get her.

Pasha: You might want to wait until morning.

Me: Why?

Pasha: She's been drinking.

Me: So?

Pasha: And she's having a good time with her friends.

Me: Just how good a good time?

Crickets.

I've already given Stefan the address, which I know surprises him, but he's not paid to give an opinion about where I go. I'm clenching my fists so tightly that my fingers ache. I'm pissed Pasha hasn't answered, and I'm hurt thinking about Tina enjoying a lap dance and whatever else happens at a male strip club. I've never been to one, but they can't be that different from the ones I run. I keep thinking about her getting wet for some other guy, maybe going home with one. Fuck it. It's been ten minutes.

Me: Answer my fucking question.

Pasha: Sorry. Had to take care of something.

Me: What the fuck?

Pasha: It was nothing. She dealt with it.

Me: Dealt with what? Stop being evasive.

Pasha: Are you coming here? Do I need to keep her here until you arrive?

Me: Of course I'm headed there. What do you think?

Pasha: Fine. Hurry up. It's almost last call.

I noticed he still hasn't answered my question, which

means he knows I'm going to lose my shit if he tells me. I'm getting fucking tired of my family keeping things from me. It only gets me pissed when I might otherwise handle whatever it is calmly.

We get to The Hangar Club, and Stefan comes around to open the door. I don't get out. I don't need her friends making a scene when they recognize me. I watch them each leave, then Pasha leads Tina out to the sidewalk. She stares at the car until I get out. I doubt for a moment that she'll come to me, then it's as if an invisible force propels her to me.

"It's time to go home, *malyshka*."

"No. I'm not going anywhere with you. You dumped me."

"I did not, but you seem to have forgotten about me easily enough."

"You think I've forgotten about you? Who texted who, Bogdan? Who left voicemails? Who didn't fucking answer any of them?"

"I had a family matter to deal with."

"So your brothers and cousins said. What kind of issue keeps you from using a fucking phone in this day and age, Bogdan? Stop lying to me and go home. Without me."

"*Malyshka*, get in the car, and I'll explain."

"Fuck off."

"I'm going to ignore that because you're drunk, and I get why you're pissed."

"Pissed? I'm past pissed. I'm hurt. I feel like an idiot, especially when I ask your family, and they just say you're busy. I feel humiliated. And having a fucking shadow everywhere I go to remind me of you makes no goddamn sense when you don't give a shit about me, but your brothers refuse to call them off. Why do they care more than you? Are you worried I'll be some dirty little problem to clean up that'll be inconvenient if someone whacks me?"

"Get in the car now, *malyshka*."

"No."

"You know I won't force you, but we're getting way too much attention. Get in, and I'll tell you enough that my brothers are probably going to kill me."

"Make me."

It's a whispered challenge, but I know she's given in.

"If I have to force you, then I'm going to spank that fine little ass of yours."

I shift, so I now stand almost behind her and place my hand on her lower back. I press, and she takes a step forward. Once I'm blocking anyone's view from the sidewalk, I squeeze her ass enough to hurt. I feel the muscles clench, but I don't relent.

"Daddy."

She looks back at me, and I see a wealth of emotion in her eyes. Some of it is discomfort from my hold on her, but most of it is so much deeper. I'm seeing just how badly I hurt her, and I hate myself for it.

"Get in, baby girl, and let Daddy take care of you."

She nods as her lip trembles. She slides in, and I follow after I tell Stefan to take us to her place. I want her to have the comfort of her home when she's upset, but part of me also wants to be sure she can't bolt. She watches me get in and open my arms to her, but she stays where she is. She looks lost and way younger than her years.

"Why couldn't you answer at least one of my texts?"

"Because my phone wasn't on, *malyshka*. Where I went, we don't keep our phones on. It was a family matter because my brothers were involved too. But it was mostly about work. Will you let me hold you while I explain? I've missed you so damn much, Tina. I know you're hurt, and even if you don't think so, it's obvious you're pissed. But I've been hurting being away from you, too. Please."

She studies me for a long moment as the car moves. She nods and inches closer. I lift her into my lap, and she instantly snuggles closer.

"This is where you belong, *malyshka*. I wish you were never out of my reach, and I hate admitting there will be times when you have to be again. I'm going to tell you everything that I can, Tina. If you ask questions, I may not be able to answer them. I have to think about keeping you safe and about keeping my family safe. If those weren't an issue, I would tell you everything. Even the things that would make you despise me. I hate that there are secrets I have to keep, but most of them aren't mine to tell."

"I assume this was bratva stuff, not just Kutsenko stuff."

"It was, but in this case, it's all tangled up. Do you want me to tell you what I can about the past week first? Or do you want me to tell you a little about the bratva?"

"You'd tell me about that? Is it one of those things where, if you tell me, you have to kill me?"

"Funny, *malyshka*." I kiss her forehead and close my eyes. Her scent fills my nose, and I feel like I can finally breathe again. The feel of her in my arms soothes my battered soul. "Which do you want, baby girl?"

"Tell me whatever you think I need to know in whatever order you think makes sense, Bogdi."

I shudder.

"I thought I'd never hear you call me that again. I really wasn't certain you'd get in the car."

She sits up and cups my jaw in her hands.

"Bogdan, I know you're going to tell me things you have told no other women in your life. I know you trust me, and that means the world to me. I still trust you. As hurt and embarrassed as I am, I still trust you. But I need to know what we are. Either we're together and partners, or don't tell me anything and we part ways. It can't be in the middle. I can't do this week again. You can't disappear and leave me wondering what the hell is happening."

"I know, Tina. I'm all in. I know your job makes this complicated, but—"

"No, it doesn't. Anthony took your project today. I wanted to tell you days ago that he was going to, but I had no way. Didn't Niko tell you?"

"I haven't talked to him in a couple days. I told you, where I went, we don't keep our phones on. He can reach me, but he must not have thought I needed to know. I did. It would have changed at least the past few days. He's going to know I'm pissed about that. Tina, I would have come home sooner if I'd known."

"Didn't you still have to do whatever you were doing, regardless?"

"Yeah. But I'm not the only one who can do it. I thought it was all right to stay away because I thought my brothers and cousins made it clear that I had to be away, but nothing changed about how I feel about you. I thought I still couldn't be with you because of your work. If I'd known I could be or that my idiot relatives let you think I dumped you without a word, I would have come to you immediately."

"What does this mean? Are we all in, then?"

"Yes, *lapochka*. We're all in."

"What does that mean?"

"Sweetheart."

"What can I call you?"

"Whatever you like, baby girl."

"No, I mean in Russian. What can I call you? I want to learn."

I think I just fell in love. She's so earnest in her request.

Other women have asked, but none seemed as serious as Tina does right now. None actually bothered to remember them.

"*Solnste* is sun, and *zaychek* is bunny or little rabbit. Maks and Laura use those with each other, and I think it means more than any of us want to ask. I think they're like us."

I cock an eyebrow, and I see she understands. I've heard Maks call Laura *malyshka* plenty of times. But their other pet names come out when baby girl and Daddy wouldn't be appropriate to say out loud or when their dynamic shifts. I've seen it. I never thought I would have that for myself, but with the woman in my arms, I think I might. I never wanted it, even when I saw Maks and Laura like this. Now it's like my next breath depends on it.

"You can use *katyonak* for men or women. It means kitten."

She chokes on her laughter.

"Kitten? More like lion or tiger. I've seen that tattoo on your back. Those aren't kittens."

"They're not. They represent my brothers and me."

"How do I say lion?"

"*Lev.*"

"I can remember that. I can even say it. Can I call you that? *Lev.*"

"Yes, *lapochka.*"

She hesitates, and I wonder what she wants to ask.

"Can I call you my lion?"

My heart is going to burst. I don't even remember to answer. I'm kissing her as though it's been decades, not days. She's shifting on my lap to straddle me. She's unfastening my pants as I push up what little skirt she's wearing and move aside her thong. I don't bother silencing my groan as she slides down my cock.

"Don't move for a second, Tina. I'm going to come if you do. I've been aching for you, and I haven't had a chance to do a damn thing about it. I haven't been alone long enough to jerk off. But you filled every free minute I had, every dream."

"You really missed me that much?"

"Like crazy, *malyshka*. I promise you this will not happen again. I will not disappear without telling you. I can't promise how long I'll be away. This was unusual. It's not normally this long, but I will never let you wonder if I'm coming back to you. I'm always coming back."

"Bogdi—"

She hesitates, then seems to decide better than to say what's on her mind.

"Tell me, Tina. Don't hold back from me right now. I need you."

"Will you make love to me right now? I don't want to be fucked."

"Yes, baby girl."

We're complete equals this time. I'm not controlling how she moves. She's free, and she knows it. She rocks on me as we kiss. My hold on her hips is light as I thrust up. I pull her shirt—if you can even call it that—over her head. No pasties tonight. She's unbuttoning my shirt until we can press chest to chest, skin to skin. Neither of us is in a hurry. Our hands roam over clothes and bare skin. I'm fighting not to come until she has at least once.

"*Lev*, I'm so close."

"I want to feel you come on my cock. You don't have to ask for anything tonight, Tina. Take what you want, what you need. I'll give you anything to make you happy."

"You do. I realized that's why I was so miserable. It's because I'd been happy with you for just a few days, then it felt like you ripped it away."

She rocks and rises over and over until her body stiffens. I suck her tit as her cunt squeezes me. I fight not to spill, but I watch her as she keeps riding me. When she finally looks down at me, her eyes are glazed, and her lips are plump from our kisses. She looks entirely fuckable, but I want to make love for the first time. Not just the first time tonight. Not just the first time with her. The first time ever. I loved my last girlfriend, and I think I may have loved at least one before her. But we fucked. Even when it was slow and tender. I realize now, compared to what I'm sharing with Tina, it was still just two people getting off. I know it was because I always held something back emotionally. I always felt disconnected, and I did it on purpose. But I'm surrendering completely to Tina. I'll give her my entire heart if she wants it.

"I want to watch you on top of me, Bogdi."

I roll us, so she's lying on the car seat. Her hands are running up and down my abs. I had the sense to put my gun in the compartment under the seat. Her fingernails are scratching down my back and driving me wild. My thrusts get harder and faster as our gazes meet. We watch each other. Sweat drips from my cheek to her chest. Neither of us notices. I'm holding myself up on my knuckles, but she pulls me closer. Her legs wrap around my waist as we're once again chest to chest. I slide my arms underneath her back and hook my hands over her shoulders as she wraps her arms around my back. We're clinging to each other as we come together. I bury my face in the crook of her neck as her forehead rests on the top of my shoulder.

Even as our orgasms end, we don't move. We stay together, our bodies still joined. It isn't until my body refuses to cooperate with my heart or my mind that I pull away. She straddles me again as she rests against me.

"Baby, we're at your place."

"We're home?"

She sits up and looks out the window, her voice drowsy.

God, how I wish it were our home. I know she doesn't realize how what she said sounds. Or at least I didn't think so until she looks at me. She's biting her bottom lip.

"Let's talk about all of it once we're inside. I'll tell you everything I can, then we can talk about what's next."

She pulls her top back on before I slip off my suit jacket and wrap it around her shoulders. Neither of us bothers to button my shirt. We go inside after I wave and shake my head at Pasha. He followed us, but I'm letting him know he doesn't need to stay the night. I watch Stefan, then Pasha, drive away. I walk into Tina's house and really look around for the first time. I would trade every property I own to call this my home. My penthouse feels so sterile compared to her place. She has art and photos on the walls. I can see into her office as we walk to the living room. There are framed blueprints and designs on the wall, and I suspect they might be hers.

The furniture begs me to get comfortable and take a nap. She hits a button on a tiny remote, and the fireplace comes on. She drapes my jacket over the back of an armchair, kicks off her shoes, and grabs a blanket. She shakes it out before taking a seat in the middle of the sofa. I sit to her right and accept the half she offers. She curls her legs up as I kick off my shoes and put my legs up on the ottoman. She inches closer as I wrap my arm around her shoulders.

"I'm deciding as I go along what's all right to tell you, Tina. I don't even know what exactly I'm going to say, so bear with me, baby girl."

She nods and looks up at me with such trust in her whiskey-brown eyes. She's tired, but she doesn't seem at all tipsy like when she first came out of the club. There's clarity and attentiveness in them.

"My father, Anton and Pasha's father, and Sergei and Misha's father were all KGB together until the fall of the Soviet

Union. But the Podolskaya bratva in our neighborhood in Moscow forced my father and uncles to join. They were actively recruiting—forcing—men to fight against the Chechens. Everyone knows the Podolskaya are organized and basically paramilitary. Maks was born not long after the Soviet Union fell. My parents had been married a year and a half when he arrived. They'd already drawn my father into the bratva, and they were scared for my mother's safety each time he had to be away for even a night. As soon as she could, my mother got pregnant again. She did the same thing each year until I was born. My parents wanted each of us, but they purposely had us close together. A woman who was always pregnant or had delivered so many children wasn't desirable as a sex worker. It's why my family will never trade flesh. We might own strip clubs, but the women who work there come willingly. We don't recruit, and we don't force them. Hell, I fired Zora the other night for banging Todd. We do not run whorehouses or brothels. None of us have a taste for that, and our mother would flay us alive."

"You must have been born around when the Chechen War started. I wasn't alive yet."

"Yeah. I was born a year into the Second Chechen War. How old are you?"

"Twenty-six. When's your birthday?"

"It was in March. When's yours?"

"Three weeks."

I smile as thoughts of ways to celebrate leap to mind. They all involve us alone somewhere far from New York and work.

"Don't think I will forget, *malyshka*." I give her a quick kiss. "My father died when I was ten, fighting the Chechens. He'd already been trying to get us over here, but it became urgent when my mother became a widow. Sergei and Misha's father moved their family to America as quickly as he could after my father died. We arrived a week after I turned eleven. Anton and Pasha's father helped smuggle us out of Moscow and into St. Petersburg. We left from there. He didn't want his brother's sons to be recruited into the bratva or, worse, what was left of the Russian army."

"How are Sergei and Misha related to you again? On your mother's side?"

"Yes. Our mothers are sisters. The Podolskaya found out fast what our uncle did, so it was no longer safe for them. They followed us to America pretty soon after. We moved here and lived in Queens. We started in an apartment in a Russian neighborhood, but once we could, we bought our mom a house. It's actually close to here, like fifteen minutes. You live pretty near where Laura lived before she moved in with Maks. He has a house about ten minutes away."

"That's funny. I grew up about twenty minutes away."

"We were here only four or five months before a man who ran the Ivankov bratva noticed our family. At first, he was only interested in my uncles. But once he realized there were so many young boys in our family, we became a feeding ground for him. My uncles could keep my cousins out longer than my mother could. We were already doing things we shouldn't to get by. We spoke little English, and it was hard for my mom to find work in the beginning. Tina, we all have rap sheets. None of us have recent charges, but we've all been arrested for petty crimes. Some of them were so we could pay rent or have food. Some of them were jobs gone wrong for Vlad."

I stop myself. I didn't mean to say that bastard's name. But it's too late.

"Vladislav Lushak."

"How do you know his name?"

"I grew up in Queens. I heard rumors. I also met him once when I was interning during college. The man had no soul."

"Did he try to do anything to you?"

He may be long dead, but rage is rising in me at the thought that he might have hurt her. He had no decency, no boundaries, or limits with anyone. A beautiful young woman like Tina was exactly the prey he stalked.

"He made a comment, but my boss back then stopped him. He gave me the creeps, and I didn't walk around alone for like three months. But he never did anything."

"Then you can imagine what he did to four boys with no father. My uncles did what they could, but they couldn't stop the Ivankov bratva once Vlad decided we would join. He trained us to do things I pray you never ever find out I can do. My brothers, cousins, and I learned early on never to betray our emotions in front of him. It's a habit that I will probably always have. It doesn't mean I don't feel things. I do, but he would torture us as punishment whenever anyone even blinked as a reaction to what he did. Maksim learned the fastest because I was the youngest and smallest. I was Vlad's favorite target. He would hurt me to train Maks."

"That's horrid."

She nestles closer to me, wrapping her arm tightly around my waist as though she might shield me or comfort me. My arms go around her waist, relishing the comfort she offers.

"You've seen how big we all are. We got that way from the physical training he put us through, along with the sports we played. Maks is a bare-knuckle champion. He took the brunt of the mental and emotional torture because he was the oldest. He's always felt responsible for the rest of us, particularly Aleks, Niko, and me. Anton, Pasha, Sergei, and Misha had their dads to enforce some boundaries with Vlad. Not many, but no one came to their doors at night and forced them to steal cars or rob convenience stores. We did it to keep Vlad away from our mom as much as to provide for us and to protect ourselves from his men. He used to threaten to sell our mom if we didn't do what he said. I was eleven, and Maks was only fourteen when we arrived. We believed every threat he made until Maks entered his twenties, and I became a teen. By then, we were bigger than most of the older men and even the other guys our age. Only our cousins rival us in size. Vlad learned quickly never to pit us against each other."

The first man I ever killed was a man who pulled a knife on Misha. I took it from him and stabbed him through the eye. I went to Orthodox Mass an hour later that Sunday and served as an altar boy. I keep that anecdote to myself.

"We rose through the ranks, starting as *boyeviks,* or foot soldiers. That's when we were stealing cars and pick-pocketing tourists in Manhattan. We knocked off liquor stores and ran illegal gambling rings. Vlad tried to force us into animal fights, but we refused to do anything that involved hurting animals or women and children. We made sure Vlad understood that. We'd been here about six years when he tried that. By then, even I was bigger than him. He was aging and arthritis was slowing him down. He couldn't dole out the beatings himself quite as quickly or easily. His youngest son was my age. I put him in the hospital for nearly a month to prove to Vlad that we weren't sex traffickers. I thought he would kill me for nearly killing his son. He promoted me. For nearly a year, I was senior to Niko. He hated it."

I loved it. I made him get me lunch whenever I could. I did that in front of a girl he liked. He didn't speak to me for a month. The power lost its novelty fast after that. My brothers are my best friends. I hate being at odds with any of them. It's always been us against the world. Our cousins are basically like our brothers, but there's still a difference. I know Sergei and Misha feel the same, just like Anton and Pasha do. Something about coming from the exact same blood, I suppose.

"I had opportunities that Maks and Aleks didn't because they were the two oldest. Maks didn't inherit his role as our leader. He took it. Vlad thought that because we'd all moved into our places since we were well on our way to being wealthy that we wouldn't notice him trying to coerce our mom. We knew he was making bad business decisions, and people had already lost faith in him. But he forced his way into our mom's house one night but didn't know we were there and having dinner in the backyard. He grabbed my mom, and she screamed. Maks was in the kitchen. Vlad was dead before he knew Maks was there. Vlad had already groomed Maks instead of his other sons. The rest of the bratva already looked to Maks to lead. So inevitably, he became our *pakhan*."

"What does that mean?"

"It's the boss. It could mean someone in charge at a business, but in the bratva, it means the senior most person. The person who runs everything. He'd be called a don if he was Italian or *jefe* if he was Cartel. He stepped into the position when he was barely twenty-three. I was in college. Niko and I both got to go, but Maks and Aleks didn't. Sergei and Anton also got to go to college. They both got athletic scholarships and went to school in Philly."

"Can I ask you something about them?"

Oh, shit.

"Of course."

"Do they not like me?"

"What?"

"They kept giving each other a look when we came back into the trailer after talking outside."

"They definitely like you. They say you remind them of Laura, which is probably the best compliment they could give. She doesn't take shit from Maks, and she's as loyal as the day is long."

"Then what did that look mean?" Her eyes widen as she leans back. She's figured it out. "Are they…"

"Yes. And you can never breathe a word about it. Ever, Chr—Tina."

"I won't. Is it really that dangerous for them over here?"

"We live in Little Russia, Tina. Everything we do is connected to the Russian community and to being bratva. It doesn't matter that it's America. The bratva is Russian, and they won't condone that relationship."

"I won't say a word. Does Laura know?"

"I don't know."

That isn't something anyone but Maks would ask her about. No need to put ideas in her head if they aren't already there.

"Maks became *pakhan*, and eventually my brothers and I became members of the Elite Group. It's like his senior advisors, his inner circle. Sergei and Anton lead the two divisions that handle intel and enforcement. Pasha and Misha have men working under them."

"And yet, they're both just acting as lowly bodyguards and drivers for me."

"There is nothing lowly about that, Tina. You keep saying that. I don't trust anyone outside my family to keep you safe. No one. If I can't be with you, then I only want one of my brothers or cousins. No one else will ever be good enough."

She slowly nods her head.

"Part of why I was gone was because I had to deal with someone who could have become a threat to you. He was already a threat to our business." She opens her mouth. "Don't say his name. If you never hear me confess, you have no truth to tell anyone. And I don't want to lie to you. Another development kept me away even longer. Some people hired to create problems with our other businesses thought to use Laura to get to Maks."

I twist to look at Tina directly.

"There is a place we go where we control everything that happens there. I will never tell you where it is. I will never take you there. I need you to never look for this warehouse or ask about it. Knowing puts you and everyone else close to me in danger. It's where we take care of things that no one needs to know about. When we go there, we remove ourselves from the outside world until we are done. It's why I couldn't contact you, and why my phone went straight to voicemail. I will let you know if I can before I disappear. If it's going to take longer than three days, I will make sure someone tells you. Beyond that, I will not tell you anything else."

She nods but remains silent.

"Sometimes we can't control everything. If I say I need space because I don't want you to see me, it's just that. It's not the other way around. It's not that I don't want to see you. It means something went wrong, and I'm not in the right head-space or physical condition for you to see me."

"Physical condition?"

I show her my knuckles.

"It can be worse than this."

"I'm guessing you don't go to hospitals when it's like that, do you?"

"No. We have a doctor."

"Can I ask one question about this part?"

"I will try to answer."

"If something happens to you that's really serious, how will I know?"

"One of my brothers or cousins will get you or call you."

"Okay, that leads to one more question. Sorry."

"Don't be sorry. This is a lot."

"It is. What if I'm with you and something happens, like I can't take you to the hospital, but I need to?"

"Give me your phone."

She reaches across the sofa to where she dropped her purse and gives me her phone. I program my brothers' numbers, plus Anton's and Sergei's.

"You call one of them or take me to them."

"All right."

"Am I scaring you, *malyshka?*"

"Worrying, not scaring. I just want to be prepared."

"I know. And I appreciate that."

"You've never told any other women in your life any of this, have you?"

"None of it."

"What did they think when you disappeared?"

"That I went on an out of the country business trip."

"Why didn't anyone tell me that?"

"I don't know. That's a good question. I think they know something is different between us. My guess is they truly don't know what to tell you."

She nods again but remains quiet for a long time.

"Thank you for telling me, Bogdi. I have a lot to digest, but none of it makes me want to tell you to leave. It just makes me want to hold you closer."

"Do you think this is something you can live with?"

"Yes."

"You're not shocked and horrified?"

"My dad was in the military before my parents moved here from Scotland. He's killed more people than he'll ever admit. Sometimes it was kill or be killed. Sometimes it was a righteous cause, I suppose. I guess I can equate what he did to what you do in a lot of ways. I don't think you enjoy it or do it for sport. You do it to protect yourself and the people you care about. As for your businesses and those crimes, well, as long as you aren't buying and selling people, I suppose I can justify it to myself."

"After what my parents went through to protect my mom, none of us would ever be part of that. She would never forgive us, and we would shame our father's memory."

"Then I think I'll figure out how to work my way through all of this."

Our kiss is slow at first, but as always, it builds until we're pulling at each other's clothes. I carry her upstairs, where we strip each other and fall onto the bed. It's dawn before we finally fall asleep. She's tucked against my chest, and I'm holding my baby girl. We're where we both belong, even if the world insists upon intruding.

Chapter Eleven

Tina

I was sober by the time we got to my place last night and while we were talking. I listened to everything Bogdan told me and tried to digest it all. There was so damn much. I was certain when he carried me upstairs that I could handle everything. We were both exhausted once we stopped having sex, so we fell asleep quickly. But now that sunlight is shining into my room, and he's sleeping next to me, I'm hesitating.

What am I supposed to tell my friends and family when he disappears? How often does that even happen? Do I tell them what he used to tell his girlfriends? He's on an international business trip. What if he's gone more than he's here? I don't know that I want to carry on a relationship with someone who's gone and keeping things from me more than he's with me. I know he doesn't want to keep secrets, and I understand why he has to, but do I want to be kept in the dark about most of his life? I'd feel like a toy he takes out to play with sometimes.

Then there's the most basic question. Am I safe with him?

It would devastate my parents if something happened to me. How would I explain it? How would he? I can't tell them anything, which means keeping secrets from my family. If I told them even a hint, they would freak out and want me to stop seeing him. Then I would have to pick, which is something I really don't want to do. I don't even know if his family likes me enough to trust me. He says they do, but is he sure? Is he just telling me that?

"*Malyshka,* you've been tense since the moment you woke up. What's wrong?"

He's spooning me, so I roll over to look at him. I think he knows already, and whatever he sees in my expression confirms it. He strokes my hair back from my shoulder and kisses me softly.

"You're having second thoughts."

"I'm having second, third, fourth, hundredth thoughts, Bogdan. It's not as simple as I wanted to believe last night."

"Do you have more questions?"

"Tons."

"Such as?"

"Do you go away often? What do I tell people? How much danger am I in? What happens if people know we're together, then something happens to you? Am I in danger for the rest of my life? I'm thinking about all the lies I'm going to have to tell my friends and family."

"I know. Your questions are the reason I've shared none of this with someone. It's hard on everyone. I know there's a lot for you to think about, and I don't want to rush you."

"But?"

"But what? I know how I feel about you, and I think you know how you feel about me. There's also a lot to think and feel about the situation. I won't rush you."

140

"I don't want you as a fuck buddy, but we've had a lot of sex already and have never been on a date. What kind of relationship does that really make this?"

"One I don't know how to define. Would you go out to dinner with me tonight?"

"Yes."

That was simple. I would love to go out to dinner with Bogdan and finally do something like a normal newly dating couple.

"I want you only to myself, *malyshka*, but I won't demand it. If you still want to see other people, I understand."

"Do you?"

"Not in the least, but I know you have other—arrangements —that you might not be ready to end."

"Todd? That's been over, regardless of how I feel about you. There isn't anyone else."

I push onto my elbow. I feel like I need to sit up to think properly. His hand rests on my waist. I'm tempted to roll on top of him and ride him. I can see he's hard from the way the sheet drapes over him. But we still need to sort shit out.

"Give me a month, Tina. If you don't feel comfortable or you realize you don't feel that strongly about me, then we go our separate ways. I won't pressure you."

"I won't be at the site anymore."

"And I rarely spend that much time at them. I have the bars and clubs to manage. Niko usually handles our casinos in Jersey, but this has been keeping him busy."

"When will we see each other?"

"Whenever you want. I will make my schedule work."

"Does that mean one night a week? Whichever is your slow night."

"If that's all you want. But I'd like to see you more than that."

"Fridays and Saturdays must be really busy for you, so I suppose those are out."

"They don't have to be. I know you work a regular Monday to Friday job, so weekends might be the only time you want to go out."

I shake my head. I want to see him all the time. But I see the sense in having a trial go of this for a month.

"What if we see each other twice a week for a date?"

"That works. You pick the days that work for you."

"Can we..."

I can't believe what I want to ask, which is ridiculous considering how we met.

"Can we what, baby girl?"

"Can we have one night a week that's just sex?"

There. I said it. He's grinning like it's Christmas. He pulls me down to kiss me, and I move to straddle his leg. I grind my pussy against him. I want him to know how much I like the way he feels, so I moan. He grabs my ass with both hands and squeezes to where I whimper. It only makes me ride him faster.

"Do you need a good fuck, baby girl?"

"Yes, Daddy. Rough."

The tenderness from last night is gone. He flips me onto my back and snags my arms. He pins them over my head as his other hand dives between my thighs.

"Oh, *malyshka,* you're already so wet for me. Do you want me to fuck you right this minute?"

"Yes."

"Yes, what?"

He pinches my clit, and I practically buck off the bed.

"Yes, Daddy."

"Yes, Daddy, what?"

"Yes, please, Daddy."

He releases my clit and thrusts into me. I fight to free my

hands to touch him, but he only holds firmer to my wrists. He wraps his hand around my throat, just enough pressure to remind me who's in control again. My eyes are wide as I watch him. There's determination in his gaze and sheer dominance. I'm here for that.

"I'm going to fuck you hard, Tina. If I'm hurting you, speak up. What's your safe word?"

"Olives."

"That's right, baby girl. Now you're gonna take Daddy's dick as I fuck you. Does it feel good?"

"Yes."

I'm already panting. This reminds me of the first night we spent together, and I want that all over again. Every time he slides out of me, I miss the feel of him being inside. Every time he fills me, I clench my muscles, trying to keep him there. But he doesn't ease up. He doesn't slow down. He just keeps pounding me until I scream. My orgasm hits me like a Mack truck. I writhe beneath him until it's done. I claw at him when he pulls out and lets go of my hands.

No! I don't want it to be over. He didn't come.

I shouldn't have doubted him, and I don't as he flips me over and pulls me onto my hands and knees. His hand lands across my ass over and over. When he pauses, I wiggle my hips. I get a chuckle and another spanking. We go back and forth until I nearly say my safe word. He knows when I'm reaching my limit. He understands. He pulls my hips back and pushes his dick in me. Holy fuck.

Then I feel it. He licked his finger. And now it's in my ass. Everything from my belly button down tightens.

"All of you is mine, Tina. Your mouth, your pussy, your ass. They're mine to pleasure and to punish. Do you want me in your ass?"

"Yes!"

It's a strangled sound. Normally, I'm not a huge fan of anal, but with Bogdan, I'll do just about anything.

"Tonight. After our first date, I'll fuck you here."

He slides his finger in and out twice more. How funny it sounds, and he knows it. How many first dates end in anal? How many first dates are planned while fucking?

"Now."

"That's not what I said."

I get a spanking for my insistence, and I knew I would. I wanted it.

"Now."

I make sure I'm not whiny. I don't need to sound like a brat, but I can sound insubordinate. His fingers dig into my hips as he pounds me. Our skin slaps together. He pulls his finger out of me and uses that hand to hold me in place while the other travels up my back, between my shoulder blades, and under my hair until he can grasp my throat. This time his hold is much tighter.

"Are you all right with breath play?"

"Yes, Daddy."

It's one of the ultimate tests of trust along with being arousing as hell. I'm putting all my faith in Bogdan to know what I can take, especially when I'm facing away from him. The pressure begins heavier than before, but not enough to constitute what most people would consider breath play. I can still breathe easily, but I feel restrained, not able to take deep breaths. I'm relinquishing control, and I feel free. The strain over the past week of wondering what went wrong, worrying about the work situation, and now the fear of being involved with a bratva member slips away as I focus on what Bogdan is doing and the sensations it elicits. Allowing him to have control allows me to live in the moment.

He leans over me and whispers.

"You're such a good girl, *malyshka*. You have faith in me to take care of you, and I know that doesn't come easily." He pulls me up so I'm kneeling with my ass on his lap while he thrusts. He tightens his grip. "Rest your head back on my shoulder. Daddy will do what you need."

His free hand pinches my nipples hard enough for me to shudder. Then it slides down to my clit, and circles it until I'm trembling with the need to come.

"Daddy, please."

"Yes, baby girl. Come."

My legs are shaking, and I'm gripping the sheets beneath me. He tightens his hold until I nearly see stars. And then I'm coming. It's the most intense orgasm I've ever had. I see stars, and I'm about to claw at his hand when he releases my throat. I sag back against him as I feel him finish. He wraps his arms around me, holding me in his embrace. It's like a giant Russian bear hugging me. My Russian bear.

I pull away and spin around. Before Bogdan can react, I've dropped onto his still erect cock. I'm clinging to him as though my life depends on it. I've explored levels of intimacy with him I never did with men I was involved with for months. I never trusted them like that.

"Daddy."

It's somewhere between a whimper and a whisper. I just hold on, and he doesn't put me down or push me away. He holds me just as tightly. He murmurs in Russian against my cheeks as he strokes my hair. I'm limp and sated.

"Are you all right, Tina?"

I hear concern, and I realize that while I feel wonderful, he fears he's hurt me. I sit back and kiss him. I pour every emotion I can't articulate into that kiss. All the emotions I can't separate and don't want to dissect. They go into this kiss as our tongues tangle, and we share the same breaths. When we finally come up for air, I kiss both his cheeks, his forehead, around his mouth, and finally drop a short, hard kiss to his lips.

"I'm more than all right. That was incredible."

"I didn't hurt you? I didn't scare you?"

"Neither. I was just spent and needed a moment. Now I feel like I could either run a marathon or take a nap."

"How about a bath?"

I laugh.

"Will you take it with me?"

One of the best features in my bathroom is the giant soaking tub that stands on claw feet. I have the best of the vintage style, with all the amenities of modern plumbing. I don't use it as often as I should, but when I do, I never want to leave. It's also big enough for two, though I've never shared it with anyone before.

"I'll wash behind your ears for you."

Bogdan teases, then kisses me before he climbs off the bed. He reaches out his hand, and I take it as I get to my feet. He sweeps me into his arms, and I squeal. He carries me into the bathroom and perches on the edge of the tub with me in his arms. He holds me securely as he leans forward to flip the plug lever and to start the water. He adjusts the knobs until he's satisfied. I point to a bottle of lavender bubble bath. He smirks but squeezes in a healthy dollop.

"Bogdi, I've never done that before or this."

"Breath play? A bath with a man?"

"Breath play to that extent. I haven't minded having someone hold my throat, but I've never agreed to that tight. And I have had baths with guys before, but none have ever used this tub with me."

"I rather like knowing I'm your first for a few things."

I twist and look up at him.

"You're my first for a lot of things, Bogdan. You're the first man I've ever trusted implicitly. You're the only man I've let take complete control of me. In the past, guys might have thought I submitted completely, but in my head, I always rebelled a little. I don't with you. Not being in control feels better."

"I will do my best to never disappoint you, Tina. It will never be willfully or without care. Your trust means everything to me."

"You trust me just as much. You've trusted me with your life and those of people you love. I don't take that lightly."

"I know you don't. That's why I've told you what I have. But I also know that one round of good sex doesn't get rid of your doubts and questions."

"It doesn't."

I sigh and look down. I feel badly that I'm having doubts because it's at odds to how I feel about the man holding me. But reality and fantasy are opposites, and they're tugging at me.

"Tina, we stick to what we agreed to. Two dates a week and a third night for sex." I feel his chest rumble as he chuckles silently. "If, after thirty days, it isn't working, then we reevaluate or go our separate ways."

"When do the thirty days start? Today, with our date tonight?"

"It can. Is that what you want?"

"Yes."

"In a rush to get it over?"

Lines form around his mouth and eyes as he grins at me, and I swear his eyes twinkle. He looks boyish and yet mature at the same time. How does he do that? He turns off the water after testing the temperature. We ease in together, and I lean back against him. Neither of us talks as we soak. I move my hands through the bubbles as his hand strokes my belly. My sigh comes from my soul as I relax against him and close my eyes.

"Tina. *Malyshka*."

I jerk awake. I hadn't realized I drifted off. Bogdan is laughing, and the vibration rumbles through my back.

"How long have I been asleep?"

"About fifteen minutes. I had to wake you because you're getting goosebumps. The water is going cold."

"Fine." I try to sound as beleaguered as I can, and it garners another laugh as he helps me to my feet. He steps out and moves to the glass-enclosed shower, where he turns on the water. I follow him, and we step in once it's warm enough. As the waterfall fixture rains down on us, we step into each other's arms and kiss. The feel of being pressed chest to chest, belly to belly, thigh to thigh with him is everything I've imagined while watching the sappiest movies or reading about it in romance books. I've always longed for it and felt like I was missing out. Now I have it. It's sensual, erotic even, but it's also tender and affectionate. It's a fantasy come true.

"Turn around, and I'll wash your hair, *malyshka*."

It's heaven. Absolute heaven. He's so gentle as he massages my scalp, and once again, I feel like I could drift off. Only the fact that I'm standing keeps me from doing it. As the shampoo runs free from my hair, he leans forward, so I can wash his hair. Then we're running the bath poofs over each other. I had a fresh one that I gave him the morning he barged into my house. It's been hanging in my shower ever since. That definitely didn't help when I thought he'd dumped me, but I couldn't bring myself to toss it out. I'm glad I didn't. I glance at the sink counter and think about whether he'll ever keep a toothbrush and razor here. He follows my gaze, but neither of us says anything.

He kisses my throat, then down between my breasts, and

over my belly. He kisses each hip bone before spreading my pussy open. I have to rest my forearms on the wall behind him to keep from collapsing as his tongue works me. I wasn't wrong before. His tongue is surely a national treasure twice over. My clit is already tender from last night and this morning. He's careful with me, as always, but he's unrelenting. He grips my ass as my kneecaps tremble, holding me up as I come. He straightens, and before he can say anything, I drop to my knees. I stroke him, then lower my mouth onto him. I don't particularly enjoy giving blow jobs, but I enjoy pleasuring Bogdan. My head bobs in tandem with my hand. I just can't take all of him, even when the tip brushes the back of my throat.

"Tina!"

His hand fists my hair as he holds my head in place. I continue to suck and swallow until the last of his cum slides down my throat and leaks from my lips. He helps me to my feet on the slippery floor and kisses me. Our hands roam over one another until there's no excuse to remain, and our fingers are shriveled.

"Let me dry you off, baby girl."

He wraps a fluffy towel around my hair, then rubs one over me. He hands me my robe from the hook on the back of the door, quickly dries himself, then wraps the towel around his waist. When we go back into the bedroom, I realize that I have all my clothes available to me, but he only has what he wore last night. He's looking at the same thing. I wonder what the day will bring since neither of us seems in a hurry to get dressed.

"I guess I'm just going to keep you naked all day."

I laugh as I tug his towel free and fling it behind me. He bends low and scoops me up around the legs and tosses me over his shoulder. He lands a playful slap on my ass over my robe. He drops me onto the bed, and I bounce. He follows me onto the mattress and tugs my robe open. He latches onto a nipple and sucks hard before he tickles me. He sucks on my breast while making me giggle. It lightens my spirit to laugh after last week.

I reach down and stroke him, but he catches my hand and pulls it away as my stomach grumbles. He leans forward and blows a raspberry on my belly. Never would I have imagined Bogdan has a silly side to him.

"If you intend to keep me as your sex toy, you shall need your energy. Come, baby girl. Let's see what I can make you for breakfast."

"You cook? Or are you hoping to find cereal and milk?"

"Yes, I can cook, thank you very much. You know I live alone, and I don't exactly look like I'm starving."

"I don't know. Maybe you have a maid show up in a skimpy little outfit. Maybe you order in a lot. Maybe your mom drops off food."

"No to the first two, and only once or twice a week to the third." He winks at me, and I'm uncertain if he's serious or not. "I'm the baby of the family. She takes care of me."

"Does she do that for your brothers?"

Bogdan just grins and winks again. I'm completely clueless now.

"She only sends us home with leftovers when we make it over there. She doesn't drop off food, *malyshka*. We don't see her as often as we should, and we all know that. But we all talk to her several times a week. We like to check in on her, and none of us feels like getting a replay from a brother is enough."

"You said she lives kinda near here. Does that mean you grew up near here too?"

"No. When we moved here, we got a place in a Russian neighborhood near Brighton Beach. We all saved up once we were making decent money and bought her a house. Maks and Aleks had already moved out, and Niko and I were in college."

"Where'd you go to school?"

"NYU."

"Like me."

"Yeah. We must have been there at the same time."

"You know I studied architecture. What did you study?"

"I majored in finance, but I minored in medieval literature and art."

"You did?"

"I'm an enigma, baby girl."

One I hope I can figure out. I just need the time.

Chapter Twelve

Bogdan

I know my answer shocked her. I don't tell many people about my minor since most don't believe me. It's hard enough to convince some people that I even attended a university like NYU. They look at me and assume I'm a mobster or a trust fund baby. Maybe a pro athlete. I went on a full academic scholarship. Knowing that we were on campus at the same time makes me wonder what we would have thought of each other if we'd met back then.

"Eggs? Pancakes?" I look in her fridge and pantry. There's plenty to choose from. "French toast? Bacon or sausage?"

"Yes."

Her stomach rumbles at just the right time.

"We can't have you starve. Pancakes or French toast?"

"French toast, please."

I'm soon moving around the kitchen as I discover where she keeps everything. The quality of her kitchenware and the clear use of her pots and pans tell me she likes to cook, too. Or at least she cooks often. I whisk the eggs as the griddle in the center of her cook range heats.

She gathers what she needs to make coffee with her French press. The aroma of fresh brewing coffee fills the kitchen, but I notice that she's only making enough for two cups. I'm not a big coffee drinker, and I suppose she isn't too.

"Will two cups be enough for you? I prefer tea."

"Yes. I would have been happy with the tea. You didn't need to make that especially for me."

"I don't mind. I only use this when the girls are over or my family visits."

"How did you and your friends meet? You seem really close."

"We are. We all lived in the same dorm our freshman year, and Kelsey was my roommate. I'm the only native New Yorker in the group. Sarah and Kelsey are from Massachusetts, and Tracey is from Arizona."

"And they all stayed here after college?"

"Yeah. Sarah went to med school at Colombia while I was there for grad school. Kelsey works in advertising and got hired by a firm straight out of school. Tracey moved to Philly for a year and hated it, so she came back. She works in pharmaceutical sales."

"Do they live near here? My sister-in-law and her friends all lived in Queens and still do. She and Maks spend a lot of time in Manhattan, but they prefer his house here in Queens."

"No. We're all spread out. Sarah and her boyfriend have an apartment on Staten Island. Tracey lives in Harlem, and Kelsey lives in Brooklyn."

"And you still get together pretty often?"

"We're not that far apart."

She rolls her eyes at me. I pinch her backside before laying the first four slices of bread on the griddle. I lay out strips of bacon above the soon-to-be French toast, then I crack four eggs into a pan. While I'm manning the stove, she puts a cup of coffee next to me and fills the kettle. She sets the table in the breakfast nook and puts two plates next to my coffee mug. It's domestic tranquility that I haven't experienced in three years. I missed it when my ex-girlfriend and I first broke up, but then I relished the freedom. As I watch Tina in her robe with her wet hair hanging down her back, I realize how much I miss it. The difference with Tina is that I want this to last. In the past, I knew it would come to an inevitable end. It was just a question of when.

I don't doubt that Maks and Laura will have kids one day. I wonder if Laura realizes the role her children will step into, but I wouldn't touch that question with a ten-foot pole. While I don't have to worry about my son ever inheriting the role as *pakhan*, I've been against the idea of children because sons would eventually take my place in the bratva. It's a role I would have end with me. At least, that's what I thought before really looking around Tina's home and seeing her in the kitchen like we're a real couple who lives together.

When she comes to stand by me to see how I'm progressing, I wrap my arm around her waist and settle my hand on her belly. I've always been careful not to get anyone pregnant, so it's really unusual that I'm having sex without a condom, let alone having sex with Tina every time without one. The idea of having a life growing inside her and beneath my hand is oddly appealing. When she looks up at me, I suspect she's thinking the same thing I am. She rises on her toes to kiss me. The moment our mouths meet, we can't get enough. I'm ready to lift her onto the counter, drop my boxers, and sink into her. But the kettle whistles, and we both come back to reality.

"Do you want butter and syrup?"

She goes to stand next to the fridge and looks at me. I can

only nod as I try to get my thoughts and my lust under control. What is she doing to me?

"What do you want to do today? Do you already have plans?"

I carry our food to the table. I'm nervous as I wait for her answers. She hasn't hinted that I need to leave soon, and we agreed to a date tonight. But there are a lot of hours between now and then.

"To be honest, I'd originally planned to mope all day and maybe cry a few times. I went out with the girls last night because I couldn't stand looking at the walls for another night. But even while I was out, I wanted to spend today at home."

"Baby girl."

I feel utterly horrible. She says it with such reluctance that I know she hates admitting it because she feels weak, and I know she isn't saying it to be spiteful. Her gaze dashes to the food I put on the table before returning to me. She joins me in the breakfast nook.

"It's all right now, Bogdi. I understand, and I don't plan to cry today, unless it's because you tickle me again. Do you have plans?"

"No. I'd hoped to see you."

Her cheeks pinken as she beams at me. I take her hand and lace our fingers together for a moment before we eat.

"You need some clothes, I suppose."

She sounds regretful, as though she assumes that means we have to part company. I have no intention of doing that unless she tells me that's what she wants.

"We could go to my place, and I could get dressed. Then we could do whatever you want. A walk, museums, art gallery, one of our construction sites."

She rolls her eyes again, then looks half tempted before she shakes her head.

"A walk would be nice. Then maybe we could watch a movie or something before tonight."

"Anton can grab some clothes from my place and bring them over. He won't be doing much while Sergei is traveling with Maks and Laura."

I didn't flat out confirm what she'd suspected last night, and I'm not doing it now. But I know she understands my meaning.

"I understand why you insist on Misha and Pasha, and that them guarding me is part of their job. But would Anton do this as a favor for his cousin and friend, or is it part of his job?"

"It would be a favor. Anton and Sergei were Laura's guards while she and Maks were dating, but that was because Pasha and Misha were traveling. A childhood friend of theirs died, and they went to Moscow for the funeral and stayed to see family. When Maks and Laura get back, they'll probably go back to taking turns guarding Laura. Though it was Sergei more often than Anton, since Sergei lives in the same building."

I get out my phone and call Anton. Tina listens attentively, but I know she can't understand anything I'm saying since I'm speaking Russian. Unless she shocks the shit out of me like Laura did and starts speaking Russian like a native. I should have known that day that she and Maks would end up together. He'd watched her like a fucking hawk during that meeting, and I knew she'd seriously impressed him at the end of the meeting. I didn't know until later that she'd threatened to bury us if we used a newly gained building for sex trafficking. I'd just seen the bewildered look on Maks's face when he stepped out of the conference room and how he'd been lost in thought the rest of the day.

"I think Kelsey is interested in Pasha. Should I introduce them properly?"

I'm not prepared for that question. Pasha dates, but he never gets serious. Only Anton, Sergei, and I have been in long term committed relationships since high school, and they really only count as one person in this case.

"Only if Kelsey understands he won't get serious. I'm the only one who's had long relationships. The others keep them short or not serious."

"Oh."

I don't know which part she's reacting to. That Pasha won't get serious or that I've had *relationships*. We haven't spoken about our pasts to each other, and I don't think either of us wants to, but our pasts keep coming up. I know about Todd and Jared, and I barely know much about the second guy, other than he was a boyfriend who wants to get back together. Or at least he wants to fuck Tina again. That isn't happening, but I can't blame the poor fucker. She's addictive.

"Anton'll be here in half an hour. We can go for a walk around here or wherever you want."

She bites her bottom lip as she considers what to say.

"Is it safe for us to walk around in my neighborhood? I mean, is it safe for people to see where I live when I'm with you?"

They're fair questions, and ones I've already thought about, but I hate she has to ask.

"Yes. Misha's already outside, and Anton will be here soon. He's watching Laura's mastiff, Sebastian, while they're out of town. They've grown to like each other. Sergei is the fucking Dog Whisperer, so Sebastian's glued to him if he's not with Laura. Anton has had little choice but to like the daft animal. He's going to bring Sebastian with him after he feeds Cleo and gets my clothes. He'll follow us on the walk. He'll look like a guy out with his dog, and we'll look like a couple having a nice stroll. Misha will drive ahead of us."

"Is all of that really necessary?"

I can see she's getting anxious. I take her hand in mine and squeeze.

"Until I know your neighborhood a little better, and until we know if anyone's going to take an interest in us, I would feel better doing this. It's only a precaution, and I'm sure I'm overreacting. I just won't take any chances with your safety."

"All right."

The time passes quickly before Anton arrives. I run upstairs to get dressed while Tina plays with Sebastian. The dog is the sweetest beast you'd ever meet. He's protective of Laura, but he's a gentle giant the rest of the time. It wouldn't surprise me if Tina talks about getting one by the time we walk out the door.

It's a beautiful day, so we walk for an hour and a half. Some parts we're holding hands, and some parts we're walking with our arms around each other. There's a tree with bright red leaves barely hanging on. We stop to take a selfie under it, and it feels like we're a real couple.

When we get back to her place, she insists Anton and Misha stay for lunch. She makes a mountain of sandwiches that we devour. She eats hers while we eat three times as many. She just smiles throughout, laughing when my cousins and I tease each other. Misha helps her clear the table, and I jerk my head toward the door. Anton nods and gets Sebastian's leash. Misha notices, and they both say a hasty goodbye.

"What do you want to watch, *malyshka?*"

"Doctor Zhivago? War and Peace? Crime and Punishment?"

"All the books were better than the movies. Especially the untranslated versions."

I smirk, knowing she's teasing me. I might introduce her to Russian cinema one day, but I doubt she wants to read subtitles. She offers to make popcorn while I pull up a streaming app on her TV. We're soon under the blanket, nestled together like we were last night. I'm holding the bowl of popcorn in my lap while she leans against me. She suggests a slasher movie, and I don't have the heart to tell her I hate them. They're a little too close to my day job. I think she realizes that because she flushes bright red and scrolls down the list until we find *The Princess Bride*. Who hasn't watched that movie at least a dozen times and wouldn't mind watching it a dozen more?

By the time the credits are rolling, we're both nearly asleep. I know I barely slept over the past nine days, but it's obvious neither did Tina. I feel guilty all over again. The sofa is extra deep, so we shift until we're lying down. I stroke her hair as her head rests on my chest, but we're asleep within minutes.

"Where are we going tonight?"

"It's a surprise."

"But I need to know something, so I wear the right things. Is it a jeans and kicks kinda night or cocktail dress and heels?"

"Cocktail dress and those heels you had on last night. You looked amazing, even if I wanted to gouge out the eyes of every guy in that place."

She laughs, but I don't think she realizes how serious I am. Never have I experienced such potent jealousy in my life. There are basically eight of us who have shared everything our entire lives. I'd gladly give any of them everything I have. But knowing that a strip club full of basically naked men were ogling her drives me to the brink. It took every ounce of restraint I could dredge up to keep from going in there and beating my chest.

"Do you want me to wear something like I did last night?"

"Fuck no." Okay. That might have come out a little fast. "I'd rather you save that little ensemble for a night in."

"You didn't love my tits and ass half hanging out?"

"I loved that. I just didn't love other men seeing that."

"What's yours, you mean?"

I freeze. How do I answer that? I know what I want to say, but we're having a thirty-day trial, and I said I understand if she wants to see other people.

"Bogdan, it's not a trick question. I already told you. I don't want to see other people. I'm all in while we figure this out."

"Then yes, that's exactly what I mean."

"Fair enough. But that means I don't want you wearing those tight button downs."

"Why not?"

"Because you're way too hot to begin with. I see how women stare at you when you're wearing a suit. I'll be beating them back if they see you like that."

She jerks her chin toward me. I've just finished getting dressed while she stares at her closet. She turns back to her clothes and moves a few things back and forth. I slide my arms around her waist and kiss her neck.

"Jealous?"

"Yes."

She sounds purposely petulant, which lands her a swat on her backside as I kiss her neck.

"What would you have me wear instead?"

"A baggy sweatshirt that doesn't show any of your muscles."

"Then I insist on a floor-length muumuu for you."

"Not happening. So I guess I have to give in a little with your wardrobe. Keep your jacket on, sexpot."

She picks out a silver cocktail dress with an asymmetrical strap that goes over her right shoulder and across her back. It has a slit in the back that's only a couple inches long, but it's enough to hint. She grabs a shawl of some sort and carries her heels downstairs. When we get outside, Pasha is in the driver's seat, and Anton is in the passenger seat. She glances at me but says nothing other than to greet my cousins.

We head into Manhattan, and I can tell she's curious where I'm taking her. She knows I want to surprise her, so she doesn't ask. She just watches the skyline go by as we chat about our upcoming week. Her eyes widen as she realizes that we're at a Michelin star restaurant. It's the same one Maks and Laura had their engagement dinner at. I reserved the table they were supposed to have before it became a family event. That was quite a day, and Maks's proposal didn't go at all how he'd planned. It was the saddest and happiest day of their entire relationship and nearly didn't happen.

The maître d' leads us to a chef's table set in a secluded area next to the kitchen. We can see what the chef's doing, but there's also a door that closes when we want privacy, putting us in a separate nook. I pull out Tina's chair and kiss her neck before I take mine. I don't give it much thought as I take her hand and place it on the table between us while we lean together to look at the wine menu.

"Why is that woman staring at us? It's more than just because you're hot. She looks like she wants to fuck you and murder me?"

I look at Tina as she whispers, then follow her gaze. Fuck my life.

"I used to go out with her."

"She doesn't look over you."

"It wasn't a nice break up. We were together a while."

Tina looks at me, and realization dawns. She's too fucking perceptive.

"What's her name?"

"Chloe."

"She named your cat, didn't she? Chloe and Cleo."

She studies the menu as she talks, but I can tell she's uncomfortable. I don't blame her. Chloe is glaring at me like she wants to stab me with a steak knife. I nod to her, which only seems to piss her off more. I realize she's staring at my hand holding Tina's, and I get it.

"She did."

"Didn't you say you dated for a few years? Did you live together?"

"Yes, to both. We dated for three years, and she lived with me in my penthouse."

"Is she not over you?"

"I don't know."

"She must not be. She's pissed."

"She's angry because I'm holding your hand in public, and we're sitting so close."

"Didn't you do that with her?"

"No, and it's one of many things she complained about. I never displayed any affection in public. She gave up trying to get me to not long after we started dating, but she would remind me that she didn't like it."

"No wonder she's pissed."

"Ignore her. I'm here with you, not to think about my ex-girlfriend."

"Easy for you to say. Wonderful. She's coming over here."

I want to groan, but I remain quiet. Chloe is beautiful and intelligent, but she has a tongue that will cut you to the quick. I didn't know that until she moved into my place. She'd played nice until then. I learned to pacify her, but that grew old. She complained I was emotionally shut off. I wonder why. It wasn't worth the arguments about things I couldn't discuss. I would change the subject and offer her whatever I thought would calm her down.

"Hello, Bogdan."

She ignores Tina, and it irritates me even more.

"Hello, Chloe. This is Tina."

Tina's watching everything like a hawk. She has a warm smile on her face, but it doesn't reach her eyes. I squeeze her hand in reassurance, and I can tell Chloe sees.

"I thought about reserving our special table, but it was already taken. I see why."

Tina doesn't flinch, but I feel her arm stiffen.

"Yes, that older couple has it."

Fuck her. She's not ruining my first date.

"It's been too long since we caught up, darling."

She has a Southern drawl since she grew up in Mississippi. The endearment could just be a Southern thing, but Tina and I know it isn't.

"I lost your number."

"I'll have to call, so you have it again."

I deleted it from my phone, but I still remember it. I'm not answering.

"It looks like you're about to leave. What do you recommend on the menu?"

Tina's voice is sweet, but there's no missing that cue. Chloe looks ready to lash out. Before I can say anything, she does.

"I recommend you stay away from Bogdan."

"Oh? Is it because he isn't affectionate? Or is it because he doesn't display emotions?"

"Been telling tales, Bogdan?"

"Hardly. He seems so new to these things. At our age, it's nice to be someone's first."

Tina, don't piss her off. Fuck me with a pogo stick.

"I was going to say because he isn't over me."

Tina laughs.

"That wasn't the case an hour ago. He was definitely over something."

"Chloe, your friends are waiting."

I need her to leave before it turns into a war between them.

"Let them."

Her tone is defiant, and I'm surprised she doesn't pull up a chair.

"I'm not doing this, Chloe. I'm having dinner with my girlfriend. I know for sure you and I are through. We have been for three years. Leave or I'll have you escorted out."

"Bastard."

"Don't talk about my parents."

"Or what? You'll have one of your mobster brothers take me out? I know what you are, even if you never admitted it."

"If you're so sure, then you must realize what a bad idea it was to come over here."

"You wouldn't hurt me, Bogdan. You couldn't."

"You forget I broke up with you, not the other way around. I have felt nothing toward you for years, but you are aggravating me now. Go away."

Chloe opens her mouth to speak, but Tina beats her.

"Chloe, I can understand why you loved Bogdan, and I suppose I can imagine why he loved you. But there's more to a relationship than good sex. That's rather a thin type of love. Your wedding ring tells me you know there's more to it than that. Isn't it so nice when you find a partner who reciprocates? I know it is."

I glance down at the hand farther away from me, and I notice what Tina did. There's a moderate sized engagement ring and a wedding band behind it.

"My congratulations to you and your husband, Chloe."

"I think you know my husband, Bogdan, or soon will. His name's Anthony Lake."

Our new inspector is my ex-girlfriend's husband. Tina reacts faster than I do.

"Congratulations. I'll have to mention that when I see him in the office on Monday. No one knew he was even engaged."

Chloe glowers at Tina until one of her friends calls her over. The girl, whose name I can't remember, waves at me. Chloe casts me one last look before she turns away. Tina got the last word, but what did it gain us? Nothing. Chloe's even more likely to fill her husband's head with bullshit, and my brothers and I will pay the price. Literally. I expect heavy fines are suddenly going to roll in.

"I didn't know Anthony was married, and especially not to your ex-girlfriend. If I had, I wouldn't have traded projects."

"I know, *malyshka*." I turn toward her. "You know what she said isn't true, don't you? I don't have feelings for her. At least anything other than annoyance."

"I believe you. I know it's true, and that's why she's so pissed. I probably shouldn't have said anything, but I was feeling possessive."

"I have no issue with that. I feel that way about you. You know the last time I had a girlfriend was three years ago. How long ago was your last boyfriend?"

"A year ago. Isn't this exactly the topic people aren't supposed to talk about on a first day? We are the most ass-backwards couple."

"I suppose we're getting it over early."

"I suppose."

The waitress comes and takes our order. We lapse into silence as we both consider what happened, or at least that's what I'm thinking about. I can't tell what Tina is from her expression.

"Am I your girlfriend? Or did you just say that to make a point?"

"I guess I think of you that way. I just said what I felt."

"What about now that she's walked away?"

"I feel like I want to have a romantic dinner with my girl-friend and only think about her."

I bring her hand to my lips, and I watch how she blushes. If I could have her even closer to me, I would. I can't imagine what came over Chloe to approach us, let alone say what she did. Our conversation moves to our childhoods, and I discover Tina has two older brothers. She's never mentioned them, but she says she sees them every couple of weeks.

"Did you tell them about me when you thought I ghosted you?"

"And have them beat the crap out of you, or get the crap beaten out of them for trying? Uh, no."

"I would never hurt your family, Tina."

"True, but your family travels in a pack. I don't think your brothers would let you go down without a fight."

I shrug.

"They might. If you mean enough to your brothers for them to find me, then my brothers will understand how protective they are."

"Will my family ever be able to meet you?"

"Of course. It's not like I'm in the Witness Protection Program or the CIA. I live a normal life most of the time. I have friends who aren't bratva."

"Do they know you are?"

"Some have guessed. Some I've hinted to. You really are the only person I've admitted it to."

She takes that in for a moment before she nods, but she looks in the direction Chloe went when she left with her friends.

"Will you tell me about your mom?"

"Happily. She's one of the two most beautiful women I know." I see her tense. "You're the other one."

She turns doe eyes to me, surprised by my comment. I realize she doesn't see herself as I do. I slide my chair closer. Place settings be damned.

"*Malyshka*, you're so damn beautiful it makes my heart ache."

"You must like me a lot to think that. You work with beautiful women every day."

"That doesn't mean I think they're more beautiful than you."

"I have carrot colored hair, tons of freckles that practically cover most of my face, and my eyes—well, they're my best feature."

"I love looking at your freckles. I could spend a lifetime counting them, and I'd still want to do it more."

Where the hell did that come from? Don't be stupid. I know that's what I want, or I wouldn't bring her into my world. She smiles again, but I can see she's getting uncomfortable. I don't know if it's talking about her looks or it's me mentioning a lifetime.

"You're also super smart. It's not like anyone gets into NYU and Colombia. I know since I fully expected to get rejected from NYU, and I did get rejected by Colombia. I know how perceptive you are, too. I see how you take everything in and process it quickly, then offer solutions while most people are still trying to understand the problem. You read people well."

"I try. It's difficult being in a male dominated industry, so I've learned to be succinct, and to notice body language to gage how I should come across. When I was an intern, I got treated like shit a few times, and my boss back then gave me the advice to keep it short and plan how to approach people before the conversation starts. I try to take cues to keep things on track, and sometimes I just have to let people ramble or vent."

"Do people treat you better now?"

She laughs.

"When I can shut an entire site down, it's amazing how quickly people can become polite."

"So you're in it for the power."

She laughs along with me and nods. A leaping flame in the kitchen draws our attention, so we watch as the chef prepares our meal. I can tell she's fascinated, and that's why I wanted this table. I wanted to give her a night that she wouldn't normally have. Chloe excluded. We talk while we eat, and we share things about when we were kids with our brothers. I volunteer stories about growing up in Moscow and how much better our life is here. She's cautious when she asks if I miss it and would ever want to move back. I can answer that without thinking. No.

By the end of the evening, I feel like we know each other's life story. She's a hilarious storyteller, and I can't remember the last time I laughed so much. Maybe this is merely infatuation, but I don't think it is. I wonder how she feels.

Chapter Thirteen

Tina

It's been a week since our nearly disastrous first date. I have never been so uncomfortable as I was when Chloe approached our table, and never have I felt more physically inadequate than when she stood in front of me. I sat there counting my flaws until she got to the bit about Bogdan still being in love with her and not being over her. Then I couldn't hold back. I know what she said wasn't true. I believe Bogdan, and nothing about his demeanor made me think he was pretending for my sake. But I was fed up. We finally had a chance to do something like a normal couple. The day had been perfect up till then.

It went back to being the perfect date, but I haven't stopped thinking about Chloe telling Bogdan that they should be in touch. I wonder if she's called or texted him. If she has, did he answer? I'm dying to ask, but I don't want to sound like the crazy girlfriend. And that word was unexpected. I thought he'd said it just to give Chloe a strong hint, but then he said that's how he thinks of me. I suppose I sorta think of him as my boyfriend, but I wasn't ready for a label. What happens if things go to shit before now and the end of the month?

We've had our two regular dates and one sex night. All of it has been amazing. We went to the movies, since we realized it's something we both enjoy. We sat in the back and made out for part of it, like we were teenagers again. And our sex night. Holy shit. We spent the night at his penthouse. He held nothing back. We were loud enough that Cleo meowed several times to let us know we annoyed her. I discovered an assortment of newly purchased toys and—implements. It's a regular date night this evening, and I'm looking forward to it. Maks and Laura are back from their honeymoon and having people over. I'm going to meet her and some of her friends.

"It's casual, baby girl. I promise."

Bogdan's standing behind me as I pick out what to wear. We've spent all day together, just like we did last Saturday. We had our sex night last night, and we went grocery shopping together today. Plenty of sexual innuendos, especially in the produce section. He picked out ingredients to make me a Russian dinner later this week. I'm really looking forward to it. But I'm paying extra attention to what I wear because his mother's going to be there. I want to make a good impression.

I end up in a shimmery top, jeans, and ankle boots. I top it off with a navy blazer and silver clutch. I feel sophisticated, which doesn't take much considering I wear a hard hat and steel-toed boots every day. The party is at Maks and Laura's Queens house, so we're there in a few minutes. I look around at the veritable mansion and notice a woman who is absolutely stunning. Like breathtaking. I know in an instant she's Bogdan's mother. She has the same blond hair as Sergei and Misha. Her sons resemble her strongly but aren't replicas. Since Anton and

Pasha look so much like them, their father's genes must have had a strong influence too.

"Come meet my mom."

Bogdan steers me in the woman's direction, and she must notice us approaching. She turns and beams. Bogdan doesn't hesitate to engulf his mother in a hug that lifts her off her feet. She giggles and sounds much younger than her years, but it's infectious. I'm grinning by the time Bogdan lets go. He turns to me and wraps his arm around my waist, drawing me next to him.

"Mama, this is Tina." I reach out my hand. "Tina, this is my mom, Galina Kutsenko."

"It's nice to meet you, Mrs. Kutsenko."

"Galina please. It's nice to meet you too." She looks at her son and winks. "He can't stop talking about you. I can't get a word in edge wise."

"Mama."

Bogdan hisses, and his cheeks are bright red. I've never seen him blush, but he's mortified. I realize I haven't told my parents a single thing about him, not even that I'm dating. That takes the edge off my excitement. I feel guilty now. He squeezes my waist, and I look up at him.

"It's true, Bogdan. I've been eager to meet you, but I wasn't sure he would share you with anyone."

"Mama."

"I have to have some fun at your expense. You were the wildest of my sons and gave me the most gray hairs."

"I was not, and you're still as blonde as you were in your wedding photos. Don't blame me."

"Who was?"

I'm dying to know since all the brothers seem so reserved. I'm still looking up at Bogdan, so I don't see Niko approach.

"I was, and Bogdan used to follow me everywhere."

"Until college, maybe."

Bogdan looks less than thrilled by this conversation, so I try to come to his rescue.

"Where'd you go to college, Niko?"

"NYU like you and Bogdan."

"We must have been on campus the same time too. What did you study?"

"Finance. Pretty exciting stuff."

"Did you minor in anything cool like Bogdan? I didn't expect medieval literature and art."

Galina and Niko stare at me. Did Bogdan not tell me the truth?

"I can't believe you told her that. You never tell anyone."

Niko recovers faster than Galina, and Bogdan merely shrugs.

"I minored in—"

"Music theory."

Bogdan blurts out before his brother can finish. I look between the two and can see the good-natured teasing between them. Renaissance men. I also watch Galina as she looks at her sons. The pride radiates from her.

It's not long before I'm introduced to Laura, who I think is about the greatest thing ever. She's a corporate lawyer, and I learn how she met Maks. She's a complete rock star the way she maneuvered the merger to her clients' benefit. Her friends are nice, but I can tell they feel a little out of place. Their conversations appear awkward, like they aren't sure if they should talk. I wonder how much they know about Maks and his brothers.

Bogdan gets drawn into a conversation with a couple of men I don't know. They're speaking Russian, so I assume they're bratva too. It tempts me to ask Laura what they're saying, but I figure if they wanted everyone to know, they'd speak in English. Niko joins me where I'm sitting on the sofa alone since Bogdan just got up.

"Wait until the food starts. I hope you came hungry."

"Typical guy. Thinking with your stomach."

"Better than the other thing typical guys think with."

I choke on the sip of beer I just took, and he thumps me on the back. He's not as gentle as Bogdan. I can't help but laugh and nod as he moves back to where he was sitting at the end of the sofa.

"Now you sound like my brothers."

"Maks and Laura had the event catered, but my mom and aunt insisted on making a few dishes. Have you met Aunt Svetlana?"

"No, not yet."

"She's the lady speaking to my mom and Sergei."

"Wow. I didn't expect her to have red hair."

"Yeah. It used to be closer to your color when I was a kid, but it's darkened as she's gotten older."

"Do redheads get teased in Russia as much as they do here?"

Niko thinks about that for a moment.

"I don't know. I didn't know any redheads when I was a kid. I was twelve when we left, so I don't remember at least a quarter of that time. Did you get teased a lot?"

"Mercilessly. Especially since everyone assumed I was Irish. I made the mistake of not wearing green on Saint Patrick's Day when I was in fourth grade. My mother and father were livid when I came home covered in bruises from kids pinching me. I almost got suspended for pushing a kid, who fell backwards and rolled down the hill in the playground. I would have taken that suspension with pride. He was an asshole."

Niko laughs, and it's the first time I've seen him do that.

He's a handsome man for sure, but when he smiles, I bet he gets whatever he wants with most women. But I don't find it nearly as alluring as Bogdan when he smiles. We keep talking for another fifteen minutes about work, and he tells me some embarrassing stories about Bogdan that I will tuck away in my arsenal. We're facing each other, and Niko's arm is resting on the back of the couch. I'm just beyond his reach, but when Bogdan joins us, I realize how it must have appeared to anyone behind us. Shit.

"Thanks for keeping Tina company, Niko." There's an edge to his voice that surprises me. "Thanks for keeping my seat warm."

Niko's brow furrows for a moment before he stands up and nods to me. He walks away, and I don't see where he's going.

"Bogdi, what was that about?"

I can tell he's reining in his temper. I put my beer down on the table. He sticks his hand out to me and helps me off the sofa. I look around to see if anyone is watching us as he leads me up the stairs to a guest bedroom.

"I'm the one who should ask what that was about. You looked awfully cozy with my brother."

"I can guess how it looked, but he couldn't reach me. We were just looking at each other to make the conversation easier."

I step toward him and put my hands out to rest them on his chest, but he grasps my wrists.

"*Malyshka*, I know you don't know how things work among the men, but Niko does. I'm not angry at you, but I need you to understand. There's a lot of posturing and machismo that goes on. Everyone here knows I brought you and that we're seeing each other. Sitting where it looks like Niko has his arm around you makes me look like a chump, and it makes you...You can guess. He knows better than that, and I believe he just wasn't thinking about it. But people were already talking. If I look weak, then so do my brothers. That's a dangerous ground for us to tread. And more importantly, I don't want people to talk poorly about you. I don't want rumors that will taint people's opinion or put you in danger."

"I didn't think about any of that. He had his drink in his hand, anyway."

"I know. It looked like he was passing it to you."

"Bogdan, I'm sorry."

"It's not your fault, so you have nothing to apologize about, Tina. I'm just trying to let you know."

"So it was how it looked and not that I was talking to him?"

That makes him pause. It wasn't just about the way it looked.

"I was jealous."

"Why? You know I want to be with you. Until you told me the other day, I thought Niko didn't even like me."

"He likes you all right."

"As his brother's girlfriend. Nothing more. We were talking about you nearly the entire time."

He takes a deep inhale before he nods.

"You were at Pussycats with someone. I know it's not the first time you've been to a strip club with Todd. Were you two planning to add a third?"

"What? No. I'd never go home with a stripper."

He cocks an eyebrow.

"Male or female, Bogdan. Why are you asking this?"

"Because I watched you before I approached you at the bar. You were into the first few dancers who came on stage. It was the last one before you got up who didn't hold your interest. I saw the way Todd's hand kept sliding up your thigh and under your skirt."

"I still don't understand why we're talking about this."

"Do you want a threesome?"

I stand there with my mouth open. It's a fantasy, but with two guys, not two girls.

"You're not denying it, Tina."

"I'm not into girls. They might be hot, and it might be arousing to watch them give a guy a lap dance who you know is going home to fuck you, but I'm not into them."

"Why's that hot to you?"

"I don't know. I get something they don't. I get to be the one who gives the guy real pleasure. It just is to me."

"Then you want two guys."

"If I were to have a threesome, then yes, that's what I would prefer."

"Have you had one before?"

"No. Have you?"

"Yes."

I take a step back. Now I feel sick. I don't want to have this conversation. I look around before I look at the door. I want out.

"I didn't say that to hurt you, Tina. But I won't lie to you. If you ask me a question that I can answer, I will. We both know there are plenty of questions I can't. I won't add to that list if I can help it."

"You didn't have to be so blunt. Was it two girls or you sharing a girl?"

"Yes."

"Both? I don't want to hear this, Bogdan. I want to go back downstairs."

I move to turn around, but his arm captures me and hauls me back against him. His hand goes to my throat and rests heavily there. I feel him getting hard, and all I want is to rub against him.

"Is that a fantasy you want, Tina? Do you want me to share you with another guy?"

"Would you?"

"For one night, if that's your fantasy, then yes."

"Do you expect me to share you?"

"No. That's not your fantasy, and I don't want that."

"Do you really want to see me with another guy? Sucking his dick or getting fucked?"

"Not particularly. But I told you, if that's your fantasy, then I will."

"Let me turn around, Daddy. I want to see you while we talk about this. I need to."

He releases me immediately, and I spin around. His arm goes back around me, and his hand is back on my throat.

"You looked like you appreciate Niko's good looks."

"You'd share me with your brother?"

"It wouldn't be a first."

"Fuck you."

I try to push him away, but he tightens his hold.

"Such a dirty mouth is going to get washed out. With my cum. Behave yourself, *malyshka*."

"No. I'm Tina right now. Don't control me on this. I don't want to be some woman you and your brother fuck, then compare notes on later."

"That is not what would happen. I would fulfill your fantasy if that's what you want, Tina. And I trust Niko to be discreet and to respect our boundaries."

I swallow as I look at him, then I glance back at the door. This isn't my darkest fantasy, but it's one I've had plenty of times. I know it's twisted that it's between brothers, but Bogdan is right that Niko would respect our boundaries. But I have no idea if that's even something his brother would agree to.

"Do you want me to ask him, Tina?"

I keep staring at him. I don't know what to say. This wasn't what I expected. Niko's hot, and if he's anything like Bogdan in bed, then I'm the luckiest bitch on the block. But can Bogdan really do this and not resent Niko and me later? Can I look at Niko and forget that we've slept together? How awkward is that going to be?

The longer I look at Bogdan, the clearer something else becomes to me. It doesn't matter if it were Niko or any other guy. I know what my answer is with certainty.

"No. I don't want this with Niko or anyone else. I don't want anyone else, Bogdan. If I have to choose between my fantasy and something that could fuck up my new relationship, then I want nothing to do with it. And before you say it won't get between us, that's bullshit. Even if it isn't a big deal, I'm too into you to want another guy touching me. I don't want to share myself with someone else."

I see him relax. It's not his body. It's not even his mouth. It's all in his eyes, and I see it. He would have done this for me if I wanted it, but it would have hurt him. I slide my hands up his chest and around his neck. I go up on my toes and press his head toward me. He allows me to and brings his lips to mine. Once again, I imbue the kiss with everything that I'm feeling but am too scared to say aloud.

"I'll do anything to make you happy, Tina. You're everything to me."

"This was asking too much of yourself. If I wasn't so into you, then maybe. I don't understand what's between us, Bogdan. I don't know why I feel the way I do about you so soon after we met."

"I don't either. Do you believe in Divine Intervention?"

"Yes, I believe in God, so I believe He plays a role in many parts of my life. Do you?"

"I have a conflicted relationship with God, but yes, I do."

"Why do people meet? Why are they in the same place at the same time? Maybe it's a coincidence. Or maybe sometimes someone is guiding them. There's no law on how long it takes to realize you care about someone. There's plenty we don't know about each other, but on a fundamental, atomic level, I feel like I've known you my entire life."

He tucks hair behind my ears before he cups my face. It's his turn to begin a gentle kiss that makes me melt against him. We're still kissing when someone pounds on the door.

"Bogdan, we have to go. Now."

It's Aleks, and it's not like he's mentioning the party's winding down. It's urgent. Bogdan looks at me, and all I can do is shrug. We hurry to the door, and I can tell it surprises Aleks when we open it so soon. He glances past us at the bed, which remains untouched.

"We were talking."

Bogdan clearly doesn't appreciate his brother's assumption.

"We need to go. Something's come up."

I want to ask if he's going to be away for days. I want to know how much danger he's facing. I want to know...But I can't ask any of it. We hurry downstairs, and Laura comes toward me.

"You're going to stay with me tonight. If that's all right with you."

"Is something wrong with me going home?"

I turn toward Bogdan, panicked. Is he in that much danger? Am I in danger? Holy shit. This is intense. Is this what I signed up for? Does this happen often? I look at Galina, who's hugging each of her sons. I see Misha, Sergei, Pasha, and Anton all hugging their parents. I look back at Laura, but she's stepped aside to talk to her friends, who are gathering their things. Everyone is leaving but me. Even the other guests. The men crowd together talking, and the women are saying quick good-byes and leaving in pairs and trios.

"*Malyshka.*"

Bogdan walks up to me and tucks me against his chest. I bite my tongue to keep all my questions from tumbling out. Maybe I can ask Laura some of them. But I can only assume Maks has told her as much as Bogdan has to me.

"I may be gone a couple days. If it's more than two, I will get a message to you. If it's more than four, I want you to stay with Laura or my mom."

I don't know what to say. I'm terrified. What's going on that I might need to stay with his mother or sister-in-law?

"I will explain as much as I can once I come back, but I don't have time now. Something happened with a shipment, and we need to take care of it."

"All of you?"

I look past his shoulder. There are ten men not including Bogdan, his brothers, and his cousins. Some of them are as big as Bogdan, and others are skinnier and older. They're the ones who scare me the most. They look like the most unforgiving. The ones who've killed enough people to have lost count. If they're still alive, maybe that means it's safer for Bogdan to be with them.

"Yes, baby girl. We all have our roles. Stay here with Laura tonight."

"Bogdan, please be careful. I—"

I just stand there with my mouth open.

"I will, *lapochka*. I feel the same way. When I get back, I'm taking you away for a long weekend. You won't need to pack anything but a toothbrush."

"*Moy lev*, I will hold you to that." I stand on my toes and whisper. "Daddy, no more thirty days. I know what I want. I'm yours."

"And I'm yours."

He cups my face again like he did upstairs, but this kiss is quick and hard as Aleks calls his name. I'm left standing there as Maks and Laura share one last kiss. Maks is the last one out of the house, closing the door behind him. Laura and Galina wrap an arm around me and each other. The three of us embrace, and I sag against Bogdan's mother. Only my mom is this comforting. I see Laura doing the same thing. What broad shoulders Galina has to carry the weight of our fear and her own so stoically.

"Let's put the food away. There will be plenty of leftovers for you both."

Galina squeezes our shoulders. Laura looks as reluctant to let go as I do. I stare at the table full of food before my feet work. I carry dishes into the kitchen with the other women and put things in containers and cover others with aluminum foil. Everything goes into the fridge, but Laura convinces me to take half of it home tomorrow. Laura lends me a t-shirt and sweat-pants. We try to convince Galina to stay longer, but I think she needs to be alone. She's being strong for us, but I don't know how strong she really feels. Two of the men stayed behind and are Galina's guards. I saw the security around the house when we arrived. There's a small army patrolling the estate.

Laura and I sit on the sofa in silence, each of us covered in a blanket. I don't know what to say when the silence grows awkward.

"How much do you know, Christina? Maks said Bogdan told you everything."

"As much as he can, and still keep everyone safe. Are they going to that place?"

"Eventually. Maks told me Bogdan's been there since you two started dating. He said you thought he dumped you without saying anything."

"Yeah. Aleks and Niko just told me he had family stuff to deal with."

"I don't think they'll be gone that long. If they are, someone will let us know. That's the one thing that I insist upon with Maks. We had something similar happen, and it was Galina who had to explain to me that sometimes they're gone for days. I went for a walk to her place, and my guard that day left with his wife to go to Atlantic City after I got to Galina's. No one told Maks where I went. I suppose our guards thought Galina's guards told him and vice versa. Or they all thought Ilya told Maks. He went ballistic when he came home and couldn't find me. Those few days were among the hardest of my life. I didn't want you to be alone, and honestly, I don't want to be alone. Thanks for keeping me company tonight."

"Thank you for inviting me. Does it get easier?"

"Sorta. I don't know where the place is that they go. But Maks promised to text me before he goes inside. Right now, I don't know who controls the situation, because I know nothing other than there's an issue with a shipment. Once they're on their property, they have control. I just have to make it until that text comes. That's why I need your company."

"Are you scared? Because I'm terrified."

"Yes. I'm always a little scared, I suppose. But I've figured out how to manage it."

"Any suggestions?"

"I remind myself of how much I love Maks. Part of what's scary is that I love him so much, and I can't bear the idea of losing him. But I also know that I don't want to live without him, so there's no way I'm walking away. I don't want to miss out on all the good stuff because I'm scared something bad might happen."

I think about what Laura says, and that's what I realized too. That's why I nearly said I love you. Being with him for the good stuff outweighs my fear. I just pray I'm not wrong.

Chapter Fourteen

Bogdan

Donovan O'Rourke has some balls. I'll give him that. He runs guns and other weapons down the St. Lawrence River from Canada into New York. He's been the head of the Irish syndicate for years. We leave him alone, and mostly, he leaves us alone. But he just stole a three-million-dollar shipment of weapons headed to South America. Apparently, he's turned pirate because he didn't dare try to steal from us while the crates were on shore. He had men board the container ship our cargo was on and steal the crates from there.

The Irish control most of the docks, and what they don't, the Cartel does. Right now, the Cartel is staying out of the way. Laura's childhood friend turned out to be a complete prick, but his uncle heads the Colombian Cartel in New York City. Maks let Enrique know Juan fucked up royally when he set his sights on us. Juan's brother, Pablo, is in line to inherit from Enrique since the guy has no kids.

At first, I wondered if Salvatore Mancinelli was behind this since the Irish and Italians tend to run together, but Sergei's intel says this is all Donovan. We knew he'd been surveilling our warehouses down here, but we didn't expect him to go out to sea. He sent men far enough off the coast to still be in international waters. Not that it matters. We can't exactly cry foul and try to enact maritime law when they're already stolen goods that we're selling illegally to overseas nongovernmental entities.

Right now, I'm crouched at the corner of a shipping container, wearing all black with night vision goggles and a rifle. An hour ago, I was talking about a threesome with my girlfriend. That was a fucking awkward conversation, but I hadn't lied. I would have dealt with it if that was a fantasy she wanted to act out. Obviously, sex is a pretty important part of our relationship. But the fantasy isn't just about pleasure. It's about trust and intimacy. And I don't want to share that with anyone else. But if she did, I would have made it work.

I didn't want to lie, so I answered her questions honestly. But I saw the pain I caused her when I admitted I'd had threesomes before. A couple were in college, and a couple have been since I broke up with Chloe. The ones in college involved Niko. I know that would creep some people out. A little too incestuous, but our dicks never touched inside or outside the women. Not even close. The two times after I broke up with Chloe were with two girls. I thought at first that they were rebound sex, but I realized something else. I loved Chloe, but not deeply. I loved things about her, and I loved the fun time we had together when things were good. But I replaced her pretty damn fast, and I didn't think twice about it.

I'm trying not to let my mind wander when I'm supposed to be focused. All I need is to get shot while thinking about Tina. I can't guarantee I'll never get hurt. She's seen my scars. But I don't need to get injured the first time I'm forced to leave her behind. I don't know how well she would deal with that.

Aleks taps my shoulder. I look where he's pointing, then he holds up two fingers. We fire simultaneously, silencers on our weapons. Both men fall. I gesture for us to move forward. Niko and Maks are on the other side of the container. I peek around the corner and find Maks looking at me. We nod to each other before inching across a three-foot gap between storage units. We're getting closer to where the ship's docked that has our weapons. I take out another guy, who turns and looks straight at me. I have quicker reflexes than him.

I glance left and watch three of our guys jog forward. Then it starts. Raised voices and guns without silencers. Amateurs. Pasha and Misha are in charge of this mission as our *avotoritets*. Right now, the rest of us, even Maks, are their *brodyaga* or *bratok*. We work for them as our brigadiers. This isn't just some petty crime for a regular foot soldier. We're not hustling some guy outside a casino or strong arming someone who owes us money. I wish it were so mundane. I'd be in bed with Tina tonight if it were.

I have my rifle raised as I run forward. I glimpse Sergei and Anton, who are side by side. Each of them has their gun pointed in an opposite direction. I see the muzzle flash from Anton's rifle. Then I see him. The guy aiming for my cousin. I charge forward, rifle pointing at the guy. As I squeeze the trigger, I slam into Anton and knock him forward. I press my hand on his back to keep him down before I fire another round. My cousin and I watch the man crash to the ground from the top of a container.

"You need a diet."

Anton and I scramble to our feet. He's grinning at me and claps a hand on my shoulder as I scowl.

"You're welcome, cousin."

Pasha whistles, and we know it's time. We pour onto the ship's deck, having used the two gangways connecting the vessel to the dock. There's only a skeleton crew aboard, and we want them alive. My brothers and I put hoods over their heads and restrain their arms behind their backs before we get them onto the dock and into our armored SUVs. The others will deal with reclaiming our cargo and getting it away from the harbor. My brothers and I head to the warehouse with our guests.

"String them up."

Maks's command echoes in the cavernous building when we get there. We get the six men stripped and attached to the meat hooks, their arms straining above their heads, their toes grazing the floor. Maks plows his fist into the face of the ship's captain. We're certain this isn't the original ship captain. Oh, no. The head of the original ship's captain arrived by courier to Maks's penthouse. No packages go up to Maks and Laura without being x-rayed first. Needless to say, they alerted Maks immediately.

"How much did Donovan O'Rourke pay you?"

Maks starts the questioning. No one answers. Not so smart thinking they can hold out. I hold up a pair of pliers in front of the youngest man. He can't be older than me, and he looks an awful lot like the captain. I click them open and closed before going down on one knee.

"He will cut off your crewman's toes until we get an answer. If he gets through all ten toes, he'll move onto the guy's balls. He won't be able to walk or fuck."

Maks has a handful of the guy's hair and yanks the captain's head back. We all wait, but no one speaks. Fine. I put the pliers around the young guy's left pinky toe and squeeze. As expected, the guy tries to kick me. I ram my fist into his junk. I squeeze a little harder with the pliers and blood drips. I've cut through skin and fat, and I'm almost to the bone.

"Dad, he's gonna cut off my toe!"

Just what I thought. Father-son duo.

"Shut up." The captain can barely talk until he spits out a wad of blood. "We're all as good as dead, so don't say a damn word."

"You are as good as dead," Maks agrees. "But you can decide how painful the death will be. Tells us what we want to know, and it's quick. Lie or remain silent, and we will make your agony last for days."

I watch him raise his hand. That's the signal. I snap off the little toe, and the guy howls. I cut the next toe off and throw them both at the captain. They smack him on the cheek, but he says nothing. He doesn't plead for his son's life or for mercy from my torture. He'll forsake his own son for their mission. My father would have been insisting that he take all the torture, and he'd be fighting until his last breath to get us free. He might have been former KGB and Podolskaya bratva, but he was a father first.

Maks signals me again, and I take off another toe. I jump back when my victim pisses himself. I expect it, but I thought he might have lasted through the first foot. We'll leave him like this until he's dead. He'll hang in his own filth. The other men we captured are looking around, not sure who to watch. The father and son? Each other? The men who will kill them? Hard choices. I come back to stand in front of the young guy. I put the plier around his nose, squeeze, and yank. Howls of pain fill the air.

"You could talk, and I would move onto someone else."

I can see him considering it. He knows his father was right that they will all die. It's just a question of how much agony they'll suffer first.

"O'Rourke hired us to take our trawler out and look like we were in distress. The cargo ship's captain offered us aid. We came aboard at his invitation, then we took it over. We kept the crew alive long enough to dock, then we sliced their throats, gutted them, and tossed them into the harbor. Nothing will float to the surface."

"See, that wasn't so hard."

I slap the guy's face before drawing my knife across his chest. The wound bleeds heavily, but it won't kill him. I move to the man standing next to him. Niko takes my place, driving his fist into the guy's face over and over, until it's mangled, and the crewman passes out. The new guy in front of me looks old enough to be my father.

"Are you fishermen usually?"

Maks is standing beside me now, questioning the guy as I put the pliers around his puffy nipples. There's so much hair, I worry they won't grip his skin. But they do. I squeeze, slowly increasing the tightness.

"Fuck! Yeah, we're commercial fisherman. It was a good payday."

"Was it though?"

Maks smirks at the heavyset fisherman. The man glares at Maks, so I pinch him harder until the skin breaks. I draw back and step away from the men. They've seen what we're willing to do. Now we see how much they're willing to talk.

"How much?"

I'm curious to know how much they decided their lives were worth. I doubt it'll be much.

"Ten grand each."

More than I expected the fisherman to say. Donovan's supposedly forking out the good money. Sixty K for this lot. Not worth the investment.

"You know he would never pay you, right?"

Aleks has been quiet and watching until now. He steps forward with his arms crossed as Maks steps back.

"He paid us each half already."

The heavy fisherman is ready to sing like a canary while the captain seethes.

"He might have let your families keep that, but likely he would have taken it all back, maybe with interest. And he had no intention of letting you live long enough to collect the rest."

"It's his fucking men on the docks that botched this. We did what we were supposed to. He would have hired us again."

Now the captain is feeling chatty. We all laugh. Aleks explains why we find it amusing.

"No, he wouldn't. You could talk in between. He wouldn't take that risk. Those men on the docks were to move the cargo, then kill you. If he bought you off so easily, he'll find others just like you."

"I'm his second cousin. He won't stand for this."

I squint in the dim light. I guess there's a resemblance if I try really hard. But Donovan O'Rourke would sell his mother to the Devil. The only family he cares about is his uncle in Ireland who sends the weapons, and his cousin Colin. Other than that, he couldn't give a shit.

"He might not stand, but he'll sleep like a rock at night and won't think twice about you. He'd probably just put a bullet between your eyes. We could do that too if you tell us more. Otherwise, you'll be here a few days."

That's the last thing I want to hear, even if I expected it. I want this over with, so I can be with Tina by morning. But I can't shirk my responsibilities just because I have a girlfriend again. It was different when Maks and Laura were dating. Maks hadn't had a girlfriend in such a long time and had sworn off women, so when Laura came in, we all stepped up and took our turns here. We wanted them to work from the get-go. But I've had girlfriends before, and I've never put them before my role in the bratva. Besides, I don't think any of them realize how serious I am about Tina. I think they believe she's just another girlfriend to keep me company until I feel like we're getting too close. Then I'll pull the plug.

The night drags on as we take turns getting only a small detail here and there. It's three a.m., and the men are passed out and drooping from their hooks. My brothers and I are in the office while Misha and Pasha organize men to guard them. Anton and Sergei went back to Maks's place to guard Laura and Tina. They'll tell the girls that we're all right.

"We have the weapons back, and we can get them down to Miami within the week. Donovan must know by now what happened. Either he's going to strike back or not, but these men aren't any use to either of us."

I can tell Maks is eager to get home to Laura, and I want to get back to Tina. Aleks and Niko look at each other before Aleks speaks.

"Go home to your women. We'll take care of them. Meet us at the gym to work out at seven."

"Later. We can work out while Laura's at Mass."

When it comes to religion, how such a faithful Catholic girl wound up with my extremely lapsed Orthodox brother is anyone's guess. Laura goes to Mass almost every Sunday at her church in Queens. It's near their house.

"Fine. I wouldn't mind the few hours of sleep before working out."

Niko sleeps like the fucking dead and is the one who can sleep anywhere.

"I don't know if I'll make it. I need to see how Tina's doing with all this." I've never had to worry about this before because no one outside the bratva used to know what I was doing. "Her birthday is coming up. I'm taking her away for a long weekend."

"Do you think her boss'll let her take the time?"

Fuck. That reminds me.

"I don't know. We ran into Chloe at dinner the other night."

"How'd that go over?"

"It fucking sucked. Chloe was a straight up bitch to Tina. She told her to stay away from me and that I'm not over her. Tina insinuated I'm over Chloe because I was a different kind of over Tina an hour earlier."

"Good for her."

Aleks says what my brothers are thinking as they all laugh.

"Yeah, well, it got worse. Turns out Chloe is now married to Anthony Lake, our newest inspector. I'm sure she filled her husband's ear."

"Wait. Your vain, designer name only, gold digging ex-girlfriend married a lowly city employee? I call bullshit. Something isn't right. If she were happily married, she wouldn't have said anything to you."

Niko's right.

"He must have more money than what he gets from his salary."

Maks states the obvious, considering my brothers know exactly how expensive Chloe's tastes run. She makes good money in advertising, but she definitely benefited from my deep pockets. I think that was one thing that disappointed her the most when we broke up. I wouldn't be taking her on any more luxury vacations or buying her expensive gifts. She was the type to expect it. Tina is not. All the more reason I want to take her somewhere nice.

"Who's lining his pockets if it isn't us? Salvatore?"

"Probably. I know it shocked Tina to hear Anthony was married, let alone to Chloe. I think she believes Anthony's a stand-up guy. I don't know if she's figured out that he probably isn't, if he can afford to keep Chloe."

"Take your girlfriend on vacation. We'll deal with Anthony when he shows up. Go home."

Niko grins and waggles his eyebrows at me. I still need to talk to him about being careless with Tina earlier, but not right now. It's not the time nor the place, and if he says Maks and I should go, neither of us is going to argue. Maks and I shower and change before we leave. Aleks will take care of the clothes we leave behind. They'll be ashes in the Flushing River before we get to Maks's house.

We go in silently, unsure if the girls are still awake. The TV's flickering, but we find them both asleep on the couch, head-to-head. Maks whispers to me.

"Stay. Take one of the guest rooms."

We each scoop up our woman and climb the stairs. Maks goes to the master bedroom to the left while I go down the right hall to the room where Tina and I were talking earlier.

"Bogdi?"

"Yes, baby girl. I'm back."

Her eyes flutter open as she tries to focus in the dim hallway light. She wraps her arms around my neck and rests her head back against my chest.

"I didn't think you'd be back so soon. I tried to stay awake, but I couldn't keep my eyes open. Was Laura awake?"

"No. You were both passed out. Maks is carrying her to their room."

"You're okay?"

"Yes, *malyshka*."

"Good. Will you hold me while we sleep?"

"I'm not letting go until you tell me to."

She yawns, and I can tell she's more asleep than awake.

"That'll be never."

I look down at the woman in my arms, and my heart feels like it's going to burst. This isn't lust. This isn't infatuation.

This is finding my soulmate. But is that how she sees me? I think so from the way we talked earlier. I lie her on the bed before I strip. I slide in next to her, and she wriggles backwards into my arms. She's already back to sleep, but my mind is still whirling despite being exhausted. I reach back and grab my phone from the bedside table.

I spend the next half an hour booking our getaway. I know her birthday isn't for another week, but I want to make sure I get what I want. If her boss doesn't give her the time off, I might just insist she quit and let me take care of her. That's likely to blow up like an atom bomb if I suggest it, but I would gladly do it. I have another contingency plan if her boss refuses. I've gotten the sense he's been giving her a hard time ever since she traded cases with Anthony. She hasn't said as much, but she changes the subject when her office comes up. She'll talk all day about the build sites she visits. Something's up there.

"*Malyshka*, I'm meeting my brothers at the gym while Laura's at church this morning. Do you want to stay here and hang out while we're all gone? Do you want to go to your place or mine?"

"I usually go for a long bike ride on Sundays. Can I still do that?"

I think about who could go with her. None of us are cyclists. Does that mean one guy drives a pace car? Before last night, I thought I might spend most of the weekend with her, so my cousins could have the time off.

"Where do you ride?"

"To Central Park, take a loop around, then ride home."

"That's like thirty miles."

"Yeah. It takes about three hours."

Shit. I don't want to tell her no, but she'll be too easy to lose in traffic going into Manhattan. And then, once she's at the park, no one could drive alongside her.

"Bogdan, if it's going to stress you out, then I won't go. I can set up my bike in my garage and ride there. I use two sawhorses, and it's like a spin class."

"I don't want to make you give up something you enjoy."

"Then I'll just have to make a cyclist out of you. I wouldn't mind seeing you in those tight shorts."

She smacks my backside as we come out of the bathroom. Laura dropped off a couple of toothbrushes. Tina hasn't asked me about last night. I'm not sure if she just doesn't want to know, or if she doesn't want to ask.

"Come with me to the gym."

I hope my brothers don't care. We don't bring friends. It's our time to just be ourselves as a family. Sometimes we talk business, but most of the time, we just hang out.

"I don't want to intrude."

"We have some of the high-end bikes there that you can ride. Maks and I may go a few rounds in the ring while the others lift. Then he and I will join them. You can lift too."

I see something speculative in her eyes as she considers my offer. She nods, and I can't decipher her expression. What have I just gotten myself into?

Chapter Fifteen

Tina

We make a quick stop at my place, so I can change. Bogdan borrowed clothes from Maks. I'm carrying my water bottle as we walk in. This is a boxing gym with some cardio equipment and weights. The ring takes up the entire center of the space. Bogdan points to the bikes, and I get on. I program it for a steep ride to make up for not having three hours. I watch all the guys hop on treadmills. None pick the bikes. We're all doing cardio for nearly an hour before the guys hop off. Maks and Bogdan let their brothers wrap their wrists before they get into the ring. Once they're sparring, Aleks and Niko join their cousins at the free weights. I watch Bogdan in the mirrors. It's clear he and Maks are skilled, but they're taking it easy on each other.

They stop for a break after a half an hour, and I've come to the end of my programmed workout. I get off and grab my water bottle. I'm sweaty and thirsty. When Bogdan comes over, I hand him his water.

"Good workout, *malyshka?*"

He keeps his voice low, and I duck my head. I don't know why I suddenly care if any of them hear the pet name. Maybe it's because we're in such a masculine space. As I'm looking everywhere but at his relatives, I spot the weight bag.

"Can I use the bag?"

"Sure."

I hear Bogdan's surprise. He brings over a couple boxing wraps and covers my hands and wrists. He's sweating, but he isn't winded or anything. He looks like he could go a few more rounds.

"I knew you were into boxing, but I never thought to ask if you're into wrestling or MMA."

"A little MMA. As you can see, we don't have a cage."

"So you guys just stick with the boxing?"

"Mostly. Are you into MMA or wrestling?"

"Real wrestling, not the pro shows. And yeah, I like MMA."

"You are a wealth of surprises."

I grin and shrug.

"You up for a round or two? Or are you worn out?"

"Our rounds this morning wore me out, *malyshka*. But I think I still have it in me to go a few more."

My ears are on fire. I'm pretty sure his brothers heard him, and I don't want Maks thinking we were having sex at his house. We waited until we got to mine. Well, we waited until we got to the car, then we did it again at my house.

"Shh."

Bogdan just chuckles as he signals Aleks to come over to wrap his hands. We each put on a headguard before I toe off my shoes and socks. I don't think he was ready for me to vault myself onto the raised boxing ring. He's beside me a moment later and ready to lift the rope, but I'm already sliding between the bottom and middle one. He's watching me with curiosity, and I can tell he's questioning what he's agreed to.

"Straight boxing or MMA?"

He looks at me as though I've lost my mind. I just raise my eyebrows.

"MMA. I like you under me, *malyshka*."

I flutter my eyelashes before backing into my corner. I raise my hands and take my stance. I see more surprise. Aleks rings the bell, and we move forward. I studied him through the mirror, and he knows I was watching since our eyes met a few times. But he has no way of predicting what I'll do. It's rather thrilling.

We circle each other. I make to jab with my right fist, and he shifts away. Right into my left hook. He staggers back a step and stares at me. I shrug and back off. He blocks my next two punches, but I land one in his ribs. Again, he looks shocked.

"Bogdan, are you going to spar with me or just keep taking the hits? Can't you tell I know up from down?"

"I've never hit a woman before."

I pause and tap the palm of my right hand on top of my left fingers and signal a time-out.

"Bogdan, you're not trying to beat the shit out of me. We're working out. I trust you not to go too far."

"I don't trust myself."

"Aw, sweet man."

I can't help it. I bounce onto my toes and peck his lips before I dance back away.

"Fight like you normally would, just maybe with a little less force. I know what to do, Bogdi. Trust me as much as I trust you."

He still looks doubtful, but I signal the end of the time-out, and he comes out ready to swing. He lands one to my kidneys

199

that nearly sends me to my knees, but I get him in the gut and the jaw with a combo. I retreat and come from another angle.

"MMA, right?"

"Yeah."

He's not even remotely ready for my leg sweep. He goes down with a thud, and I'm on top of him in an instant, my knees pinning his biceps to the mat. I have my legs spread wide enough that my knees are almost on his elbows, so his hands can't reach me. I lean forward and give him another kiss before I jump up. I reach out to help him, and he pulls me forward. He's quick to roll me onto my back and pin me, but I'm just as quick. I slide myself back until I can hook my leg around his neck. I squeeze my thighs together, careful not to truly choke him.

I nearly come out of my skin when he rakes his teeth against my upper thigh, then licks me. I glance to his brothers and cousins, who are way too amused. I pray they can't see what he just did, but Pasha and I lock gazes for a split second, and I know they did. I twist and squeeze, rolling him onto his back. I'm scrambling again to get on top. He reaches to get me in a headlock, but I get to my feet and back toward my corner.

"What the fuck, Tina? You could have warned me."

"That I can fight?"

"Yeah."

"My dad told me to never give away the upper hand. Here, it was you not knowing I can fight."

"Tina—"

"What, Bogdan? Are we done? Or are we going to keep going? If you just want to box and no MMA stuff, then that's fine."

I see him glance at his family. I glance in the mirror. Half of them are laughing, and the other half are stunned. I'm not sure which is dissuading him more.

"Please. I never get to box anymore. There's no one for me to spar with now that I don't live at home, and I'm not teaching women's self-defense classes."

"You taught those?"

That was Misha.

"Yeah. In college at the gym."

"Oh, shit. I saw you there. Your hair was a lot shorter then, wasn't it?"

"Yes, Niko."

Bogdan looks completely conflicted. I pull the strap from my headguard and tug it off. I pull the Velcro loose with my teeth and let both hands unravel. I walk to Bogdan and place my hands on his waist.

"*Lev*, I should have told you. I'm sorry. I wasn't trying to trick you or embarrass you. I just wanted to have a little fun in the ring. I didn't know if you'd believe me or think I just meant I took cardio kickboxing or something."

"Why'd your dad teach you that?"

"Are you angry?"

"No. Just shocked as shit. Why'd he teach you?"

I move to the side of the ring and accept Niko's help when he lifts the ropes. I wait for Bogdan to jump down beside me.

"My dad's a retired British Royal Marine, and I have two older brothers. When I was a kid, it was because I wanted to keep up with my brothers and do what they did. My freshman year of high school, a creepy guy followed me home from swim practice. I told my dad, and he decided it was time I learned to fight for real. My brothers were already gone, so we used to spend an hour together every night practicing in the basement. He wanted me to do more than just swing a punch. He wanted me to get out of any hold. He warned me that if I ever get tied up, I can expect to die. The goal has always been never to get restrained or taken to a secondary location."

I give them a pointed look. They all know that's exactly what happens when they take someone to the warehouse. I don't have to say it out loud.

"Your dad's smart. I would teach a daughter the same thing."

I look at Maks and see his appreciative smile. It puts me a little more at ease. I'm still a little worried that I embarrassed Bogdan since he isn't saying anything anymore. He's just watching me. When no one else speaks up, the guys go back to their weights, but Bogdan leads me to the office. He closes the door and snaps the blinds down. Before I know it, I'm pressed against the wall with my wrists pinned next to my head. Bogdan is devouring me, and he's hard as a pole. He rocks his dick against me, and I can feel my clit throb.

He pushes his basketball shorts down while I peel off my cycling shorts then kick them free. He lifts me, and I wrap my legs around his waist. He's inside me in one thrust, then he's slow, teasing me until I pull his hair.

"No, *malyshka*. Daddy decides now."

I do a Kegel and hold him in place. I don't do it on purpose. His words make me shiver, and I squeeze to relieve the ache. He's torturously slow as he surges into me over and over. He pulls my tank top and sports bra up and latches on to my nipple.

"Fuck, Bogdan."

"That's exactly what I'm doing. You have the sweetest tits."

He goes back to sucking on them as he presses me harder against the wall.

"Daddy, may I come?"

"No."

I whimper. I need to. I can't stop it when it happens. He pulls me away from the wall and lands a jarring slap to my ass.

Two more follow in quick succession. That only pushes me into another orgasm. He spanks me three more times.

"You're doing this on purpose."

"Yup."

He speaks between suckling one breast, then the other. I do a Kegel every time he's balls deep until I know he can't wait any longer. I feel him twitch inside me as he keeps rocking against my clit.

"I need to come, Daddy."

"Now, *malyshka*."

It's not just permission, but a command. I bury my face in the crook of his neck as I shudder. He walks us around the desk until he can sit on the chair.

"Did you do that because you really were mad at me?"

"No. I did it because you're the hottest woman I've ever met. Because if my family weren't here, I would have stripped you and wrestled you naked, then fucked you right there in the ring. Do you have any idea how much restraint it took not to put my mouth on your pussy when you straddled me? I barely restrained myself enough to only lick you when you put me in a headlock."

"Yeah, your family saw that."

"I'm sorry. I didn't realize they could see. I was way too turned on."

"You don't mind that I didn't tell you first?"

"I won't lie and say I wouldn't have appreciated a heads up before you took me to the mat in front of seven of my male relatives. But I'm so damn proud of you I wanted to show you off to them."

"Are you saying you could have fought back harder?"

"Maybe. At least when you pinned my arms. I saw stars when you put me in a headlock."

"And I didn't even squeeze as hard as I could."

"Good. I would have passed out. But also, good because it reassures me you can really defend yourself. You know I worry."

"I know you do, *moy lev*. It makes me feel good to know you're proud of me."

"I'm always proud of you, Tina. You've accomplished a lot in a pretty short life, and you're wonderful."

"I think you're wonderful, too."

"We need to go back out there."

"I know."

We end up kissing instead until we know we can't wait any longer. I pull my shorts back on, and we adjust our clothes. No one looks at us when we come out, and I'm relieved. I join the guys at the weights for another half hour before we leave.

"I'd like to request Thursday, Friday and next Monday off, Tom."

"A long weekend. Why?"

"I have plans to go away for my birthday, which is on Friday."

"Where're you going?"

"I don't know. My boyfriend is surprising me."

"Your boyfriend. You mean Bogdan Kutsenko."

The cat's out of the bag. I can guess exactly how Tom knows. Chloe told Anthony, who told Tom.

"Yeah."

"You haven't been together that long to be going away together."

You're not my father, dipshit.

"It'll be fun."

"Where's he taking you? Moscow? Thailand?"

"That's not funny."

I find nothing humorous about him joking that Bogdan's taking me to places known for sex trafficking and prostitution. But he has said nothing outright, so there's nothing for me to complain about formally. He did that on purpose. He knows what he's doing with his veiled insults.

"So where's it going to be?"

"I told you. I don't know. He's surprising me. I'm asking you at the beginning of the week. Can I have those days off?"

"No."

"Why not? I'm ahead on all my paperwork, and I don't have any field work scheduled those days."

"Because I said so."

I'm not your fucking kid.

"I have the days on the books, and I have no outstanding assignments. I'm entitled to use my days."

"And I'm entitled to deny your request."

I won't get anywhere arguing with him. I nod and head to my desk. Two can play this game. Tom isn't the only person with connections. Mine might have all been legal before meeting Bogdan, but I already have friends at the Main Office. It's how I know I'm in line for a promotion.

I turn my phone on.

Me: Hey, Max. I'm sorry I didn't respond earlier. I have a new boyfriend, and we were hanging out all weekend. My phone died, and I didn't have my charger.

That is true. At least for part of the time.

Max: Hey. No worries. A new boyfriend?

Me: Yeah. We started dating a few weeks ago.

Max: Serious?

Me: Yeah. He even wants to take me away for my bday.

Max: That's why I was texting. I wanted to see what you're doing for it. Some of us were talking about taking you out.

Max and I went to grad school together. He and I have stayed in touch with all our friends who stayed in New York, and we get together every couple of months.

Me: Thanks for the offer. My boyfriend and I have to change our plans, but I know he has something in mind.

Max: Change your plans?

Me: He has a getaway planned, but I can't get any days off.

Max: Why not? Don't you have them on the books?

Me: I have more than a month on the books, but my boss won't let me. He doesn't approve of my boyfriend.

I know I have to confess at some point.

Max: Who're you dating?

Me: Bogdan Kutsenko.

Max: And Tom said no? Idiot.

Me: Don't believe the rumors, Max.

Because they don't even touch on reality.

Max: Consider the days yours. Have fun! I want to see pics when you get back.

Me: Thanks! You're the best.

Max: Anytime!

I lock my phone and put it on my desk.

"That wasn't cool, Christina."

Damn, Max moves fast. It hasn't even been five minutes.

"What isn't?"

"Getting the borough chief to tell me to give you the days off."

"I didn't. Max texted me to ask if I had plans for my birthday. I said I did, but that they'd changed. He asked why, so I told the truth."

"And that just happened to be right after we talked."

"He texted me over the weekend, but my phone died, and I didn't have a charger with me."

"Convenient. I'm still denying your request."

I say nothing. I just stare. He can't look at me, so he turns around and storms off. I unlock my phone again.

Me: Lev I can't get the days off. We'll have to reschedule. Maybe around Thanksgiving.

Bogdan: Why not?

Me: Tom denied it. He's being a DB about it but he's still my boss. I tried pulling some strings with a friend who's the borough chief and works in the Main Office. It didn't go over well.

Bogdan: We'll figure it out. Don't worry.

Me: I'm sorry. I hope it isn't too hard to change what you planned. I'm bummed.

Bogdan: I'll sort it out and it won't be a problem.

Me: Thanks, Bogdi.

Bogdan: Anything for my malyshka.

I send him a heart-eyed emoji and a kissy face emoji. He responds with the blushing one and a kissy face one too. I sigh in frustration and then again in resignation. This blows.

I spend my morning working on reports and filing various documents with the city and county. I don't have any field visits, so I'm already bored. It makes me wonder if a promotion to the Main Office is what I really want. I'd rather be outside all day than cooped up in an office. I need fresh air and sunshine every day, even in winter. I'll brave the temperatures for as long as I can bear it just to breathe in the crispness.

I don't look up from my computer until someone's standing at the entrance to my cubicle. It makes me jump when I see Bogdan. I glance at the clock on my computer screen and realize it's noon. I didn't realize three hours had already passed.

Chapter Sixteen

Bogdan

"Are you hungry?"

"What're you doing here?"

"I came to take my girlfriend to lunch. Are you hungry?"

"Yes, but I planned to eat at my desk."

"How long do you have?"

"An hour."

"Were you going to work while you ate?"

"Part of it. Hasn't Misha or Pasha told you I usually go for a walk when I have lunch here?"

She can tell from my scowl, they haven't. I see her mouth "woops."

"I'm taking you out. Grab your sweater and purse."

The command in my voice sends a shiver skittering down her spine. She doesn't hide it. She follows my instructions, then pushes her chair in.

"I'm more than happy to skip the frozen meal I brought."

We're almost to the elevator when Tom steps out of his office. He looks at my suit coat, which has a visitor sticker I don't think Tina noticed since no one called up to her.

"It's not appropriate to have guests at work, Christina."

"She doesn't. I walked to her desk, invited her to lunch, and now we're leaving."

I take her hand and move toward the elevator.

"That's still a visitor. His sticker says so. You know that's not permitted."

"Says who?"

I can tell she internally cringes since her grip tightens. I need to stop, but I'd bet my penthouse that there isn't a policy about it at all. Tina's mentioned his wife and kids stop by, and so do other people's. I bet she's pretty much the only person who's doesn't have visitors at work.

"Your lunch isn't for another thirty minutes."

"I'll be back within sixty. I don't have a set lunchtime, only what time I usually stop."

"I'm saying your lunch isn't for another thirty minutes."

"Show me your employee handbook. I want to see where it says supervisors set policies on visitors and lunchtime."

I know I appear like an immovable object, and I am, since I'm not backing down. But I relax my stance because even if Tom gives in, Tina will pay for it later. I don't need her to send me away and let Tom win. That's a precedence I don't want, but I also don't want her to get written up. She squeezes my hand hard. It doesn't register at first because I'm still staring at Tom.

"I don't have it handy."

"Odd. I would think it would be with other protocol binders. Since you won't let Christina leave for another thirty minutes, we have time to wait."

"You don't order me to do anything, Kutsenko."

That merely gets me to raise one eyebrow.

"Leave, or I will have you escorted out."

"You'd really do that?"

My smirk says everything. It's not the obvious threat Tom issued, but Tina's boss understands. He narrows his eyes and huffs.

"You're not worth the trouble. Either of you. I'm warning you, Christina. Only this once. You're on thin ice for insubordination and defiance."

"For what? Texting a fellow city employee? For having a visitor when your family stops by at least once a month? For going to lunch without permission when I don't need it in the first place? Please, tell me, Tom. What rules have I broken? I'm sure the Main Office would love to know how exacting you are in your expectations."

Tina pulls out her phone and unlocks it. She presses on a contact I see named Max and holds up her phone. His first and last name are entered, so Tom sees them both.

"You will regret this."

Tom turns around and slams his office door. I glance around and notice the entire office watched that scene. Most people look stunned or mortified. A few appear disinterested. Those who are reacting are staring at me like they expect me to open fire in the office.

"Rough day, Christina?"

She twists to see a guy approaching. I can't read his expression, and I can't tell if he's being patronizing. He sticks out his hand to me, which I shake, but I watch him closely.

"Anthony, this is my boyfriend. Bogdan, this is Anthony. He's the new inspector for your flex building project."

"It's nice to meet you. Niko said you're very thorough."

I can tell Tina's holding her breath.

"Just keeping up with Christina's standards. I understand you're my wife's ex-boyfriend."

And there it is. The elephant in the room just stomped its foot.

"I am. Small world."

"She mentioned she ran into you the other night."

"Did she?"

"Yeah. Said it surprised her to see you."

"Oh?"

"She said you two used to stay in most nights. You preferred to be homebodies."

"That's not what I remember."

Motherfucker will hint that I used to fuck his wife regularly just so he can rub it in Tina's face. I never expected Anthony to be this way. It's a shock. But then again, he married Chloe. I know what type of man I am, and I was with her for three years.

"You must have married recently, since you aren't wearing a wedding ring. Is it still being sized?"

Tina points to his left hand. There's not even a hint of a tan line from him wearing one.

"They're not practical on the job."

Bullshit. It's not like he's working construction. He's inspecting it. He walks around with clipboards and watches other people work.

"You knew the connection when I asked you to take the case. You didn't think to mention your conflict of interest?"

"What conflict? They broke up three years ago. It's a coincidence. It's not like I'm the one involved with any of the business partners."

I bite my tongue to keep from repeating what Chloe said that night. There's nothing to be gained. Tina squeezes my hand again, but much lighter. I nod to Anthony, and we say goodbye. We're finally in the fucking elevator. I pull her in for a hug.

"Shitty day?"

"You could say that."

"Call in sick and don't go back this afternoon. I have a doctor on the payroll who'll write you a note."

"I can't do that. What illness do I mysteriously have?"

"Lovesick?"

She gazes up at me, and I wait for her to react.

"Why would I be lovesick when I have you right here with me, and I'm right where I belong?"

I lean down and kiss her as the elevator pings and the doors open.

"Food poisoning."

"That suggestion might work, since my stomach is in knots, and I'm not sure I can eat without heaving. Let me think about it."

We get into the waiting car, and I take her hand again. We ride in companionable silence as she leans her head against my shoulder. I let go to wrap my arm around her.

"What are you in the mood for, *malyshka?*"

"Surprise me, Daddy."

I wish we were going to my place or hers for a little afternoon delight. Instead, I can tell she's worrying about going back to her office after I drop her off. I lower the privacy glass and speak to the driver in Russian.

"That's Ilya." I nod toward the driver as the glass finishes rising. "Sometimes he was Laura's driver and guard when Sergei couldn't be."

"Maks trusted someone outside your immediate family?"

"We're second cousins."

"Ah."

"I trust him, too. I'd prefer my brothers or cousins, but if one of us can't be with you, then I'll make sure it's Ilya."

She nods. I bet she's wondering if I mean when we're all at the warehouse. We arrive at a busy restaurant, and her expression tells me she is confused why I picked somewhere so popular.

"I don't hide during the day, Tina. I'm not a vampire. I can show my face in public."

"I know. I just wasn't sure how you feel about being seen with me."

"Why wouldn't I want to be seen with my girlfriend?"

"It's not like that. I just mean, I don't understand yet what's safe and what isn't. I don't know if I should be nervous about it."

"Baby girl, I will not purposely put you at risk. That's the whole point of why I've been cautious. But I won't hide you away and keep you from the real world. We bring security with us, and we go about our lives."

"All right."

That seems to reassure her a lot. We've gotten coffee or gone out to lunch on the weekends, but it's always been in her quiet neighborhood in Queens, not somewhere so busy. We take our seats, and a waiter is quick to take our drink orders. I see her scanning the menu and looking like she can't choose. I want the entire left side and half the right. I don't think she knew this place existed, and it's only ten minutes from her office.

"I would offer a recommendation, but everything is good here."

I grin at her, hoping I look relaxed. It's a complete one-eighty from my fierceness in front of Tom, but I don't want her to stress while we're together. Once the waiter takes our order, I reach both hands across the table and take hers. It feels so natural, yet this is new to me.

"Tina, I want to talk to you about something my brothers and I have discussed a few times. Today just makes it seem like the right time to bring it up to you."

"What is it?"

Her shoulders round, and she sucks in a breath as though she's preparing for something horrible.

"I know you have a career plan already, and I know we've barely started dating. But Kutsenko Partners would like to hire you as the head of our construction branch. You'd oversee all our building projects. You'd be in charge of hiring the foremen, handling inspections, filing permits with the city and county, and budgeting. Right now, Niko handles a lot of the build sites, but all four of us head up different ones. It takes away from the other businesses we each run. You'd report to Maks."

"You want me to quit my job and work for you?"

"No. You'd work for Kutsenko Partners. I'm only one fourth of the business."

"And if we break up, do I get fired?"

"Definitely not. That would be stupid for our business. And we're not breaking up, Tina."

"You don't know that."

She stares at me long enough that I want to squirm.

"Tina, you know what's between us isn't typical. We are not typical. I need you to understand that I'm in this for good. I've brought you into my world because I want you to stay."

"I know I've already said the thirty days don't matter anymore. But neither of us can be sure this soon that we're going to work out."

"I am."

She sits there staring at me for a moment before she whispers, "So am I."

"Then why deny it?"

"Because I don't want to lose my heart to you, Bogdan."

"And if I want to give you mine?"

I'm so earnest that she knows I'm not joking at all.

"Then I will do all that I can to protect it and treasure it, Bogdi. And if I give you mine?"

"There's nothing I won't do for you, Tina. I will always treasure what we have."

"Can I ask you something?"

"Of course."

"Did you ever cheat on your old girlfriends?"

"Never. Why?"

"Because people who do it once...If you could do it once, it means that you don't value the commitment as much as you might think or say. If you didn't value the promises made once, why would I believe you'd value them in the future?"

"Is that how you view infidelity?"

"It's what makes me cautious about trusting anyone who has cheated."

"Did an ex-boyfriend?"

"Yes. I didn't know until I agreed to move in with him that he'd had a girlfriend the entire time. I was the side piece. He was going to move her out and move me in. I thought we loved each other so much. That he couldn't live without me. But I wasn't ready to live together, so I didn't move in. I stopped by his place one night because I'd left a sweater there. He'd foolishly given me a key. I let myself in and went to his bedroom. He was fucking his supposed ex. Turns out they reconciled, and I was still the other woman."

"That's disgusting. I'm sorry you went through that."

"Yeah, well, I know other people who've cheated before. Rarely is it only one time. Even if it is, it still happened. They let it happen."

"Tina, why would I choose someone else when I can be with you?"

"Isn't that the sixty-four-thousand-dollar question? I don't know that even cheaters enter relationships planning to cheat. Why commit to someone, then?"

"Tina, beyond never wanting to hurt you, my family would kill me. Not just because they all like you. I suppose there's honor among thieves because infidelity just doesn't happen in my family. My father and mother sacrificed so much to keep my mother safe and with my father. It would dishonor them and all they did for our family. A lot of my memories of my father have faded. I can barely see his face anymore. But I remember how much he loved my mother. I can remember how he used to come home every day. He would pick us each up, give us a loud kiss on the cheek, then he would kiss my mother like he hadn't breathed all day until he was with her. I finally think I've found what my parents had."

She's so choked up she can only nod. I watch her swallow several times, and her eyes are watering.

"What are you saying, Bogdan?"

"I'm saying that we aren't some passing fling, and I think you know that."

"You want me to come work for your company, and you're also telling me you think we're going to spend our life together."

"Yes."

"Wow."

"You don't have to decide right this minute."

"I already have. I'll take the job, and I told you before that I'm all in. I understand now what I really meant. I'm all in for good, not for however long this lasts."

"Do you believe in soulmates?"

"I didn't use to. I mean, I figure some people really find the right partner, and they have marriages that last because both people work to make it last. Other people aren't so fortunate. But I've been infatuated before. I've thought I was in love when it was really being in love with the idea of being loved. And I think I have genuinely been in love too. But never has it felt like this. Never have I felt so unquestioningly certain about anything. Not what I wanted to be when I grew up. Not picking a college. Not when picking a house or a job. It's like my mind is at rest when I think about being with you. It's simple, like being with you is just how it is. There are no maybes or what ifs. It just is."

"That's how I feel. I know you might need more time before we move beyond dating."

She shakes her head as I answer.

"Why would I, after what I just explained?"

"Because strong feelings for someone don't mean being ready for major life changes."

"Are you not ready for major life changes?"

"Do you really have to ask that? I've been making major changes since I met you."

"Fair enough."

Okay. That feels better. My heart is already racing.

"I want more than three nights a week with you, Tina."

"Are you asking me to move in with you?"

I blush, and now I've really made her curious. She leans forward and cants her head to see my face better. I know my answer and don't have to give it any thought.

"I like your place better than mine."

"You want to move in with me?"

"Maybe not officially if you aren't ready for that, but I'd rather spend every night with you than be apart."

She bites her bottom lip. She must think this is insane. She poses a question instead.

"Can we figure out a getaway together and see how that

goes?"

"Of course. But what about Tom?"

"What about him? You offered me a job."

"We haven't discussed anything like salary and benefits."

"I don't think you're going to screw me over, Bogdan. And just about anything will pay better than being a civil servant."

"You have a lot of faith in me."

"I do. But I also know you and your brothers aren't stupid. You must know what I'm worth if you're trying to poach me. It's obvious I don't need a new job, so you're going to offer me some type of incentive to get me to quit. Otherwise, why would I? So what if my boss is a douche? If that mattered, I would have quit years ago."

"That's true."

"My only concern is what will people think about me sleeping with one of my bosses?"

"There might be some raised eyebrows at first. But it won't take long for everyone to see exactly why we hired you. And it's not so I can stop by for a quickie."

I wink at her, and my smile is wicked. I might ask Ilya to drive around the block a few times before we go back into her office.

Our food arrives, so we sit back. I got a club sandwich with chips, and Tina got a French dip with fries. We each look at the other's plate, then pick up half of our food and swap. We don't even say a word. Instead, we laugh. It feels a bit like being an old married couple. Jack Sprat could eat no fat. His wife could eat no lean. Between the two, they licked the plate clean.

The service is fast considering how busy it is. But I suppose that's so they can keep turning the tables over and get more people in. We're done with our meal within thirty minutes from when we arrived. Maybe there is time for that afternoon delight.

Chapter Seventeen

Tina

I still have twenty minutes before I have to be back at work. As we walk out, I notice we're close to the public library. I nod toward the building.

"Do you have time to come in with me?"

"I'll clear my entire afternoon for you, Tina."

"I'm glad you said that."

I take him inside and make a beeline for the public computers. I log in and pull up the word processing program. It only takes one paragraph to write what I need to say. I pay the librarian then print out my letter. I save it to my cloud and log off.

"Are you sure, Tina?"

"Yup. Will you come back up with me?"

"Are you scared?"

"No. I have stuff for you to carry."

I grin and wink. As much as I thought about having a quickie in the car, I'm in a hurry to get back to work now.

Bogdan comes up with me, but he waits by the elevator. I go to Tom's office, and it shocks the shit out of me to see Tom, Jeremy, and Anthony inside. I didn't even know Jeremy was back. I can see them through the glass beside the door. What the ever-loving fuck?

I knock on the door and wait to be told to enter. I nod to them before I stick out my hand with my open letter. Tom takes it and scans it.

"Effective immediately."

"What does this mean? Other endeavors?"

"I've been offered a better position. After consideration and this morning, I've taken it."

"You're walking out today without giving two weeks' notice. I thought you were more professional than that."

I tilt my head to the side as I look at Tom, then each of the men in the room. I return my gaze to Tom. They know I know. I know they know I know. Bureaucracy is one thing, but corruption is another. New York City is infamous for it. I can tell Tom's calculating what to say to get me to stay. He doesn't want me blabbing. Not interested.

"I'm going to gather my things. I'll leave all my paperwork where it is. Enjoy the rest of your lunch, gentlemen."

I walk away without another word. I gesture for Bogdan to follow me. I grab some boxes from the copier room and hand them to him.

"I need to clear my computer of anything personal. It'll only take a minute since I don't use it for that. Too many eyes that can see. I want to wipe my passwords. Can you box up my personal stuff, please?"

"Sure. How did it go?"

"He called me unprofessional. I managed not to call him a dick. Bogdan, I'm certain they know I'm aware of their connections without me even seeing them having lunch together." I look up at him. "They're going to cause trouble."

"Let them. The only reason nothing's happened to any of them for their negligence and coercion is because I told my brothers to stay out of it for your sake."

"What do you mean, nothing's happened to any of them?"

"They're city employees. They're not that hard to get fired."

For a normal businessman, yes, they are. Firing a city employee that's been around as long as those three practically requires an act of God. But few people have the billions the Kutsenkos do, or their connections. I think of something.

"I haven't seen Jim's name listed on any site records since Niko fired him. Why is that?"

Bogdan shakes his head. He won't answer, at least not out loud. I think I know. It's worse than what he alluded to the night we talked after the Hangar Club.

"I'll tell you what I can, but not until we're in the car."

It only takes five minutes, and then we're headed to the underground parking garage. Bogdan puts the boxes on the backseat and offers to drive. I pretend to hesitate before I hand him the key fob. It's not until we're on the street that he speaks.

"Jim made unwise choices. As far as anyone knows, he stole money from us and ran away to Latin America. We were glad to see the back of him, so we haven't pursued him for our losses."

"Okay."

It's better that I know nothing else. I'm certain that matches whatever they've told anyone who's asked. I wonder where we're headed until I realize we're going into Manhattan. That surprises me until I see we're almost at his apartment. He hands off the fob to the valet, and we go up to his penthouse. Our clothes are practically off by the time we get inside. We leave a trail of them as we head to his bedroom. I almost can't ignore how disapproving Cleo looks as she follows us to the bedroom, then has the door closed in front of her furry little face.

"Get on the bed, *malyshka*. Face down."

I'm quick to follow his directions. He opens the drawer where he keeps everything he bought just for me. I hadn't cared that much our first night that he already had toys and stuff because I didn't think I would ever come back. But once I knew he'd bought things for only me, I realized how much it relieved me that I wasn't sharing anything he'd used with other women.

He slips a blind fold over my eyes before he takes each wrist and snaps handcuffs onto them. I expect him to wrap them over the crossbar on his headboard, but he doesn't. That must mean he wants to roll me over at some point. I feel him tug on the chain between the cuffs, then I find myself attached to the bed. This way, he won't have to unlock my hands to move me.

"What's your safe word, *malyshka*?"

"Olives."

I hear him moving around, but I can't tell what he's doing until I feel something cool drip between my ass cheeks. We've only done anything anal that night he told me he was going to fuck me in the ass. He did. I've done it in the past because a couple guys wanted to over the years. Bogdan is the only one I enjoyed. I feel the plug pressing against my hole. I relax as best I can before he presses it in. I'd guess it's about medium-sized.

"Your ass makes me hard just thinking about it. Looking at it makes me want to fuck you right now. But I have plans, *lapochka*. Can you tell what this is?"

He trails something between my shoulder blades after he moves my hair aside.

"A riding crop?"

The first slap lands across my ass and stings.

"Yes. This is only for pleasure. Do you understand?"

"Yes, Daddy."

"Good girl."

The crop bites into my skin, and my ass soon burns. I breathe through it, but my skin feels like it's on fire by the tenth one. I do my best not to kick my feet, but one lands in just the right place along my horizontal crack, and I can't help it.

Just when I think I can't take any more, I feel his cool fingers slide into me. I'm dripping, and I know he can see that. He starts with two, then adds a third finger. With the plug and his fingers, I feel so full. I try to grind my clit against the mattress, but his hand lands across my ass.

"Not yet."

"I'm sorry, Daddy."

He finger fucks me until I come to the edge, then he pulls back. He does this three times until I'm begging.

"Daddy, please. I need to come. I need that or a break."

"Say your safe word if that's the case, *malyshka*."

He knows I won't. I kick my feet again when he withdraws all the way. He unhooks my cuffs from the headboard but keeps them around my wrists. He rolls me over, and I feel him climb onto the bed.

"Open for me, baby girl."

I don't hesitate. I open my mouth and keep my tongue flat.

"Lick me."

I feel the tip of his cock on my lip. I swirl my tongue over the head, and I taste his precum. I draw my tongue from his balls back to the tip as slowly as I can.

"You think you can tease me?"

He presses his cock into my mouth. I feel him move to lean forward against the headboard. His cock is touching the back of my throat, and I know there's more that I can't take. I relax and breath through my nose. I swallow, and a little more slides down my throat. I hear his breath hiss. He wasn't prepared for that.

"Stroke what you can't take."

That's why he freed me. I wrap one hand around his cock and the other cups his balls. I still tease him, changing the speed and pressure. He lets me. I know he's enjoying it from how hard he's breathing. He pulls away, and I tsk in protest. I feel him get off the bed and move around near my feet. Then he's fastening a spreader bar to my ankles. He lifts my legs straight in the air until my ass is almost off the bed. He connects the handcuffs to it, so I have no way to move unless I lower my legs, which would force me to sit up.

I'm not ready for the lash to land across my still-burning ass. It's a cat-o'-nine-tails. He isn't using much force, but my ass is already sensitive. He trails the thongs along the inside of my legs, and it tickles. He draws it up over my pussy, and I squeeze my eyes shut even though I'm still blindfolded. He brings it down onto my ass with a crack that fills the otherwise silent room. He teases me over and over in between each time the thongs whip across my ass. With my legs in the air, I can't kick them. He did that on purpose. This time, when it lands, it's on my clit and netherlips rather than my ass.

"Daddy."

It's surprise and need. He's driving me crazy, and he knows it. I squeal when I feel his tongue lick me, then dip inside me. I tense my core and lift my hips toward his mouth. He chuckles and presses my hips back down.

"I decide, *malyshka*. Or did you forget who's in control?"

"I didn't forget, Daddy."

He shifts and kisses my lips before he goes back down on me. I hear a buzz before I feel the foam end of a vibrating wand slide over my belly, up my left thigh, and down my right one. It presses against my clit as Bogdan's tongue slips back inside me.

"Daddy, please. I really can't stop it. I'm going to come. Please."

"You can come, baby girl."

It only takes a few seconds more before I finally feel it. God. It feels amazing to come. But now all I want is to touch him, hold him as he fucks me. He catches me by surprise when he releases my arms from the spreader and unfastens the handcuffs. He extends the spreader until my legs are as far apart as I can go.

"Keep them up in the air."

I hear the wand turn off, then something else turn on. I'm still blindfolded, so I don't know what he plans to do next. I hear a bottle cap flick open, and I assume it's lube. I take several deep breaths as I prepare myself. He slides the anal plug out, and I hear it land in what sounds like a box. More lube drips over my ass. Then I wait. It seems like forever, but I know Bogdan is putting some on his cock. Then it's there. His cock is pressing into me.

Once the head has gotten through the tight ring of muscle, he slides a dildo in me that hits the spot he knows makes me crazy. The vibrator's extension rubs against my clit as he eases farther into me. Everything is so damn tight. I feel so fucking full. It's almost too much and yet not enough.

"Are you all right, *malyshka?*"

"Yes, Daddy."

"Hold the vibrator and move it where you need it."

I feel his shoulders press between my raised legs. Now I understand why he spread them so widely. As he brings his upper body over mine, he slides the rest of his cock in until I feel his pubic bone touch my ass. He rocks gently as he removes the blindfold from my head. I blink several times as I adjust to the daylight coming in through the window. He kisses me with a tenderness that starkly contrasts with the spanking he gave me with the crop and whip. That was trust. This is intimacy. The two things I crave most with him. The two things I've never had so much of with another guy.

"May I touch you, Daddy?"

"Please do."

His voice is strained, and I can tell he's yearning for the same thing as me. The hand that isn't holding the vibrator in place travels from his waist, up his back and around to his chest before tunneling into his hair. This kiss is everything. It doesn't stop as he helps ease my legs down over his back. He's not thrusting, just rocking. When we finally come up for air, we gaze into each other's eyes. We say so much without a single word. We're gazing at each other as we come together.

Whatever it takes, I'm making a life with this man. My parents sound like Bogdan's. I'm lucky my father retired from the military and is home with my mother. Galina wasn't that lucky. History is repeating itself. My mother lived through my father going away to war. Galina did the same. Both of them survived loving men constantly in danger. I can hardly equate what Bogdan does to combat, but I'll live with the same risk of him not coming home. But if I can have the love our parents experienced, then I will take the risk.

He eases out of me, and I watch as he gathers everything we used. He cleans them with some foamy stuff as I slide off the bed and hurry to the bathroom for a moment of privacy. He's still naked as I slip my bra and panties back on. He gives me a disapproving look, to which I smile and shrug.

"Did we come here so you could get some clothes to take to my place?"

"Is that what you want me to do?"

"Yes. And a razor and shaving cream."

"Really?"

"Yeah. I already gave you a toothbrush, but I want to see your stuff on my counter. I suppose it makes all of this feel real instead of some marvelous daydream."

"You think I'm dreamy?"

He snags me around the waist and pulls me against him. He kisses along my neck to just behind my ear. It tickles in the most erotic way.

"Very."

"What other dreams do you have, Tina?"

I lean back because I'm not sure what he means.

"In life? Or sex-wise?"

"Both."

"You know what I thought my career plan was, but that's taken a sudden detour."

"A detour takes you back to your original path. Is that what you want?"

"To ever work for Tom again? Fuck no. To work for the city? Who knows? I suppose my career has taken a turn."

"What else do you dream about?"

"Do you mean what do I fantasize about?"

I'm not ready to tell him I want to be a wife and mom. I don't know if a family is even a blip on his radar.

"I'd like to know that too."

Too? Is he hinting at whether I want a family? Let's stick to my fantasies.

"You know what one of them was. My only other one is dark. I'm not sure I want to share that."

"Is it something I could act out with you?"

"Yes."

Don't ask me anything else. But I know he's going to.

"Does it involve anyone else?"

"Once upon a time, it did. But not anymore."

"Now you have me seriously intrigued."

Do I really want to do this? He's going to think I'm totally fucked up. He tries to encourage me to open up.

"Considering how we got together, I think nothing about our sexual wants is something to hide. I have my fantasy, and it's dark as fuck. I would never ask it of you. It's that dark."

"Tell me yours. I might feel a little braver about telling mine."

Bogdan looks around and grabs his boxers. Okay. This is serious if he can't tell me naked. The man would be a nudist if he could. Not that I blame him with that body. I'm rather disappointed that he's covering up. He looks around as though he doesn't want to do this standing. He pulls back the bedcovers and waits for me to climb in. My brow furrows, but I slide in and move to the side I've slept on before. I notice for the first time that it's the one farther from the door. He's always positioned himself, so I'm on this side.

"Do you have me farther away from the door on purpose? Or do you just like that side better?"

"It's on purpose. If anyone ever came in, I could get to them without having to get past you. I'm also the first target."

He sees that bothers me, so he brings me to cuddle against him. We slide down until we're lying on our sides facing each other.

"I've had a fantasy since I first realized sex was for more than making babies." He pauses, and I nod. "I want to tie a woman up and keep her there at my mercy. I don't want to hurt her or even spank her. I just want to come and go, staying long enough to tease her or even get a blow job. I want her to get to where she's begging for me to let her go, but she's grown to depend on me for everything." He closes his eyes. "I know that's totally fucked up."

"I would do that for you."

I speak without thinking, but I know I'm not wrong. I would do it. How fucked up am I that it intrigues me?

"You don't have to say that."

"I'm not. I would really do that. You know I enjoy being restrained, and you know I like to beg. The idea of being at your mercy, that I'm wherever we are for your pleasure, those things give me pleasure."

"I don't mean for just an hour or two, Tina. I mean, for like a day or two."

"Would you let me eat and drink? Could I have a break long enough to go to the bathroom if I needed to?"

"Of course."

"Then I'd do it."

He stares at me for a long time. He's incredulous, but he finally nods.

"What's your fantasy?"

"Maybe mine isn't so fucked up after all. It's about as twisted as yours, though."

"Then I'm pretty sure I'm going to want to try it right now."

"It can't be right now. It can't be at either of our places."

"Oh, are you into voyeurism?"

"I don't mind being watched. But that isn't part of this fantasy."

"Do you enjoy watching?"

"We met at a strip club, Bogdan."

"You might like to watch strippers, but that doesn't mean you like to watch sex."

"It's not like I haven't seen porn."

"That's totally different from people live and in front of you."

"Do you?"

"Do I what? Like it, or do it?"

"Either. Both."

"It doesn't bother me if people are having sex around me, but it's not something I try to watch. Now what's your fantasy?"

"I—"

I can't do it. I'm too ashamed to say it out loud.

"Tina, I won't judge you for it."

"Yeah, but what I fantasize about is a crime in real life. A horrible crime."

"And mine isn't? Forced kidnapping and being detained against someone's will. That's pretty fucking illegal in the real world."

Oh. I hadn't thought about it being against my will.

"Can I ask you why that's your fantasy? Is it because you do that in real life, but there's nothing pleasurable about it?"

"I suppose. But that desire started before I ever did that for the bratva. It has gotten stronger over the years. I've never even hinted at it to anyone. Does the forced part make you want to reconsider?"

"Not at all. Just the opposite. I like the idea even more. It's —it's basically the second half of my fantasy."

He nods as I think he's guessing what I mean.

"Do you have a rape fantasy?"

I pull my lips between my teeth. I can't look at him as I nod. He kisses me on the forehead, and I close my eyes. He kisses my nose and my cheek.

"Do you know why you want this?"

I nod. I need a moment before I can find my voice.

"When it first started, it was because I'd seen a book on the woman's body and health. It explained everything from the top of a woman's head to the tips of her toes, inside and out. It talked about how a woman's body reacts during sex. It described the difference between consensual and forced. I was too young to understand the power dynamics and harm truly being forced causes. As I got older and got teased for my hair and freckles, it made me feel isolated when all I wanted was to be pretty like my friends. I was pretty nerdy, too. I didn't get approached much by boys, so the idea of being so desired that a guy or guys wouldn't stop when I said no intrigued me. I don't actually want to be raped. Who does? But the fantasy is to be desired that much."

"I understand. That is dark, and I don't think most people would understand. But the human mind works in common ways across the species. Most fantasies and fetishes aren't entirely unique. I'm certain neither of us has fantasies no one else ever has."

"True. But—I don't know...It seems darker that I want to have this happen to me rather than do it to someone else. Fuck. That doesn't sound any better, either."

"Tina, what we do together is consensual. If we roleplay a fantasy, then that's our business. So what if they aren't what most people would want? If it's what you want or you agree to, then I want to fulfill your fantasy."

"How would we do that? I mean, I don't have a job anymore, so it's not like I have to worry about being gone for a day or two."

"I'm still taking you away this weekend, Tina. When we get back, we can plan something."

I know my face lights up like a kid on Christmas. That sounds perfect. A vacation with Bogdan and sharing our desires. We just need to make it to Thursday.

Chapter Eighteen

Bogdan

It's all set. I have everything for our getaway planned. We talked more about it after we got to her place. I suggested making it longer since she doesn't have a job where she has to be back on a specific day. She'll start with Kutsenko Partners when she's ready. If that's in a few weeks, then we'll make it work. She said she has the savings to do that, but I would never suggest she not work and dip into those reserves.

It's Wednesday, and we're leaving a day earlier than I originally suggested, and we're going to be away for an entire week instead of four days. I haven't told her the destination, and I know she's dying to ask. I thought about the Turks and Caicos and the house Maks rented when he took Laura away for her birthday. They'd been together about as long as Tina and me. I want something different, something unique to her. I suppose I don't want her to think I copied my big brother. I considered Europe, but for this trip, I don't want to lose an entire day each way just traveling. I picked something a little closer.

"Are you going to tell me or not?"

"Nope, *malyshka*. You must be patient."

"That's not one of my finer qualities."

She playfully huffs as we arrive at the private airfield. She knows we're flying, so I don't blindfold her for this part. I watch her look around as steps descend from the plane. The pilot and flight attendant appear to greet us. Both smile and offer us their best wishes on a wonderful vacation. She looks back over her shoulder, and I know she's looking for any luggage. I grabbed a few things from her closet this morning while she was in the bathroom putting on makeup. I had to hurry because she doesn't wear much. I told her I was headed to the kitchen to make breakfast, but first, I handed a bag to Anton. He'll make sure it gets aboard the plane discreetly.

I learned from Maks's error and am bringing Anton and Pasha with us. Maks and Laura left New York alone, but a threat to her made Maks order Niko, Anton, and Aleks to fly down and join them. There have been no threats to Tina, but I'm not taking any chances. I warned her ahead of time that they were coming. I know she isn't thrilled, but it's more about having bodyguards than it being my family.

"Get comfortable, baby girl. It's a three-hour flight."

Everyone fastens their seatbelts, and we're soon taxiing then taking off. Once we've gotten to our cruising altitude, and there's nothing but clouds to watch, she leans against me. Neither of us has gotten much sleep in the past two days. We've been too busy enjoying our bubble. I think my brothers understand now how serious I am about Tina. Niko teased me about going ring shopping for her. All four of us were with Laura when she picked out her ring. It was a disaster. Maks fucked up, since he's not the most communicative of the bunch. It worked out in the end, but it was uncomfortable for a while.

My mind has wandered many times to whether I would

bring Tina with me to pick out a ring or whether I would surprise her. I think we're moving toward that. I glance down at her, and she's asleep. Her left hand is resting on my chest next to her cheek. I unfasten our seatbelts and scoop her into my arms. We're on a jet we own, and it has a bedroom in the aft. Once she's settled, I slip out to talk to my cousins.

"Are we any closer to knowing what's going on with Salvatore and the threats against Laura?" I ask as I sit next to Anton and across a table from Pasha.

"Are you certain it's Salvatore?"

Anton is the most skeptical of all of us. He's a "I'll believe it when I see it" kind of guy. It's wise to have him around.

"No. We're uncertain of anyone. Robert Simms doesn't want to be found, so he won't be. All we know is he contracted out for-hire mercenaries. We have no way to know who paid him. The man keeps his money under a mattress and uses burner flip phones. He's off the grid despite living in New York."

I have no idea how that's possible, and I'm stating what we already know.

"There was the incident at Pussycats, the attack on Maks's rooftop, and the photos. But it's gotten quieter since they got married."

Pasha's right. Maks believes Laura's childhood friend, who still has the hots for her, is behind at least part of it. Detective Juan Diaz has connections on both sides of the law since he's a police officer and his family is Colombian Cartel.

"Even if nothing else happens, Maks won't overlook what already has."

I state the obvious. Maks can't afford for anyone inside or outside of the bratva to think he's a pushover, that he'll just roll over and take it.

"They're going to that event at Gracie Manor this weekend. Hopefully, it's uneventful, but good for business."

Pasha sighs as he says what all three of us are thinking. There are a few wealthy investors who'll be there, plus a couple councilwomen who could help us get our Queens projects back on track. Salvatore's been a pain in the ass even more than usual. We know he didn't dump the bodies that were found. Someone marked them, so we know who did. But Salvatore's paying off people left and right in the Queens planners' office. We're losing men because no work means no pay. Our Russian guys will stick around no matter what. But the Americans and others won't. I can't blame them. They have families and bills.

"At least the Irish are quiet for now. Sending them the box of toes may have sent the right message."

"It didn't hurt that we burned down a warehouse, too."

I remind Anton—not that he would forget—that we did more than just interrogate the ship's crew.

"Something's going on with them. They haven't given us trouble in ages."

Anton's always the skeptic.

"We also haven't had such a large shipment of weapons in a long time. Maybe his connection in Ireland hasn't sent as much as usual. We track what goes in and out, but we don't know what's actually in the crates."

That's one of Aleks's duties. Maks oversees everything, so he doesn't have one specific business venture or crime area. Aleks doesn't really have a singular focus either since he's Maks's second-in-command as the next oldest brother. But he oversees a lot of our monitoring of rival syndicates. He's not the hacker that Sergei is, but he's good at eying cargo and appraising it, even from a distance.

"We need—"

Pasha sends me a warning look before shifting his gaze past

me. I turn to see Tina standing in the doorway to the cabin. How much did she hear? It couldn't be much since Pasha didn't stop me sooner. I go to stand with her and give her a quick peck. I keep my voice low.

"You didn't sleep long, *malyshka*."

"I guess I've already gotten used to not sleeping alone."

"Are you suggesting I join you?"

"No. I mean, I didn't intend to interrupt your conversation. It's about work, so I'll go inside."

I shake my head and take a step forward, which makes Tina take a step back. I close the door behind me.

"This is our vacation away. Nothing is pressing enough at work to pick that over being with you. If you want me to stay with you while you're asleep, I will. We were just discussing a few things that have come up recently. We weren't planning anything or talking about anything new."

"But—"

"No, *malyshka*."

I infuse some command in my voice, and I can tell she'll back down. Now I regret it. I don't want her to retreat from me.

"Baby girl, truly. It wasn't anything that important. You know about what happened at the Queens building site. There was a break in at Pussycats a while ago, just after we met. A few other inconvenient things have happened, and we were just rehashing that. We were chatting to fill the time. I don't want to think about work when I'm with you."

"All right. I know work doesn't go away just because we leave town."

"To me it does. What do you want to do? Are you hungry because I can have the attendant bring you something? If you want to sleep more, I'll stay with you."

Tina glances back at the bed before looking at the cabin door.

"I'm not a member of the mile-high club."

"Neither am I."

I see my answer shocks her. It does me too, now that I think about it. Chloe used to be on her phone most of the time, so I read or scrolled social media on mine. She was never interested in having sex aboard the jet.

"Do you want to be?"

"*Malyshka*, do you really have to ask if there's a time when I don't want to have sex with you?"

She giggles and blushes.

"I suppose not. You are a bit like the Energizer Bunny. You just keep going and going."

"Can't keep up?"

I wink at her.

"Something certainly keeps up."

She palms my cock and finds I'm already hard. I have been since I saw her sleepy expression in the doorway. We strip quickly, and I back her toward the bed until we fall onto it. We're both careful to stay quiet. My cousins must know exactly what's going on in here. I'm certain they don't think we're sleeping, but I don't want to embarrass Tina by broadcasting it.

Her hands slide over my back and cups my ass before her fingers pass over the divots at the base of my spine. I've found she likes them. One hand returns to my ass while the other squeezes between us to wrap around my dick. Damn, that feels amazing. She's watching me and knows she's driving me crazy. I tug her nipple between my teeth, and I see her press her lips together to remain silent. She's already wet when I press my fingers into her, and I feel her sigh. It's as though she's been needing this and finally gets relief. I work her and rub her clit with my thumb. Her nails dig into my ass as she gets close to coming. Her eyes plead with me, and I nod my head. She goes stiff beneath me, and her cheeks flush.

Neither of us can wait any longer. She spreads her legs wider and guides me into her pussy. I swear, entering her is almost as good as coming.

"Daddy, that feels almost as good as coming."

"I was thinking the same thing, baby girl."

This isn't a quick fuck, or even one that's about power exchange. We're making love as we move together. We're equals in this, and I revel in it. I'm a jumble of emotions: affection, lust, admiration, happiness. And dare I say it? Love. I'm falling in love with this woman. I've known it all along, and I see my feelings mirrored in her eyes. I know she almost said it that night at Maks and Laura's.

"Bogdi, I'm so close.

"Me too, Tina."

And then we're there. We're clinging to each other and kissing. We've had a lot of memorable sex before, but nothing has been like this. Ever.

We've just touched down in Miami, and I think Tina knows where we are. But she's clueless about the next leg of our trip or our final destination.

"Close your eyes, *malyshka*."

I whisper in her ear as we reach the bottom of the plane's steps. She follows my instructions, and I slip the blindfold I've used on her at my place over her eyes. I wrap my arm around her and guide her around the plane.

"A helicopter?"

"Yes, baby girl. Now bend forward."

I help her get onboard and snap her seatbelt together before doing mine. Pasha and Anton sit facing us, traveling backwards. It's noisy, so I put the headphones on Tina before putting mine on. The pilot looks back, and I give her a thumbs up.

"You're making me miss some of the best part, Bogdan."

There's a radio system built into the headphones, so we can talk to each other. I consider what she says, and I realize that's true. The view is spectacular as we fly south over the Atlantic.

"You can take off your blindfold for now."

She yanks it down without hesitation, which makes me laugh, and peers out of the window.

"We're headed south. Are we going to the Caribbean?"

"How do you know?"

"The water's to the left, Bogdan."

She playfully rolls her eyes but gives me a peck on the cheek, too.

"Yes. We're headed to the Caribbean, and that's all I'm telling you for now."

She nods and goes back to looking out of the window. She points to islands as we fly past, and she recognizes some of them. When the pilot announces we're landing in five minutes, I insist she put the blindfold back in place. She scowls but does as she's told.

"If you're a good, *malyshka*, I'll give you a surprise as soon as we get where we're going."

"Isn't all of this a surprise?"

"True."

The helicopter lands, and we wait for the blades to stop spinning before I help Tina off. I lead her ten feet, then stop. I slide one arm around her waist as the other slips off the blindfold. Spread out before us is the bow of the super yacht I booked and the sparkling water of the Caribbean. The Bahamas is in the distance. She shades her eyes as she looks around. She takes in the deck with the cabana and lounge chairs. Below us is a pool and a hot tub. The crew is weighing anchor and preparing for us to get underway.

"Bogdan, this is incredible. I never dreamed of being on a ship like this. Thank you."

The kiss she gives me doesn't last long enough because I know she's eager to explore. So am I since I've only seen photos. The chief stewardess greets us and takes us on a tour. We meet the captain and the rest of the crew before we're shown to the master cabin. Now that we're alone, she unleashes her full gratitude as she kisses me. I pick her up after she unfastens my belt and pants. For once, I'm not wearing a suit, just a button down and pants. I push the dress she's wearing up to her waist and practically rip her thong as I pull it to the side.

"Hard, Bogdan."

"Don't worry, baby girl. I'll give you whatever you want. Hold on."

"All right, Daddy. Holy fuck... Yes... Just like that. Don't stop."

"Your wish is my command, birthday girl."

"Not until Friday."

"All week, *malyshka*."

As she rides my cock, neither of us is interested in arguing over semantics.

"I'm close."

"So am I, baby girl... God, you're tight... Fuck."

As soon as I feel her pussy and thighs squeeze tighter, I don't hold back. Her back slams against the door, the rhythm an undeniable proof of what we're doing. I wrap her ponytail around my hand and tug until I can rake my teeth down her throat. We're both left breathless as I lower her to her feet. She grins at me and stands on her toes to peck my cheek.

"Bogdan, how am I going to swim if I have no bathing suit? And I can't live in the bathrobe over there for a full week."

"I wouldn't mind if you did."

"Seriously."

"I told you I would give you your first surprise since you've been a good girl."

"That wasn't it?"

She points her thumb over her shoulder and waggles her eyebrows. Her grin is infectious.

"No. That was a spontaneous surprise. This one I planned."

While we were on the tour, one of my cousins brought our bags into the cabin. I don't think she's noticed them yet. Anton and Pasha excused themselves and said they were going to sweep the ship and talk to the captain about security while we went on our tour. I look in the closet and find them on the floor. I pull out a box that's small enough to fit a book and not much more.

"What's this, Bogdi?"

"Open it. It's not your birthday gift, just a little something to start the trip."

She pulls the ribbon off and opens the lid and peels back the tissue paper. She lifts out the bikini, and her cheeks match her hair.

"This isn't a gift for me, Bogdan. This is a gift for you. I can't wear this in public. My dental floss is thicker than these strings."

It's skimpy, but not that skimpy. It'll cover all the necessary bits. Just not very well.

"You can use the robe as a coverup to go out to the cabana or the pool and hot tub."

"Then what? You really want the crew and your cousins to see my tits and ass hanging out and on display."

I don't, but my cousins are smart enough to not only avoid looking, but to keep anyone else from looking. The entire point of picking the yacht is for the privacy. I even considered requesting an entirely female crew, but I didn't think that looked too good.

"Baby girl, no one is going to watch us. The cabana will shield you, or you'll be in the water."

"And if I want to swim in the sea? I've seen those shows where people go to the Med on the private yachts. There are always crew members to watch them when they're swimming off the boat."

I knew she'd be hesitant, but she's getting really agitated. Far more than I expected.

"Tina, what's the matter?"

She looks at me and bursts into tears. Holy fucking shit.

"*Lapochka,* I didn't mean to make you cry. What's wrong? If you don't want to wear it, I brought a couple of your own bathing suits. I'm sorry."

She holds up the string bikini as tears stream down her face. This is not how I wanted our vacation to start. I take it from her and toss it on the bed and pull her into my arms.

"I want to be confident enough to wear that for you, and I probably could in here. There's no part of me you haven't seen. But that isn't easy either."

"What isn't easy? I don't understand."

"Not everyone can be a nudist as confidently as you. Your body is perfection. Not everyone's is."

"Tina, yours is."

"No, it's not. Do you have any idea how scary it was to undress in front of you once I realized just how hot you are? I wasn't feeling that confident when we went into your bedroom the first time. And now..."

"And now what?"

"And now I've met your ex-girlfriend. She's gorgeous."

"And a bitch. Have you been feeling like this since that night?"

"Not really. But the thought of being on display in that thing made me think of how beautiful she is, and how she would have no problems wearing it and rocking it. Even if she weren't perfect in it, she has the confidence to pull it off since she had the balls to come up to us."

I chuckle at her metaphor. It wouldn't surprise me if Chloe had a pair hidden all along. Brass ones at that. But I don't want to think about her. I'd gladly forget any woman in my past to keep the one I have right now as my partner in the future.

"I didn't know you felt this way. I wouldn't have guessed."

"Because I don't want anyone to know I'm insecure about stuff. That's the thing about being insecure. You make me feel incredible, Bogdan. Like I'm precious and beautiful. I got past my nervousness with you. But the idea of other people seeing me and judging me, even if they aren't, is too much for me."

"I'm sorry, *malyshka*."

"You couldn't have known. I didn't tell you. And I am flattered that you want to see me in something like that. I'm just too embarrassed for anyone else to see me. Do you have a rooftop pool at your place?"

"Yes. It's private."

"Can I save this for there?"

"Of course, baby girl. Whatever you want."

"Thank you for understanding. And I'm sorry I burst into tears. I think I'm a little more stressed out than I thought."

"I considered that, and I have a couple's massage booked for tomorrow."

"You do?"

I see the excitement back in her eyes, and I breathe easier.

"Yes. They'll come by tender around ten o'clock. We can sleep in. Then after the massage, we can have lunch. I have snorkeling planned. I didn't know if you scuba dive or not. If you can, we can do that too."

"Sleep in? And miss enjoying being on this yacht with you. Pshaw! I'm enjoying every moment I can."

"So you're happy that we came?"

"Bogdan, beyond happy. Please don't let my little freak out ruin this for you. I'm sorry."

"You didn't freak out. It was insensitive of me. I knew from grabbing them that none of your other bikinis are that revealing, and your day-to-day clothes are pretty modest."

"Yeah, but my clubbing clothes aren't. I can see why you think I might be okay with it."

"They're not as wild as some women. I should have thought about this better."

"Fear not, Daddy. Your gift to yourself won't go unused. It'll just have to wait seven days."

She grins and flicks her tongue at the corner of her top lip. She darts around me and gets to the closet as I wrap my hands around her waist and lift her off her feet.

"Uh-uh, *malyshka*. Consider this Santa's workshop, so it's off limits. You're not discovering your presents before I'm ready to give them to you."

I set her down and pull out the duffle bag with her clothes in it.

"You packed more than just my toothbrush."

She lifts out clothes and puts them on the bed until she gets to an aquamarine bikini. There's no string to the bottoms, and the triangles will cover way more than the one I picked. If this is what she's confident in and will leave the cabin in, then it's perfect.

"Come on, Daddy. Hurry. You're wasting daylight."

Chapter Nineteen

Tina

Other than my little breakdown when we first arrived, the past two days have been beyond perfect. Once we changed, we headed out to the deck and laid in the sun for a while before pulling the cabana up. We made out like we did the night we went to the movies. Nothing more than kissing and heavy petting since the sun was still up and anyone could see us, but it was fun. I convinced Bogdan that if the captain said it was fine for me to dive from the side, that he shouldn't look so panicked.

The drop from the sundeck to the water was about ten feet, so not that different from the diving boards I used to compete on. It's been years since I tried anything, but I've still got it. Two rotations into a swan dive with only a little splash. I came back up to the surface to find Bogdan looking down at me in awe. A moment later, he was over the side and tucked into a cannonball. He's not heavyset, but his bulk is dense. It was like

249

being hit by a tsunami. We both came up spluttering and laughing.

We had a beautiful dinner on deck with white glove service before going into the main salon. Bogdan arranged for someone to turn on a mix of slow songs, and we danced while we watched the sun set. We were swaying to the music long enough to see the stars come out. Once it was dark, I reconsidered the bikini he got me. I wore it out to the hot tub, and he helped me get in and out with the robe on. I sank under the bubbles the moment it came off.

I'm lying under the cabana now, remembering what we did in that hot tub.

"This has been a fantasy for as long as I can remember. Sex in a hot tub or in the ocean. Even a pool. Any body of water. The tub's been good enough until now, but you're fulfilling a fantasy I didn't even think to tell you the other night."

"Then we share the same one, malyshka. Even though my pool's heated, it's been too chilly to take you up there. I've been thinking about making love to you in it since the night we met."

"If it's heated and we take robes with us, then we should be fine. We're christening your pool."

"Baby girl, I can read your thoughts. I know you just thought about whether I've done that with anyone else. I haven't. Despite being in a few long-term relationships, I haven't done everything a couple can. I could wonder the same thing."

"Most of the guys I've dated have been very vanilla compared to you."

"What am I?"

"A Neapolitan."

"Why? Because I have a sweet side?"

"You do. You can joke that you don't, but between your mellow side and your dark side is a sweet man who is doing

everything he can to make this a vacation I can never forget. Thank you, Bogdan. I—I'm so lucky to have you in my life."

I nearly told him I love him. It's been on the tip of my tongue for days, but I really thought I was about to blurt it out last night. Then I caught myself. I think he wanted me to say it, that he was waiting to hear it. Maybe he's nervous too. If I had said it, maybe he would have reciprocated. What if he hadn't? It would be horrible. I don't want to risk ruining the trip.

"Tina? You awake?"

"Yes, Bogdi. I didn't fall asleep, but I was dozing. Is it time to get ready for dinner?"

"Yes. We're going ashore tonight. I have something special planned."

"You mean making love in the hot tub, a couple's massage that ended with us making love in the shower, two delicious dinners on deck, breakfast in bed twice, and dancing in moonlight two nights in a row hasn't been special?"

"Another special thing planned. How's that?"

"You're spoiling me."

"Today's your birthday."

"And you gave me a gift at breakfast and at lunch, *moy lev.*"

I woke up to a set of high-quality sketching pencils and a pad. Bogdan saw a sketch book on my desk one time, so he must have remembered that I enjoy drawing building designs. At lunch, he presented me with a tube wrapped in ribbon. When I popped off the lid, replicas of the blueprints for the Empire State Building and Sears Tower slid out. I can only imagine what he has planned for tonight.

"That was just the morning and afternoon. We still have tonight."

We return to our cabin, and I spy a garment bag hanging on the back of the closet door. It wasn't there when we left for lunch. I look at Bogdan, and he nods. I unzip the bag and instantly see a tuxedo. In front of it is a gorgeous evening gown. It's emerald-green with a fitted bodice that flairs out to a mermaid hem. It has only a single strap and a plunging v between the scalloped neckline. As I take it out, I realize it's backless to where my shoulder blades will be. It's the most gorgeous piece of clothing I've ever seen in person.

"Try it on."

"Not until after I shower. I'm not getting sunblock on that."

I spin on my heel and toss my robe and bikini on the bed. Bogdan is behind me as I turn on the water. We step under the showerhead, and I wet my hair, then lather shampoo into it. I don't think we've taken a shower together without having sex. There's a first time for everything.

"Later, Bogdan. This is a real quickie. I want to try on that gown. I'm so excited."

I'm rinsing out the shampoo as I talk. He follows suit as he answers.

"You like it?"

"Yes. And I will show you how much later tonight. Right now, I just want to get clean, get my hair dry, and put on that gown."

"I have something to confess."

"What?"

"On Monday, when you called Kelsey, you put your phone down before it locked. When you went into the kitchen, I took a picture of her number. When I stepped onto the balcony to make a call while you played with Cleo, it wasn't work. I called Kelsey to ask about your dress size. I didn't want to guess and get it wrong."

"Bogdan, you put so much thought into everything. You make me feel so special."

"You are special, Tina. You deserve someone who'll remind you of that every day. I want to be that someone."

I've just finished washing myself, so I put down the bar of soap and rest my hands on his chest. He put his bar down next to mine. We opened another one after our second shower together. We realized we were going to be late to a meal again because we'd taken our time having sex, then had to share the bar to get cleaned up.

"I can easily guess what people think about you, whether it's just by looking at you or by the rumors. I know some of it is true. I know a lot of it is worse than what most people can guess. But the man you are with me is considerate, gentle, thoughtful, and caring. Even when we're being rough, you're still always careful with me. I know I'm safe with you. We met in an unusual way, and nothing about this relationship so far has been conventional. But it is, to an extent, predictable. I know you will always treat me well, and you put me first whenever you can. I didn't realize how important it was to me to rely on a partner until I met you. I realized that I've never let myself truly depend on anyone. People have disappointed me enough times to not trust many to be there or do the things I need. You're the only one."

Bogdan turns off the showerhead and grabs a towel. He dries me off before drying himself off. He hasn't said anything yet, and I'm feeling a little uncomfortable. He helps me into a robe before putting one on. We lace our fingers together as we step onto the cabin's balcony. He turns me to face him, so the sun isn't in our eyes. There's an island in the background, and the water is crystal clear. Everything on the ship is polished to gleaming. It matches the sparkles from the sunlight hitting the water. It's the most idyllic scene I've ever witnessed in real life.

"Tina, I love you."

"I love you, Bogdan."

He cups my face, and I do the same to him as we kiss. Finally. It feels like such a relief to speak my feelings aloud. It sure as shit feels amazing to know he feels the same way. One of his hands slips down to my throat. There's no pressure there, but it still feels sexy as all get out. His other arm goes beneath my backside, and he lifts me off my feet and twirls me around before setting me back down.

"I didn't want to say it while we were still in the shower. It didn't seem right to say something so serious there. I was going to wait until tonight, but I couldn't. I knew if I didn't decide to say it now, that I would blurt it out at any moment."

"I felt the same way. I've nearly said it more than once."

"I know, *malyshka*. I think I was hoping you would, so it would be easier for me to admit it, too."

"And I didn't want to because I wasn't sure if I was the only one feeling it. I'm glad one of us is brave."

"You're right that we have done nothing the conventional way. I haven't even met your parents, but I want to keep moving forward with our relationship. I don't want to go back and forth between two places. I don't want to spend any nights apart when we don't have to. I want to have dinner with you every night and climb into bed beside you, so I can wake up to you every morning. You know I like your place better, but if that feels like too much, like you don't have a way out if you need it, then move in with me and keep your place."

"Honestly, I hate admitting it, but I don't really enjoy going to your place. Not after meeting her. Everything in your place, everything we do there, you've already done with someone else."

"And your place? I feel the same, but I still like it better."

"I've never lived with someone, Bogdan. Not in that house or anywhere. Only my family and my college roommates. And why do you think that, as foolishly risky as it was, I went to your place instead of inviting you to mine? I didn't want to wake up to someone in my house. I wanted to slip away and go back to the privacy of my space. I've only had a few guys over. Usually, I've gone places with them or to their apartments or houses."

"Would you share your house with me? Or would you rather start somewhere fresh together?"

"I like my place, but Queens doesn't seem practical since you're in Manhattan most of the time."

"But Laura and Maks are spending more time there, and I think eventually, they'll only use their penthouse if they have to come into Manhattan for something. My mom and your parents are in Queens. We could find somewhere else there."

"That's a big step. There are logistics to figure out."

"Keep your house. Rent it or not. That's your choice. You can always have it if you feel you need to leave."

"I can't just live off of you."

I see something spark in his eyes, and it makes me wonder if his intentions go further than just cohabitating.

"Tina, I am a very wealthy man. It's unlikely anyone I could date will earn what I do. Incomes will always be unbalanced. You will not be living off me. You make it sound like you're taking advantage of me, or that you're lazy and won't do anything to contribute. Even if I paid for every single thing in our home, which I would gladly do, you are not the type to sit and be served. Are you worried about losing your independence and having to rely on me?"

I shake my head.

"I just told you. I rely on you in a way I don't do with anyone else. And I don't fear losing my independence. You've suggested I keep my house. Fine. Maybe I will. I don't know. But I'm not worried that I won't have anywhere to go if we don't work out, or that I'll have to ask you for things. I have a job, after all. I work for these really rich guys who are going to pay me exceptionally well."

I wink at him.

"Is it too soon, *lapochka*?"

"No. I mean, pretty much everyone I know would say it is. But they aren't us, and they aren't in this relationship with us. Can we table the worries that we're not doing this the way most people would? Can we stop worrying about whether other people will think we're doing this wrong?"

"Yes. As long as we're comfortable with whatever happens, then I don't give a fuck about anyone else's opinions."

"Good. The only thing I ask is that before you move in or we find a place together, I want you to meet my parents. It's more of a courtesy to them than anything else."

"I'd like that."

A knock at the cabin door makes us look inside.

"Bogdan. Christina. The tender is here."

It's Anton. I haven't finished getting ready. My hair is still wet. I hurry to put it in an updo, so my damp strands don't ruin the gown. It only takes me five minutes to do that and put on my makeup. Bogdan is in his tux by the time I need him to zip up my dress.

"You are too dashing for anyone's own good."

"You look stunning, Tina."

We look at ourselves in the mirror as I stand in front of him. We look good together. My red hair and brown eyes against his dark brown hair and light blue eyes are a remarkable contrast. I've never felt so pretty as I do right now. Each time I think I feel my best, Bogdan tops it.

We hurry out to the tender. The crew has blankets, since the air is crisp once we move toward the island. They also keep the spray off our formal wear. It only takes five minutes, then we're inching toward a private dock. The sand looks like the finest grains of sugar and feels just about as soft. I don't put my strappy heels on until we reach a tiled patio. I look around, unsure of where we are. It's a bungalow with a table set for two.

The chairs are next to each other, so we can both look out to sea. There are a couple lights on inside, but no one is in sight. Even Pasha and Anton, who came ashore with us, have disappeared. The tender is already heading back to the ship.

Bogdan pulls out my chair and eases it forward as I sit. He takes my hand and entwines his fingers through mine once he's sitting next to me. He kisses my knuckles before resting our hands on his thigh. We sit in pleasant silence for a few minutes before a man dressed as a chef appears. He explains tonight's menu with a lilting accent that makes everything sound twice as good. An assistant wheels out a trolley with salads and appetizers ready to serve while the chef sets up at an outside grill. We watch as he prepares our entrees.

After our main course is served, the chef and his assistant return to wherever they'd been before they came onto the patio. I sip my wine as I watch my boyfriend. The candlelight from the table flickers across his face now that the sun has set. How'd I get so damn lucky?

"I have one last present for you, Tina."

I smile as he hands me an oblong box that's clearly for a necklace or bracelet. I unwrap it and glance up at him before I open it. It takes my breath away. There are two necklaces in the box. One with a thin chain, and the other with a thicker one. One for a woman, and one for a man. On both of them hangs a lion. I trace my finger over the fine craftmanship. The filigree is astonishing. There are so many fine details to each. But what stands out to me is that on the daintier chain hangs a male lion, and on the thicker chain hangs a lioness.

"Turn them over, baby girl."

Bogdan's voice is soft and reverent as his hand rests against the base of my neck, his thumb stroking my shoulder.

There's something written in Cyrillic on both of them, but I can read what's beneath it. The necklace that must be for me, which has a lion with a full mane, says *my love, moy lev*. The necklace that must be for Bogdan says *my love, my malyshka*.

"*Ya lyublyu tebya.* I love you."

I turn my head, and he snares my mouth. As we kiss, my fingers continue to trace the pendants as my other hand cups his jaw. When we finally need to breathe, our foreheads rest together.

"*Tha gaol agam ort.*"

"What does that mean?"

"I only know a few Gaelic phrases here and there, but I know that one. It means I love you. Will you put my necklace on me, please?"

"Gladly, *malyshka*."

"I shall endeavor to make you roar tonight, *moy lev*."

We chuckle as he lifts the necklace from the box and places it around my neck. I keep running my fingers over the ornately crafted pendant. I look at the one still in the box. Bogdan wears a watch, and that's it for jewelry. I've seen where he sets his watch in his room, and there are no other pieces. The chain is long and sturdy enough for me to lower it over his head without unclasping it.

"You don't wear jewelry, Bogdi."

"I know. But I want this close to my heart."

"Will anyone comment that it's a lioness if they see it?"

"Let them. I'm proud to wear a reminder of you wherever I go."

"This means so much to me, Bogdan. I don't even know what to say other than thank you."

He helps me out of my seat and leads me to a pergola. As he wraps his arms around me, a firework explodes in the sky. It's a heart. More erupt like starbursts, and I can't help but ooh and ahh. I love fireworks, and he knows it. The final one is an enormous interlocking B and T. They share the same vertical line, and the horizontal line on the T passing through the top loop of the B. We are one.

"Can we stay here forever?"

"Yes. It's a private island I bought right out of college because I could. I was already in my current position, so I earned more than any recent college graduate I knew, except for Niko, who finished a year before me. I've only been here three times. And you are way better company than my brothers and cousins."

"Are you serious?"

"Yes, baby girl. We can come here whenever you want. If you want to have a girls' trip and bring your friends here, you can. We can arrange a temporary staff whenever we need it."

I've never met anyone who owns a private island. I've never been on one before either. I assumed there was a town somewhere past the bungalow. Bogdan takes me for a tour of the house, which is far larger than it looks from the back. Our final stop is the master suite. Freshly baked cookies sit on a plate in the center of the bed. Some girls might like rose petals. This is way better to me. I snag one as he unzips me. He eats one while I undo his bowtie and unbutton his shirt.

The rest of the night is pure bliss. We leave the doors open to the veranda and pull the mosquito netting around the bed. We don't fall asleep until the sky is lightening to a soft, deep blue, and the stars are fading. Would that life were always this peaceful.

Chapter Twenty

Tina

Bogdan and I pull into my parents' driveway the night we return from our vacation. I called my parents yesterday and asked if we could come over for dinner. I want them to meet Bogdan before we live together. I know that's going to go over like a lead balloon, since I've only mentioned dating someone a few times since Bogdan and I met. I've been careful about what I say, but now they'll either guess, or I'll be evasive. Neither appeals to me, but I can't think of any other way.

"*Malyshka*, it will go well. Don't worry."

"I hope so."

He kisses my cheek before I open the front door. I can hear my brothers, and I almost turn around. I didn't know they would be here. If they are, that means their wives and kids, too. I wanted to ease Bogdan into the family, not inundate him with names and faces.

"It sounds like your whole family is here."

"They are. I'm sorry."

"Don't apologize. I want to meet them. You've known my entire family since the very beginning. It'll be good that I know yours, too."

I'm not so certain, but I nod and plaster a smile on my face. "Mom? Da?"

I can hear everyone is in the kitchen, so I lead Bogdan toward the organized chaos.

"Auntie Christina!

My five-year-old niece slams into me and would have knocked me backward if Bogdan hadn't caught me. His hands are at my waist, but he drops them quickly. I look up to find my entire family staring at us. I look down at my niece again and realize she's a younger version of me. I looked just like her as a child. I think it's jarring for everyone to see what my new boyfriend and I would look like if we had a family together. *When not if.*

"Hi, Therese. I've missed you."

I pick her up and slide her to my hip as she kisses my cheek. I wipe a smudge of something that looks suspiciously like my mom's chocolate mousse from the corner of her mouth.

"Who's that, Auntie?"

"Everyone, this is my boyfriend, Bogdan Kutsenko." I twist to see Bogdan. "Bogdan, this is my family. My mom, Catriona, and my da, Liam."

My parents step forward, and Bogdan stands next to me. He extends his arm to shake my mother's, then my father's, hand.

"Mr. and Mrs. MacNally, thank you for having me over. I've been eager to meet you."

"Welcome to our home, Bogdan."

My mother speaks first. Her Scots accent flavors every

word. My father's deeper voice sounds like it could belong to a voiceover actor.

"Welcome, Bogdan."

"Bogdan, these are my brothers, Daniel and Tristan." I point to each. "And this is Danny's wife, Susie, and Tristan's wife, Mary. The three at the table are Danny and Susie's. Alice, Timothy, and Steven. This little monkey is Tristan and Mary's oldest, Therese. Somewhere probably sleeping is their six-month-old Saoirse."

"Good evening." Bogdan shakes the adults' hands and waves to the kids. I put Therese down, so she can go back to coloring with her cousins. I offer Bogdan a drink, and he asks for a soda. There's wine already open, and my dad and Danny are holding beer bottles. I appreciate that he's trying to make a good impression.

"What do you do, Bogdan?"

I hold my breath at Tristan's question.

"My brothers and I own a real estate development company, and we're venture capitalists. We own a few small businesses too."

"Bogdan grew up in Queens. His mom lives like fifteen minutes from me, and his oldest brother and sister-in-law are about ten minutes from my place."

"You grew up in Queens? You don't sound like it."

I glare at Danny. Bogdan's hand rests at the small of my back for a heartbeat before he withdraws it.

"I was born in Moscow, but we moved here when I was eleven. I suppose I'll never lose all of my accent, but I'm an American now."

"We didn't move here until we were in our mid-twenties, after Liam got out of the military."

I'm looking up at Bogdan and see something flash in his gaze. I realize he's thinking about his dad and how he didn't come home from war. My dad doesn't realize it when he speaks next, but he pours salt in the wound.

"What do your parents do?"

"My mother is a widow. She's a pharmacist. My father died in the Second Chechen War, a year before my three older brothers, mother, and I moved here."

"I'm sorry for your loss."

It's my dad's turn to have something flash in his eyes. I recognize the sympathy he must feel, since he lost friends while in combat.

"Do you watch football?"

Danny points to the television in the living room.

"Yes. I played American football and real football in high school."

My dad laughs, and I relax. The men move into the living room. It has nothing to do with gender and everything to do with giving my mother a chance to riddle me with questions. My sisters-in-law conveniently decide to watch their children.

"What do you need help with, Mom?"

"The roast needs to come out of the oven in two minutes. In the meantime, can you make this salad?"

"Sure."

"Where'd you meet?"

My mom keeps her voice low, but here comes the inquisition. I shouldn't be so snarky. It's fair that they want to know these things. I didn't tell them about Bogdan like he talked to Galina about me.

"I was out with a friend, and we started talking. We hit it off, so he asked me out. Turns out I was the inspector for one of their Bronx projects. We didn't know that until I went to his build site, and we recognized each other. We've been pretty inseparable ever since. He has to travel sometimes for work, so there was a week when he was away. There've been a few days here and there since, but otherwise, we're together."

"Seems serious."

"It is, Mom. Really serious."

"Like marriage serious?"

"Probably. It's living together serious right now."

"What?"

My mom freezes and glances toward the living room. I'm warming my mom up, so maybe she can prepare my dad. I haven't brought a guy home to meet my parents since I was in grad school. The last few boyfriends didn't last long enough to bother.

"Yeah. Bogdan has a beautiful penthouse in Manhattan, but he likes my place better. We don't know exactly when it'll be. We haven't ordered a moving company or anything, but it'll be soon. At the very least, he's going to move in, even if he doesn't bring all of his stuff right away."

"That vacation must have been pretty incredible."

"It was. But we were both thinking about living together even before then. It's just neither of us spoke up because we were sorta worried we weren't doing things the right way."

"The right way?"

"Yeah. Most couples don't move as fast as we are. We were both a little stuck thinking that we should do it the conventional way. Then we realized we'll never be conventional. Mom, he is so completely different from any other guy I know. Everything about being with him is like coming home or putting on my favorite sweatshirt. It just makes me want to sigh with relief when I'm with him."

I have my back to my mom while I work on the salad. I turn around to look at her.

"Tina! Watch out!"

"Ow."

I didn't realize my mom was also turning toward me, but she has a pot of boiling water in her hands. My arm grazes the scalding metal. Bogdan was the one to warn me, and he is at my side before I see him coming. He guides me to the sink and turns on the cold water. He sticks his finger under the faucet, then moves my arm under it.

"Could we have some ice, please?"

Bogdan's looking at my arm while he asks anyone to help. I notice my mom hovering, like she wants to step in. I prefer Bogdan, but I feel bad for my mom since she's the one who's always tended my wounds or injuries. Susie hands Bogdan an ice pack. He turns off the water and snags a kitchen towel. He dabs at my wet arm before wrapping the towel around the icepack and laying it on the burn.

"*Malyshka*, are you all right?"

"It hurts, but not as badly as when it happened. Thanks, *moy lev*."

Neither of us notices how my family watches us, hears our terms of endearment, even if they don't understand them. I turn toward everyone, and Bogdan wraps his arm around me to help keep the ice pack in place. I'm leaning against his side.

"Are you okay, Christina?"

"Yes, Da. It hurts, but it isn't too bad. I heard Bogdan in time to pull away. I just grazed my arm against the pot rather than pressing it."

"I thought you were watching the game."

Danny takes a swig of beer.

"I was. But I was watching Tina, too. I'm enjoying seeing her with all of you. And I admit, I'm a walking stomach. I was curious about dinner."

I know I can't make a move without Bogdan noticing. He's aware of everything that goes on around him. And I'm grateful for it since he just saved me from burning myself badly. The oven timer goes off. I put the icepack down on the island and reach for the oven mitts. Bogdan takes them from me and slips them on before opening the oven. He withdraws the pan and places it on the trivets my mom hurries to set out next to the stove. He puts the mitts where he got them, puts his arm around me, and places the icepack back on my arm. He kisses the side of my head before we both notice the shocked expressions on everyone's face.

"I was closest."

That's all Bogdan says to explain, but that doesn't seem to register.

"Thanks, Bogdan. My arm's feeling better. Can you look?"

The burn is on the outside of my forearm and difficult for me to see. He pulls back the ice and raises my arm gently.

"It might blister and will probably leave a small scar, but it isn't serious. Do you have any burn ointment to put on it? That should take away the last of the pain."

"It feels better already."

"Are you sure, *malyshka*?"

"Yes. Thanks for taking care of me.

"Always."

He whispers his final word, but everyone in the kitchen hears. I look straight at my dad, waiting to see his reaction. He's watching us like a hawk, but when our eyes meet, he nods. Thank heavens. I just got his blessing. He's never been over the top protective. Just the right amount of protective. But I understand living with a guy is a huge step, and it's one that might make any parent worry. I'm glad he approves so far. Maybe he won't get too upset when he finds out.

All the adults carry something to the table. There are twelve of us for dinner, so my mom has a children's table set up in the dining room. The eight adults find our seats. My brothers and I have our usual spots, and our partners pick chairs beside us. Bogdan pulls out mine, and I'm certain my brothers and sisters-in-law notice. My sisters-in-law playfully glare at my brothers, and I smirk at them as I sit.

The meal progresses well, and when my mom stands to get dessert, Bogdan rises too. He offers to help, so they go into the kitchen.

"Eager to impress."

"No, Danny. His parents taught him to stand whenever a woman gets up. He's American now, but he spent his early years in Europe. Since he was up, he offered to help."

"You were awfully lovey-dovey earlier."

"Because he felt badly that I got hurt, Alice? He's my boyfriend. Shouldn't he care?"

"Care or coddle? You've never needed anyone to take care of you, *Christina*."

Danny stresses my full name since I've always insisted that people call me that.

"It's nice to be taken care of sometimes. He knows I can do things for myself, but he's also considerate. It's nice to not have to do everything by myself. And to Bogdan, I'm Tina. I like it."

"After all these years, now it's Tina?"

"Not to you, Tristan."

"So only he gets to call you that?"

Tristan won't let it go.

"Yeah. I prefer it."

My mom and Bogdan return with strawberry shortcake and a bowl of whipped cream. My mom points to where Bogdan should put it before she puts down the bowl she's carrying. It's already sliced, so Bogdan plates pieces. He hands the first to my mom, then one to each of my sisters-in-law. He hands the fourth plate to me. After that, he serves my father and brothers before putting a slice in front of him. It's clear he prioritizes my mother and father while ensuring ladies first. When my mom hands him the bowl of whipped cream, he takes a dollop, then passes it to Tristan, knowing I don't like it. He doesn't reach across me, but my dad narrows his eyes.

"Did you want some?"

He must have seen my dad's expression.

"No thanks. You know I don't like it."

Dessert feels like it drags compared to the rest of the meal. It's finally over, and my sisters-in-law offer to clear the table. The rest of us go to the living room, and Therese crawls onto my lap again.

"You sound different. Why?"

Therese is looking at Bogdan, who smiles at her.

"I was born a long way away. All the way across the Atlantic Ocean in Russia. I was eleven when I moved to America. I learned English here, but I still speak Russian with my family. I have an accent to you. Did you know that you have an accent to me?"

"I do?"

"Yup. You don't sound like me, so to me, it sounds different from what I'm used to."

"Wow. Dad? Did you know I have an accent?"

"Only to me. You sound just right to everyone here."

Bogdan's quick to correct Therese before my niece runs around proclaiming it. He doesn't want to offend anyone.

"Grandda and Grandma have accents, too."

"They do. I think it's interesting how people sound different when they come from different countries. When I was little and just moved here, I liked to guess where people were from by how they talked."

"Cool. My grandda and grandma are from Scotland. Is that close to Russia?"

"Sort of. Scotland and Russia are closer to each other than they are to America. But they're pretty different."

"Therese, what did you learn in school today?"

If I don't distract her, Therese will single-handedly lead the inquisition.

"I learned how to skip count. Two, four, six, eight."

"Who do we appreciate?"

I cut in and tickle her before blowing a raspberry on her neck.

"That tickles, Auntie."

"Good."

She settles against me and listens as the adults talk.

"You mentioned having older brothers."

My dad seems to relax as he watches Bogdan with my niece. I want my brothers to like Bogdan, but their opinion doesn't matter as much to me as my parents'.

"Yes. I'm the baby of the family. Maksim is the oldest, then Aleksei, Nikolai, and me."

"Are you close in age?"

"Very. A year apart. My parents were eager to start a family, and it seemed like the right time. Do you have family in America, too?"

"Just the kids. Everyone else is still in Scotland. I met an American on deployment who offered me a job when I finished my time in the Royal Marines. It was too good to turn down."

"Oh?"

"Yes. I'm a national security contractor. I travel overseas a lot."

And then there's that. Bogdan's leg is against mine, and I feel him tense. It's not that I purposely kept it from him. I honestly just didn't think to tell him. Now my dad's studying him even more closely. Bogdan's expression is impassive. He won't reveal a single emotion or thought unless he wants to. My dad can tell. They're the same that way.

Bogdan relaxes, but I'm still tense. He takes my hand and

rubs his thumb over the back. It's subtle, and no one else notices, except for my dad. Bogdan seems to relax as the conversation carries on and moves away from him explaining himself. Therese is asleep on my lap by the time everyone is ready to head home. I struggle to stand and lift her, so Bogdan scoops her up. Therese opens her eyes for a moment before burrowing her head against the crook of his neck and falling back to sleep. I help put her coat on before Bogdan hands her off to Tristan. My brothers mellow when they see how careful and gentle he is with Therese. Finally.

Bogdan and I hang back after saying goodbye to everyone else. I'm certain my parents have something to say. I'm not wrong. The moment the door closes, my dad turns to Bogdan.

"I know who the Kutsenkos are. I know what you do, legal and illegal. Do not underestimate what I will do to protect my little girl. It's obvious you love Christina, but I will leave no trace of you if you hurt her. I'm trusting you with her. Keep her safe because I know you won't be able to keep her out of your bratva life."

"Dad!"

"Tina, he's right. I knew you were aware of who I am as soon as you saw me, even before you heard my name."

"What? How?"

"I work in national security, Christina. My work isn't with syndicates, but I'm aware. You said your father died fighting the Chechens."

"He was conscripted."

"By the Russian army?"

"No."

Bogdan and my dad stare at each other before my dad nods. "Former KGB?"

"Yes. Conscripted there too."

"Did having four children in four years work?"

"Yes."

Bogdan is holding my hand as he and my dad go back and forth with their veiled comments. I understand what they both mean, but it keeps Bogdan from having to say too much while appeasing my father.

"Your brothers and you once you got here?"

He's hinting at the Kutsenko brothers being forced into the bratva without making Bogdan admit it.

"Survived."

"I know Maksim's position."

Bogdan's gaze hardens.

"I also know Donovan O'Rourke. The man talked too much over a pint a few weeks ago at the Gaelic Society's Braemar Games watch-party. He's the only Irishman betting on the Highland Games. I've known him for years, and he knows who I am. He assumes we're more alike than we are, so he talks. He tried to hire me for some private activities, but I turned him down. I like my security clearance and job too much. But he mentioned a bratva member was dating a redhead. Keep Christina safe."

I listen to everything my dad reveals, and I'm speechless. I don't know who this Donovan O'Rourke is, but by his name and how my dad's talking, he must be Irish mob. I look up at Bogdan, who's looking at me. He pulls me into his embrace, and I sink against him. This is the most scared I've been yet since dating him.

"I will, Mr. MacNally. I love Tina. I can't change who I am, what I've done, and what I will have to do in the future. But I will always make Tina's safety a priority. She's everything to me."

"I know. It's obvious. That's why I'm warning you. And it's Liam, Bogdan."

"Thank you."

"Da, it's late. I'm exhausted, and it's been a long day with the travel. We're headed home now."

"I love you, lass."

"I love you, Da." I hug my dad, then my mom. "I love you, Mom."

"I love you, too." My mom turns to Bogdan and hugs him. "It's Catriona. There's no point in being formal when we're family."

I stare at my mom and swallow back tears. I hug her again.

"Thank you, Mom."

I whisper to her, and she kisses my cheek. Bogdan and I get into the car that's waiting for us.

"Except for you getting hurt, that went well."

"What my dad said didn't freak you out?"

"Tina, like I said, I knew he figured out who I was as soon as I arrived. I would have wondered what's wrong with him as a father if he hadn't said what he did. I'm glad he spoke up. Now I know where I stand."

"If you say so. I enjoy knowing where you're going to lie from now on."

"In our bed, beside you. Don't you doubt that, *malyshka.*"

Chapter Twenty-One

Bogdan

We've been back from our getaway for a month, and it's been one fire to put out after another. Tina started with Kutsenko Partners three days after we got home, and she hasn't been done with work until nearly nine o'clock each night. She decided she should go through every record Jim kept, and she found discrepancies that will cost us several thousand dollars if our client discovers them. She's been working with Anatolii to rectify everything, but it's meant stripping down an entire section of the second floor and starting over again.

Turns out, Jim intercepted an order and sold it to Salvatore. With what Salvatore paid him, he bought shit quality steel trusses and drywall, then made off with what was left over. Our story we made up about him wasn't too far off, and Salvatore was surely laughing as he dicked us over. That was just the Bronx project. Apparently, we had a cold snap while Tina and I were away. In Queens, a water main break flooded half of a strip mall build site and turned it into what looked like shit soup. It was a fluke of nature.

That'll set us back two weeks while the city takes its sweet ass time to send out a crew. That's with Tina pulling strings left and right. Who knows if they would come without her? We would be paying for the cleanup ourselves if she hadn't convinced them. She filed the insurance claims too. That's paperwork all of us loathe because adjustors ask too many questions none of us want to answer.

There was an altercation at one of our New Jersey casinos. A drunk guy got too rowdy at a blackjack table and started touching other people's cards. Security had to escort him out, and once outside, right at the end of the casino driveway, he fell over and dislocated his shoulder. At first, he claimed our guys roughed him up, but security footage shows every step he took from the table to the edge of our property. Now he's claiming the paving is uneven. He's suing for two and a half million dollars. He won't win. He won't even get it on a judge's docket, but he doesn't want to settle for us covering his medical bills. We'll force him to make a choice: accept what we offer or get a shadow that follows him everywhere until he shuts up. Anton's taking care of it.

The bright side of this past month has been staying at Tina's place. She's made room for me in her dresser and closet. She and Cleo are the best of friends. My cat refused to consider going with Chloe. She hissed every time my ex-girlfriend came near her when Chloe was packing her shit. She would hide in my closet. She even pissed on some of Chloe's shoes. If I hadn't already loved my cat, I would have after she did that.

Cleo cried the *entire* way from Manhattan to Queens. It sounded like I was strangling a baby. But the moment she saw Tina, her entire body vibrated while she purred. She kept wrapping herself around Tina's ankles. My cat's basically forgotten about me except at mealtimes. Then she's back to being my best friend.

We stayed in the night after we returned from the yacht and had dinner with her family, but since then she's come to work with me each night. Her friends join her sometimes at Ivy and Envy, but only she comes to Pussycats and Dolls, Dolls, Dolls. Sometimes she watches a few of the dancers at Pussycats, but she abandons it once I go into my office. She comes back there and helps me get caught up on the liquor inventory while I deal with emails.

Tonight, I'm meeting with Carmine and his little crew at Dolls. His uncle called a truce after an interesting conversation with Laura at the governor's mansion. Now we're hammering out the details, and part of that means meeting with the douche. Tina stays out of the way once he arrives. I don't like that he knew about her the last time I saw him. I trust him about as much as I would a scorpion or piranha.

"Kutsenko, your sister-in-law impressed my uncle. That's hard to do."

"From what I hear, she practically had his balls in a vise."

"Are you trying to pick a fight?"

"And let you and your little groupies fuck up another one of my bars? No. Unless you want to take it outside. I'll gladly beat your ass where there isn't any of my inventory to break."

"You talk a big game, but you're not the prizefighter in the family."

"Who do you think taught me to fight? Carmine, I have a business to run. I know your uncle's terms. We stay out of each other's lane. Fine. My brothers and I are good with that. You do you, and we'll do us. There's nothing more to talk about. You showed up in good faith, now you can leave."

"But there is so much to look at here. I've been searching for a pretty little redhead I heard works here now."

I don't react. He's antagonizing me, but I won't let it show. Vlad did too good a job of beating any reactions out of me. Carmine could slice me to pieces, and I wouldn't blink twice.

"I hear she has tits to die for."

I look at Carmine's best friend. He's just as much of an asshole as Carmine, but his Italian accent makes it hard to understand him half the time. Beyond shifting my gaze, Gabriele gets no reaction from me. Ridiculous name. There isn't a damn thing angelic about him.

"Remind Salvatore that it's in his best interest to stay away, or Laura will bury him in so much red tape, it'll look like a bloodbath."

I raise my hand and gesture to the door. My bouncers materialize and herd Carmine away. I scrub my hand over my face before going back to my office. I've never enjoyed strip clubs that much to begin with, and doing any type of business here just makes me wish I wasn't the manager. Maybe it's time Pasha or Misha take on a new responsibility. Having tits and asses in my face all night, when they're not Tina's, is annoying more than anything else.

"*Malyshka*, come with me."

Tina looks up from her phone. I know she's reading one of her romance novels. I teased her once about it, and she set me straight in no time. Never again will I consider them frivolous. She hears my command and takes my offered hand. She follows me until we get to the club's backdoor. It leads to an alley with a dead end. We keep nothing back here and put up a fence years ago, so no one could easily sneak in through the back. I gesture for her to go down the steps ahead of me.

"Bogdan?"

"Keep going."

I let her get a few feet ahead of me before I rush forward

and wrap an arm around her middle, pinning both her arms to her side, and my other hand covers her mouth.

"Scream, and you will regret it. Do you understand?"

She nods.

"Pretty girls like you shouldn't walk in dark alleys. Do you know what might happen?"

I press my right arm against hers while I keep her mouth closed. My left arm keeps hers pinned tight while my hand cups her pussy.

"I bet you have a tight little cunt waiting for a big dick to fuck you. Is that what you want?"

She fights me. She shakes her head and tries to stomp on my foot. I feel her leg move, so I move mine. She struggles to elbow me, but her arms can't move. She throws her head back, knowing she'll only hit me in the chest. I press my fingers between her legs until I can dip them inside her pussy, even with her clothes in the way.

"You're awfully hot down there for someone who doesn't want this. I bet you're wet for me."

"Nmmm."

She tries to mumble something. Probably no. But she can barely get any sound out past my hand. I push her forward with my body until we get to a wall. I'm careful not to smash her face when I press her against it. I rock my cock against her ass.

"Do you think you can take all of this, baby girl?"

I uncover her mouth and wrap my hand around her throat.

"No...No... Stop... No."

She's playing along, and I can feel her pulse thrumming under my fingers. I lean close to her ear and whisper.

"I'm going to fuck you whether or not you want it. You're mine now."

"No."

She keeps trying to fight me. It's enough for me to ease my

hold. I'm scared I've gone too far. But her hand presses mine harder against her pussy.

"You want it, don't you, you little slut? Maybe I should make you suck me off. Or maybe not. I want your cunt dripping on me."

I spin her around as I unfasten my belt and pull it from my pants. I'm quick to snatch her wrists and bind them with the strip of leather. Then I unbutton my pants and pull down the fly. The skirt she's wearing comes to mid-thigh. It's not clubbing or bar attire, but it still lets me slide my fingers inside her.

"You are wet, aren't you? You can say no, but we both know you want it."

"No. Let me go. My boyfriend will kill you."

"But not until after I've fucked you, baby girl."

I spin her back around, lift her bound hands over her head, and rip her thong off. It's lacy and sheer, so easy to do. I shove it in my pocket. I still have the first one I took from her. I nudge her feet wider as I lick her neck. Then I'm inside her. She moans.

"That's right. Your cunt is mine."

"No... Stop... Stop."

She tries to kick back at me, which pushes her hips away from the wall. It only makes me sink deeper into her. She fights harder, knowing it's just driving me farther into her pussy. I pull out and turn her back to face me.

"You're going to see me while I fuck you."

"Why're you doing this to me? I don't want it. Stop."

"Because I can. Because I want you."

"No."

"I don't care. You don't get to decide."

She whimpers, but I can see her eyes. I can see she's enjoying this. I can feel how she does a Kegel around my cock each time I thrust. I pull her arms above her head again, hook her left leg over my hip, and surge into her. My hand goes back around her throat and squeezes. She chokes, then calms. We're watching each other. I'm looking for any sign that this stops being a game. She sees my moment of hesitation and tilts her hips toward me.

"You are mine, baby girl. I want you, and there isn't a damn thing you can do to stop me fucking you."

I thrust harder and harder as I keep her pinned to the wall. She's moving along with me, and I feel her come.

"You like it when I take what I want. Naughty little girl. I felt you come. You're going to keep taking it until I'm done. You're so fucking tight. I know where you live. I'm not even nearly done with you."

"Nnnn."

My hand is still around her throat, so she can't speak. We keep moving together, and I can feel she's on the verge. But she suddenly stops. She goes completely still. I release her throat.

"Olives. Olives."

I pull out and step back.

"Freeze! Step away from the woman and put your hands up."

Fuck me.

"I'm fine. He's my boyfriend. We're roleplaying, officers. I consent. I'm fine."

Tina hurries to push her skirt down and holds out her wrists to me. I foolishly reach out to undo the belt.

"Move again, and I'll shoot."

Tina steps around me and between the two male officers and me.

"Shoot him, and I'll make sure you lose your badges. I told you, he's my boyfriend. It was a fantasy roleplay. Lower your guns and let him undo my hands."

She twists toward me as one officer lowers his gun a few

inches. When I reach for her, the other shoots. I push her aside and cover her body as we fall. I can't cushion her fall and still protect her, so she takes the full brunt of my weight.

"Tina!"

"I'm all right, Bogdi. Are you? Did it hit you?"

I can feel the burn in my arm. It's a graze, but it fucking hurts. What the fuck are they doing back here? The police don't come around unless someone calls, and it's never us. We have an arrangement. This isn't how tonight was supposed to go down. At least I got her off before it went to shit.

I stand and help Tina to her feet as the police race forward.

"I swear to God, if you touch him, I will make your life hell."

I get the belt unfastened, and it unravels, landing at her feet. She stays in front of me, so I don't think she sees how I'm holding my arm.

"I'm going to reach into my pocket, and I'm going to make a phone call that I'm putting on speaker."

She moves slowly, keeping her right hand visible as she reaches into her left pocket. She doesn't make any hurried movements as she holds the phone in both hands. The screen lights up as she unlocks it. I watch her pull up her contacts. I think I might shit myself when I see whose number she dials.

"Bogdi, remember how I said I had a boss while I was an intern who taught me some important lessons? Now he has a really important job."

We all listen as it rings.

"Ms. MacNally, it's been ages since I've heard from you. It's a bit late, though."

"I know, Mr. Mayor, and I'm sorry. But I'm having a bit of trouble with two NYPD officers. One of them just shot at my boyfriend, Bogdan Kutsenko. They're still holding us at gunpoint."

"They're what? Where are you?"

"Behind one of the Kutsenkos' establishments. We were sharing an intimate moment when these officers arrived. They thought something nonconsensual was happening. Then they wouldn't believe me when I explained. My boyfriend tried to help get something off my wrists, and—what's your name?"

"Officer Benson."

"And Officer Benson shot at us."

"Are you all right, Christina?"

"I am, but—"

She turns back to look back at me for the first time. Her eyes go wide, first with shock, then with fury. She spins back around.

"Officer Benson didn't just shoot at Bogdan. He hit him. Bogdan is bleeding. What's your name?"

She's speaking to the other officer now, who looks like he's about to shit his pants. Good.

"Officer MacMichaels."

"MacMichaels? As in Stanley MacMichaels?"

"That's my father's name."

"Oh, you really effed this one up. I'm Christina MacNally. Your father and mine are best friends."

"Christina? I didn't recognize you."

"Are they still pointing guns at you?"

The mayor jumps back into the conversation. Both officers have lowered their weapons and are looking at each other.

"No. They're holstering them. Mr. Mayor, you can imagine why I wouldn't want this on a police blotter, or why I wouldn't want a weapon discharge report filed."

"Yes, I can. Consider this night forgotten. The NYPD was never there. Gentlemen, I would quietly leave, if I were you."

I watch them look at each other before they both speak.

"Yes, Mr. Mayor."

No one talks as they rush out of the alley. Once we're alone, Tina spins back to look at me.

"Christina, do you or Mr. Kutsenko need anything? You said they shot him."

"I'll think about it and talk to Bogdan. I'll let you know if we do."

"Mr. Kutsenko."

"Yes, Mr. Mayor."

"I regret this inconvenienced you."

"Yes, being shot is a bit of an inconvenience."

"Your brother and his wife already have an invitation to the charity gala I'm holding at the Peninsula in two weeks. I'd like to invite you and Christina too. I'm sure you'll find it's a useful evening for all of you."

"I'm sure we will."

"Christina, are you sure you're all right?"

"I'm fine. Thank you, though."

"Any time. Let's talk at the event."

"Sounds good. Goodnight, Mr. Mayor.

"Goodnight, Christina, Mr. Kutsenko."

Holy shit. Maks is going to explode. He's been maneuvering for an invitation to this stupid event since his wedding reception. I got one by knowing Christina and getting shot.

"Bogdi, we need to look at how bad this is. You said you have a doctor on call."

"Yeah. This isn't bad enough to need him. Can you pull my phone out? The code is 1-0-0-3."

"My birthday?"

"Yes, *malyshka.*"

She hurries ahead of me and opens the door as I tell her to call Sergei. Ten minutes later, I'm stretched out on the sofa in my office, with Tina pressing a bar towel over my wound. I was right. It is only a graze, but it's still bleeding when Sergei arrives.

"What happened to you?"

"NYPD."

"I'm calling Maks."

"Not yet, you aren't. I need you to stitch up my arm."

"Sergei's doing it?"

Tina appears panic-stricken as she looks between the two of us. It's clear she doesn't believe my cousin should come anywhere near me with a needle and thread.

"Sergei's a trained paramedic, Tina. He and Anton both got certified while they were in college. They handle anything that's bad enough to need more than a band-aid but isn't bad enough for a doctor."

She doesn't look convinced.

"What the hell were the cops doing here?"

"I'm pretty sure Carmine called them."

"Why?"

"I don't know. He was here earlier to settle things. I had him shown out, and I watched him leave. I think our guys came back inside and didn't watch them get into their cars, or they doubled back. Tina and I were in the alley. Do not ask why. I think they saw something private and sent the police after me."

"You think Carmine saw us?"

Tina's horrified. I can see the shame as clear as day. I glance at Sergei, who is purposely looking anywhere but at her.

"I don't know for sure, *malyshka*. We pay a lot of money for the NYPD to skip the blocks with our bars and strip clubs. They only come when a patron calls. Not even the neighbors do. No one opened it, so no one saw us from the door because I could see it. I kept checking."

"But if they stood at the edge of the alley, they were in the dark. Neither of us could see them. I didn't notice the cops until they came out of the shadows."

"Hey. Easy there."

I grunt as Sergei pours hydrogen peroxide on the wound. Motherfucker that stings. He cleans around the wound before opening a suture kit. I look back at Tina, who's staring at my arm. Her eyes are watering.

"Sergei, give us a minute."

"No, Bogdan. Sergei already cleaned the wound. I'm fine. He needs to do this."

I reach out my free hand, and she takes it in both of hers. I sit up, and Sergei grumbles but moves to keep working. I pull Tina onto my lap. She hasn't let go of my hand, and I'm fine with that. She's watching every movement Sergei makes, but she remains silent. It only takes six stitches for Sergei to close the wound. He bandages it and cleans up. He leaves without a word.

"*Malyshka*, I'm so sorry this got so messed up. I don't know if it was Carmine or not, and I don't even know if he saw anything or just heard me and fucked with me."

"But he might have seen us. It's even worse if he heard. I never should have said anything about this fantasy. Or we should have acted it out in my backyard or basement."

"That wasn't what you wanted. Tina, look at me. I know you're embarrassed, but I would do it all over again, if it was what you wanted. I'll play out this fantasy as many times as you want if it makes you happy."

She swallows and nods.

"It was really great until it wasn't. It was what I wanted. I didn't expect it, and you did all the things I've dreamed about. Though you could have talked dirtier."

"Next time, baby girl."

"Yes, Daddy."

"Are you ready to go home?"

"So ready."

"Do you want to go back to Queens or crash here in Manhattan?"

She considers it for a moment. She suddenly looks so exhausted and young. I slip my good arm under her legs and my bad arm around her back before I lift her.

"Bogdan, put me down. You're going to rip your stitches."

"No, I won't. Sergei knows what he's doing, and he knows this won't be enough to bench me. He made sure I can still use my arm and let the wound heal."

"That's ridiculous."

"I was hoping you would believe me. I'm not putting you down until we get into bed. Now Manhattan or Queens?"

She studies me for a moment.

"Manhattan."

She picked that for my sake.

"Wrong answer. Our home is in Queens."

Chapter Twenty-Two

Tina

I'm wearing the emerald gown Bogdan gave me. He treated me to a spa day since I've been working fourteen- to sixteen-hour days. I'm still completely humiliated that someone might have heard us in the alley. Even if it wasn't Carmine and his goons, the two officers heard us. I feel like a pervert, but Bogdan keeps reassuring me we did nothing wrong. It's hard to believe that when your boyfriend gets shot because you have a twisted sex fantasy.

"Are you ready, *malyshka?*"

"I am."

I got a massage this afternoon, then a mani-pedi. Bogdan also arranged for someone to do my hair and makeup. I'm wearing the lion necklace he gave me. I feel like a princess. It could be my wedding day for how pampered I feel. And this gown. I'm Cinderella, but nothing better happen at midnight to take my Prince Charming away.

"You take my breath away, Tina. I'm the luckiest guy alive."

"I think Maks would disagree. He thinks he's pretty lucky to be married to Laura."

"He's a close second."

He's careful not to smudge any of my makeup, so his kiss is soft and quick. He helps me down my wood stairs and out to the car. It feels like we make it into Manhattan in a matter of minutes. They cordoned off the sidewalk for the mayor's guests. People have gathered, and there are news crews filming. When it's our turn to get out of the car, Bogdan lends me a hand. I feel like an old-time movie star as I swing both legs out first.

"Maks, Laura."

Bogdan spots his brother and sister-in-law first. Sergei is with them, and Anton is getting out of our car. Niko and Aleks get out of the car behind us. We join Bogdan's family. Laura and I hug, and it feels like I have a sister. We totally hit it off, and we keep talking about going to yoga together. We go inside and make our way through the reception line.

"Ms. MacNally, it's nice to see you again. Mr. Kutsenko, you look no worse for wear."

I grit my teeth. Maks looks back at Bogdan. It seems like my boyfriend's big brother doesn't like the reminder.

"It's nice to see you, Mr. Mayor. Thank you for the invitation."

We make our way to the bar as Anton and Sergei move through the crowd. I noticed they have earpieces in, so they can talk to one another. From the back, their builds match. The only difference is their hair. They look like the perfect pair. Niko and Aleks are still near the entrance with their earpieces in.

"What're you drinking tonight, Laura?"

I just ordered a glass of Riesling, and the guys have ordered vodka.

"Just a Sprite for me."

My eyes jump to her stomach as they widen. I look back up at her and grin.

"Damn. You're too quick. Please don't say anything. We haven't told anyone."

"Haven't told anyone what?"

Bogdan looks at me, then Laura. He must realize the answer to his own question because he grins at Maks and hugs him. He kisses Laura's cheek.

"Please don't say anything, Bogdan."

It's phrased as a request, but Maks is staring down Bogdan.

"Do you think I'm that big of an ass that I'd give that away? It's your good news to share."

"I know, but Aleks and Niko don't know yet. We were going to tell the three of you tomorrow."

"Don't worry. I'll even act surprised."

"Maybe. Let's see how it goes."

"Let's talk when we get to our table."

I nod and squeeze Laura's hand before Bogdan puts his hand at the small of my back. I love it when he does that. It's just the right amount of possessive and protective. I lean closer, so our bodies touch as we walk.

"Do you know most of these people?"

"Several, but not most."

Bogdan stops for a step before turning us in a different direction.

"What's wrong?"

"There are three men here that I'd rather not see you."

"Why?"

"Two of them already know about you, but I don't think either have actually seen you. I don't know about the third."

"Is one of them Donovan O'Rourke?"

"Yes."

I glance over my shoulder.

"Bogdi, I already know Salvatore. I can't pretend like I don't if he sees me."

"You know him?"

"We've met a few times in passing. I've been at sites when he's stopped by. Who's the third?"

"Enrique Diaz. He's the head of the Cartel. He's also the uncle of one of Laura's former friends."

"Former?"

"I'll tell you when we get home. It's not a story for other people to overhear."

"You don't have to."

"Yes, I do. I know you and Laura are becoming friends. I heard you talking about going to yoga together. There have been threats against Laura ever since she started dating Maks. Some of it was her former friend. The guy used his connections to do some shady shit. But he's not responsible for all the threats. Now that she's married to Maks, she should be safer."

"Because she's his wife?"

We move closer to the band. It's noisier, but it also means fewer people can overhear us.

"Yes. There's an unwritten code that women and children are left out of mafia business. They're untouchable. Whoever else is behind the threats clearly believes it's okay to target wives and children."

"Does that mean I could be a target, too? I'm not your wife."

He looks at me for a long time, and I see the possessiveness in his gaze. Movement breaks his focus for a moment. He shifts to block me from whomever is walking by.

"I'm trying to keep you from becoming one. I won't hide you and force you never to come out, but I will be cautious. And I will be vigilant about who sees you."

"My dad said Donovan already knows about me. Do you think Enrique does?"

"I don't know, but he's the only one who isn't a threat right now. He was practically like an uncle to Laura while she was growing up. She lived next door to Enrique's brother and his family. He won't touch any of us or our women, for Laura's sake."

"So I'm your woman?"

I flash him a saucy smile, hoping to lighten his mood. He slides the arm people can't easily see around me and squeezes my backside. It's to the wall, so no one notices.

"Yes. You're my everything, *malyshka*."

"And you're my man. I love knowing that."

"Always, baby girl. I love you."

"I love you, Daddy."

I wink before I notice a former colleague waving to me. I sigh in annoyance.

"What's wrong?"

"There's a woman coming over here who works for the Department of Buildings. We went to grad school together. We worked in the Bronx city planner's office for a few months before she magically got a promotion."

"Magic?"

"She has the golden vag, apparently. She slept with two guys and suddenly got a massive raise and a cushy job."

"Hi, Christina!"

"Hi, Jenny. Long time no see."

She pulls me into a hug before I can stop her. I almost spill my drink, but Bogdan grabs the glass for me.

"It's been forever. Are you still with the city planner's in the Bronx?"

"No. I work for a private company."

"Oh. Which one?"

And now I'm going to look no better than her.

"Kutsenko Partners. Jenny Baker, this is my boyfriend, Bogdan Kutsenko."

I see the recognition the moment she hears Bogdan's last name. She grins at me before she turns to Bogdan. I know that smile. I've seen it before. Right before she hooked up with a guy at Lady's Night when we were in school together.

"It's nice to meet you, Bogdan. What a unique name."

"Not in Russia. It's nice to meet you, Ms. Baker."

Fortunately, Bogdan's hands are full, so he has an excuse not to shake Jenny's.

"I've heard so much about your various projects. They're so big."

Fuck this bitch.

"I get to work on them."

I can insinuate things too. I take my glass back when Bogdan offers it to me. He wraps his arm around me and smiles at Jenny.

"I hope you enjoy your evening, Ms. Baker. I see someone we need to say hello to."

I don't know if he really does, but it gets us away from her.

"Not very subtle, is she? Has she always been like that?"

"Willing to fuck a girl's boyfriend right in front of the girl? Yes."

"I like it when my woman plays hard to get."

Bogdan smirks at me, and I give him what I hope is come-hither eyes.

"Keep doing that, *malyshka*, and I will get us a room, and we'll miss the entire party."

"Promise?"

"Yes."

"Bogdan Kutsenko. It's good to see you."

I turn toward a balding man with a potbelly. Was this who Bogdan spotted? Or is it a coincidence?

"Ely Westman, this is my girlfriend, Christina MacNally. Christina, Ely was my roommate freshman year."

They're the same age? No fucking way. Ely looks at least ten—no—fifteen years older than Bogdan.

"It's nice to meet you."

"You, too. How long's it been, Bogdan? Four years? Last time I saw you, you were at one of these with—"

Wonderful. He brought Chloe with him to these events. Not that it should surprise me. It's not like I didn't bring old boyfriends to work events, too.

"That was a long time ago. How's Tanya?"

"I guess you didn't hear. We got divorced two years ago."

"I'm sorry to hear that."

Bogdan doesn't sound sorry at all. And I suspect he knew. He glances at me as he presses his hand heavily against my waist.

"I heard Kutsenko Partners just acquired RK Capital Group, and it cost you a small fortune."

"They merged with us, and it did. Do you see the woman with Maksim?"

"Yeah."

"That's his wife. They met while she negotiated the merger. She's a shark and got her clients way more than we were prepared to pay."

"So Maksim married her?"

"Not that day. A couple months later."

"Wow. Was it like love at first sight?"

"Something like that."

"What about you two? How long have you been together?"

"A while. Christina was the city inspector for one of our projects."

A while? It feels like it, even if it's only been two months. Holy shit. Wow! When I think about it, I can still count it in weeks. My chest hurts when I realize just how fast we're moving. When I picture a calendar, I realize we were apart for a week after we met. Then we were together for a week before our trip and then there was the trip. We've been home about six weeks. So roughly two months.

"Was it love at first sight for you, too?"

"Yes."

Bogdan and I answer, even though I'm still a little distracted. We look at each other and know it was. I didn't realize it, but that's because I didn't want to. The image of a calendar in my head vanishes, and the tightness in my chest eases. Bogdan's arm comes up and around my shoulders, and I lean my head against him. I can breathe again. I'm where I belong. I'm home. I'm wearing that favorite sweatshirt.

"We should find our seats. The meal is going to begin. It was good seeing you again, Ely."

"You, too. Nice to meet you, Christina."

"You as well."

Bogdan and I find our places at the same table as Laura and Maks. I look around for Niko and Aleks. I spot them at different exits. Anton and Sergei are near the doors leading to the hotel lobby. We say hello to the other two couples at the table and make small talk. A conversation about a company Kutsenko Partners is in the midst of buying out engrosses the four men. I'm sure it's becoming another shell company. I'm only half listening. The other two wives are practically old enough to be Laura's and my mothers. They take little interest in us, so Laura and I chat.

As the wait staff circulates, it takes forever for our food to come. Laura shifts in her seat a few times and looks a little green around the gills. She keeps sipping what now looks like ginger ale. Maks notices too and covers her hand with his.

"Are you all right?"

"The smell is a little much. I'm going to the restroom for a moment."

"I'll come with you."

"No, stay. It'll look odd if we both leave the ballroom. Can one of the guys come with me?"

"I'll come."

Bogdan and Maks both stand as Laura and I rise. I notice Anton and Sergei are ready to accompany us out of the ballroom. I sweep my gaze over the crowd as Laura and I weave through the tables. I saw Salvatore and a man I assume is Donovan. I don't see anyone I think is Enrique. Donovan and I lock eyes, and I know the moment he recognizes me. I look like my dad.

"I'm glad you mentioned going to the restroom. I wasn't sure if I would make it through the whole meal. Let's hurry."

"Who'd you see?"

Laura's smarter than anyone I know.

"Donovan O'Rourke. Apparently, he knows my dad. We had dinner with my family when we got back from our trip, so Bogdan could meet them. My dad warned us about him."

"Yeah. He seems to make all the guys uneasy. He was at the same restaurant as we were for our engagement dinner. Everyone got tense, but I didn't know who he was until Maks explained. He creeps me out."

"Me too."

Anton and Sergei are behind us as we get to the restroom. Sergei knocks. When no one says anything, he opens the door and looks around. He bends over to look beneath the stall walls. Once he's convinced we'll be alone, he lets us pass. The cousins wait outside.

"How're you feeling?"

Laura looks better than when we were at the table. I go into a stall while I hear her turn on the water. I flush and am about to step out when the entire building shakes, and there's the sound of glass shattering. I've been in California during an earthquake, and this is way worse. It's like a bomb just went off. I turn toward the door, but I never open it. The stall wall across from me slams against my head, then lands against my chest. I'm pinned to the wall behind me. I can't move my arms easily, but I try to push against the partition. As I strain, my head throbs. I realize that I'm bleeding when it feels like my pulse is outside my skin.

"Laura!"

"I'm by the sinks. Are you okay?"

"I can't get the door open. The stall wall came loose and is pinning me."

"I'm coming."

There's screaming outside, and I expect to hear Anton or Sergei burst in. But no one does. Laura's face appears beneath the stall door. She lies down and puts her hands beneath her shoulders.

"I'm going to slide under the door and come up next to you. We have to push together. Can you get your arms up?"

She pushes forward and comes onto her feet. She crouches with her shoulder against the wall that's practically crushing my chest.

"Yeah. I already tried, but it's wedged."

"We're going to push together. Are you ready?"

"Yeah."

"All right. Now."

We both strain and push as hard as we can. The wall gives way just enough for me to drop free of it.

"Come on."

Laura crouches as she speaks. I kneel while she crawls under the door. I follow. Laura leads me to the sink and grabs three terry cloth hand towels that are barely bigger than wash clothes. She hands me one while she keeps two. I can feel bruises forming on my chest and arms.

"Press it against your head. I'll press these to your chest. We need to wait here. Bogdan and Maks know we came here. Anton and Sergei have to be nearby."

The moment Laura finishes talking, the door bursts open. For a heartbeat, I thought it was Bogdan. But it's not. It's not even Anton or Sergei. It's what my dad's and Bogdan's nightmares are made of. It's Donovan O'Rourke. He barely glances at me. He goes straight for Laura and grabs her hair while he wraps his hand around her throat. She manages the loudest, most blood-curdling scream I've ever heard. Anton and Sergei must hear her.

"Shut the fuck up."

Donovan is going to crush Laura's throat. He's squeezing so hard his knuckles are turning white.

"Going—to—puke."

I don't know if she's lying, but it gets Donovan to ease his hold. I'm inching toward him and the door when it bursts open again. A man I don't recognize with an Irish flag tattooed on his forearm storms in. He takes one look at Laura, then turns to me. His fist plows into my temple. It feels like a metal truss slams into me, and I collapse. Laura screams. I hear Donovan speak before everything goes black.

"I told you to shut the fuck up. Want to wind up like her?"

Chapter Twenty-Three

Bogdan

Something doesn't feel right. I watched Tina and Laura leave the ballroom. I noticed Colin O'Rourke sitting at a table when the meal began. He's Donovan's right-hand man and his cousin. He was a prizefighter like Maks, except he no longer fights. Maks gave him such a severe concussion during one bout that he had to give up boxing. He's never forgiven Maks. He'd been staring at us, but now I don't see him.

"I'm glad we brought the others."

I look at Maks, who's staring at where Colin sat only minutes ago.

"Something's going on. I need to find Laura."

I was thinking the same about Tina. We push back from the table and get to our feet. Before we can do anything, an explosion bursts through the building, knocking Maks and me to the floor. He grabs my tux jacket and pulls as hard as he can. I roll toward him, and barely get to his side before a chandelier lands where I was just lying. Where is Tina?

"What the hell happened?"

Maks bellows as we get to our feet. We're both running toward the doors leading to the lobby. I can hear Aleks and Niko yelling to us, but neither Maks nor I slow down. We storm into the lobby and turn toward the restrooms.

"Maks, look."

My heart sinks as I point to a silk pocket square on the ground. I know in an instant that it's Sergei's. Maks grabs it while we look around. There's no trace of our women or our cousins. I hear a door open and look up. I'm certain my heart stops. Fear unlike anything I have ever experienced, washes over me. Not when Vlad beat me for the first time. Not the first time I killed someone. Tina tumbles out of the restroom door. There's blood sliding down her cheek, and it covers her gown's neckline. There's a gash on her forehead and her chest. I bolt to her.

"Tina!

I catch her and ease her to the ground. She's ghostly pale as I hold her and push the hair out of her eyes. I kiss her forehead, away from the cut.

"What happened, *malyshka*?"

I catch Maks's surprise from the corner of my eye, but I'm focused on my baby girl.

"They took her, Bogdi."

"Who, *malyshka*?"

"Irish. I recognized a tattoo on the man who hit me. He's not the one who got Laura. She fought, but they took her. The guy knocked me out and left me in the restroom. She saved me, Bogdi. I was pinned in the stall. She helped me get out from under the partition. Then I let them take her. I didn't save her when she saved me."

Guilt and shame fill her expression as she trembles. I'm certain it was Colin who hit her, and Donovan who grabbed

Laura. Neither woman could have resisted them. Not even with Tina's skills. Colin is nearly as good as Maks, and Maks has been undefeated for almost a decade.

"Take her home, Bogdan. Get Boris to check her out. If it was Colin who hit her, she's got at least a concussion."

"I will kill that motherfucker."

Tina whimpers and tears wet her eyelashes. I feel badly now. I should have controlled my outburst. It's not helping. I lift her into my arms and turn toward the hotel's backdoor.

"Aleks, go with him. Niko, stay with me."

"No. Michail will take us home. Aleks and Niko stay with you. I have my own men once I get to my penthouse."

"This is Anton's."

Niko holds up an almost identical pocket square to the one I spotted. It's one of the few ways the couple can display their connection. Matching socks and pocket squares. I wish it wasn't like that. The only jewelry they've ever exchanged is watches that have each other's initials on them.

"They have them both, and Laura."

I'm conflicted about leaving with Tina when my cousins and sister-in-law are missing. But Tina needs medical attention. For the first time in my life, I choose someone over my family. As far as I'm concerned, Tina is my family now. She'll be my wife by the end of the week if she'll agree.

I hurry through the door Niko holds open for me. I can hear Maks saying that none of their trackers are working. My cousins' watches and Laura's bracelet have them. I need to get something like that for Tina. What if those fuckers had taken her too? I hate thinking it, but Laura is more valuable to them than Tina. They would have dumped her body somewhere and kept Laura alive.

Michail, a man who's been bratva since before I was born,

pulls up and rushes to get the door open. He helps me hold Tina while I climb in before I settle her in my lap.

"Take us to my mother."

I wrestle my phone out of my pocket and unlock it. I don't have many numbers stored in my phone, but this one is on speed dial. An older man answers, and I speak in Russian.

"Boris, meet me at my mother's house. My girlfriend Christina's hurt. Colin O'Rourke punched her. She was also trapped under a restroom stall wall. It hit her head and landed on her chest."

"Did she pass out?"

"Yes."

"How is she now?"

I look down at Tina. She's awake, but her eyes are half shut. Her head and chest are still bleeding.

"She's awake, but her head and chest are bleeding badly."

I struggle but shrug out of my tux jacket. I pull my bowtie free and press it against her forehead. I whisper to Tina.

"Can you hold this here?"

"Yes."

It's more of a croak than anything else. I rest the phone between my ear and shoulder as I cover her with my jacket. I can feel her shivering, and I'm scared shock is settling in.

"Keep pressure on it. Where are you coming from?"

"Manhattan."

"Can she make it to Queens? Do you want me to meet you at your penthouse?"

I run my gaze over Tina. She's still pale, but not as white as before. I pray I'm not making the wrong choice, but I haven't felt like I needed my mom this badly since the first time Vlad put a knife in my hand.

"No. Go to my mother's."

"I'll be there by the time you arrive. I'll be ready."

"Thanks, Boris."

I hang up and reach for a water bottle in the wet bar. We brought limos tonight instead of town cars. Part of it was for appearances, and part of it was to make sure the ladies were comfortable without crushing their gowns. I unscrew the top and help Tina sit up. I hold the bottle while she sips.

"It hurts, Bogdi."

"I know, *lapochka*. Boris is our doctor. He'll take care of you, then my mom and I will spoil you."

"I just want you."

"Baby girl."

"Daddy, I was so scared something happened to you. It hurt so much when that wall landed on me, but Laura helped me. We kept thinking Anton and Sergei would come. When I saw Donovan, then Colin, instead of you, I thought maybe they'd already hurt you. I didn't save Laura like she saved me."

"*Malyshka*, Colin is a golden glove boxer. The only person better than him is Maks. I wouldn't have stood a chance against one of his punches to my temple. Besides, you were already bleeding. I was coming for you just before the explosion. Maks and I both felt something was off. Neither of us could see Colin, so we'd just stood up when the bomb went off.

"It all happened so fast. It felt like forever when it was happening, but now I know it was only a few minutes."

"I know, baby girl."

"When I woke up, all I could think about was finding you. I needed to make sure you were okay."

"I needed the same thing."

Tina tries to sit up further, but she winces and sways. I support her back as she keeps holding the bowtie to her forehead. I can see blood seeping through my tux jacket. I peel it away. The cut on her chest is way deeper than I thought. I try to get her to lie down, but she pushes my hand away.

"Bogdan, I want to marry you."

"I want to marry you, too, Tina."

"I don't mean in the future. I mean, like today. This week. Now."

"Baby girl, you have a concussion. Let's get you to my mom's and have Boris take care of your injuries. Then we'll talk after you rest."

"Don't patronize me, Bogdan. If you don't feel the same way, say so."

"I'm not patronizing you. I'm fucking terrified. I just want to make sure you're going to be okay. I can't marry a fucking corpse."

"Daddy, I'm not dying."

"I'll let Boris tell me that."

"Bogdan, I'm not dying. I need some stitches and to lie down."

I know I don't look convinced because now she's the one offering the sympathetic smiles.

"I will marry you, Tina, the moment you are well enough to tell me that's what you want. You cannot be bleeding or concussed."

"Fine. I'm holding you to that."

"And I'm holding you right now."

She settles back against me, and it is the longest fucking ride to Queens of my entire life.

"Bogdan?"

My mom is running down the stairs as she pulls her robe around her. Her security detail must have alerted her we were here. She has guards patrolling the property around the clock. She has a gate that a guy in a guard shack has to open. No one gets near our mom without my brothers or me being aware, and I'm glad to know no one arrives without her knowing.

"Is Boris here?"

"No. I didn't know he was coming."

"I thought he would beat us here. Tina's hurt."

"What happened?"

"Mama, all of us are all right, but Donovan and Colin took Anton, Sergei, and Laura. Tina got hurt when a bomb went off at the mayor's gala."

"Let's get her upstairs. Where are your brothers?"

"They're going after Laura, Anton, and Sergei. Last I heard, none of their trackers were working. I don't know anything else."

"Christina, I have a room you can use. It's Bogdan's when he visits. What do you need, *pchelka*?"

Tina looks at me.

"That means little bee. It's what Mama called us when we were kids."

She looks down and notices her gown for the first time. Tears well in her eyes.

"My gown's ruined. I only got to wear it twice."

"I'll get you another one."

"Not the same. Can you call my mom and dad?"

"Of course."

"Galina, will you stay with me until my mom gets here?"

"Of course, *pchelka*."

"Mama, can you get one of my t-shirts?"

My mom hurries ahead of us and opens the door to my bedroom. None of us have lived here with our mom, but we all have our own bedrooms. She goes to the dresser and grabs a shirt. She drops it onto the bed as she rushes into the bathroom. She closes the door, but I hear her opening cabinets. I know she's giving Tina privacy while I help her out of her gown. I realize that a t-shirt won't work because it'll cover her chest wound. I get her out of the evening gown and unfasten her strapless bra before pulling back the covers. I put her in bed and rush to my closet. I have several suits and shirts hanging there, so I grab a button down. I finish buttoning it, leaving the top open just as someone knocks on the door. My mom comes out of the bathroom and answers whoever is knocking.

Boris steps in after greeting my mom. He makes his way to the bed, and I step back. Tina flings out her arm, trying to catch mine. She's panicking. I look at Boris and really notice him for the first time in years. He was an army surgeon before he worked for the KGB with my dad and uncles. He's a mountain with bushy eyebrows and piercing brown eyes. He's sewn me up more times than I can remember. He's taken bullets out of all of us and stitched most of our knife wounds. Despite the impression he makes, he's gentle as a lamb with his patients.

"I'm Boris. I've been Kutsenkos' doctor since they were all in diapers. This one used to pee on me every time I had to take his diaper off. At least his older brothers had better manners."

What the hell? He's making Tina laugh. He might be gentle with all of us, but he's never this nice. His accent is thicker than mine, but his English is almost as good as mine, so Tina understands him.

"I'm sure he wouldn't pee on you anymore."

"I don't wear diapers either."

I move around the other side of the bed when Tina pats the open space. I climb on, and she sags against me. Boris gets his medical supplies out, and my mom listens to his directions as they set up what he needs. He goes to the bathroom, and I can see him scrubbing his hands thoroughly. Is he about to perform surgery?

"Ms. Christina, I'm going to put some numbing ointment around wounds. Lidocaine won't take away all sensation. You'll still feel pressure. If you feel anything other than that, let me know."

"Thank you, doctor…"

"Just Boris."

Tina glances at me, then understands. It's best if she doesn't know his full name.

"Thank you, Dr. Boris."

She makes the older man smile, which is something my brothers, cousins, and I never do. We only make him scowl and swear. He talks to Tina the entire time, explaining what's he going to do before he starts. He hasn't done that with any of us since we were toddlers. We didn't go to the hospitals when we lived in Moscow. It was safer for Boris to come to us. Whenever he was away fighting alongside my father and uncles, my mother forbade us from getting hurt or sick. We were young enough to believe that she would not allow us to get sick. It seemed to work, and we kept our injuries to when he was home.

"I'm going to call your parents, Tina."

She looks at me while I'm talking. She puts her hand on my arm as I reach for my phone.

"Dr. Boris, is there anything really serious about my wounds? I want to know before Bogdan calls my parents. They're going to be upset regardless, but if they need to be warned of anything, I need to know now."

Boris looks up from his suture kit. While he was talking to Tina, he'd been checking her eyes and testing her reflexes.

"You have concussion. You're going to need both lacerations stitched, and they may leave scars. But you'll heal well from everything. Galina, could you get me glass of water, please?"

I watch my mom glance at Boris in confusion before she leaves the room.

"Ms. Christina, is there any chance you could be pregnant?"

Tina blinks several times before she looks at me, then she looks back at Boris.

"I have an IUD. I rarely get a period because of it. I don't think I am. I've had no reason to take a test."

"When you feel up to it, I'll get sample from you and send it to lab. I can have someone courier it tonight and get results within hour."

Tina nods, but I can see she's shaken. We've never talked about kids before. I'm not sure what to make of her reaction. Boris turns to accept the glass of water when my mom returns. I lean to whisper in Tina's ear.

"I want to have a family with you, Tina. Whether it's in a few months or a few years. If it's never, that's fine too."

"I still want to marry you soon. Regardless."

"I feel the same. But you heard Boris. You have a concussion. We'll discuss it when you're better."

"That's like ten days from now."

"Are you going somewhere? Because I'm not."

Her lips thin before she nods. I pull out my phone, and she tells me her mother's number. It rings three times before Catriona answers.

"Hello?"

"Catriona, it's Bogdan."

"Oh, my God. Where's Christina? We saw the news."

"She's beside me. She was in the restroom when the explosion went off. She got hurt, but it's only two cuts and a mild concussion. My doctor is about to stitch her up. She asked me to call because she wants you and Liam to come. We're at my mom's here in Queens."

"She's all right?"

I hear Liam in the background.

"Yes, she's with Bogdan at his mom's." She's muffled, as though she has her hand over the phone. She's much clearer when she talks to me again. "We'll be there as soon as we can."

"There's security at the gate. What kind of car do you drive? I'll let them know that you're to be let in."

"A dark blue SUV with a sunroof."

She gives me her license plate number, and I give her my mom's address before we hang up. My mom takes my place as I hurry outside to tell the guys to let her parents in when they arrive. By the time I get back to my room, Boris is done stitching Tina's head and is about to start on her chest. My mom has her arm behind Tina's neck, and my girlfriend is resting against my mom's shoulder with her eyes closed. My mom is stroking her hair like she did mine when I was sick or scared. She's humming a Russian lullaby she sang to all of us. Tina is completely relaxed, so I stay by the door.

"Bogdi, will you hold my hand? Everything hurts. I can already feel how sore I'm going to be."

"How'd you know I was back? Your eyes are closed."

"I sensed it, then I smelled your cologne."

My mom moves to make room for me.

"Don't go."

My mom glances at me before she settles back to stroking Tina's hair. I sit at the foot of the bed and put my hand on her ankle over the covers. We sit like that as Boris finishes sewing up her chest. It's a nasty gash, but he's made a neat line of stitches that should make it heal without too bad of a scar.

Tina's asleep by the time her parents arrive. I meet them at the door and show them upstairs. She's still leaning against my mom, who's still humming. I think it takes Catriona aback to see Tina leaning against another woman like she would her mom. But then Catriona smiles. She comes to stand next to my mom.

"Mrs. Kutsenko, thank you for taking care of my lass."

"Mom?"

Tina sits up, and my mom trades places with Catriona. Boris moves out of the way so Liam can stand beside Tina. She looks so tiny in the bed with her parents around her. My mom gives me a hug, and even though I'm a foot taller than her, I lean against her as we talk softly in Russian.

"She's going to be all right, *pchelka*."

"I know. But she was there because of me."

"I thought the mayor invited her, and she invited you."

"She got the invite because she called the mayor for a favor. There was an incident at a club two weeks ago. The police were there, and they would have arrested me if she hadn't called the mayor. She was in danger then, and she was in danger again tonight. Maybe this isn't right. Maybe I shouldn't bring her into our life any more than I already have. She could have gotten hurt so much worse."

"And she could have been at the party without ever knowing you. Life might have put her there anyway since she knows the mayor. At least you were there to help, and you're here now to take care of her."

"But Colin wouldn't have gone anywhere near her if it weren't because of me. She wouldn't know Laura or Maks. She wouldn't have been in that bathroom with Laura."

"You don't know any of that for sure. You can't second guess fate, Bogdan. She's your soulmate. Just like Laura is Maksim's, and just like your father was mine. You'll both be miserable without each other now that you've found one another. You're her other half as much as she's yours."

"Do you really believe that?"

"If I hadn't been in love with your father, maybe not. But I still am and always will be. I know what it is to find your soulmate. I hope Niko and Aleks are as lucky as you and Maks.

Look at Sergei and Anton. Their life is harder than any of ours, but they're proof soulmates exist."

My mom is right. They've been in love since we were all teenagers. They've missed out on so many opportunities to share a life and home like most committed couples do. But they are so perfectly matched that they make it work within our world.

"Bogdi?"

I look over and find Tina watching my mom and me.

"Yes, *lapochka*."

I'm careful what I call her around my mother.

"I need to learn Russian."

I laugh as I give my mom a squeeze, then walk to the end of the bed.

"What you need is rest."

"After that."

Tina yawns and struggles to cover her mouth. She's so tired, she can barely lift her arm. I think about the stitches Sergei gave me the other night. It felt like a scratch compared to what Tina's endured tonight. I watch her parents as Tina dozes off. I'm waiting for them to tell me to break things off, to leave their daughter alone. Liam is the first one to walk over to me.

"She's going to be all right, Bogdan. I know you're still going to worry, but you don't need to panic."

I glance at him before I turn back to watch Catriona adjust the covers before she gets up. Tina burrows into the pillow. I've watched her do that every night we've slept in the same bed, even the night we met.

"I am going to worry. But that's not what's going to make me panic."

"You expect me to tell you to break up with her."

"Yes."

"And make her miserable? No. She might not understand

313

all that goes on in your world yet, but she's going to stand beside you no matter what. If we try to get between you, she will pick you. We can't blame her. You come first now. I can see what you're feeling, even if just about everyone else can't. You are going to put her first whenever you can. And when you can't, you're going to make sure she's taken care of."

"I am."

"Catriona never lived with the same danger as your mother did or as Christina will. But she understood when I couldn't put her first, even though I always wanted to. I was already a British Royal Marine when we met. You were already bratva."

I sense my mother stiffen. I have told no one yet that Liam and Catriona know.

"Not only will we not stand between you, we will stand beside you. When Christina is well again, you and I need to talk about our many mutual acquaintances. You are not the only one who straddles the line between legal and illegal."

I look at Liam, and I suddenly realize that when he says he's a national security contractor, he doesn't mean domestic. Catriona gives me a hug before she stands next to Liam.

"You, your brothers, and your mom are going to be our family soon, aren't you?"

"Yes."

"Good."

"You don't feel like this is going too fast, Catriona?"

"We eloped to Gretna Green when we were nineteen. Our parents went berserk. We called it our destination wedding since we're from the Highlands, and Gretna is on the border with England. We've been married for nearly forty years after knowing each other for two months."

"I was about to deploy to the Middle East. I didn't want to leave without Cat knowing for certain I was going to do everything I could to come home to her. And I did."

Liam kisses Catriona's forehead as she looks up at her husband. It reminds me of the faint memories I have of my parents. I look at my mom and realize for the first time in years how much she misses my father. She catches herself when she realizes I'm watching her. I hug my mom, and it feels good to be the one giving the comfort rather than receiving it.

"Liam, Catriona, if you'd like to spend the night, I have a room for you."

"That would be nice, Galina. Thank you. I don't think Liam nor I want to leave."

My mom takes them to a room down the hall, and I strip off what's left of my tux. I realize Boris left without saying anything. Typical, but appreciated. He's discreet in everything he does. I climb into bed next to Tina and spoon her.

"I love you, *moy lev*."

I didn't realize she was still awake.

"I love you, *malyshka*."

I watch as she falls asleep. I feel her body go lax. But my mind is whirling. I don't doubt Donovan and Colin are as good as dead, because Maks will not let them live. But if they survive, I will burn the world down before they look in Tina's direction ever again.

Chapter Twenty-Four

Tina

Everything aches. Breathing is the last thing I want to do. Every time I inhale, the stitches on my chest tug. My entire body is bruised, and my head feels like a herd of rhinos ran across it. I've been asleep almost all day, and now it's night again. I woke up when I heard Bogdan and his mom talking. When I asked, he explained that Maks, Aleks, and Niko found Laura, Anton, and Sergei at some warehouse all the way in Rochester. It's such a complicated story I can't remember half of it, and none of it makes sense. But the Irish threat is gone. If only I could breathe easily, I would.

Bogdan's been beside himself with worry. He's hiding it well, but not well enough from me. I've learned to read the subtlest expressions and how he carries himself. I can tell he's stressed. I woke up in the middle of the night. I didn't move, but I know he was awake. I'm pretty sure he was watching me sleep. He looks like shit tonight.

"Bogdi, I'm going to live. You need to rest, not watch me sleep."

"I can sleep when I'm dead."

"Which will happen sooner than I want. I know there's a good likelihood you're going to the warehouse soon. I want you alert and thinking straight. Please, will you try to sleep? I'm still tired. Hold me, and we can deal with whatever is going on in the morning."

Bogdan lifts the tray with my half-eaten dinner off the bed and slides beneath the covers. He's careful not to jar any of my bruises or touch my stitches as he wraps himself around me. I can feel myself getting drowsy again. Boris left behind pain medicine and antibiotics to make sure I don't get an infection. I was able to give a sample that a courier collected. It was negative. Bogdan kisses my shoulder, and I finally feel him relax.

I could have sworn I just fell asleep, but the clock on the bedside table says eleven o'clock at night. I know without looking that Bogdan isn't in bed with me. I reach behind me, and the sheets are cold. He hasn't been there for a while. My pain medicine has worn off, but I feel better than I expected. I ease myself up to sitting and look around. I can hear voices outside my room. I recognize Galina's and my parents'. They've stayed, and I appreciate it. I ease out of bed and stand up for the first time in hours. I expected to be stiff, but I'm not.

I'm still wearing one of Bogdan's button-down shirts. I'm swimming in it, but there's a pair of pajama pants at the end of the bed. I slip those on and cinch the waist tight. I follow the voices downstairs and into Galina's living room.

"The Irish won't let this go. We all know that."

What's my dad talking about?

"Bogdan won't let this go. They'll reorganize like they all do when power shifts. Donovan wasn't the only one trained to lead. There are other men to take his place."

What won't Bogdan let go? What's Galina talking about? Donovan and Colin are dead.

"Is he with his brothers?"

Why is my dad asking that?

"Yes. They're taking care of things."

What things? Why is Galina telling my parents this? Bogdan wouldn't want this.

"Bogdan cannot tell Christina about any of this."

Now my mom's chiming in. What the fuck?

"He won't. He'll protect her. My sons have never told me exactly what goes on there, but I know. I was raised in Russia. My husband was KGB before he was Podolskaya bratva. Christina doesn't need to know any of it."

"What don't I need to know? What other secrets is Bogdan going to keep from me?"

My parents and Galina turn toward me as I enter the living room. It's clear from all three faces that they didn't know I was awake, let alone behind them.

"Only things that will keep you safe."

"But you can know, Da? Mom can too. Galina, you obviously already know. So everyone but the woman he intends to marry."

"I don't know any specifics, Christina. But I know how syndicates handle rivalries. It's no different from anywhere with different factions battling for control over disputed territory."

"You make is sound like there's a war going on, Da."

All three go silent. Galina has a grandfather clock, and the tick of every passing second seems to echo in our silence.

"Where is Bogdan right now?"

"Taking care of something."

"If Donovan and Colin are dead, and I assume whoever was with them, who's left?"

No one wants to answer that either. My anger is growing with each passing moment. I feel like a child, and the grownups have stopped talking because I can hear. But I'm twenty-seven-years-old and plan to marry into the bratva soon. Treating me like this will not work.

"How am I supposed to know who to trust? How am I supposed to know what to look out for? How am I supposed to know what not to say?"

"Bogdan will protect you from that."

"Like he did from Donovan and Colin, Galina? Last I checked, I'm the one with the stitches, concussion, and bruises. Am I supposed to just walk around ignorant of what's going on in my life?"

"That's for Bogdan to decide, Christina."

"Et tu, Mom?"

"He loves you, Christina. He will put you first, but he won't want you to know what he's doing."

"Because I'll think he's a monster? I'm not stupid. I can imagine exactly what he does, and it probably doesn't even touch on half of it."

"That, and it'll keep you safe if the police ever question you."

"Bullshit."

"Christina!"

"It is, Mom. Him telling me nothing won't stop the police from believing I know. They'll hound me until I say something, which will only be lies. Even if I say nothing, that'll only get me locked up for aiding and abetting. They'll probably name me an accessory after the fact. Even if we're married, it won't stop them from interrogating me. I might not have to testify against him, but they'll still pressure me."

Galina walks to me and puts her arms around me, careful not to press on my bruises or wound. At first, I freeze. But I close my eyes and lean against her. I'm suddenly so tired again. Maybe I should have taken more pain meds.

"Christina, there were threats against you yesterday. No one realized it until last night because everyone but us was at Maks and Laura's. Even when you're not there, Bogdan has someone watching your house. People broke in. We think they assumed you went there after the bombing. When they didn't find you or Bogdan, they ransacked it. Bogdan went over there to see the damage. That was a couple hours ago. We haven't heard from him since. We might not. You know why."

"All three of you knew they trashed my house, and you weren't going to tell me."

I pull away from Galina and run back up the stairs. Fuck. Every step hurts. I get back to Bogdan's room and realize I don't have any of my own clothes here. It's not like I can put my bloody evening gown back on. The best I can do are the clothes I'm wearing now. I don't even have shoes.

"Tina!" Bogdan's yelling my name. "Tina!"

I hear him running down the hall before he bursts into the bedroom. His wild eyes settle on me and where I'm standing by his closet. He pushes the door closed, but he doesn't get any closer.

"They were not supposed to tell you any of that. It wasn't their place."

"Were you?"

"Yes."

"All of it?"

"No."

"That's not okay with me. Nothing my parents or your mom told me was anything you should keep from me, Bogdan. You promised you wouldn't keep things from me unless it was absolutely necessary. You should have woken me and told me about my place."

"I had no idea what I was going to find there. I wanted to see for myself, so I could tell you the truth."

"The truth? You just told me you weren't going to."

"You asked if I would tell you all of it, and I wouldn't. I won't. That doesn't mean I would lie."

"A lie of omission is still a lie."

"And you knew from the beginning that would happen."

"It's my house, Bogdan. You might stay there, but it's still mine."

I see the hurt that I intended to inflict. I regret it, but I'm livid. I'm striking out however I can.

"After what they did, it may as well be nobody's. We can get a new place together."

"Together? There is no together, Bogdan. Not if you're going to hide even basic things from me. And what the fuck do you mean, after what they did?"

"They did more than trash it. There was a fire in your garage. They put sledgehammers through walls and broke all the windows."

I stand there dumbfounded. I'm frozen for what feels like forever. Then I'm pushing past Bogdan, who tries to stop me.

"Touch me, and I will tell my dad you hurt me."

"Tina, you wouldn't."

"We don't know each other that well, Bogdan. Yes, I would. Move."

He steps aside, and I'm out the bedroom and down the stairs. I look around and spot his keys on the entryway table. I snatch them and bolt outside. I'm in his car as he gets to the front door. I reverse and head down the driveway. The guard at the gate barely gets it open before I plow through it. I'm grateful I didn't take any of the narcotic painkillers Boris prescribed. I wouldn't be up to driving if I had.

I recognize where I am, so I know how to get back to my

house. I'm certain at least Bogdan, if not his mom and my parents, will follow me. I don't care. I need away from them, and I need to see my house. It's not about my belongings, though I'm worried about them. I want to see what these people will do to me. I need to see what life with Bogdan would really be like. He won't tell me the truth, and neither will anyone else. I'm not refusing to have a future with him. But I won't go into it ignorant.

The light I approach is green, so I speed up. As I pass through the center, headlights from my left blind me. Then I'm spinning as I try to steer into the swerve. But the semi is still pushing my car. Then I'm rolling. I feel like a pea in a tin car as my car keeps tumbling. Then it slams into the side of a building, and everything is black.

"Tina!"

Bogdan? Why's he screaming my name?

I open my eyes, and it all comes back to me. The truck, rolling, crashing. I try to look around, but I can't move. My seatbelt has me pinned in place. All I can see is shattered glass. I wiggle my toes and fingers to make sure I can. I hear other voices, but I can only make out what Bogdan is saying.

"Let me pass. She's my fiancée."

Am I? Why can't I remember what happened before the crash? I close my eyes again as a light shines into my car. There's a metal crunching. I try to look at my door, but my airbags are in the way.

"Tina!"

"Bog—"

My voice isn't working. No sound comes out. Is that permanent? What if I can never talk again? What if...

"Tina!"

Each time Bogdan says my name, he sounds more panicked. I've never heard him like this. Never imagined my never-so-much-as-blink boyfriend could sound so terrified. I look down and see blood everywhere. My arms are slashed from the shattered glass. I feel the blood trickling from my head. But I remember I can move my fingers and toes. I can't get my hands under the airbag to the horn, and I don't even know if it will work since the airbag deployed. I move my foot and find the brake pedal. I pray somehow at least one of my brake lights works. I tap the pedal four times.

"Tina! Tap the brake again if you hear me!"

It must work. I do it again.

"Ma'am, we're going to have you out in just a moment."

The sound I hear must be the jaws of life cutting away my door. Then the airbags pop. I flop forward as my seatbelt suddenly goes lax from someone cutting through it.

"Bogdi."

My voice works this time.

"Tina, I'm right here."

Two firefighters lift me out of the car and place me on a stretcher. People are around me, and someone is putting an oxygen mask on me. I shake my head, making it impossible.

"Bogdi, I'm sorry. I shouldn't have. But you would be dead if you'd been with me."

As they pulled me out, I saw the passenger side of the car. There's no way anyone sitting there would have survived. My side was horrible since the truck plowed into it. But the way the car landed would have crushed anyone there.

I let them put the oxygen mask on me. I'm not sure what else they're doing, but I try to reach for Bogdan, who's standing behind a paramedic.

"Him."

My word is garbled in the mask, but I lift my hand and point to Bogdan. I wave him closer, but the paramedics ignore me as they work.

"Christina!"

It's my mom.

"Catriona, she's awake."

I'm thankful Bogdan tells her.

"Move. I'm her mother."

She doesn't use the restraint Bogdan does. She shoves a paramedic hard enough that the guy almost falls. Luckily, he hadn't already stuck me with the needle for the IV. He would have ripped it out of me.

"*Mo chridhe.*"

My heart. My mom has called me that my entire life. God, how good that sounds right now. She takes my hand and strokes the top of my head. I feel tears seeping from my eyes. I can't turn my head because they've immobilized it, but I look to my mom. I see my dad behind her. I can't see Bogdan.

I panic.

I can't breathe, and I'm fighting against the belts they have over me. I'm trying to move my head to look around. I can't do anything but bang my free hand on the stretcher.

"Bogdan!"

I don't know if anyone can understand me.

"Bogdan, she needs you."

My dad speaks over his shoulder, then moves aside. My mom doesn't want to let go, but she does. She rests her hand just above my knee as Bogdan reaches for me. I don't know how or from where I find the strength, but I cling to his hand. My nails are biting into his skin. I breathe easier once he's touching me.

"*Malyshka,* I'm not going anywhere. Shh. Let them take care of you. I'm right here. I love you, *malyshka.*"

"I love you."

Something is making my eyelids so heavy. Is it whatever they have in the IV? Why is it hard to breathe even with the oxygen? I swear, I'm still squeezing Bogdan's hand, but I can't feel it anymore. I hear people shouting, and I'm moving. There's a bump. Then there's nothing again. This is happening too often.

Chapter Twenty-Five

Bogdan

One moment Tina's hand is gripping mine, and the next hers goes lax. The paramedics push me aside as they start CPR. The guy doing chest compressions is standing on the stretcher as two more push it to the ambulance. I don't even think about Liam and Catriona. I climb in behind the stretcher. I know an EMT is about to stop me, but my expression makes him think twice. I perch next to her head as they work around me. I have to let go of her hand when they put the defibrillator pads on her chest. I can see where several of the stitches on her chest ripped open.

I glance out the ambulance doors and find Catriona and Liam standing with my mom. They're huddled together as they watch the doors snap shut. The gate hadn't even closed before we followed Tina onto the street. I was driving my mom's Mercedes, with Liam in the front passenger seat. My mom and Catriona were in the back. We saw everything. We saw the truck ram into her. We saw it push her car until it rolled four times and slammed into a building.

Liam and I did everything we could to get her out, but the truck smashed the door shut. I don't know if she even realized that she was upside down when they pried off her door. I'd tried to get in through the rear window, but it was impossible. I always carry a knife, so I tried to get to her seatbelt to cut it away. I was making progress when the firetruck and ambulance arrived. I had to give up and move out of their way. I don't know how many times I called her name until the brakes flashed. My legs nearly gave out when I realized she was doing it on purpose. She's alive. My *malyshka* is alive.

But as I watch them try to resuscitate her, I wonder if my thanksgiving is premature. There's so much blood everywhere. She looks so tiny as the two EMTs work on her. I don't understand half of what they're saying because none of it registers. She was right that I would have been dead if I'd been in the passenger seat. She would have been dead if I was taking her to her house. I know that's where she was heading. But she was going there because of me.

It's my fault Declan O'Rourke—the piece of shit—tried to burn her house down. Stefan saw six of them break in. He called the police and made an anonymous report. The entire garage was in flames by the time the firefighters arrived. They saved the house, but the inside is almost destroyed. The roof is sagging since they did the most damage to the weight-bearing walls. The police didn't want to let me in. The firefighters already had Cleo.

Once I told them my name, they were still hesitant, but two firefighters led me through the house. They gave me one of their hats to wear as I made my way around the ground floor. I grabbed a couple garbage bags from under the sink and hurried to gather up anything I thought mattered most to Tina. I grabbed the art supplies and the blueprints I got for her birthday.

I passed the framed ones from her office wall through a window to Niko, who went with me. I gathered her jewelry and some clothes. I remembered the teddy bear she's had since she was three weeks old. He used to sit on her dresser. I put that and all the photos I can find into the bags. Finally, I remember to grab her laptop.

The police try to stop me, claiming it's all evidence. I agree to hand everything over for them to dust for prints, but I stand near the crime scene evidence team while they check all Tina's belongings that I rescued.

I'd gone straight to my mom's to tell Tina what happened. I called my mom on the way. I think she assumed I was at the warehouse or coming from there. I told her not to say anything to Tina about what was happening. I told her I wanted to be the one to explain. I understand why my mom did it, and I'm trying not to blame her for the car crash. It's my fault. Not my mom's. Not Tina's. Mine. Being angry at anyone right now won't help Tina. But I can't help it. I'm pissed at my mom, and I will make Declan O'Rourke's death so long and painful that even the Devil won't recognize him.

"I got a pulse."

I look up as a line jumps to life on the heart monitor above Tina's head. The EMTs keep working on stopping the bleeding now that her heart's beating again. I feel the tears falling. I haven't cried since I was eleven. Vlad beat Maks every time I cried. I learned quickly not to because I believed Vlad would kill all my brothers, starting with Maks. I didn't know then that he was bluffing. He saw way too much potential in four boys without a father who were all tall and muscular for their ages.

I'm crying tears of relief and fear. Tina's heart works again, but there's just so damn much blood. And her eyes haven't opened. Is she in a coma?

We arrive at the hospital, and I wait for the paramedics to get the stretcher out of the ambulance and for the legs to drop open. I run behind them as they burst into the Emergency Room, calling out stats about Tina as though she were stocks to exchange rather than a person. I'm forced to stop when they wheel her through doors and into a hallway that will probably take her to an operating room.

We said I love you before she blacked out, but does she know how deeply I mean those words? That she is my everything. If I lose her, I lose myself. Rage boils beneath the surface. I've never felt this much hatred and anger before. It's scaring me. If I didn't need to be here for Tina, I would go on a killing spree. There isn't an Irish mobster who is safe now. If I lose her, then my life is as good as done. I'll take every fucking bastard with me that I can.

"Bogdan!"

My mom is calling to me. She's with Catriona and Liam as they rush to me. She pulls me into her arms, and I get a moment's reprieve. But the instant I look at Tina's parents, that rage boils over. Liam and I lock gazes.

"It's time we had the conversation."

I shake my head, but his focus on me is unrelenting.

"Liam, I won't understand half of what you tell me right now. And if I do, I don't think I'm going to remember. I can't right now."

I'm watching the doors they took Tina through, waiting for someone to come out and tell us what's happening. My mom leads me to a seat and pushes my shoulders until I sit. I can still see the door as she wraps her arms around me again.

"*Mama, a yesli ona umret? Kak vy zhili posle smerti papy?*" Mama, what if she dies? How did you live after Papa died?

"*U menya bylo chetvero synovey, radi kotorykh ya zhil.*" I had four sons to live for.

"*I nichego u menya ne budet.*" And I will have nothing.

My mom doesn't disagree with me. She knows from her own grief that she won't convince me otherwise. If she hadn't had my brothers and me to raise, I don't know that she would have survived losing my dad. I thought her grief had eased over the years, but I saw it last night. It's still raw sixteen years later.

"Bogdan?"

I sit up as Aleks and Niko run through the ER entrance. I know Maks is with Laura, who was in pretty bad shape after being drugged. Anton and Sergei are both recovering at Sergei's. As far as anyone is concerned, Boris insisted it was easier to take care of them at the same place, so he only has to go between Sergei's, and Maks and Laura's place in Queens.

"They took her through there, probably to surgery."

I stand to talk to my brothers. I don't know how my legs are holding me up.

"What happened? Pasha heard there was an accident over the police scanner. They described you as being there when the police and paramedics arrived. No one said your name."

Aleks stands to my left as he explains.

"We knew for sure when they said a redheaded female was driving an Audi."

Niko is on my right as he talks. I don't know that I could do this without my brothers here.

"Declan fucking O'Rourke happened. This wasn't an accident. A semi slammed into her and pushed her until she rolled into a building. They..."

I catch myself when I realize I'm speaking English and nearly said that Tina's heart stopped in the ambulance. Her parents can hear me.

"We have people following him and his family."

"Niko, no one touches his nephews. This will never end if we do."

"We aren't them. We're just watching. It's your call what happens. Maks is with Laura. She's pregnant."

I nod.

"You knew?"

I hear Aleks's surprise, and I know he's hurt.

"Only because Tina guessed and asked Laura at the gala. The plan was to tell everyone today. Or I guess yesterday. I don't even know what time it is."

"Bogdan, she's going to be your wife. Tell us what you want to do."

Normally, with Maks unavailable, Aleks would decide. I appreciate that my older brother is deferring to me. But I can't wrap my head around any of it. If I speak aloud what I want to do, I'll say things I wish I hadn't. I'm in no state of mind to plot a revenge that will work. Right now, I'm likely to get us all killed. And I'm not leaving until Tina is in our bed at my penthouse. It's the only place, other than the warehouse, where I can be absolutely certain of the security. And I will never take her there.

"Give him some time."

Niko pulls me in for a hug. Aleks wraps his arms around both of us. I miss Maks. But I understand why he isn't here. It's the same reason I didn't go to his place. We both have women we love more than anything. Our place is beside them. If I could walk away from everything in my life but Tina and my family, I would. But we're safer in our positions now than if we struck out on our own. We would be targets for every syndicate in the country, never mind our overseas rivals.

When we pull apart, I introduce my brothers to Tina's parents. It's not long before her brothers and their wives arrive.

Apparently, Susie's parents are watching all the kids. Hours slide away. I don't know how many because it's an eternity.

"Mr. Kutsenko?"

A woman in scrubs walks through the door. I'm on my feet before she speaks. Tina's parents rush forward with me.

"We're her parents."

Catriona stands in front of Liam and me. The doctor looks at them, and I realize they're the ones who have the right to be informed and decide on Tina's behalf. I'm not really her fiancé. I'm not entirely sure I'm still her boyfriend. I have no say in anything that happens.

"Ms. MacNally suffered significant internal bleeding. We had to remove her spleen. A broken rib punctured her right lung. We feared the impact shattered her pelvis, but x-rays showed no signs of that. But the bones are bruised. She's in stable condition right now and in recovery. Once the anesthesia wears off, she'll be taken to a room."

"A private room."

I don't know why that matters to me right now. The doctor looks at me, then nods.

"How long will it take for her to recover?"

Catriona reaches back for Liam's hand. He wraps his arms around his wife. I know what they fear. I fear it too. She won't recover.

"The splenectomy takes four to six weeks. The lung usually takes six to eight weeks. But I can't give you an exact time frame because her injuries are extensive."

"Will she be able to walk?"

"Yes, Mr. Kutsenko. There was no damage to her spine. The airbags did what they were supposed to. I suspect the impact pushed Ms. MacNally's right side against the stick shift, and that's what caused her most severe injuries. The impact from rolling several times likely bruised her pelvis."

"When can we see her?"

"When she's out of recovery in a couple hours. Mr. Kutsenko, she woke while we were taking her to the operating room and while we prepped. She asked for you until she went under."

"Did she ask for anyone else?"

The doctor looks at Catriona and shakes her head. I see Liam tighten his hold on his wife, and I feel horrible. Their daughter is asking for the man who nearly got her killed instead of her parents. I'm ashamed and feel wretchedly guilty. But part of me is also relieved because she still wants me by her side.

The next two hours are interminable. The others make small talk, but everyone takes my cues and stays away. I've had a tenuous relationship with God ever since I killed for the first time. I confessed in silence for that crime and many others, but after a few years, I wasn't convinced God could forgive me that many times. It's not that I stopped believing. We were all raised Russian Orthodox, and my brothers and I were even altar boys before we moved to America. We served during the Sunday church services for a year once we moved here. Then it just seemed sacrilegious to continue.

I've prayed many times since then. It's not that I think God's forsaken me. I prayed when I suspected it was time to call things off with Chloe. It helped, and I felt at peace with my decision. But I still struggle to believe that confession is enough for redemption after the mortal sins I've committed. But I'm not praying for myself right now.

Heavenly Father, please grant Tina Your grace. In this hour of her suffering and need, please pass Your healing hand over her.

My mind switches to Russian as prayers drilled into me as a child come back.

Vo imya Ottsa, i Syna, i Svyatogo Dukha. Amin'. In the name of the Father, the Son, the Holy Spirit. Amen.

Raduysya, Mariya, blagodati polnaya, Gospod' s Toboyu, blagoslovenna Ty mezhdu zhonami, i blagosloven plod chreva Tvoyego Iisus. Svyataya Mariya, Mater' Bozhiya, molis' o nas, greshnykh, nyne i v chas smerti nashey. Amin'. Hail, Mary, full of grace, the Lord is with thee. Blessed art thou amongst women and blessed is the fruit of thy womb, Jesus. Holy Mary, Mother of God, pray for us sinners, now and at the hour of our death. Amen.

Slava Ottsu, i Synu, i Svyatomu Dukhu, i nyne, i prisno, i vo veki vekov. Amin'. Glory to the Father, and to the Son, and to the Holy Spirit, and now, and forever, and forever and ever. Amen.

I repeat these prayers that I memorized as a child over and over. I add my own intercessions in between. I'm praying when a nurse rests her hand on my shoulder.

"Mr. Kutsenko? Ms. MacNally is asking for you and her parents."

"Can all three of us go back there?"

I want to push my way past everyone, but I still feel horrible that Tina was saying my name instead of asking for her parents.

"For a few minutes."

I stand and wait for the nurse to explain to Tina's parents. I meet Niko's, then Aleks's, gaze. When I turn to follow the nurse with Catriona and Liam, my brothers follow. It's Danny's angry voice I hear.

"Wait! Why are they going? Hasn't your family done enough, Bogdan? This was because of you, wasn't it?"

I turn to Danny, but I look back to Catriona and Liam. I can tell all they want is to go to Tina. I want the same.

"They aren't coming inside with us. They're staying by the door. Until I say so, my brothers go nowhere."

"Why?"

I stare at Danny. Do I really have to say it out loud? He fucking knows. He just accused me of causing this.

"You fucking piece of shit!"

Danny rushes toward me, but Liam steps between us.

"I will send you home. Do not speak that way in front of your mother. Bogdan is as good as Tina's husband. Accept it. With him comes his family. They're her brothers now, too. They can do things you and Tristan can't. It's not my place to do them anymore. At least not for Christina. You may not want to, but you have to trust Bogdan. Right now, he knows what needs doing."

I glance to Niko and Aleks. We're all as shocked as each other. We're not sure what Liam just implied, but we understood he just gave me his blessing to marry his daughter. Even after all this. I didn't pray and ask for anything for me. I didn't ask God to forgive me, or to heal Tina for my sake. I don't know if it's Divine Intervention after all, like Tina and I once talked about how we met. But I'll take it.

I follow Tina's parents, who follow the nurse. Niko and Aleks stand with their backs to the door as her parents and I go in. She looks so tiny, with so many machines hooked up to her. She opens her eyes and tries to smile, but it's more like a grimace.

"Mom, Da."

She lifts one hand to them, but she's looking at me. I hang back as her parents stand on each side of her bed. She frowns. She doesn't know why I'm hesitant, but suddenly, I feel like I'm intruding on a family moment. I know Liam said I'm practically her husband, but I don't know if that's what Tina still wants. When her lip trembles, I move to the foot of the bed. She draws her lips in between her teeth. I reach over the footboard and put my hand on her ankle. I don't know the extent of her injuries, so I'm careful how much pressure I put on it. Her shoulders relax. I didn't realize she was that tense.

"Christina."

Catriona's careful as she hugs her daughter. Tina's eyes drift closed as she soaks in her mom's love. Liam kisses the top of her head, and I can see his eyes are misty.

"I love you, lass."

Liam kisses her head again before he steps closer to the IV stand, making room for me. I look at Liam, and he nods. I take his place and slide my hand into hers. She grasps it with more strength than I expected. It's the same death grip she had when they pulled her out of the car. She turns her face up to me, and I gladly offer her a kiss. I intend to keep it chaste, since her parents are here. But the moment our lips touch, there's nothing either of us can do. I cup her cheek. When I know we'll make Liam and Catriona uncomfortable if we keep going, I kiss her cheeks, her eyelids, her nose, her forehead, and her lips once again.

"I love you, *malyshka*."

"I love you, *moy lev*."

"I'm so sorry."

"Don't."

I open my mouth, but she shakes her head. She releases my hand to cup my cheek. She brushes her thumb over my bristly chin. I haven't shaved in nearly two days. I turn my head and kiss her palm before she reaches for my hand again.

"Bogdan, what I did was self-centered and exactly why you're trying to protect me. I did what I wanted because I was angry. I wanted to be treated like an adult, and instead, I acted like a child. I had a temper tantrum that nearly killed me. You didn't want me there because you knew what would have happened if I had been. I should have realized that wrecking my house wouldn't be enough. The only thing I'm not sorry about is not having you in the car with me. You wouldn't be here with me if you had been. Someone saw me leave. I don't know if they thought we were together, or it satisfied them that it was just me. I need to know what's going to happen, or I will never stop being scared. You can't keep this from me."

"I won't, *lapochka*. But I don't have a definite answer yet. I don't know what's going to happen. Whatever it is can wait. I need to know you're going to be all right. That's the only thing that matters to me."

"No, it's not. Maybe I matter most, but we both know this isn't over."

Liam speaks up as he shifts, so Christina can see him again.

"Christina, when you're well enough, I'm going to talk to you and Bogdan. I know things you should, too."

"From the Highland Games watch party?"

"And from well before that."

Tina and I stare at Liam, then we look at Catriona. She doesn't appear surprised by what her husband says.

"I'm more awake now than I was when you came in. I think you better talk to us now, Da."

"Hold on."

I cross the room and stick my head out the door.

"Can you find us another chair? We're going to be here for a little while."

Aleks looks back at me and nods before he goes into the empty room across the hall. I roll my eyes. I would have been happy with a folding chair. My brother gets the recliner meant for a patient's guests who spend the night. He hefts it into the air and carries it across the hall. I hold the door open as he inches through the doorway. He puts it down as soon as he's in the room and leaves in silence. I move the chair closer to Tina's bed. Liam and Catriona take the loveseat. I hold Tina's hand through the bed rail.

"You know I work for a defense contractor. I've been with them for over twenty years. There have been questionable things that happened during that time, but I didn't ask questions above my rank and pay grade. But about a year ago, I discovered that the company's owner has been supplying us with weapons and ammunition that aren't issued by the government. They're black market. Some of them come from the Ivankov bratva, and some come from the Irish. I didn't know until after the fact that Donovan intended to sell that shipment he stole from you to my boss."

"We assumed he was going to sell them in South America, like we were."

"From what I understand, he had this complicated plan to have his crew sail south, past Florida, before going farther out to sea and coming back up north. He was going to have them bring it down the St. Lawrence to Rochester."

"Like he does the guns his uncle used to send from Ireland."

"Yes. When he talked to me at the Gaelic Society, he told me about the shipment. He wanted to hire me as a mercenary. He wanted me to go after Laura. Why he even suggested something like that is beyond me. He knows I don't go near women and children. I've almost lost my job countless times over the years for reporting colleagues who violate the Geneva Convention by assaulting women and children. The only reason they haven't fired me is because I'm too good at what I do."

I want to ask what that is. But his stare tells me to remain silent. Maybe one day, but not today.

"I also had no wish to put myself in Maksim's crosshairs. I didn't want to get in the middle of that war. You hadn't started dating yet, and my guess is Maksim and Laura had just gotten together. Donovan was angry that I refused. He thought he could back me into a corner and force my hand. He threatened Christina. I left before we got in a fight, which he wanted. Colin was there, too. He wanted an excuse for Colin to have a go at me. He thought having his cousin beat me to pulp would convince me."

"Donovan didn't know you used to be a close combat instructor, did he, Da?"

"No. After that, I had a couple of colleagues take turns watching the building sites when Christina inspected them. One guy saw you come out of a trailer together. He couldn't see where you went, but he noticed you came back looking much more comfortable together. Then you were gone for more than a week, so I thought it wasn't anything serious. But once I knew you were dating Christina, I called off my men. I knew she was safe with you, and I didn't want anyone watching you too closely."

"That's why it didn't surprise you when I arrived at dinner with Tina."

"You look exactly like Maksim, who I've been aware of for years. Even if I didn't know your brother's name, I know your family name. My company has bought guns from you before, and you've washed some money for them too."

I glance at Tina. I've never explicitly told her what our illegal business ventures are. She shrugs.

"I didn't know Christina was still on Donovan's radar. My guess is he knew she survived the encounter at the Peninsula and wanted to clean up loose ties, so he ordered the break in before your family arrived in Rochester."

"He and Colin are dead."

"I know that now. I got a call last night. It was Declan O'Rourke. You were already at Christina's house when he told me. I was going to talk to you when you came back to your mom's, but I didn't get a chance. He threatened Christina since he can't get to Laura now.

"They planned it. They're watching me."

Tina's looking at me, and I don't blame her for being terrified. I stand up and drop the bed rail and perch on the edge. She leans forward with a grunt and wince, so I can slip my arm behind her neck. Liam continues to explain.

"He's forced my hand. Now I can't ignore him. He thinks he can take up his cousin's banner and force me to side with them. They couldn't bribe me with money, so they think they'll win by harming my family."

"What're you going to do?"

I'm uncertain I want to know, but I have to. I don't want to do anything that could put Liam in the middle.

"Your brother just got a new *vor*."

"What?"

"No."

Tina and I speak at the same time. Liam's gaze locks with mine. I recognize that expression. I've seen it in plenty of men just before they kill. Liam won't get in my way, but neither is he going to let this go. Either he can be on our side, or we end up competing to get to Declan. I look back at Tina as I explain.

"*Vor* means thief. In your father's case, he'd be a made man. Maks would have to decide that."

"What's a made man?"

"Someone not born into the bratva or isn't Russian. An outsider who works for the bratva or joins."

"Da? You're joining the bratva?"

Tina looks at her mom, who nods. This isn't news to Catriona. It's clear she and Liam have talked about this. I don't know that Maks will agree. We don't bring in anyone from the outside. Ever. Either you're born into it, or you're not. If you're not, you aren't welcome.

"You'll lose your job if your boss finds out."

"I'm not a billionaire like you and your brothers, but I have enough to never work another day in my life. Cat and I could both retire right now without a second thought."

"Da, you can't be serious."

"Lass, I am. I have connections the Ivankov bratva couldn't get on their own in this lifetime or the next. I know things about the Irish, the Italians, and the Colombians that could make me a rich man if I sold my secrets. The only continent I haven't been to is Antarctica. Our government has interests every-where, and those sometimes need protecting by people not directly employed by them."

"And the secrets you have on us?"

"Go to my grave. Even if you and my daughter don't work out, telling anything I know about you is as good as putting a bullet in her. You and I both know she's marked for life."

"Marked? What're you talking about? Bogdan, what does my dad mean?"

"It's why I've brought no one into my life the way I have you. What you said at my mom's house is true. It's not just the police who won't believe you know nothing."

Tina leans away from me. I don't know what she's thinking from her inscrutable expression. No one says anything. Her parents and I watch her.

"You need to get me one of those trackers Niko said your cousins and Laura have. You need to teach me Russian. And you need to teach me about the bratva. You may not get me even proficient in Russian before we get married, but you can do the other two things. I'm banged up right now, but the one thing the doctor said I don't have is a concussion. It's time to talk wedding plans, Bogdan."

Chapter Twenty-Six

Tina

Bogdan's looking at me like I'm a puzzle to solve. I think I was clear about what I want and what needs to happen. My parents are silent while Bogdan and I look at each other.

"Do you want to come ring shopping with me? Or do you want me to surprise you?"

"Surprise."

"Do you want a civil service or a religious one?"

"You decide."

"Russian Orthodox, if you don't mind standing for an hour. A new house or my penthouse?"

"Penthouse until we find a house. I like your mom's neighborhood."

"Children?"

"Many and soon."

"Dogs?"

"If Cleo approves."

It's like a round of speed dating. Things normal couples usually learn about each other over several months boil down to one conversation with us. But none of Bogdan's questions or my answers are a surprise.

"When?"

"Can you find an Orthodox priest in the hospital?"

I wink as I look up at him. He gives me a smacking kiss and whispers in my ear.

"When you're well enough, *malyshka*."

I know he's not talking about the wedding. I wink at him again. If only we were alone. But I grow serious.

"Mom, Da, I need to talk to Bogdan about something alone. Just for a minute."

They leave, but I wait until I hear the door click closed. Bogdan shifts, so we're facing each other.

"I don't want to hurt our parents' feelings. Before whatever happens happens, I want to get married. I'm selfish, Bogdan. I want to be the one the doctors talk to. I want to be the one who decides what to do. I want you to know first. I want you to be at my side first. We can't do that unless we're married."

"I feel the same way. I knew letting your parents in here was the right thing to do, but it was hard. When the doctor came out and asked for me, I thought I would faint. I thought I would have to wait to hear from your parents."

"If something happens, I'll have to wait for someone in your family to remember to tell me. No one from the hospital or the police, or even the morgue, will call me if I'm not your wife."

"Tina, my family will not forget to tell you. How could they? If I'm not with you, then one of my brothers or cousins is."

"True. But you know that's not the same. I want to be your emergency contact, and I want you to be mine."

"Is that the only reason to get married?"

"Of course not. We love each other to distraction. That's why this matters to us. Do you want to marry because you feel obligated to keep me safe by making me untouchable as your wife?"

"I'm marrying you because I don't want to spend my life without you. And unfortunately, the Irish have proven wives and children aren't off limits to them. Look at what they did to Laura."

"Bogdan, we have to go."

No, no, no. Not fucking now. That's the same thing Aleks said the last time Bogdan disappeared.

"What happened?"

"They hit Deuces Wild."

I recognize the name as one of their casinos in New Jersey. But I don't know what this means. How bad is it? It must be pretty bad if Aleks expects Bogdan to go with him and Niko. I can see Niko talking to my parents. My mom and dad come back into the room, and Aleks steps aside. Bogdan and my da nod to each other. What the hell does that mean?

"*Malyshka,* you know I want to stay."

"And I know whatever this is, is big enough that you can't."

"Your dad is coming with us. Your mom is going to stay here. I'm sending Stefan, Michail, and Ilya here. You can draw the curtain, but one of them is in this room with you at all times, unless privacy is essential. The other two are always outside the door. Catriona, I need you to meet every charge nurse, nursing assistant, and doctor who comes on shift as soon as they arrive. No one you don't meet at the nurse's station comes in this room. Do you know how to shoot?"

"Yes."

Bogdan pulls the gun from the holster attached to his belt. I've gotten used to it being there or holstered under his arm. He hands my mom his pistol, stock first. I'm stunned as I watch them. My mouth drops when my mom handles the gun like an expert. She checks that it's loaded and pivots to aim toward the bathroom door. She makes sure the safety is on before she tucks it under the pillow on the loveseat.

"Do you know how to shoot, Tina?"

"Yeah."

I answer and nod, but I'm still staring at my mom. She shrugs.

"Your da's job isn't to make friends, and I'm home alone a lot."

Bogdan leans over and weaves his hand into my hair. I cup his cheeks with both hands, ignoring how it tugs at the IV needle in my hand. This time, we don't care that our family is there to watch. When we pull apart, Bogdan whispers in my ear so quietly I barely hear him.

"The things I'm going to do to you, *malyshka*, when we get home. You are mine for at least a week. I'll make you beg."

"Yes please, Daddy. Do you promise?"

"Everything under the sun and moon, baby girl."

"I love you, Daddy."

"I love you, *malyshka*."

We kiss one more time before he stands up. We're certain no one heard us since no one's close enough. My dad gives me a hug and kiss on the cheek before he does the same for my mom. Their kiss is just like Bogdan's and mine. Then three out of the four Kutsenko brothers and my dad are gone. My mom picks up the TV remote and finds a reality show she knows I like. There's nothing to do but watch TV and wait.

Chapter Twenty-Seven

Bogdan

It's just before dawn when we approach the docks. Maks was in the armored SUV that picked up Liam, Aleks, Niko, and me. He's livid. It has nothing to do with the casino and everything to do with having to leave Laura. My mom left the hospital after I went back to see Tina. I didn't know. She went to Maks and Laura's to stay with her. Watching my future father-in-law climb into the backseat with me didn't make Maks any less angry. I'd told my other two brothers that I would explain once we were with Maks.

I spoke in Russian in case Maks unleashed his disapproval, but he listened to me. As I explained Liam's background, he recognized the value of having my future father-in-law with us. When I finished, Maks sized up Liam, then nodded.

"Who do you work for?"

"Alpha Yankee."

My brothers and I stifle our laughter, but Liam doesn't.

"Ridiculous name, isn't it?"

Liam's shaking his head as he says what we've always thought. Maks sticks out his hand for Liam to shake as he repeats what we've often said.

"They certainly think highly of themselves."

With that handshake, Liam MacNally became a *vor*. There is no backing out for him.

As we near the docks, I reach into the back of the SUV to pull rifles from the racks installed along the sides. I hand them to my brothers and Liam. Maks takes an extra one for Pasha, who's driving. Even though we all know our guys checked the weapons before loading them into the car, we all check our own. I toss more ammunition to Maks, then give some to the others.

Misha's driving the car behind us with the men Maks trusts the most. There's only a dozen of us. Any more than two SUVs makes it too obvious. The vehicles are armor plated with bulletproof glass, tires that will still roll even if shot, and extended bumpers for ramming. We've modified their engines to give them more horsepower. They're basically tanks.

"According to the street cameras we tapped, Declan was behind the truck that hit Christina. He stayed until her car hit the building, then he turned off. We tracked him here. But we don't know which building, since the city-owned cameras don't cover this area. They hit the casino as a distraction."

Pasha's information doesn't surprise me. We have warehouses near the docks too, and none of them have cameras monitored by the city, only us. I'm certain it's the same here. Actually, maybe not. This is the second time we've come here, and the first time, Donovan had no clue. I wonder if Declan is more vigilant. I have the answer to that question the moment the thought pops into my head.

We're still half a mile or so from the docks. The first bullet hits the rear left passenger door. If the glass wasn't shatterproof, the bullet would have struck Liam.

"Down."

Everyone but Pasha and Liam duck. He opens his window just enough to get the end of his rifle's barrel through the crack. He has a sniper periscope that allows him to align his sights and fire without having any part of his face exposed to the open window. He releases a stream of bullets before he pulls back and shuts the window.

"That was someone's personal SUV. No armoring. Driver and passenger dead."

Liam speaks with clipped efficiency as he reloads. No one responds since there's no need. We're all looking for points of attack. They know we're here. Apparently, Declan is more attentive than Donovan was. They pepper the vehicle with bullets on Maks's side. Pasha turns toward our attackers and speeds up.

Niko and I are in the third row, with Liam and Aleks in the second. Maks, Aleks, and Liam lower their windows. There's nothing Niko and I can do since we don't have moveable windows on either side. My two oldest brothers and my future father-in-law open fire as Pasha continues to drive faster. We race through the streets, exchanging fire. We need to get to the docks before Declan flees.

"Brace yourselves."

All of us grab the "oh shit" handles and hold on. We plow into the town car in front of us. Pasha keeps going until we pass through the gates and into the shipping yard. We slam the car backwards into a shipping container. This vehicle is metal plated, too, so our bullets aren't doing much. Its occupants lean from their windows and return fire. Everyone ducks back into the SUV. There wasn't time for us to don our body armor, so we have to rely on the vehicle to protect us. I glance back and through the rear window. Misha's SUV isn't in sight, so he's still on the move. I don't know when we lost them, but it means he's still in control.

As I turn back to see what's happening in front of us, I see Misha swerve toward us, then make a sharp right. The SUV following him isn't as agile and slams into the same shipping container as we pushed the town car into.

"Reverse!"

I shout as I slap the seatback in front of me. Someone in Misha's car must see what I do because they're backing up, too. Pasha guns it, and our wheels squeal. We put just enough distance between us and the other two cars to not die when the shipping container explodes from the chemicals I saw leaking. The town car and SUV are engulfed in flames. Pasha's still reversing, using his rearview mirror and backup camera to guide him. I see what he does just before we drive over something. There's no way that guy survived.

Pasha stops, and all four windows go down. Niko and I scramble into the back, and we each unlatch a small window above the rear quarter panel on each side. They were a custom addition just for this reason. We slide the barrels of our rifles out and add to the gunfire.

"Fuck!"

"Maks! You hit?"

I can't take my eyes off my sights.

"No. There's Declan. The fucker is heading to a boat. If we have to board it, we're as good as dead. Who knows who's on there?"

Pasha leans far out his window, opting for his handgun instead. He fires.

"Shit. I only got his leg." I hear him switch to his rifle. "Who the hell is that behind him?"

"I don't know. But I got him."

I glance back when Liam speaks. I can see out of his window. I squint and notice a body sprawled on the ground about a hundred yards away. It's missing the back half of its skull.

"We're going."

That's Pasha's only warning before we're moving again. I hear two windows go up, so someone's reloading. Niko and I keep shooting as men pour out of the warehouse. Most are armed and firing back at us. They're spraying bullets left and right, whereas Niko and I are methodical. We only shoot people we know we can hit.

We're nearly to the edge of the dock when a car appears to our left. Pasha swerves to avoid it, and the tail end of the SUV spins and knocks me against the side panel. But it also gives me a clear line to shoot. My bullet goes through Declan's neck and out through his throat. The second one goes through his heart and never reappears.

"Declan's done."

"Aleks, get Misha's car on the radio. Tell him to take out the warehouse."

I listen to my brother bark the order in Russian. A moment later, something large fires out of the side of Misha's SUV. The projectile is a grenade, and it detonates on impact. Another sails through the air and hits the other side of the warehouse. We came prepared for war. The walls burst apart as two fireballs leap into the sky. There's no one left standing.

I hear Misha's muffled voice through Aleks's earpiece. It's turned up, so he could hear over the gunfire. But it's quieter now.

"We need Boris. Yuri and Igor are hit. Ivor's dead."

That's half the occupants of that SUV. This was Yuri's first mission. Depending on what happened, this might be his last. Maks will decide when Misha debriefs him. Igor and Ivor were cousins. They were young men when Vlad forced my brothers and me to pledge our loyalty. They were there when each of us got our first bratva tattoos. They were both good to us and often protected us from the men while we were still kids. I'll miss Ivor.

"Maks, take Liam and me to the hospital. I'm not going to your place."

"I know. Thank you for coming, *bratishka*." Little brother. "You did well today."

"You're welcome, *starik*." Old man. "Pasha, hurry."

"I'm going. You know it's going to take longer. I can't take any major roads where people are going to see a shot up car."

Pasha takes side streets with no cameras and few people who are up this early. He blows through red lights and stop signs. It's probably faster than if he had taken major roads. When we get to the hospital, Liam opens his door before the SUV even stops. I scramble over the seatback, not waiting for him to slide it forward. We go in through a side door I conveniently have a key card for. It's not the first time one of us has had to use it. We keep one in every car we own.

Liam and I take the stairs up to the third floor. I pull open the door and look both ways. I forget about Liam and let go of the door as I bolt down the hallway.

"Where the hell is my fiancée?"

Chapter Twenty-Eight

Tina

"Oh, crap. It sounds like someone woke my Russian bear from his hibernation."

My mom swings my wheelchair around and hurries to the end of the hallway. As she turns, I wave both hands.

"Bogdan! I'm here!"

One moment his face is flushed, the next it goes pale. He's running toward me and barely stops in time not to trip over my wheelchair. He crouches in front of me, and I can feel his relief.

"What are you doing out of bed, *malyshka?* Does your doctor know?" He lifts me out of the chair and into his arms. "Grab the pole."

He walks slowly enough for me to drag my IV stand with me. I look back at my parents, who look shocked at first, then amused. My room's door is open, but the moment I get the IV stand inside, he kicks it closed. He yanks the privacy curtain before carrying me to the loveseat.

"Daddy, I'm all right. The doctor said it was okay for me to leave the room for a few minutes. She said I'm not allowed to walk farther than the bathroom, but she knew I was anxious about you being gone. Your men were with me the whole time. Didn't you see them?"

"No. All I saw was no one at your door. There's no way they would still be there if you weren't."

"I'm fine. What about you?"

I looked for any bleeding as he ran toward me. He was sprinting, so I figure any injury couldn't be that serious.

"I'm fine. No one in my car got hurt."

"But people in the other cars did?"

He sighs and nods.

"No one you know, baby girl. But a man I've known since I moved here died. His cousin got hurt, and so did a younger guy."

"What happened?"

"Something that hasn't happened since I was a teenager."

"Was it the gunfight at the O.K. Corral?"

"Basically."

That wasn't what I expected. My eyebrows shoot straight up.

"It was a street war that started just outside the docks. We were about a half mile from the shipyards when the first car appeared. It was violent. That's all I will say. But Declan can never be a threat to you again."

"He's dead?"

"Yes, *malyshka.*"

"Did you kill him?"

He hesitates.

"Good. I hope his soul rots in hell. Thank you, Daddy."

We finally kiss. It's like air and water and all things essential to my survival flow into me through this kiss. I can breathe again now that I'm in Bogdan's arms. He'll live to fight another day, which is inevitable. But I'm with the man I'm going to marry, and we're both safe. For now, that's all that matters.

Chapter Twenty-Nine

Bogdan

It's been nearly two months since I brought Tina home from the hospital. She was there for a week, and it was the longest seven days of my life. I didn't leave once I returned from the shipyard. Our moms brought us food. Technically, they brought me food, but I shared it with Tina when none of the hospital staff was looking. Aleks brought me clothes, so I had something fresh to wear every day.

We spent one night in my penthouse, and we both knew we didn't want to stay there again. The ghosts of my past lingered there, and as much as I liked Tina's house, she admitted she felt similar about her place. We bought a place together. My penthouse sold in two days. Apparently, luxury and being owned by a Russian mobster made it highly desirable. We stayed with Maks and Laura. The ladies are as close as sisters, and they enjoy most of the same things. We put a bid on a house in my mom's neighborhood that was accepted without a counter since we paid cash.

We closed in two weeks and have been here for four. At first, Tina tired easily, so she did a lot of the move-in directions perched on my lap. That suited me just fine, even though she blushed nearly the entire time. We sold my penthouse furnished, and nothing was recoverable from her house, so we've started fresh here.

"*Malyshka*, where do you want this holly?"

"On the mantle."

We're celebrating our first Christmas together, and it's snowing outside. Our families are coming for Christmas Eve dinner, and I'm helping Tina finish decorating. We put up the tree last night after driving an hour outside the city to find a place where you can cut your own tree. We would have done all of this sooner, but Tina wasn't up to it yet. I can see she's still tired, so I'm offering to help wherever I can.

"What do you need me to do in the kitchen?"

"Not eat all the deviled eggs. I saw you pinching them earlier."

"You're one to talk. Are there any maraschino cherries left?"

"Yes. An entire bottle."

"So you bought two."

"Maybe."

"Did you really eat that entire jar?"

"Did you really eat a dozen of my chocolate chip cookies?"

I lift her down from the stepladder where she's hanging the last few ornaments that arrived today. We have tinsel for her nieces and nephews to hang on the lower branches. We head into the kitchen, which smells amazing. We both love to cook, so we've been teaching each other traditional dishes that we grew up with. Tina's pulling a batch of *priyaniki*, Russian spiced gingerbread cookies, out of the oven when the doorbell rings.

I hurry to answer it and find my entire family on the other side. They must have carpooled. My three brothers, Laura, my mom, both my aunts, both my uncles, and my four cousins, are grinning at me.

"Shh. She doesn't know."

I'm still gathering coats to put in my office when the door-bell rings again. I appreciate it when Laura offers to answer it. I can hear Tina and her family before I return to the foyer. I wrap my arms around her lower back as she wraps her arms around my neck.

"*Malyshka*, you make wherever we are a home. Are you happy?"

"Beyond anything I could imagine. You are my home, *moy lev*. Wherever you are, as long as we're together, I'm home."

We watch as the kids drape the tinsel on the tree before everyone finds seats in our massive living room. Maks and Laura recently bought a house down the street. We had the same requirements as them. We had to have enough room for both sides of the family to gather. Laura has a sister and her parents. They're also expecting twins. I still can't picture Maks as a dad. He used to torment me as much as he taught me.

"*Malyshka*, what's that on the mantle?"

Tina's brow furrows as she looks. She walks over and finds a small box and grabs it.

"I don't know."

"Did Santa come early?"

Santa had nothing to do with this.

"Should I put it under the tree?"

"Look to see who it's for."

She opens the little card and smiles.

For my love, my malyshka. Open me.

She looks at me as she lifts the lid. Tears come to her eyes as she covers her mouth with her fingers.

"Can I see?"

I pretend to peer into the box. I lift out a smaller one. I turn it and open it as I go down on one knee.

"My *lapochka,* I love you with all that I am and all that I have. Will you marry me?"

She nods her head as I take the ring out. I whisper my command to her.

"I need to hear you say it, *malyshka.*"

"Yes, Bogdi."

I slide the ring onto her finger, and she throws her arms around me. I pretend to cough as she squeezes. I stand up and lift her off her feet. Just like I did when we were on the yacht's balcony after we said I love you for the first time, I spin her around. Our kiss probably has her brothers and sisters-in-law covering their kids' eyes. Damn, I should have waited until after dinner. Now I have to make it through an entire meal before I can make love to my fiancée.

"I love you, *moy lev.*"

She looks at her ring as she fingers her lion necklace. She wears it every day, just like I wear mine.

"I love you, *malyshka.* You will always be my *lapochka.* My sweetheart.

Epilogue

Bogdan

"I told you. The more you struggle, the longer you remain tied to that chair. You should have listened."

Sparks fly from Tina's eyes as she fights against the silk scarves binding her arms and legs to the chair. She's been here for twelve hours. We've suspended the roleplay for her to eat, drink, go to the bathroom, and walk around every couple of hours. Otherwise, she's been my captive.

"And I told you I'll bite your dick before I ever suck it."

"Are you testing me, baby girl?"

I don't let her answer. My hand is around her throat, pressing just enough to make it hard for her to breathe. I tip her chair back against a bench we have set up in our basement. It puts her at an angle where I can straddle her chest while putting none of my weight on her. I coil her hair around my hand and yank. I know it stings because her eyes water, but her mouth opens with a scream. My pants are unbuttoned and unzipped already. I've been stroking myself, forcing her to watch. I know she hates it. I know she feels like I'm robbing her of the pleasure and power of arousing me.

No woman has ever made me as hard as my wife. She doesn't have to touch me to do that. A glimpse, a whisper of a thought, a sniff of her scent. It's been a year since our wedding, and we still can't keep our hands off each other. Once we settled the main parts of the house, I had a crew come in and finish the basement. That includes a nook set aside for when we wish to roleplay. It's not a sex dungeon. There aren't any swings or restraints hanging from the walls. It looks like a man cave. But we enjoy it for other purposes.

I slide my cock between her lips and deep into her mouth. She grazes her teeth along the sensitive skin. I tighten my hold on her throat and her hair. I harden my gaze. Her reaction is immediate, and God bless, it feels fucking amazing. She sucks me until I'm almost cross-eyed, but it's not the right time for me to come yet. I pull away, releasing my hold on her. As I step away, I tug the chain that connects the nipple clamps she's been wearing for the last fifteen minutes.

She watches me intently as I grab the massage wand and turn it on. She shifts in her seat, anticipating and dreading in equal parts. I watch her fingers tighten around the ends of the armrests. The *Ben Wa* balls I inserted must press against her g-spot. I have the wand on the lowest setting, but as I press it against her clit, I turn it on high.

"Don't come, or I will be very disappointed in you."

We've roleplayed this scenario plenty of times, but our actions still affect each other as powerfully as the first time. Her defiance flares as the hours pass, but it's nothing like in the beginning. By now, she wholly depends on me for pleasure and relief. She wishes to please me as I dominate her, and I'll do anything I can to please her.

Her breathing increases, and I can see her belly quiver as

she fights against the need for release. Her eyes close as she concentrates. Uh-uh-uh.

"Watch me, baby girl."

"Daddy, I need to come."

"How badly?"

"So badly it hurts. I need it."

"Who decides what you need?"

She glances down before meeting my gaze.

"You do, Daddy."

"And why's that, baby girl?"

"Because you'll always take care of me."

"Is that what you want? I thought you were so independent."

"I was. I am. But I—I—like it when you take care of me. All I have to think about is how good you make me feel."

"That's right, my sweet little captive. I will give and take away pleasure, but I will always give you what you need."

I kneel between her spread thighs and latch onto her clit. I tongue her pussy before sucking on her clit.

"Daddy, please!"

I reach up and lace our fingers together.

"Come, *malyshka*."

I feel it when I return my mouth to her pussy. It gets wetter as she digs her fingers into the back of my hands. When she finally shudders through the last wave of her orgasm, I untie her from the chair and remove the nipple clamps before easing the Ben Wa balls from her pussy. It's not one of her breaks, so it surprises her. I lift her from the chair and carry her from our basement.

"Daddy?"

"Yes, Tina."

Our roleplay is over.

"I can go longer, Bogdi."

"I can't. I need you, Tina."

When we reach our bedroom, I lie her on the bed as I strip before joining her. I encourage her to straddle me before she sinks onto my cock. That moment of pure bliss. That instant our bodies become one. It's her turn to entwine our fingers as she rests my hands beside my ears. She leans forward and presses her body to mine as she rides me. Our kiss is languid and filled with love. Eventually, my hands roam over her back and ass. Her arms are tucked under my shoulders.

"I love you, Tina. You're everything to me."

"You're my everything, too. Always."

We come together as we gaze into each other's eyes. We decided last night to start trying for a baby, so she had her IUD taken out today. Perhaps it'll happen tonight. But until it does, the only baby girl I need is my *malyshka*.

Don't miss the next installment

Preorder and have it ready when you wake on Sept 20th.

She has no idea what she agreed to...

My *printsessa* thinks she's taken a regular job for a regular lawyer.

She doesn't know the devils that lurk below the surface now that she's in my world. The bratva world.

Innocent, sweet, and trusting.

All the things I am not. All the things I never knew I wanted.

But I do now. And she's mine.

Let someone try to take her. I'll burn the world down around them to keep her. She's my soulmate.

She doesn't know her limits yet. I'll take her there, then bring her back with my touch and my love.

Bratva Treasure is an interconnecting, standalone Dark Mafia

Romance with a HEA and no cliffhanger. It contains extra-steamy scenes that will make your toes curl and your granny blush. This is book three in *The Ivankov Brotherhood*, a six-book series that'll keep you warm at night.

Preorder now for Sept 20th.

About the Author

Sabine Barclay, a nom de plume also writing Historical Romance as Celeste Barclay, lives near the Southern California coast with her husband and sons. Growing up in the Midwest, Celeste enjoyed spending as much time in and on the water as she could. Now she lives near the beach. She's an avid swimmer, a hopeful future surfer, and a former rower. She loves writing romances that will make your toes curl and your granny blush.

Subscribe to Sabine's bimonthly newsletter to receive exclusive insider perks.

www.sabinebarclay.com

Join the fun and get exclusive insider giveaways, sneak peeks, and new release announcements in
Sabine Barclay's Facebook Dubious Dames Group

Do you also enjoy steamy Historical Romance? Discover Sabine's books written as Celeste Barclay.

The Ivankov Brotherhood

Bratva Darling

BOOK ONE SNEAK PEEK

LAURA

As I sit across from the four Kutsenko brothers, I press my lips together to keep from drooling. No four men should be so strikingly handsome. Not all from the same family, anyway. I fight a valiant battle against letting my gaze drift toward the eldest, Maksim, whose ice-blue eyes bore into me. After years of negotiating billion-dollar investment contracts while facing countless ruthless businessmen, I've learned to keep my expression studiously blank. But it's a true struggle today. Instead, I focus my attention on the squirrelly lawyer sitting across the conference table. While he's disingenuous with each comment, he's a good negotiator. But I'm better. How cliché am I?

While I feel Maksim watching me, I focus on Dmitry Yakovitch as he continues to argue the merits of the venture capitalist company I represent, RK Capital Group, merging with Kutsenko Partners. What he means is the merits of Kutsenko Partners acquiring RK Capital Group, then stripping it and making it another money-laundering shell corporation. While most people in New York have little awareness of the Russian mafia, I do. The Kutsenko brothers' names appear on no titles or deeds anywhere in New York City, but it wasn't difficult to determine which shell companies likely belong to them. Their assumption that I'm unfamiliar with them is proving beneficial to me as they continue to whisper amongst themselves in Russian. I think they may even believe they're convincing me that they don't speak much English.

The senior partners of RK Capital Group know who I'm negotiating with, though they may not know I'm aware of these Russians' more nefarious operations. They've given me the go-ahead to agree to a merger with an eventual acquisition, but only for the right price. A price to the tune of twenty billion dollars. Considering an investment firm like Goldman Sachs is worth nearly one-hundred-and-twenty billion dollars, my clients' asking price appears reasonable.

"Mr. Yakovitch, I shall stop you now." I raise my left hand, pen caught between my index and middle fingers. When I have his attention, I lean back in my chair and casually twirl the pen over my index finger and thumb. "Fifty billion is my clients' asking price. You know that. Your clients know that. RK doesn't oppose the merger. What they oppose is the insulting offer you've made. It's nearly noon, and I'm hungry, Mr. Yakovitch. I have a delicious ham sandwich waiting for me. I even have three chocolate chip cookies waiting for me. If we aren't going to make any progress, I shall let you go, so I can move onto my eagerly anticipated lunch."

I cant my head just enough for me to appear as though my gaze rests solely on the opposing attorney's face, but I can see each Kutsenko brothers' reaction. My face battles yet again against showing my emotions as I fight not to smirk. Their muted but surprised expressions confirm what I already know.

"Please tell your clients to make a reasonable counteroffer, or I will conclude this meeting and enjoy my ham sandwich and cookies."

Dmitry glares at me before turning to Maksim and his three brothers. In rapid Russian, he doesn't interpret my suggestion. Oh no. There's no need for that. I can't catch every word because his voice is too low. But I catch something along the lines of "The bitch refuses to budge. What now? A fucking ham sandwich. More like a stick up her ass."

Maksim swivels his chair to look at his brothers. In Russian, he says, "Fifty billion is ridiculous. She's not so stupid or naïve not to know that. My guess is they'll settle for twenty billion. We offer fifteen."

"That's barely better than what we already offered," Aleksei, the second-oldest brother, argues. "She'll be eating the fucking sandwich and dipping her cookies in milk before we walk out the door. We need the buildings."

"We offer twenty, Maks," Bogdan, the youngest, insists.

As I watch the brothers discuss, their voices barely lowered, I pull my lunch sack from the black leather satchel by my feet and set it beside my laptop. It's a ridiculously pink floral bag with an embroidered monogram, the L and D overlapping. It's an empty prop, but they don't know that. I watch as five sets of eyes narrow. I offer a smile that would appear innocent in any setting other than this meeting. It's patronizing, and I know it.

www.ingramcontent.com/pod-product-compliance
Lightning Source LLC
Chambersburg PA
CBHW050504110726
47899CB00005B/1324